Fionn: The Adversary

Fionn: The Adversary

The Fionn mac Cumhaill Series - Book Three

BRIAN O'SULLIVAN

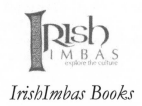

IrishImbas Books

ISBN: 978-0-9941468-1-6

ACKNOWLEDGEMENTS

Special thanks to Marie Elder.

Thanks and credit also to Chiaki & Nasrin (Chronastock) for the use of their image on the cover.

Many ancient Fenian Cycle texts were essential for the completion of this work. These included *Macgnímartha Finn* (The Boyhood Deeds of Fionn), *Acallam na Senórach* (The Colloquy of the Ancients), *Fotha Cath Cnucha* (The Cause of the Battle of Cnucha) *Aided Finn meic Chumail* (The Death of Finn Mac Cumaill) and many more.

Dedication

Pour Odile Dambricourt.

Foreword:

This book and its characters are based on ancient narratives from the Fenian Cycle and in particular from the *Macgnímartha Finn* (The Boyhood Deeds of Fionn). The *Macgnímartha Finn* was a twelfth century narrative that attempted to collate a number of much earlier oral tales about the legendary Irish hero Fionn mac Cumhaill and the Fianna. It was originally edited by Kuno Meyer in 1881 for the French journal Revue Celtique.

Many of the personal and place names used in this novel date from before the 12th century although many have common variants (Gaelic and English) that are in use today. For those readers who would like to know the correct pronunciation of these names, an audio glossary has been developed and is available at **irishimbasbooks.com**. A more basic pronunciation guide for character names and a glossary is available at the back of this book.

Chapter One

The muscular curve of Fiacail mac Codhna's buttocks was the first sight to fill Bodhmhall's eyes when she finally came to her senses. Consistent as ever, the big warrior was standing naked outside the little cave, hands upraised in salutation to the mighty yellow orb of Father Sun.

Cossetted in the woolly remnants of sleep, Bodhmhall struggled to make out what her man was saying, although the murmured pattern of words could hardly have been much different from those uttered over the time they'd lived together at Dún Baoiscne.

With that, her forehead creased into a series of deep furrows.

Her man?

Cave?

Stirred by a pressing sense of alarm she didn't quite understand, Bodhmhall sat up from her bed of crushed fern, exclaiming painfully at the burning sensation in her lower left arm. Looking down, she hissed at the sight of the rough wooden splints and crude strapping that encased it.

The shock of seeing the injured limb and the flare of pain dislodged her logjam of confusion. A wave of muddled memories flooded her head, all competing furiously for her attention: her father's summons to Dún Baoiscne; the arduous traverse across the Great Wild with their *Lamraighe* allies; the ambush at An Bearna Garbh and the subsequent leap from the waterfall with her nephew to escape their pursuers.

She felt her breath catch as she recalled the latter, the choking sound in her throat loud in the tight confines of the cave. The leap from the high cliffs had been one of the hardest things she'd ever done and even now the memory of it caused her hands to shake. Striking the water at the foot of the falls, she'd broken a bone in her arm. Afterwards, in the watery maelstrom of the mountain river, she'd also come close to drowning. Ironically, having miraculously survived both experiences, she and her nephew had subsequently been seized by The Brotherhood, a group of Tainted Ones who'd been stalking her nephew – Demne – over the seven years since his birth.

Eaters of the dead.

A surge of bile rose in the back of her throat and she had to close her eyes and focus to keep from throwing up. When the nausea finally settled, she shook her head and looked out at the naked warrior with fresh appreciation. Had Fiacail mac Codhna not arrived to save them, Demne would have been taken by The Brotherhood and she, of little or no value to their malevolent endeavours, utilised as an ingredient for their stew pot.

1

With a shudder, she pushed aside those gruesome images and set herself to inspecting the injured limb, delicately loosening the rough bandages to examine it more closely. Her probing fingers produced another involuntary hiss of pain but she ignored it, pleased to find that the swelling had almost completely subsided. Several days' rest in splints had allowed the bone to start setting and it now appeared it would heal well. Tentatively testing the limits of the limb's extension, she found it sensitive but nowhere near as painful as it had been mere days before.

Clicking her tongue in satisfaction, she slowly rose to her feet.

'Ah! The *Cailleach Dubh* – the Black Hag – awakes!'

Bodhmhall blinked as the Seiscenn Uarbhaoil man moved into the opening of the cave, a wide space between the two pillar-like standing stones. In reality, the cave was little more than an old place of worship, a rocky recess at the base of a steep cliff where the long-departed Ancient Ones must once have gathered in homage to their own gods. Displaying no fear of Otherworld consequence, Fiacail leaned against one of the standing stones and grinned broadly. He made a lazy gesture towards a glorious shaft of sunlight that struck the floor of the canyon just beyond.

'See, Bodhmhall. It pleases Father Sun to see you stir.'

She gave a desultory wave at the golden benediction. Whatever Father Sun's feelings on the matter, his golden rays were now showering Fiacail's bronze skin with disconcerting intensity, highlighting the tightness of his torso and the muscular sinews of his arms and legs. Flustered, she averted her eyes from the prominent *bod* that dangled between his legs, silhouetted against the brightness of the canyon behind him.

Fiacail, of course, exhibited no such self-consciousness. Oblivious to her discomfort, he advanced into the cave with his habitual aplomb, retrieving a pair of leather leggings and a short-sleeved, blood-spattered tunic that he lazily pulled on. 'Do you have a hunger on you?' he asked. 'A portion of yesterday's porridge remains.'

Bodhmhall felt her stomach clench at the prospect of food. Despite the hunger, her belly felt swollen and queasy. In addition to the intellectual cloudiness, this was another unpleasant side effect of the herbs she'd been using to alleviate the pain over the previous days.

'Is it hot?' she asked, biding for time as she struggled to pull her thoughts together.

'Of course, it's not hot! We can't risk the smoke from a fire.'

Bodhmhall bit her lip as she tried to absorb this fresh nugget of information. Her head had quietened and more manageable snippets of memory were now shooting through her mind but they dispersed too rapidly for her to grasp. With an effort, she managed to rein in some of those scattered impressions and coral them into a vague sense of coherence. 'Gob An Teanga Gorm and his warriors. I thought … I thought they had left.'

Fiacail regarded her with visible frustration. Although he made no immediate response, he tugged irritably at the whiskers of the impressive moustache protruding from either side on his upper lip and then scraped the thick stubble beneath his chin with his fingernails. The Seiscenn Uarbhaoil man had always had a preference for a clean jaw and invariably followed his ritual greeting to Father Sun with a shave. Recent circumstances however had curtailed that particular practice.

'They have,' he confirmed. He picked up a nearby stick and rolled it absently between his palms. 'But they're just as likely to reappear when they discover that whatever drew them away from the valley wasn't you or the boy.'

Ah!

She was starting to remember. Two days earlier, while out hunting, Fiacail had spotted Gob and his *fian* [war party] making their way down the river valley. Immediately backtracking to their refuge in the hidden canyon, he'd alerted Bodhmhall and after a hurried discussion, they'd reluctantly agreed to remain where they were. Bodhmhall's injuries meant she'd have been unable to move at speed and so any attempt at flight would have been perilous. If they stayed concealed however, the chances were high that their enemies would eventually grow discouraged and leave.

This had been their belief, at least.

Cloaked in dense forest, littered with rocky hollows and interspersed with rivers and streams, the valley was a torturous terrain to search. Despite this, the *fian* had displayed an unexpected tenacity, doggedly scouring both sides of the river, beating through the forest and combing any natural tracks or trails with resolute determination. It was as though they'd sensed their quarry was located somewhere in that particular area.

Which, of course, was impossible.

For two days, Bodhmhall and Fiacail had huddled by the entrance to the ravine, listening fearfully as the calls of the hunters drew ominously closer then mercifully faded once more. The canyon was accessible only through a narrow cut in the ridge, a gap choked with holly trees and other heavy growth. This meant their hiding place was difficult to find but it also meant that, if discovered, there was no route of escape. Neither of them had any illusions as to their fate if it were discovered.

Towards the end of the second day, one particular group of warriors had passed closer to them than at any other point during the previous searches but, once again, failed to spot the entrance. Peering through the thick screen of foliage, Bodhmhall had fearfully observed them pass by: five lean, hard-faced men in padded tunics, bearing cruel-looking, metal-tipped javelins and other weapons. Shivering, she'd watched them leave, thankful that section of the valley was so broad. Had they been caught further upriver where it was substantially narrower and, consequently, easier to search, the outcome would have been drastically different.

On the morning of the third day, Bodhmhall had awoken to an unusual silence, a hushed stillness that seemed to pervade not only the canyon but the entire valley. Nervous, she'd remained at the hidden entrance with Fiacail for the better part of the day but over the course of the morning, heard no sound of voices, no sound of movement, no indication of any kind in fact that the *fian* remained within the environs.

It was late afternoon before Fiacail finally dared venture forth to investigate further. Crawling through the undergrowth on his belly, he'd worked his way towards the river where a decayed tree on a high mound overlooked the waterway. Concealing himself within the mildewed hollow of the trunk, he'd waited and watched in silence.

For the remainder of the afternoon, he observed no indication of the *fian* warriors' presence. Towards nightfall however, a great ululation had arisen from the far side of the river, spreading quickly along the valley as it was taken up by different groups of warriors. The fading light and the thick forest canopy had prevented him from seeing the opposite bank but Fiacail had managed to catch a glimpse of warriors on their own side of the river, returning at a run from some point upstream. Speeding directly past him, they hadn't even paused to look in his direction. He'd scanned them, as well as he could in the gloom, and had spotted the hatchet-face Gob An Teanga Gorm at the forefront, urging his men on with bellows of excitement.

Bodhmhall's frown tightened as the memories returned. Clearing her throat, she made to swallow but gagged on an unexpected bitterness at the back of her tongue – yet another unpleasant side effect of the herbs.

Fiacail passed her a wooden bowl half-filled with water. She swallowed most of the liquid but kept a few drops to trickle onto her fingers which she then used to scrub her face. She needed no reminder of the precarious situation with respect to food and water. The presence of the *fian* had prevented Fiacail from leaving the canyon to hunt or replenish their water supply. They'd survived on what untainted food they'd managed to scavenge from the Brotherhood's supplies and the rainwater they managed to collect but that meagre hoard was now almost exhausted.

Bodhmhall tested her arm again. 'I am strong enough to leave, to depart for Ráth Bládhma.'

Fiacail's gaze rested on the stick between his fingers. 'Yes,' he said at last. 'I believe you are.'

The *bandraoi* gave him a quizzical look, surprised by the uncharacteristic vagueness of his response. 'Then we should leave as soon as possible. As you say, the *fian* might return.'

The warrior tapped the ground absently with one end of the stick. 'There is a ... complication.'

Something in the way he said that caused the hairs on the back of her neck to rise.

'A complication?'

'Earlier this morning ... I found tracks at the entrance to the canyon.'

The *bandraoi* felt her heartbeat stutter. 'The *fian*?' The words came out as a kind of garbled croak.

He shook his head. 'No. A single person, a big man from the depth of his print. Whoever he was, he was familiar with the canyon for his tracks led directly to the entrance.' Fiacail sniffed, tossed the stick over his shoulder and raised his eyes to consider the *bandraoi* directly. 'He was careful. He tried to hide all trace of his visit but I found a heel print he'd overlooked in the darkness. After that, it was a simple matter to find the others.'

Bodhmhall clutched her wounded arm. 'We should leave. Now. They could ret-' She stopped abruptly for the warrior was regarding her with a knowing, unharried expression. The certitude in his eyes triggered a sudden flash of insight as all the facts converged in her head: a single man, a big man, a knowledge of the canyon's location, reconnoitring and then subsequently withdrawing.

'You think it was Futh.'

Fiacail maintained his steadfast gaze but he dipped his head in acknowledgement. Bodhmhall felt a glacial frisson pass through her. One of the Brotherhood's more brutal members, Futh had treated her with great cruelty over the time she'd been held captive. Despite her broken arm, he'd dragged her by the hair through the Great Wild without regard for her screams of agony. He'd also held her down during an attempted rape by one of his comrades and the memory of the merciless amusement in his eyes still made her sick to the stomach. There'd been no pity to the man, no empathy of any kind and now, given the death of his brother during her rescue, there was even greater reason for antipathy towards her.

Bodhmhall looked down at her hands and realised they were trembling.

'The possibility of that man stalking us ... It terrifies me.'

'And so it should. That big, bald fucker terrifies me as well.' Fiacail unconsciously reached one hand up to touch the wound on his shoulder. Futh had sliced him there with a quarterstaff tipped at either end with a metal blade and although the wound had scabbed over and was healing, he hadn't forgotten how close he'd come to being killed. Futh and his brother had been the most dangerous members of the Brotherhood and although Fiacail had succeeded in slaying one, it'd been a close thing. Disconcerted by the unexpected deaths of his comrades, Futh had panicked and taken off into the forest and, in that respect, they'd been exceptionally lucky. If he'd stayed and fought it out, it was more than likely he'd have killed them all.

A sudden thought struck the *bandraoi* and she peered anxiously over the warrior's shoulder, out into the canyon. 'Where's Demne?'

'He keeps a watch on the entrance.'

Bodhmhall's eyes widened. 'You left him to guard the entrance? By himself.'

'I left him to watch it,' he corrected her. 'And to call out at any sign of danger.' He scowled then, vexed by the *bandraoi*'s accusatory tone. 'I needed rest, Bodhmhall. In your dream stupor, you were of little use and even I can only go so long without sleep.'

Rebuffed, Bodhmhall shrank back, momentarily lost for words. She raised both hands, palms outwards, in apology. 'Forgive me. The sleeping potion leaves me ... cranky.'

Fiacail shrugged, dismissing the slight with an airy gesture. 'You have endured great hardship. Some crankiness is to be expected. But...' He eyed her closely. 'Do not take the potion again. I will need your help when he returns.'

She became aware that her hands were clenched. 'You believe he'll come back?'

'If someone killed my brother I'd come back.'

Bodhmhall frowned at that, knowing Fiacail had the right of it. Futh and his brother Ruth had formed a true Man Pair, physically and mentally identical to the point of mirroring each other's actions. Unrestrained by the instruction of Rogein or Regna of Mag Fea, the two leaders of the Brotherhood, Futh would almost certainly be determined to avenge his brother, something Fiacail was quick to affirm.

'From what little I have seen of Futh, I judge him a man of basic instincts. He's had days to mull over his purpose and without the guidance of his leaders he'll fall back on basic emotions. And none are as basic as the yearning for vengeance.'

6

He rolled his head back and yawned loudly. 'And so you see. Our situation is ... complicated. We should depart for Dún Baoiscne with haste, but we cannot. Futh has had days to prepare, to scout the terrain and the most viable routes from the valley. If we leave the safety of this little canyon, there's little doubt he'll be awaiting us, preparing an ambush we're unlikely to survive.'

'But ... Then what should we do?'

'As to that ...' The warrior gave a lop-sided grin. 'I confess I have no answer. But rest assured, I will think on it further.'

**

Leaving Fiacail to take her place on the bed of fern, Bodhmhall left the cave to find her nephew standing outside, several paces to the right of the entrance. A slight figure with little more than seven years on him, he looked a fragile defence against the potential return of the brutal Brotherhood warrior.

And yet, she reminded herself, he'd taken Regna of Mar Fea down with a single sling cast, smashing his skull from the force of the bullet when the fat man had tried to kill her.

My nephew has always been more than he appeared.

She stood and watched the boy in silence for a moment. Oblivious to her presence, he continued to stare towards the thick stand of holly that marked the passage into the canyon. His sling dangled loosely from his right hand, a smooth river stone cupped snugly in the woven reed pouch. Studying him, Bodhmhall experienced a heady outpouring of affection and pride, a sensation so intense it caused her lips to tremble. She took a moment to compose herself before she called out to him.

'Demne.'

The boy's head snapped around and he stared at her briefly before twisting back to face the distant entrance. '*A Aintín*, I can't talk. I'm on watch duty. So the bad man can't creep up on us.'

Bodhmhall looked towards the holly trees and slowly drew on her *tíolacadh* – her *Gift*. After a moment, her view of the intense green foliage shimmered, fading into a beautiful pattern of tiny yellow flames, the internal lifelights of every living being within that space. Studying the vibrantly glowing spectacle, she finally allowed herself to relax. There were no flames of any substance to be seen, confirming the absence of anything larger than small birds, rodents or insects. Loosening her hold on the *Gift*, she watched the yellow colours gradually dissolve back into different shades of green and brown once more.

'You can relax for now,' she told the boy. 'I've studied the trees and no-one is in hiding. We can continue to watch while we talk.'

Because of his familiarity with his aunt's abilities, the boy accepted her assurance without dispute. His shoulders drooped with relief and he surprised her by moving forwards to wrap his arms about her waist, embracing her firmly. With a mild sense of bemusement, she stroked his head as she returned that embrace. The child's scalp was still shorn as a result of the Brotherhood's preparation for his initiation ceremony but now, after a few days of growth, a fine fuzz was discernible against her fingertips. Bodhmhall briefly wondered whether her nephew's hair would grow back a darker shade or whether he'd retain the dramatic blond colouring of his father.

With a start, she realised the child was shivering, his head trembling against her stomach. Pulling his hands away, she went down on one knee and clasped his cheeks between her palms, forcing him to face her. 'What is it Demne?'

The boy chewed his lips anxiously. 'I'm scared, *a Aintín*,' he confessed at last, his shame at the admission evident in his tone. 'Fiacail says that Futh wants to hurt us.'

'I know, little one. But an intruder cannot get to us without crossing that open ground and Fiacail is just inside the cave. We'll have more than enough time to call him should we have need.'

'Futh scares me.'

'And me,' she confessed. 'But we must find the resolve to face him down. Otherwise we allow him to win and we do not let cruel men win, do we?'

Demne thought about that. His jaw firmed up and he shook his head.

'Besides,' the *bandraoi* continued. 'I've seen you stand and fight. You killed Regna of Mar Fea when he was about to spill my blood.' She stroked his cheek. 'Do not doubt yourself, Demne. You have a rare inner strength, a mark of greatness.'

A mark that others too had noticed. According to Regna, the Brotherhood had been seeking the child since the year of his birth, drawn by some mysterious prophecy in the stars that only they could comprehend. The Adversary – that mysterious and relentless opponent – had also gone to great lengths to lay his hands on the boy, dispatching two separate war parties to capture him.

Bodhmhall played with a loose thread on the hem of her dress. It infuriated her that, after all this time, she remained ignorant to the identity and motivation of the individual who'd created such havoc with their lives.

And you bear responsibility for at least a portion of that.

That much was true. After the first assault on Ráth Bládhma, she'd foolishly allowed herself to grow negligent, lulled into complacency by the passage of time and the incessant grind of leading the settlement. Now it was clear the Adversary would never give up, would never abandon his efforts until Demne was in his grasp.

Without thinking, she drew on the *Gift* once more, using it to re-examine her nephew's lifelight. As always, the boy's unusually intense internal flame radiated power, a deep yellow flare that pulsated with the regularity of a beating heart. The *bandraoi* bit her lip. Even after all these years, the sight never failed to impress her. The exceptional fervour of that flame alone was enough to confirm her nephew unique, but as to how that uniqueness might one day manifest itself, she didn't have the slightest notion.

'Bodhmhall, is my mother dead?'

The sudden question took the *bandraoi* completely by surprise and as the *tíolacadh* faded she struggled to conceal her reaction. Since their rescue from the Brotherhood the boy had spoken very little and rarely on issues beyond those related to their immediate survival. The specificity of this particular question therefore intrigued her. 'I don't know,' she admitted.

Demne appeared to mull over the subject for a time. As he did, he pulled the stone from the pouch of the sling and rolled it between his fingers, enjoying the firm sensation of smoothness. Bodhmhall caught a glimpse of the crude image of a deer that had been painstakingly carved into the hard surface by Liath Luachra. It must have taken the woman warrior an age to produce and she'd fashioned more than a dozen such stones for the boy.

How typical! The Grey One openly scorns any thought of tenderness towards the child and yet, when least expected, performs great acts of affection.

At the thought of the missing woman warrior she had to resort to her druidic training to calm herself, slowing her breathing and her heartbeat to regain her composure. The Grey One had been supposed to follow her and Demne off the falls after the ambush at An Glenn Teann. When the *bandraoi* and her nephew had broken free of the white water and waited on shore however, she had not shown. And many days had passed since then.

'Can we go home to Ráth Bládhma?' Demne asked, mercifully interrupting such bleak considerations. 'Can we go back there now?'

He pulled back to look up at her. Close to despair, she made to embrace him again but he backed away even further. 'My mother took me away from Ráth Bládhma. I didn't want to leave. It's my home. All my friends are there.'

'None of us wanted you to leave, *a bhuachaill*. But, as your mother, Muirne had the right to make that decision.'

'It was the wrong decision.'

She continued to regard him closely, struck by the adamant condemnation. In their conversations together, her nephew had an unusual trait of switching from the typical speech of a child to that of someone with much greater maturity. Despite her familiarity with this peculiar mannerism, Bodhmhall still found such conviction in a mere seven year old quite disturbing.

Demne continued to stare at her, as though challenging her to deny the truth of it.

Bodhmhall sighed. 'Home is that place that's most dear to us, *a bhuachaill*. The place where we are – or have been – most loved. Ráth Bládhma's your home now but in later years you'll call other places home, places where you find or create love of your own.' She clasped her hands together, carefully preparing the words at the heart of what she intended to say. 'Your mother never experienced love at Ráth Bládhma. When she came to us, it was under trying circumstances and she was alone amongst strangers. I suppose, from her perspective, Ráth Bládhma was never much of a home. That may be why she was keen to take you away.

How very diplomatic, Cailleach. You defend a woman you despise out of love for her son.

'Liath Luachra says my mother is untrust-.' Demne's tongue fouled on the syllables. He tried again. 'She says my mother is un-trust-worthy.'

Bodhmhall's lips gave a wry twist. 'Liath Luachra is forthright. Perhaps overly so.'

'But she never lies.' Demne raised his hand and looked wistfully at the smooth stone held between his fingers. 'I wish Liath Luachra was here. I miss her.'

Bodhmhall looked at her hands. 'So do I,' she said.

***

Hampered by her broken arm, there was little of practical use Bodhmhall could do to pass the time but keep her nephew company while he remained on watch. This was not something that displeased her however. Over the course of their journey across the Great Wild, Muirne Muncháem had done everything in her power to prevent the *bandraoi* from spending time with the boy. The ambush at An Glenn Teann and their subsequent capture by the Brotherhood had also meant there'd been little real opportunity to talk.

Occasionally, in quiet periods within the conversation, her thoughts turned to Ráth Bládhma and the people she'd left behind. She wondered vaguely how her *lubgort* [vegetable garden] was faring, whether Aodhán was maintaining a sufficiently close guard on the valley and whether the slender Morag was swelling at the belly. At the thought of the pregnant young woman, Bodhmhall exhaled heavily in displeasure. Aodhán's spouse had specifically asked her to be present for the birth and given the couple's previous misfortune with a stillborn child, she'd given her word to do so. It was a promise she'd had every intention of keeping, although at the time of making it she could hardly have imagined her current predicament. Liath Luachra and their *Lamraighe* allies were missing or killed and the relative safety of the *Clann Baoiscne* stronghold was still some distance over harsh and unforgiving terrain. They were being hunted by killers and now, to make matters worse, they had the additional threat of Futh to contend with.

Her lips turned down as she looked around the little canyon. It was hardly the most defensible refuge were an enemy to penetrate the entranceway. Roughly rectangular in shape, it extended from the narrow cluster of holly trees, widening gradually for a distance of sixty paces or so until it reached the rock wall set at an oblique angle to the entrance, where the cave was located. On the southern side of the canyon – where the sunlight rarely touched – there was minimal growth, mostly sickly grey grass and lichen. On the northern side however, a thin stand of mountain ash – about two or three trees deep – stretched three quarters of the length of the canyon, terminating abruptly at a point opposite the cave entrance and offering a direct line of sight into the rocky hollow.

Rising to her feet, Bodhmhall crossed the rough stone floor to the ash trees. There she delved about in the undergrowth before returning to Demne, a thick bunch of *slánlus* [ribwort plantain] clutched in her right arm. Taking a seat on the rock beside her nephew, she began to instruct him on the rules and tactics behind *Gaiscíoch* – Warrior – a game she'd enjoyed playing with the other Dún Baoiscne children.

Before being selected by the draoi Dub Tíre for less childish instruction.

The *bandraoi's* grip on the cluster of *slánlus* grew tighter as she banished those memories, turning her attention instead to explaining the rules of the game.

To play *Gaiscíoch*, both players had to pull a *slánlus* stalk – the *gaiscíoch* – from the bunch, the thicker and more flexible the better. The object of the game was to behead the other's *gaiscíoch* by decapitating the seedcap. This was achieved by both players taking it in turns to hold their *gaiscíoch* out in a horizontal position and allowing the other player to make a downward strike with their own *gaiscíoch*. Sometimes, if you were lucky, you obtained a particularly hardy stalk that outlived your opponent's for the course of several 'combats'. As in life however, the wear and tear eventually took its toll and the winning stalk was, in turn, beheaded by a new victor.

They were still immersed in play later that afternoon when a bare-chested Fiacail emerged from the cave, announcing his return with a booming yawn. Standing alongside them, he stretched the muscles of his shoulders before pulling on a fresh green tunic. Bodhmhall regarded the item of clothing with interest, noting the delicate needlework of the spiral designs about the neck and cuffs. The big warrior had never wanted for good clothing, she recalled wryly. There'd always been plenty of women willing to make him a quality garment in exchange for a smile.

Or more.

She awkwardly shifted her position on the rocky seat. The uncharacteristic flush of resentment had surprised her. When she and Fiacail had lived together, his tomcat ways had caused her no end of distress but such days were long past and she hadn't considered them for many years. Any romantic notions she'd held for the Seiscenn Uarbhaoil man had long since been extinguished, even before she'd left Dún Baoiscne for a new life at Ráth Bládhma.

Despite Fiacail's own feelings on the matter.

She suppressed such considerations beneath a smile as the warrior moved closer, standing behind her right shoulder and staring towards the holly-screened entrance to the canyon. 'No movement?' he asked. He scratched absently at an itch under his arm.

She shook her head. 'Nothing.'

'You used the *Gift*?'

'Yes.'

'And there is no-one concealed there now?'

'Not at the moment.'

He grunted. 'Good. Warn me if you see anything, anything at all.'

With this, Fiacail returned to the cave, reappearing a few moments later with a set of three metal-tipped javelins. Standing directly outside the cave, he set them point first into the ground.

He took some time to place his feet, meticulously adjusting his stance before shaking his arms and allowing his hands to hang, relaxed, by his sides. Suddenly, in what seemed like a single, seamless movement, he grasped the haft of the first javelin, raised it shoulder height and launched it directly at the foremost tree of the ash stand across the canyon. Even as the first missile left his hand, he'd grasped the second and cast it, followed immediately afterwards by the third.

The first javelin shot left of the tree, smacking hard against the cliff face behind before tumbling noisily to the ground with a metallic clatter. The second passed to the right, falling into the undergrowth between the trees. The third missile, however, slammed into the trunk with a heavy *thunk*, the sound of the haft quivering violently from the force of the impact, audible even at that distance.

Bodhmhall watched her nephew nod appreciatively, impressed by the warrior's cast. The Seiscenn Uarbhaoil man however, had an unsatisfied expression while he considered the results of his efforts. Clicking his tongue non-committedly, he walked off to retrieve the javelins.

A few moments later, he was back again, taking up the exact same position, adjusting his stance and repeating the entire process.

It continued like that all afternoon, the big man targeting his tree, casting tirelessly then retrieving the missiles and trying again. As the afternoon progressed however, Bodhmhall grew increasingly uncomfortable for she could see that Fiacail's accuracy was not improving. If anything, the fading sunlight seemed to cause his aim to deteriorate for by the time the sun was out of sight behind the southern wall, he was barely striking the tree trunk once for every nine casts he made.

Finally, covered in sweat, he stopped and laid the weapons aside, gratefully accepting the bowl of water Bodhmhall was offering him. 'You should rest,' she told him. 'You press yourself too hard.'

He looked at her, arching one eyebrow.

'Are you using your *Gift* to read me, *Cailleach*?'

She couldn't repress the guilty smile. 'How did you know?'

'It's an on old habit of yours.'

'What old habit?' she asked, genuinely surprised.

'Back in Dún Baoiscne, whenever you used your *Gift* to examine me, you always nagged afterwards.'

Bodhmhall stared at him.

'Don't look so shocked. A sensitive man like myself can pick up on such womanly ways.' He guffawed loudly at the expression on her face. 'I have a question, *Cailleach Dubh*. A serious question concerning *An tíolacadh*.'

Amused but curious, she gestured for him to continue.

'When you consider me with your *Gift* …'

'Yes?'

'Is my internal flame as handsome as my external features?'

Her lips curled into a sardonic smile. 'It is even more handsome.'

'I knew it!' he exclaimed effusively, slapping his knee with enthusiasm. 'I knew I had the right of it.'

Both laughed with genuine good humour.

'Tell me,' he said and his voice was suddenly serious. 'With your *Gift*, do you see the life force of the plants and trees as well as those of animals?'

Bodhmhall took a moment to prepare an answer. 'It is more … indistinct. Like a blur. There is some light but it merges together and … It forms a moody background.'

Fiacail nodded sagely. 'So you could not, for example, distinguish that tree that I've been striking with my javelins all afternoon from the others?'

She looked at the tree. The surface of the trunk bark on the closer side was badly pitted from the rare strikes the Seiscenn Uarbhaoil man had succeeded in making and white parts of the inner trunk were exposed. 'No,' she said, shaking her head.

'Ah,' he said simply. He sounded oddly disappointed.

Bodhmhall's left eyebrow formed a sardonic arch. 'You display uncommon interest in *An tíolacadh*. Back in Dún Baoiscne, it never seemed a subject of great significance.'

His eyes dropped to her breasts and he grinned broadly. 'When we lived together there were always other … distractions. I suppose that my interests extend with age.' He raised both hands in the air and regarded her with exaggerated shock that could not disguise the true humour behind it. 'Perhaps I am growing wise!'

She gave a cynical smile. 'I never noticed your interest extend beyond a comely shape.'

He shrugged with unforced nonchalance. 'I cannot extend beyond a comely shape. You cannot distinguish between the life force of the trees.'

'I may not be able to distinguish the tree but I can make out the bird's nest in the upper branch.'

Fiacail looked at her blankly and she laughed out loud. 'The nest, oh wise one. The nesting season is well over but a *spideog* – a robin – is using it as a refuge. I can see the *spideog*.'

The warrior's eyebrows raised at that and his face broke into a satisfied smile. 'Well now, *Cailleach Dubh*,' he declared. 'Well, that is truly more interesting.

***

With their supplies exhausted, dinner that evening was a particularly lacklustre affair consisting of the previous day's porridge sweetened with a handful of berries. Sharing a single bowl, the trio ate with appetite but not enthusiasm, despite the fire that Fiacail now permitted. Normally a man who enjoyed his food more than most, Bodhmhall noticed that the warrior refrained from any comment over the course of the meal. It was evident that, even with the threat of Futh, they'd be obliged to leave the canyon if they wanted to eat.

Nightfall slunk in with the zeal of a hungry predator. Absorbed in her contemplation of the campfire flames, when Bodhmhall looked up she was shocked to discover the darkness already enveloping the canyon beyond the immediate circle of light thrown out by the fire. The Seiscenn Uarbhaoil warrior had stacked the base much higher than normal and Demne had gathered so much firewood that an impressively high pile now sat ready to be tossed onto the flames.

Bodhmhall considered the ruddy blaze with some misgivings. The rocky confines of the canyon seemed to amplify the noisy crackle of burning logs and she feared the yellow glare reflected off the walls might draw Futh to them in the same way moths were drawn to a flame.

Turning to the side, she glanced uneasily towards the canyon entrance and stiffened, a gesture which did not go unnoticed by the big warrior. 'Do you see - ?'

'Lifelight,' she confirmed.

'Is it him?'

'The flame is too large for an animal,' she confirmed. Her voice was short, her vocal chords tight with tension, but she managed to control the quaver.

Fiacail muttered something unintelligible under his breath. 'Do not turn your face towards the passage. Keep a watch from the corner of your eye.' He transferred his gaze across the fire to her nephew. 'Or you Demne. Do not reveal that we're aware of his presence. Understand?'

The boy looked frightened but he gripped his sling tight and nodded silently.

Bodhmall realised she was scratching the inside of her palms with her fingernails, a nervous habit she'd thought to have overcome. She purposely pushed both hands down by her sides, taking a deep breath before she addressed the warrior. 'What should we do, Fiacail?'

'We will ignore him and finish this delightful meal.' The Seiscenn Uarbhaoil man wiped a smudge of porridge from his chin, stroking his stubbled jaw with disfavour. 'This lack of water vexes me however. I have need of a shave.'

15

The *bandraoi* continued to stare at him, confused by his apparent nonchalance. 'Fiacail, the entrance way is the single point narrow enough to prevent him gaining entry to the canyon.'

'Rest easy, Bodhmhall. The Bald One will not be the match of me.'

She gaped, the warrior's brash confidence doing little to reassure her. 'Fiacail, I -'

'Bodhmhall please. Let me savour the full flavour of this repast.'

The *bandraoi* lapsed into anxious silence as she watched him chew on the last of the gritty porridge. Despite his instructions, she struggled to avoid using her *Gift* although she repeatedly peeked furtively towards the cluster of trees at the canyon entrance. 'Futh is inside,' she hissed urgently. 'He's positioned at the far end of the mountain ash. I told you we should have-'

The warrior's hand reached across to grip her wrist, silencing her. He turned then to the boy who'd been anxiously following their talk. 'Demne,' he said, his voice surprisingly light. 'You should return inside the cave. Take your sling and remain within its shelter. Whatever you do, do not look towards the ash trees when you stand. And do not run. Do you understand?'

With a gulp, the boy nodded. Swallowing again, he rose stiffly, eyes focussed on the entrance to the cave. As he walked towards it, Bodhmhall could see the tension in his shoulders as he resisted the natural inclination to run.

Fiacail picked up a loose twig and absently began to pick his teeth with it. Spitting out a loose white glob of crushed kernel, he spoke to her from the side of his mouth. 'Where is he now?'

She started to turn but his hand abruptly shot out, grabbing her arm and preventing her from moving. He shook his head. 'From the corner of your eye, dear one. From the corner of your eye.'

Disconcerted and angered in equal measure, she furiously tugged her hand free but did as he asked. 'He remains in the trees by the entrance,' she said after a moment or two. 'He probably watches us, forming his plans.'

'Probably.' The warrior appeared unfazed.

'Fiacail,' she pleaded. 'Futh has had several days. He may have prepared javelins.'

'I would think so. That's what I'd have been doing had I been in his place.'

She stared at him incredulously. 'But he might cast them!'

'From that position? I wouldn't think so. Even your young Aodhán, good as he is, would struggle to make an effective cast at such a distance in this light.'

'But he can move closer, work his way through the trees.'

'Then we will join Demne in the cave. The angle of the entrance means that no javelin strike will hit us.'

'Not if he proceeds to the end of the ash stand. From there, he can see directly into the cave and the strength of the fire means he'll view us clearly.'

'Bah! You worry too much, *Cailleach*.'

She glared at him with a mixture of outrage and desperation then watched with horror as the warrior dropped another log on the fire.

What is he doing? He blinds us to the darkness.

She froze then, her posture rigid for a fresh flicker of movement had caught her eye. 'He draws closer through the ash trees.' The *bandraoi* shivered, recalling the expression on the bald man's face when he'd held her in place for his aroused little comrade, the gruesome leer and the bulge against the cloth in the crotch of his leggings. She suddenly felt very sick.

Looking down at her hands, she was disturbed to find she'd started scratching the palms again. The skin was now grazed with deep lines of red scored into the flesh. She growled unconsciously, hating the tremor in her voice, hating the Brotherhood warrior even more for reducing her to such a state of terror.

Unmindful of her mounting despair, Fiacail frowned. 'Very well. We'd better return to the cave. It would be pointless to tempt fate. Or the Bald One's casting arm.'

Bodhmhall rose to her feet and regarded him in consternation. The Seiscenn Uarbhaoil man seemed oblivious to the true extent of the danger.

'I'll put out the fire.'

'No time for that. Besides, if he crosses the canyon to the cave we'll be able to see him.'

'If he has javelins he will have no need to cross. Fiacail, please! I beg of you.' There was real fear in her voice now, a discernible quaver that she could no longer disguise. The warrior caught it for he now regarded her with quiet intensity. 'Do you truly believe, dear one, that I would place you in harm's way?'

With that, he started slowly towards the cave.

Bodhmhall stared, slack-jawed, after him then, rousing herself, stumbled hurriedly in his shadow. As she drew alongside, he reached out to grasp her arm and draw her close. 'Come take my hand. Steady now. Walk easy towards the cave. See! Isn't this pleasant? You haven't held my hand in such a long time. I'd truly forgotten how soft you were, *a chroí*.'

Once again, Bodhmhall struggled to make sense of the warrior's increasingly irrational behaviour. Terrified, she glanced back over her shoulder and caught sight of a bright yellow blur, moving purposefully down the southern side of the canyon towards them.

'He's almost on us!' She almost broke into a run but Fiacail's grip on her hand tightened, holding her in place. Fearing the increasing likelihood of a javelin arching in out of the darkness, it took all of her self-control not to struggle free, despite the knowledge that any shelter in that cave would be short-lived. A soon as Futh reached the end of the trees, shrouded in darkness, he could pick them off at his leisure.

'Look here,' Fiacail crowed proudly, gesturing towards his own set of three javelins that remained poking up out of the ground by the entrance to the cave. 'See how prepared I am.' She gaped, unable to make sense of the comment. It was all as though she was trapped in some kind of surreal dream.

Or nightmare.

Without any warning, he suddenly reached forward, clasped her in his arms and kissed her full on the lips. Taken completely by surprise, she struggled to think straight as she felt his dry lips clamped upon her own. Before she had time to react, he whirled her around so that she was facing the end of the ash stand directly behind him.

'Use the *Gift*, Bodhmhall. Where is he?'

Enveloped in his embrace, she suddenly realised that the tension of his body was not a result of passion but of stress. Looking into his brown eyes, she saw them flared with furious determination. 'Towards the end of the trees,' she managed to gasp.

'Where exactly?'

'At the very end of the ash stand, now. His stands upright, just beside the tree with the nest.' Her voice went hollow. 'He has moved to the left.'

He prepares to cast.

Suddenly, Fiacail whirled away, thrusting her aside with such force that she was pitched back against the stone pillar to the left of the entrance. In one single dynamic movement, he'd whipped up the nearest javelin and flung it out into the darkness. Even before her mind fully grasped what he'd done, the second javelin was in his hand and it too went whirring into the darkness. There was a sudden terrifying, agonzied scream but already the third missile too was off, following the others. Bodhmhall stared as the warrior lunged forwards, knife in hand, and disappeared into the darkness beyond the fire.

With belated insight, she realised Fiacail had been standing in exactly the same position from which he'd been casting that afternoon, that he'd even been holding the exact same stance.

He never missed his target this afternoon! He wasn't aiming for the tree but the position to the left. The position from which Futh was most likely to cast.

All that time, over the course of the entire afternoon, he'd been training his body, establishing a muscle memory so that when he cast, he'd hit that exact spot. She shook her head. It had truly been a plan of remarkable ingenuity.

Pulling herself off the ground, she drew on her *Gift*, staring across the canyon to the trees where the invader's lifelight was now stirring weakly, much closer to the ground than before. Even as she watched, another more brazen flame rushed in and leaped upon it. A moment later, the first flame was completely extinguished.

She sat staring in shock until Fiacail returned, emerging out of the darkness and into the red glow thrown out by the fire. He was breathing heavily and his clothing was scuffed but he contrived to put on a casual air as he drew closer. Drawing to a halt alongside her, he looked down with surprising gentleness. 'You can sleep easy tonight, dear one.'

Unable to speak, she nodded dumbly. Looking very weary, Fiacail continued on towards the cave, stroking his chin as he did so. 'And in the morning,' he said. 'I will celebrate this moment with a shave.'

Chapter Two

On the southern bank of the river, the warrior Liath Luachra sat contemplating her reflection. The still pool, located to the side of a slow-flowing inlet, mirrored her haggard expression with unsettling accuracy. Her face was gaunt, her eyes framed by black rings, the high cheekbones sharpened by the shaded hollows beneath. The physical evidence from the toll of days of hard running and combat was impossible to ignore. Of more concern however was the worrying sense her internal resilience had also diminished, withered not only by the gruelling journey but the loss of Bodhmhall and Demne.

Her eyes turned to regard the coursing river with a mixture of bitterness and trepidation. A fast-flowing stretch of surging white water, just the sight of it was still enough to make her shiver. Less than a day earlier, she'd barely managed to crawl from its liquid grasp, half-drowned and at the limit of her endurance. Stretched exhausted on the sandy bank, she'd wanted nothing more than to lie there and sleep. Instead, she'd somehow forced herself to her feet and stumbled downriver, combing the bank for Bodhmhall and her nephew.

Several hundred paces later, numb with fatigue, she'd crawled into a cluster of fern inside the treeline, curled into a damp ball and promptly passed out. Later that afternoon, when she'd come to her senses, she felt stiff and cold and far from recovered. Staring up at patches of sky through the breaks in the forest canopy, she could tell from the grey quality of the light that nightfall was closing in. Despite feeling every bruise, every individual cut, scratch and strained muscle, she'd pushed herself off the ground and started searching again.

By the time dusk seeped in, she'd still found no sign of Bodhmhall or Demne although she did locate Muirne Munpáem and Gleor Red Hand. The *Lamraighe* couple had washed up together on a short mud flat over a thousand paces downriver from where she'd collapsed. Despite the gentle incline up to more solid ground however, they hadn't progressed beyond the water's edge.

Gleor, unconscious, had an ashen pallor that matched the hue of his greying beard. The *Lamraighe* leader's face bore numerous cuts and bruises and she could see washed out bloodstains on his tunic, although she was unable to tell if they were his.

Muirne – the Flower of Almhu – normally a woman obsessed with her appearance, was sitting dismally in the mud beside him, caked in sludge and filth. Marks in the surface of the mud bank revealed how her attempts to shift her husband towards the bank had been stymied by the stocky weight of his body.

The two women had stared bleakly at one other for several heartbeats, their expressions lacking any warmth. Without a word, the Grey One had abruptly turned her gaze away and started off downriver. Muirne's despairing pleas had trailed her until, finally, she'd halted and turned sharply to retrace her steps.

Cursing under her breath, she'd helped the Flower of Almhu drag the insensible Gleor up onto the bank and into a small clearing several paces inside the trees. Using her sword – miraculously, still in its scabbard – Liath Luachra had cut some saplings and constructed a rough lean-to in which they'd placed the comatose old man.

Not a single word was exchanged over the entire period the two women worked together. Holding the *Lamraighe* couple responsible for their predicament, Liath Luachra bore no love for either of them and knew the feeling was mutual. Despite this, when the shelter was complete, she'd crawled inside to sleep beside them, too tired to question why she'd returned to help them.

Too tired to do anything but sleep.

***

It was well after dawn the following morning before Liath Luachra was able to peel the lids from her eyes. It took several moments to remember where she was, to stir from the painful discomfort. Beside her, the *Lamraighe* couple remained comatose, lying huddled together in exhausted slumber.

Ignoring the growl of hunger from her stomach, the woman warrior crawled from the lean-to, emerging into a world of dark trees and shadows and greasy, low-lying cloud. Making her way through the trees, she stumbled out of the forest and down to the river, dropping to her knees at the edge of the mudflat to drink and wash her face. Finally, feeling more clearheaded, she got to her feet and surveyed her surroundings.

The waterway was broad at this section of the river valley, the low banks thick with pine and alder and hemmed in close by the steep mountains on either side. The forest, stretching inland from the river, spread for little more than a hundred paces before running up against the base of those mountains.

Liath Luachra closed her eyes and slowly exhaled, focussing her attention on the sensation of the wind in her hair. Although she tended to wear it up in taut, unyielding braids, due to the previous day's dousing she'd released it to dry more effectively. Now, the black mane hung free, thick strands slapping her forehead and shoulders in the strengthening breeze.

She opened her eyes once more and stared upwards to where clouds the colour of old porridge smeared the sky, drifting sluggishly in a westerly direction between the ridges on either side of the valley.

Move. You've rested enough. Find Bodhmhall.

With a groan, she put one foot in front of the other and started downriver.

The woman warrior scoured the riverbank for the better part of the morning, increasingly troubled by the absence of sign, yet conversely relieved given the prospect of what she *might* find. After an extended period of fruitless searching, she reluctantly headed back to that section of the riverbank where she'd left the *Lamraighe*.

She was within a few hundred paces of the makeshift campsite when she first noticed the smoke, a thick column that rose up from the distant trees. A markedly visible indication of their presence, she doubted their enemies were close enough to see it. Nevertheless, her instinctive caution made her uneasy at such careless pinpointing of their location.

With a grunt of dissatisfaction, she continued on her way.

As she approached the camp, she spotted the *rí* of Na *Lamraighe* at the edge of the trees overlooking the mudflat. Propped up with his back resting against a giant alder, his legs were sprawled out on the ground before him. He looked to have recovered some of his colour but there was a visible slump to his shoulders she hadn't noticed before.

While she was watching, Muirne emerged through the trees and squatted down alongside him, stroking his forehead and talking. Both were still too far away for the woman warrior to hear what she was saying.

Unable to face the prospect of conversation, Liath Luachra chose a secluded patch of grass beyond the mudflat and sat brooding as she stared out at the frothing water. Idly tossing pebbles into the current, she tried to work through her next course of action.

It was possible Bodhmhall and Demne had been swept much further downstream, but now that she had covered a fair portion of the riverbank, that possibility was looking increasingly unlikely. If they'd washed ashore on the opposite side of the river, the chances of finding them were even slimmer. Not only would she have to locate a ford to cross the waterway, she'd have to search the opposite bank both upriver and downriver for sign. That was simply too much ground to cover, particularly given Gob An Teanga Gorm's inevitable arrival with his men.

The Grey One ground her teeth and exhaled heavily.

Her only workable option was to continue downstream, to work on the assumption they'd come ashore on her side of the river. If, after two days, she still hadn't found any sign of them, she'd find a way out of the valley and strike overland in the direction of Dún Baoiscne. Assuming Bodhmhall and Demne were still alive, they'd be headed in the same direction. Given the rugged topography generally limited the number of viable paths, there was a possibility – albeit a slight one – their trails would intersect.

She reconsidered the plan for a moment, assessing its various merits and weaknesses but was unable to come up with a better alternative. Her lips twisted into a mirthless grin. Whatever she decided, the immediate priority was to get further downstream and out of the confines of the river valley. Bodhmhall, she knew, would have already worked that out too. The *bandraoi* was smart enough to know Gob An Teanga Gorm and his men wouldn't give up on their intent to capture them.

The thought of the hatchet-faced warrior at An Gleann Teann prompted a bitter surge of animosity just as a splashing noise upstream made her turn her head. Muirne Muncháem had moved down to the river and was kneeling, water cupped in her hands, to drink. As her view of the young woman momentarily fused with the memory of the lethal, hatchet-faced man, Liath Luachra recalled the words he'd uttered just before the battle had started.

Tell Muirne she'll have cause to regret her decision to spurn me.

The warrior woman felt a sudden fury flare in her chest. Preoccupied with the struggle for survival and her own feverish search for Bodhmhall and Demne, she'd forgotten those words and it was only now that the ramifications struck her. Muirne had known the identity of their opponent all along, and had kept that information to herself.

She betrayed us!

Leaping to her feet, the warrior woman started furiously towards the Flower of Almhu. Muirne must have sensed or heard her approach for her pretty face came up to glance in her direction. Spotting the Grey One's murderous countenance, she jumped to her feet with a cry of alarm and made to flee. Before she'd even made five steps, Liath Luachra was on her, tackling her to the ground, one hand grasping her long curls, the other clamping tight about her throat.

There was no mercy in the Grey One's eyes as she dragged the smaller woman towards the lowest section of the river bank, and forced her head out over the surging current. 'Why?' she demanded. 'Why did you betray us?'

Muirne's response was a fearful squawk. 'I didn't! I did –'

Whatever she'd intended to say was cut off, replaced by an incomprehensible gurgle as Liath Luachra pushed her head into the river.

The younger woman struggled fiercely but the Grey One lay across her, one knee pressed against the small of her back, both hands holding her head firmly below water. The angle of her body and the warrior woman's steely strength meant it was impossible for Muirne to leverage herself up and, as a result, she could do little more than beat ineffectually at the water on either side. It was only when this desperate flapping began to falter that Liath Luachra eased her grip and pulled her up.

She waited patiently as Muirne coughed and gasped and choked, spluttering water out of her lungs. When she judged the younger woman sufficiently coherent, she repeated the question. 'Why did you betray us?'

'I didn't betray you! I -'

Once again her head plunged underwater. The Flower of Almhu struggled, splashing the river violently and creating lots of spray but little in terms of effective resistance. The Grey One pulled her out of the water.

'Please! Please, my baby ...'

This time, the Grey One relented but held her head so that it lay just above the streaming current.

'I care nothing for your baby, you twisted branch. I care nothing for you and if you -'

'I didn't betray you!' Muirne yelled. 'I don't know what you're talking about.'

'I'm talking about your friend.'

'What friend?'

'The one waiting in ambush at Gleann Teann with thirty warriors. What was your agreement? Were you going to sacrifice us and your husband to ...' With this she paused, for she knew something wasn't making sense. Despite her dislike of the other woman and her contempt for her self-serving ambition, she knew Muirne harboured genuine affection for Gleor Red Hand. Liath Luachra had seen evidence of that intimacy herself back in the fortified stone circle at Glenn Teann just before the battle.

And Gleor Red Hand and his men had fought furiously against the overwhelming odds.

'There was no agreement!' A yell of utter desperation from Muirne. The warrior woman readjusted her grip on the now sopping curls. 'Tell me about Gob An Teanga Gorm.'

'Gob! I don't know anything about -'

Splash!

Back into the water.

Liath Luachra detested Muirne Muncháem, had disliked her from their very first encounter at Dún Baoiscne many years earlier. Newly wedded to Bodhmhall's brother Cumhal, the spoilt young woman had done everything in her power to undermine the *bandraoi*'s standing at a time when

Bodhmhall's existence in the community was already on shaky ground. Some years later, when Cumhal had been killed, Muirne had the gall to turn up seeking asylum at Ráth Bládhma, despite the history of enmity between them. The little community's subsequent attempts to protect her had cost the life of Liath Luachra's only friend and now, potentially Bodhmhall and Demne's as well.

Her hand tightened, gripping fistfuls of Muirne's hair.

And yet, her protests have the ring of truth.

The woman warrior frowned. Muirne was a skilled manipulator of mistruth but even so, she wondered if she might be asking the wrong questions.

She heaved the Flower of Almhu's head up out of the water again. There was a repetition of the spluttering, the sobs of fear, the gasping for breath.

'He was my father's man! My father's man!'

Now we're getting somewhere.

'Go on.'

'Gob was my father's man.'

'Yes, you've already said that.'

'I don't know what else.'

'He led the ambush in Gleann Teann. He was also the same man who organised the assault on Ráth Bládhma almost seven years ago. I can't believe two such events connect simply through chance.'

'Gob was at An Gleann Teann?'

Liath Luachra's lips compressed. The astonishment in the woman's voice sounded genuine.

'Yes. Why was he there?'

'I don't know! I don't know! I never even saw him. I was at the stone circle.'

'You were present during the attack on Ráth Bládhma.'

'I was in the huts! Hiding with the other women and children. I only heard the fighting. I never saw the attackers.'

Liath Luachra exhaled in annoyance. That much was true. Bodhmhall had told her as much many years ago.

'Gob wants your son. Your eldest son, not Gleor's unborn whelp. Why would he want Demne so badly?'

'Gods! I don't know. Please, I don't know.' Liath Luachra pressed her head down, dipping it momentarily into the water before allowing it to rise again. Muirne spluttered as river water dripped from her nose and mouth.

'He left my father's stronghold. A year before I married Cumhal.'

'Why?'

'... I don't know.'

But this time, Liath Luachra caught the pause and before she had time to expand on the lie, the woman warrior had ducked her back underwater. Holding her down, she counted to twelve before raising her again.

'He made advances to me!' Muirne spat breathlessly. 'He offered me his hand.'

'And?'

'And I refused. Gob meant nothing to me and my father had already approved my marriage to Cumhal with *Clann Baoiscne*.'

Her father. Tadg mac Nuadat of Almhu.

'Your father?' she repeated to give herself time to think.

'Yes, yes!'

'So, what happened?'

'Gob left Almhu. He never came back. I never saw him again. I don't know any more.'

Liath Luachra studied the other woman with a chilling lack of expression then grudgingly released her. Muirne hauled herself back onto the bank, weeping with terror and gasping for breath. The Grey One watched her crawl away without compassion, her thoughts focussed on what she'd learned. The new facts added little to her understanding but she suspected the Almhu woman was telling the truth for her story seemed to align with Gob's threat to kill her.

I don't understand.

She chewed furiously on her inner cheek. In hindsight, although it was evident Gob and Muirne had known one another, it now seemed unlikely the two were as tight as she'd initially assumed.

Frustrated, she glared at Muirne with fresh hostility. The younger woman's curly locks were drenched and in complete disarray, the top of her neck and her green travelling dress sodden and coated in fresh mud from the river bank. 'Go!' she said. 'Go away from me. See to your man.'

Muirne hurried off, stumbling in the slick mud in her haste to escape the woman warrior. Liath Luachra eyes followed her as she scurried back to the treeline where Gleor Red Hand had now struggled to his feet. Grasping one of the nearby trees for support, the old warrior was glaring at her with undisguised hatred for the mistreatment of his woman. Belatedly, the woman warrior realised the *Lamraighe* man would have seen everything, heard everything. Incapacitated, he'd probably been bellowing impotently at her to stop but, consumed by her own fury, she'd been too preoccupied, too far away to notice.

Liath Luachra turned away, picked up another stone and flung it out at the passing torrent. The current was so strong there wasn't any splash when it struck the water, the force of the flow compacting any ripple before it could even form. She shivered again as she recalled the bloodcurdling terror she'd experienced when the four of them – herself, Muirne, Gleor and his son Fintán – had leapt into that torrent from the falls at Gleann Teann.

Her lips formed a thin line at that. In truth, she was the only one who'd actually jumped. Obstructed from leaping after Bodhmhall, she'd driven the others over the edge while they'd been struggling at the precipice of the cliff. Three of them – Liath Luachra, Muirne and Gleor – had survived the fall but, like Bodhmhall and Demne, there was still no sign of Fintán.

No doubt Gleor holds me responsible for that as well.

She pulled at a loose thread on a tear in the left knee of her leggings. Apart from her sword – *Gléas Gan Ainm* – and the sling wrapped about her arm, she'd lost all her weapons and equipment in the flight from An Gleann Teann. Now she had little more than the clothing on her back: the faded red battle harness and tattered leggings. Muirne and Gleor were in a similar situation although the *Lamraighe* man had managed to retain his tinder pouch and knife; Liath Luachra had appropriated the latter while he was unconscious. Fortunately, the late summer meant the weather remained mild so the cold wasn't an issue. Nevertheless, the temperature had a tendency to fluctuate and the season was certain to turn in the days to come.

Her stomach growled again and a fresh wave of weakness washed over her. Light-headed, she felt her head spin and had to drop to her haunches before she collapsed. For a time, she sat hunched over, fighting the dizziness. When her head finally cleared, her armpits were wet with sweat, her heart pounding as though she'd been running hard.

She needed food.

Waiting until the vertigo had fully passed, she got to her feet and worked her way back towards the inlet where a slow-flowing stream ran down from the ridge to enter the main waterway. Placing herself near the bank, she sat patiently scanning the water until she'd spotted what she'd been looking for, a number of small shadows flitting in and out from the shallows beneath a nearby section of the bank.

Trout. Big ones.

She knew there were probably several of the fish hidden in hollows beneath the bank where the flow of water had eroded the soil. Dropping to her knees, she crawled to the edge so her own shadow didn't fall onto the water, inching her waist forward until her upper body dangled over the flow. Slowly, very slowly, she slid both hands into the water, easing them under the protruding lip and into the hollow from where she'd seen the fish emerge. With immense patience, she brought her hands together several times in a painfully-slow pincer movement until she felt her right fingertip brush the cool smoothness of fish scales.

With delicate, gentle caresses, she stroked the underbelly of the unreactive trout. Continuing the slow stroking movement, she gradually worked her hand up towards the head, increasing the tightness of her grip around the gills at the rear of the head. For a long time, she maintained exactly the same position, despite the growing strain on her shoulder and stomach muscles. Then, with a great splash of water, she yanked the trout out of its refuge, flipping it up behind her in one swift and supple movement. There was a flash of silver scales, a wet slap as the trout hit the ground and then it was flapping frantically on the bank.

Exhausted from the *dornfhásc* – the tickling – she flopped back onto the grass and rested, easing the tension of extended stillness from the muscles of her upper body. By the time she'd recovered, the other fish had returned. She settled back in place, repeating the process two more times until she had three relatively large trout lying on the bank.

Using Gleor's knife, she removed the heads and gutted the fish, then washed them in the river and carried them back to camp. Working her way through the trees, she entered the clearing and approached the fire where she started to build a light frame of green sticks. Wedging her catch onto the finished frame, she placed the woody contraption above the smoky flames.

Trembling from fatigue, she settled back onto the ground, mouth watering as she watched the flesh of the trout sizzle, the delicious aroma of cooking fish flooding her nostrils. As was often the case with food caught in the Great Wild, the hardest part was the waiting.

She let her gaze drift around the little clearing before realising, with a start, that Gleor Red Hand was seated in the shadows of the trees just beyond the lean-to, watching her with silent loathing. The waxy greyness to his skin and the vague glaze to his eyes seemed to have faded, burned off by his fury at his woman's mistreatment. Muirne, meanwhile, had retreated inside the lean-to and although she occasionally poked her head outside to regard the fish with hungry eyes, the Grey One doubted she'd risk coming any closer.

A sullen silence filled the little clearing but Liath Luachra made no attempt to fill the vacuum. She had nothing to say to either of them. Through their unbridled ambition and poor decisions, Gleor and Muirne had potentially cost the lives of the two people she held most dear. It was true to a point, that they too had lost much but that was a burden of shame they – and the *Lamraighe* leader in particular – would have to bear. From the vehemence of Gleor Red Hand's gaze however, she suspected the

Lamraighe man intended to focus on his enmity towards her rather than acknowledging the bitter truth of his own mistakes.

Reaching forward, the warrior woman used two thin sapling branches to turn the fish. From the corner of her eye, she caught Gleor's stare swing from her to the fire and then back again.

It galls him that he's dependent on my help.

She shrugged. There was nothing she could do about that, nothing she cared to do at least.

The fillets didn't take long to cook through and Liath Luachra didn't waste any time transferring them from the now-blackened frame to a flat rock for cutting. Using Gleor's knife, she removed the remaining bones, resisting the almost overwhelming temptation to stuff the freshly cooked flesh into her mouth.

Swallowing the lump of saliva congealed at the back of her tongue, she turned to address her two silent comrades. 'Do you want fish?'

'I don't want anything from you, Grey One,' Gleor snarled.

The woman warrior ignored him and focused on the task of cutting the fish into smaller morsels. That lack of reaction however, seemed to infuriate the *Lamraighe* man even further for he growled at her again. 'I've never liked you, Grey One. You are a brutal woman and you'll learn to regret placing such hardship on Muirne.'

'The withered blossom's hardship is a result of her own selfish designs.' Liath Luachra's gaze flickered towards the Flower of Almhu, who was regarding her without expression from the dubious safety of the lean-to.

'Designs that you shared,' she continued, turning her eyes back to Gleor. 'You took Demne from us. You repeatedly ignored our counsel. It was your arrogance and your errors of judgment that cost Marcán Lámhfhada his life.'

She paused then as she recalled her last sight of Gleor's massive, one-eyed bodyguard, throwing himself into the horde of attacking warriors to give his leader a chance to escape.

Misplaced loyalty, Marcán. You deserved better.

'I will avenge Marcán. Our enemies' blood will spill one hundred-fold for his sacrifice.'

Liath Luachra snorted. 'That's cold comfort for Marcán. Besides, how will you carry through on such a mighty boast? *Na Lamraighe* are a broken force. Your warriors feed the carrion at Gleann Teann.'

'There are plenty more warriors back in our territories, all eager for battle glory. *Na Lamraighe* will rise again.'

'Not in your lifetime. No warrior with a blood name will follow such poor leadership. And without your warriors, you're just another old man crawling around in the mud with delusions of authority.'

Gleor turned his head and spat at her, the glob of spittle just missing her ear. 'I piss in your mouth, Grey One.'

Liath Luachra displayed no emotion. Piling some of the fish onto a flat piece of bark, she got to her feet and started to walk away, the heat of Gleor's eyes burning a furious hole in her back. 'Choke on your fish,' she spat back over her shoulder.

Leaving the trees, she wandered down to the river and found a grassy spot to eat in peace. Father Sun had jostled his way through the grey clouds and now hung at his peak, dousing the river valley with fine, honey-coloured sunshine.

The woman warrior ate slowly, forcing herself to take small bites. After more than a day without food, the cooked trout tasted delicious, better than anything she'd eaten in a very long time. Ironically, despite her appetite, the extended periods of hunger also meant her stomach had contracted and it didn't take long before she was feeling full. Putting the bark plate to one side, she wrapped the remaining fish in wide, green leaves of *copóg uisce* – water dock – for later. With a burp of satisfaction, she sat back to reflect on her situation.

With her strength recovered, her immediate instinct was to up and set out once more for Dún Baoiscne, however the reality of *Na Lamraighe's* cumbersome presence prevented her from doing so. Gleor was still clearly unable to travel yet as allies of Ráth Bládhma, of Bodhmhall, the woman warrior had an unavoidable obligation to assist them.

She bit her lip in frustration. She had the increasing sense of wasting time, achieving nothing. In her mind she visualized the day flashing past just like the raging waterway before her. She still had no idea if the *bandraoi* and her nephew were alive, she was still no closer to finding them and it wouldn't be long before Gob An Teanga Gorm and his men came looking for them.

So find them, Grey One! Find them before that.

She sighed. Such a task was easily articulated but decidedly more difficult to achieve.

***

The woman warrior had already spent the better part of the afternoon combing the southern bank by the time she reached the low knoll of pine forest stretching down from the steep southern mountain range to the river. There, the soil where the trees touched the water was badly eroded and crumbled away in parts so that a number of the great trees had tumbled into the waterway. From the vacant spaces, she could see that some had already been flushed downriver but the remainder lay tangled together, protruding out at an angle against the current and held in place only by the sheer weight of their combined mass.

Liath Luachra briefly studied the water between the curtains of rotting foliage and mangled branches. Perceiving nothing of note, she was about to move on when a distant glitter of sunlight on metal caught her eye. Stiffening, she stared but had to move back a step before she relocated the source of the gleam. Shielding her eyes against the glare of the sun, she peered through the snarled branches of the log jam, her heart sinking when she spotted a grey bulk bobbing sluggishly, wedged half-submerged beneath one of the heavier branches thirty paces offshore.

Suppressing a mounting sense of panic, the Grey One slipped down to the edge of the water and clambered lithely onto the buttress of one of the thicker trunks, carefully working her way along its greasy surface. Reaching the point where the enormous branch forked off towards the bobbing object, she dropped to her hands and knees, wriggling her way forward through the mesh of tangled branches.

Despite its apparent solidity, the route through the broken trees was a treacherous one comprising numerous smashed branches and clumps of slippery vegetation. Whole sections had the potential to give way without notice and spill her into the river beneath. In the grip of that powerful current, the Grey One knew she'd be swept under the fallen trees, probably to snag on one of the many underwater obstructions. It would not be a pleasant death.

So, do not let it happen!

After several tense acrobatic manoeuvres, stretching and crawling through the woody debris, she made it to the point where the giant branch curved down to touch the water. At the bottom of the curve, it straightened out sharply, extending into the river for ten paces or more before dipping beneath the flow.

It was from that elevated position that she caught her first clear view of the object that had initially caught her attention. A gleaming clasp of bronze, it was attached to an item of clothing – a cloak – that bulged out of the water, inflated by a trapped air bubble. Closer now, she could also make out two bare white legs protruding from beneath the enormous bough, flailing sluggishly underwater in the flow of the current.

Her throat was suddenly very dry and, inside her chest, something shifted sideways. She stared at the feet for several moments before finally gathering the courage to slither down the slippery curve and onto the horizontal section. As it was too perilous to continue in an upright position, she dropped to straddle the bough, river water lapping above her ankles as she shuffled forwards to where the cloak was trapped.

31

It's a man.

She sucked in a lungful of air, suddenly conscious that she'd been holding her breath. Up close, she could see that the bare legs were hairy, the ankles strong and muscular. She was also able to make out the hem of a padded leather tunic floating just above the knees.

One of Gob's men.

Overcome with relief, she grasped the rough bark of the bough. An immediate and urgent craving for solid ground almost drove her back to shore but she shrugged it off. Having come so far, it would've been foolish not to investigate further.

With a great exhalation, she continued her forward shuffle, advancing until she sat almost directly above the submerged body. In the time it took her to get there however, the erratic currents had shifted the cloak and the bronze clasp had disappeared just beneath the surface.

Grasping the slick bark with both hands, she leaned out, stirring the water with her foot. Her perch was precarious, too unstable to risk scavenging the body of the dead warrior, but she was determined to recover the bobbing cloak. In the days to come, as the weather deteriorated, the extra layer might make the difference between survival and death.

She watched the current shift the cloak around for a time then, picking her moment, plunged her left arm into the water and grasped the sodden material. Because of her precarious position, hauling the waterlogged cloth out of the water was more difficult than she'd anticipated but she eventually managed it. Draping it across the bough, she threw one last glance at the ghostly legs before shifting about and starting back the way she'd come.

Shuffling along the bough, she clambered up the angled section and started working her way through the twisted woody detritus. She was shaking by the time she got back to shore, sapped not only from the physical exertion but from the strain of extended concentration.

Hauling the bundled cloak under one arm, she scrambled onto the bank and crawled up the loose soil to more solid ground. Locating a stable oak tree, she slumped against its trunk and with trembling hands withdrew the remaining morsel of fish from inside her battle harness, chewing on it listlessly while she examined her new acquisition.

The cloak was wool and from the feel of the material – admittedly sodden – of excellent quality. The bronze clasp used to fix the material into layers or to fasten it tighter was fabricated in the familiar shape of an oak leaf and seemed almost ...

She paused.

This is Bodhmhall's cloak.

She stared at the garment in her hands, struggling with the reality of what she was seeing.

This is Bodhmhall's cloak.

Raising the bronze clasp to examine it more closely, she felt a growing sense of dread. She hadn't made a mistake. She recognised the clasp as a present from Bodhmhall's brother Crimall, one of the *bandraoi's* few personal possessions. Liath Luachra had seen her toy with it on innumerable occasions over the years and there was no mistaking the soldered repair in the lower pin where one of the Ráth Bládhma children had damaged it.

She continued to clutch the cloak tightly, grappling with conflicting senses of confusion and dismay. How could it be? How could it possibly have ended up in the possession of the dead warrior?

Struggling to calm herself, she muttered quiet reassurances under her breath. There were a thousand possible explanations for how he might have gotten his hands on it.

But Bodhmhall was wearing it when she jumped.

That single realisation stymied any further attempts to assuage her fears. Dazed, she sat very still.

She was still sitting, the garment grasped tight between her fingers, when a flicker of movement by a clump of wildflowers at the treeline drew her eyes. From the colourful blossoms, two butterflies emerged – one orange and black, one bright yellow with spotted wings – fluttering out into the full glare of the late afternoon sunshine.

Butterflies?

She stared at the colourful creatures, watching as they floated erratically before moving further into the trees and then abruptly disappearing. Gazing mutely in their wake, the woman warrior recalled her last in-depth conversation with Bodhmhall prior to leaving Ráth Bládhma. The subject of their discussion – her own rare sighting of a butterfly swarm – had prompted the *bandraoi* to reveal the teachings she'd received on the role of insects as messengers of the dead.

From those who have taken the Dark Leap.
Our ancestors and those who have gone before us.

Two butterflies.

Demne and Bodhmhall.

That abrupt and devastating association crushed her, broke her more than any physical assault ever had. Keening in pain, she rocked backwards and forwards, the dripping garment clenched in her hands. A scalding grief welled up inside her chest, a wound more agonizing than any sword thrust.

For a time then the old madness came back, that violent, twisted battle fury from her mercenary days with *Na Cinéaltaí* – The Kindly Ones. Her side vision blurred, fading to a blinkered, red mist and she was vaguely aware that she was screaming. She didn't know how much time passed before she finally came to her senses but she was suddenly conscious that her throat was raw, that her sword was in her hand and the earth in front of her was scored and raked from where she'd been hacking at it.

Exhausted, she fell back on her haunches, sweating, gasping for breath, incapable of a single coherent thought.

And yet, despite her despair, some of that old fury surged forth again, a ferocious internal seething that flamed to life and burned through the grief.

She is not dead. Demne is not dead. I don't believe it.

She swallowed the sob swelling in her throat, knowing she had to cling to that hope, had to reject the weakness of grief. Otherwise … there was nothing.

Shivering violently, she got to her feet and replaced *Gléas Gan Ainm* in its scabbard. Pushing herself off the tree trunk, she used the momentum to take several faltering steps before she stopped. She had no idea where she was going.

'Grey One.'

The voice caught her completely by surprise, struck her with the force of a slap to the face. In shock, she swayed back towards the tree, staring towards a section of wood thirty or forty paces downstream from where the voice had seemed to come. As she watched, a slim figure stepped out of the shadows and started towards her, a youth of about eighteen years with ruffled brown hair and a scraggly moustache. Despite his good looks, he looked worn and bedraggled, his tunic and leggings filthy and torn, his hair greasy and unkempt. As he drew closer, she saw that although his eyes were ringed with shadow, they burned with excitement.

'Fintán!'

'Grey One! I'm so glad to see you.' This much, at least, was evident from the relief in his voice. He stopped before her, made as though to reach forward and embrace her then abruptly seemed to change his mind. 'I'd feared you drowned.' He paused. 'Have you seen my father? And Muirne?'

She returned his stare with desolate detachment, seeing him as though he was very, very far away. If it had been one of Gob's men who'd stepped out of the trees, she realised, she'd be dead by now.

Accustomed to the woman warrior's habitual lack of animation, the *óglach* did not seem slighted or even surprised. In the end, it was her ingrained fear of appearing weak that drove the numbness out and allowed her to answer. 'I… They…'

It took a moment to remember how to speak.

'They're alive,' she croaked. 'Upriver.'

'My father is in good health?'

'He's not dead.'

Fintán cocked his head to one side as he regarded her with perplexity. Dismissing the odd remark, his relief and youthful self-absorption then drove him to explain his own reappearance.

'I nearly died! Whenever I came close to the bank I was thrust back by the current, several times until I hit the shallows downriver.' He raised his hands and stared at them as though to convince himself of the reality of his survival. 'I've been working my way back since this morning. I think -'

'Bodhmhall or Demne?' she cut him off abruptly. 'Have you seen them?'

'No, Grey One. And I've searched the riverbank, all the way from where I came ashore.'

'Maybe they were driven further downriver.'

The youth shook his head. 'I don't think so. The current was slower and the banks were low where I came ashore. They must be on the other side.'

Both turned to stare across the foaming white water. The green woods and the mountains lining the far bank seemed distant and indistinct. The woman warrior sighed, confused, depleted and so numb as to be uncertain *how* she felt.

The *Lamraighe* youth turned to her then, his face full of burning intensity. 'Grey One. You pushed us off the cliff! You pushed us all off the cliff at An Glean Teann.'

Liath Luachra considered him without emotion. 'You were in the way,' she said.

***

Fintán mac Gleor chattered incessantly as they made their way back upriver but Liath Luachra let him prattle on without complaint. Too distraught to contribute anything of her own, it just was easier to slip into a passive role and let his *ráimeis* [nonsense] wash over her, filling the empty spaces in her head.

Still struggling with the traumatising demise of so many of his own tribal comrades, the youth had a complex knot of emotion to unravel and vent. His mood flitted wildly, flipping sharply from mute despondency to joyful exhilaration as he skipped from topic to topic without discussing any

35

of them in depth. It was a relief therefore when the Grey One finally spotted the thin column of grey smoke announcing their return where the *Lamraighe* couple awaited. Too dead inside to feel any sense of outrage, on this occasion the Grey One simply stared and said nothing.

Catching sight of his father by the riverbank, Fintán released a yelp of delight, dropped his satchel and rushed forward to embrace the older man. Liath Luachra watched their happy reunion, observing how the older man's cold demeanour cracked and how he wept openly as he hugged his son close.

Unable to cope with such displays of sentiment, she retrieved the *óglach*'s satchel and continued alone towards the campsite. Thrusting herself into the solid shadow of the treeline, she pushed her way forwards until she hit the edge of the little clearing. There, to her surprise, she found Muirne Muncháem sitting cross-legged on a smooth boulder near the fire, bent forwards over the green travelling dress draped across her lap. The smaller woman was naked and completely focussed on stitching a tear in the fabric of the hem.

Disconcerted, the woman warrior stumbled to a clumsy halt. She stared blankly at the Flower of Almhu, noting the smoothness of the younger woman's skin, the roundness to her breasts, and gaining an unexpected insight as to why so many men had fallen under her spell. Her gaze dropped to Muirne's belly and she noted the slight bulge that hadn't been apparent prior to their departure from Ráth Bládhma.

Sensing her presence, the Flower of Almhu glanced up with a start. Alarmed by the Grey One's mute scrutiny, she quickly pulled the dress on over her head and slipped from the boulder. Hurrying away in the direction of the river, she circled wide to avoid coming anywhere near the warrior woman.

Liath Luachra watched Muirne leave without emotion but when she'd disappeared from sight, she stepped into the clearing and moved towards the boulder, the only section of open space still bathed in sunlight. She hung Bodhmhall's cloak across the branch of a nearby oak tree and when it lay draped smoothly across its length, lifted one corner of the material to her nose in the hope of catching some remnant of Bodhmhall's scent in the fibres. To her dismay, there was nothing. The river water had washed all trace of the *bandraoi* away.

Returning to the boulder, she lifted Fintán's satchel from the ground and emptied its contents onto the hard, flat surface: a selection of berries, seven edible mushrooms, a large clump of water-cress, and a single hare. She sniffed. In terms of nourishment for four adults, the pickings were slim although it'd be a simple enough task to supplement the meal with fish again.

For tonight at least.

The problem, of course, was that this wouldn't overcome the obstacles facing them. Several days of rough terrain still separated them from their destination and they had no ready food supply. They could, of course, keep their hunger at bay through the use of snares or *dornfhásc* while they remained by the river but travelling to *Clann Baoiscne* territories meant they'd have to head north-west, away from their current supply of food. For that reason, they'd be obliged to spend a substantial proportion of each day foraging, time she'd have preferred to use reducing the distance between themselves and Dún Baoiscne.

Liath Luachra sighed and slowly got to her feet. Traversing the Great Wild without supplies was bad enough but a particular concern was that at least one member of their party was incapable of contributing to the food gathering process. At the best of times, dependents were a burden. In situations like this, they were a dangerous liability.

The Grey One drummed her fingers along the surface of the boulder and knew that, at some point, she'd have to address that directly.

Chapter Three

The prickle of sunlight against her eyelids stirred Bodhmhall from slumber. With a groan, she sat upright on the bed of crushed bracken. Squinting against the liquid glare of the sun, she smeared a dribble of saliva from her lips with the back of her hand.

Although she tried to concentrate, her head remained woolly at first, not from the sleeping draught on this occasion but from sheer fatigue. Three days had passed since leaving their refuge at the box canyon and Fiacail had been pushing them hard, eager to put as much distance as possible between themselves and Gob's *fian*. Darkness had been close upon them when they'd finally halted, settling themselves in for another uncomfortable night in a dense patch of fern at the forest's edge.

Despite the limitations of the site, the waist-high fern provided effective shelter from the late-evening breeze. More importantly, it was safe. No pursuers could have found them unless they'd literally stumbled upon them. Situated on the slope of a low hill, it also offered a fair view of the flatland stretching off to the east, the trail they'd be taking once they were up and moving again. In the fading twilight the previous evening, she'd seen a pair of hills in the distance, protruding up from the earth like the breasts of a prostrate woman. This morning, the brilliant sunlight that had woken her so brusquely shone through the narrow cleavage of those earthy curves.

The *bandraoi* plucked a twig from her hair as she stared towards the rising sun, struggling to rouse herself for yet another day of travel. She'd lost her hair clasp and comb in the river and now the dark strands were a tangled nest kept under control only through the use of a topknot held together by a length of grass fibre.

A soft snore from the ferns to her left confirmed that Demne hadn't shared her abrupt awakening. Brushing the feathery fronds aside, she found him curled on his side, the heavy material of his cloak shielding his face from the rays that had roused her. It didn't look as though the boy would willingly stir any time soon.

Turning her gaze to the green nest of crushed fern where Fiacail had been sleeping, she could see no sign of the warrior although the presence of his cloak and axes suggested his absence was no real cause for alarm. Dropping her left hand to lever herself off the ground, she stiffened at the burn of pain the movement produced, another reminder of her injured limb. Exhaling the ache through gritted teeth, she stared at the flatland with tearing eyes, seized by a sudden yearning for Ráth Bládhma, for Liath Luachra and her life back at An Glenn Ceoch.

Bodhmhall was jaded, worn down by a combination of mental and physical fatigue. She'd had enough of pain, of death, of discomfort and being hounded from one location, one danger to another.

Pull strong, Cailleach. What rattles you now, so close to the end of your ordeal?

That much, at least, was true. Although the topographical features were unfamiliar, she knew they couldn't be far from *Clann Baoiscne* territory, had quite possibly entered it already. Recovering her calm, she levered herself off the ground with her good hand and got to her feet. Weeping was wasted effort. It would not save her or Demne. It would not help Liath Luachra.

She took a moment to slap the woody detritus and flecks of dry fern from her clothes. When she'd succeeded in removing the worst of it, she studied her travelling dress with disapproval for the material was tattered and grimy from sweat and mud. And, like her, it smelled.

She thought then of the shallow pool they'd passed before stopping the previous evening. A small pond, less than four hundred paces south of the campsite, its water had looked appealingly clear and fresh. She'd been too exhausted to even consider bathing at the time, but now there seemed no better place to try and wash her troubles away.

***

Weaving her way down through the trees, Bodhmhall quickly hit flat ground and followed a tiny feeder stream until the pool came into sight.

Unfortunately, it was not the only thing that did. Standing alongside it was Fiacail mac Codhna, once again absorbed in his morning ritual to Great Father Sun.

Clicking her tongue in frustration, the *bandraoi* silently eased into the shadows of the trees, preferring to wait out of sight until the warrior was done. She stared longingly at the distant water, before transferring her attention to Fiacail. As always when performing his ritual, the Seiscenn Uarbhaoil man was naked, both arms raised towards the east through a wide gap in the canopy, in supplication to the rising sun.

As she watched, his hands dropped to his sides and he shifted back to retrieve his clothing, bearing his weight on his hips in a perfectly balanced stance. The warrior was in impressive shape, his upper torso taut and muscled, his belly rippled, his buttocks firm and tight.

The *bandraoi* took a step to the right, intending to place herself behind the bulk of a large oak trunk. Unfortunately, her foot landed firmly on a clump of dry forest debris and the sharp snap of a dry twig rang loud above the twitter of birdlife.

The warrior reacted immediately, spinning on his heel with a javelin raised, dark eyes focussed unerringly on the spot where she stood concealed.

'Fiacail! Hold your cast!' Fearful of the warrior's lethal reflexes, the *bandraoi* hurriedly stepped out of the trees.

'Bodhmhall.' The Seiscenn Uarbhaoil man's shoulders relaxed. He lowered the javelin.

Flustered, Bodhmhall waited for the warrior to finish dressing before approaching any closer. 'I came to bathe. It was not my intention to disturb you.'

'You cause no disturbance. My ritual is complete. I am satisfied, Great Father Sun seems satisfied.'

The *bandraoi* looked at him blankly then shook her head, her lips curling in a wry half-smile. The warrior raised one inquisitive eyebrow as he leaned against a nearby tree. 'What is it Bodhmhall? Tell me true, now.'

Bodhmhall shrugged. 'Nothing of consequence. I'm simply uncertain as to whether I should be impressed or disturbed that you continue this ritual after so many years.'

'Someone has to do it,' he said in all seriousness.

'But why? I understand you offer Father Sun your greetings but what else must you share with him that's of such importance?'

'I offer him words of thanks.'

'Of thanks?'

'For troubling to bathe the world with life each day. And for warming my skin. Sometimes, if he's untroubled by cloud, I'll tell him he has a handsome cast and request a boon.'

Bodhmhall laughed out loud at that. 'You attempt *plámás* [soft talk] to seek a boon from Father Sun?'

'You should never underestimate the sway of *plámás*, dear one.'

'No, I suppose not.' She chewed on her lip then, her amusement abruptly faded. 'You know, Dub Tíre used to despise you for daring to address Father Sun.'

Fiacail regarded her with an air of caution that surprised her until she intuitively, if belatedly, grasped the reason behind the response.

Dub Tíre.

In all the years she'd known the warrior, even during the time they'd lived together as husband and wife, she'd avoided speaking of the *draoi* at

40

Dún Baoiscne. On those few occasions when others had broached the subject, she'd invariably diverted the discussion to other topics.

And yet now, here she was, dropping that despised name into the conversation. It was little wonder Fiacail's response was so guarded.

Perhaps you have moved on, Cailleach Dubh. Perhaps with time, that memory does not rub so raw.

She delicately raised her injured arm to her chest, stalling for time to reframe her thoughts.

'Dub Tíre believed you interfered with his own intercessions to Father Sun on behalf of the people.'

The warrior snorted. 'I need no-one to intercede with Father Sun for me. Besides, what would Dub Tíre have known of the subjects I might wish to raise?' He shook his head with quiet conviction. 'No. It was not my interference Dub Tíre feared so much as the threat to his own authority.'

Bodhmhall made a careless gesture with one hand. 'The Druidic Order placed great faith in his skill and foresight.'

He chuckled at that. 'And you, of course, have always aligned your opinion with that of the Druidic Order.'

The *bandraoi* gave a wry twist of her lips before steering the conversation to safer waters. 'What do you ask of him?'

Fiacail looked at her blankly.

'Great Father Sun. What do you ask of him?'

The big man's eyes gaze turned inwards as he considered the question then snapped back to focus on her. 'I ask for a horse.'

'A horse?'

'Is it not proper that I should travel at equal height to the *rí* of Seiscenn Uarbhaoil? That fat old man has a horse. As do two of his warriors. Not that they're inclined to share such good fortune.' He sighed as though burdened by this great injustice then abruptly contradicted himself with a shrug of dismissal. 'Of course that's not all. I also ask that my sword arm remains strong, my *bod* remains firm and, as on every other occasion over the last ten years of course, tha-'

He paused suddenly, casting her a furtive sideways glance.

Intrigued by the big man's evident discomfort, she pressed him further 'Ten years? What is it, Fiacail? What have you been asking for these past ten years?'

He stared at the ground for a long time as though to avoid the *bandraoi's* gaze. Eventually, realising that this was not a matter she intended to let slide, he slowly raised his head and sighed. 'I ask him,' he said, his voice heavy with emotion. 'I ask him that after all these many years, Bodhmhall ua Baoiscne might deign to forgive me.'

***

'There!'

It was late afternoon when Bodhmhall's excited cry brought the little party to a standstill. Startled, Fiacail and Demne stared at her in alarm before turning their gaze in the direction indicated by her pointing finger. The target of her enthusiasm was a collection of five dome-shaped mounds sitting off to the north-east, several hundred paces from the treeline of the nearest section of forest.

The mounds – more like circular, grass-covered humps than hills – looked strangely isolated sitting out alone on the flatland. On their western side, a shallow corridor-like depression in the earth, barely discernible beneath the layers of grass, formed a passageway up to the curve of the nearest structure. Too regular and linear to be a natural form, its artificial origins were confirmed by a pair of lichen-coated standing stones that flanked the depression where it approached the base of the mound. The placement of the stones suggested they'd been set there to mark some kind of threshold, although what that might have been, even Bodhmhall couldn't begin to guess.

Fiacail mac Codhna stroked the smoothness of his chin as he considered the *bandraoi*'s excited reaction. With renewed access to water he'd taken to shaving again and now his face – bar the usual moustache – was freshly groomed. It made him look several years younger.

'I recognise this place,' the *bandraoi* told him. 'It's named Síd Na Thost.' The *Síd* of Silences.

The Seiscenn Uarbhaoil regarded the mound but displayed no discernible reaction. The *bandraoi* realised he'd have encountered many similar *síd* over the course of his extensive travels, some of them far bigger and more impressive than these.

'It marks *Clann Baoiscne* territory.'

Comprehension registered in the warrior's eyes and he dipped his head in acknowledgement. 'Oh. Well, these are happy tidings then.'

The weight of her earlier fatigue must have caught up with her for Bodhmhall found herself irrationally vexed by the warrior's lack of enthusiasm. 'It is more than that, Fiacail. It means we are safe.'

'That may be, dear one, but I'll keep my axe close to hand all the same. Our pursuers won't share your knowledge of this site's relevance and, even if they did, I doubt they'd care.' Fiacail shifted the heavy basket of supplies

42

on his back, seeking a more comfortable alignment. Noting the tension in the *bandraoi*'s stance, he tested the waters with a decidedly innocuous question. 'This territory is unfamiliar to me but by my reckoning we must be within two or three day's march of Dún Baoiscne. Is that not so?'

'Two days,' she confirmed grudgingly.

He grunted in acknowledgement and she watched as his eyes drifted back to the stretch of grassland they'd just traversed. A dark line of trampled pasture marked their passage from the south-west. Turning his gaze skyward, the warrior considered the position of the sun then the large body of cloud clumped together to the west. A knot formed in the centre of his forehead.

'Father Sun is unhappy. He will admonish us with hard rain tonight.' He whistled tunelessly to himself as he looked around, completing his inspection by pointing to the crest of a prominent hill poking up from the bulk of green forest to the north. 'We should divert our trail, make our way towards that hill.'

'Cnoc Uaigneach,' she informed him. The Lonely Hill.

'Cnoc Uaigneach,' he repeated. 'It may bear a despondent name but it should provide a sheltered cleft against the coming storm.' His eyes returned to the flattened pasture once more and his lips formed a thin line.

'You're concerned,' Bodhmhall observed. 'By the trail we leave.'

'Of course. If Gob's men are on our heels it is an effortless path to follow.' He yanked the tips off some nearby grass stalks and chewed on them silently before spitting them from his mouth. 'Still, good fortune presents itself with the coming storm. The wind and rain will obliterate all trace of our passage. If we stay alive until nightfall we can consider ourselves free of pursuit.'

'Really?'

'Of course. The purging of our trial will make it impossible to follow us. Besides, as of tomorrow, we'll have but a single night more in the Great Wild.' He stroked his chin pensively once more before underlining this conclusion with a decisive grunt. 'But we'll take no chances. For now, you should take Demne ahead to find shelter. I'll lay false trails to confound pursuit and follow when I'm done.'

Bodhmhall was about to voice her agreement but a tug on her sleeve distracted her. Looking down, she found Demne staring towards the distant mounds.

'What are they, *a Aintín*?'

'They're *síd, a bhuachaill*. Burial sites of the Ancient Ones. Their people lie at rest within those mounds.'

Demne squinted then chewed awkwardly on the inside of his cheek, a mannerism he'd recently adopted in imitation of Liath Luachra. On his young face the gesture simply looked painful. 'There must be many dead in there.'

'Not so many. They're said to contain little more than burnt bones and ashes but it's hard to be certain. In their wisdom, the Druidic Order forbids any but themselves from entering.' She paused, her eyes taking on a faraway gleam as she considered the distant *síd*. Suddenly, conscious that the others were watching, she busied herself by slapping her hand against the skirt of her dress, brushing off the few fragments of grass that had accumulated there.

'You are tempted, are you not?' Fiacail offered her a knowing smile.

'What?'

'To enter a *síd*. Do not attempt to deny it, Bodhmhall? I know that look.'

'You know nothing.'

'Would you do it? Would you truly venture inside, violate the prohibition?'

At first, the *bandraoi* simply deigned him with a frosty expression but then seemed to reconsider the matter. 'I don't know,' she admitted at last. 'I confess to a great weight of curiosity but …' She shook her head. 'No. In truth, I think I'd be too frightened. I'm not so brave or so formidable I could oppose the restraints of upbringing so easily.'

Fiacail considered this conclusion with obvious amusement. 'And yet, it seems to me that is entirely your life's work, *Cailleach*.' Chuckling loudly, he gave her good shoulder a hearty slap. Without another word, he struck off across the flatland, making no effort to minimise the trampled grass in his wake.

Bodhmhall and her nephew watched the warrior walk away. 'Why does he leave us?' the boy wanted to know. 'Is he not coming to Dún Baoiscne?'

'Rest easy, *a bhuachaill*. He goes to lay false trails for our enemy. He'll catch us up soon enough.' She took his hand in hers. 'Come. We have a distance to cover before nightfall.'

With this, she led off at a steady pace, headed towards the forest and the distant hill. The boy followed but after a short distance he approached to clutch her dress at the waist. 'What is Dún Baoiscne like, *a Aintín*?'

'It's a busy place. There can be many people there, many animals and children.'

'More than Ráth Bládhma?'

She laughed at that. 'Much more, *a bhuachaill*. The fortress dwarfs Ráth Bládhma. It has two great ditches and two embankments. The inner embankment is reinforced with stone.'

Demne's eyes widened as he attempted to imagine the scale of what she was describing. 'Will we see my grandfather there?'

'Tréanmór? Yes. As *rí* of *Clann Baoiscne*, he rules the stronghold.'

'Is he nice?'

Bodhmhall blinked, taken aback by the simplicity of the question, the naive reduction of people to those who were 'nice' or 'not nice'.

'In some ways he is … nice. In other ways, he is not.'

The boy frowned at her. 'Well,' he persisted. 'Do you think he's nice?'

'No,' she admitted. She shook her head. 'No, I don't.'

'But he's your father.'

'Yes.'

The boy looked at her in confusion, unsettled by the bluntness of her response. Noting his reaction from the corner of her eye, Bodhmhall experienced an uncomfortable twinge of guilt. Her nephew had limited knowledge of parent-child relationships. Restricted to his meagre experiences from Ráth Bládhma and what others had told him of his own father, he'd naturally assumed that all parents loved their children. The possibility that this might not be the case challenged that belief.

She continued to watch him surreptitiously as he thought the matter through. Because of his youth, he hadn't yet learned to conceal the depth of his emotions and his inner confusion was reflected across his features. The *bandraoi* waited for him to complete his deliberations but when he did so he didn't react as she'd expected.

He simply chewed the inside of his cheek and kept on walking.

***

They set camp in a shallow cleft at the foot of Cnoc Uaigneach. Bodhmhall had chosen the site with care, dismissing several possibilities before settling on a recess in the curving wall of a low cliff at the base of the mountain. It was a good site. The greater part of its exposed side was screened by a semi-circular stand of oak trees set less than ten paces out from the cliff while above, a wide promontory protruded, offering effective protection against the expected rain. Best of all, there was a tiny spring in the rocks several paces off to the side of the recess, an extremely convenient source of fresh water.

Fiacail reappeared to join them a short time before nightfall. Entering the camp, he wordlessly raised his hand to display the two hares he'd caught while laying his false trails. The *bandraoi* immediately set to making a small fire close to the cliff wall, confident that the strengthening winds would rip any tell-tale trace of smoke away.

Putting the hare furs aside for later curing, the big man cut up the carcasses, separating the meat into segments which he then diced into smaller morsels. While he popped them into his little stew pot and prepared the other ingredients, Bodhmhall helped her nephew collect firewood from the forest. It was almost dark when they returned, the *bandraoi's* face strained and pale from trying to carry too much with her arm. Dropping her bundle by the fire, she shivered and wrapped around her shoulders the cloak she'd retrieved from the body of one of the Brotherhood. It was too dark to make out the clouds gathering in the heavens above them but she could sense their oppressive accumulation. The temperature was dropping fast and there was a tightness to the air that hadn't been there earlier. The wind was also growing increasingly bitter, violent gusts battering the enclosing trees and lashing the leaves.

Fiacail had the right of it. Father Sun quarrels with the Great Mother and vents this fury to express his displeasure.

The snug recess sheltered them from the worst of the weather. Nestled beneath the promontory as they were, the rain and the gusts couldn't touch them and the heat of the fire reflected from the cliff wall to keep the chill at bay. Beyond the curve of the promontory however, the world became a different place. Five or six paces past the flickering light of the fire, the night was darker than the heart of a Tainted One. Tree leaves flailed and crackled, great boughs creaking painfully as they were pushed and stretched. The shriek of the wind was particularly frightening. Loud enough to stir the ancestors from their rest, the fact that the forces causing that disturbing howl couldn't be seen made them all the more unnerving.

Staring out at the roiling black, Bodhmhall knew she should feel relieved to be huddled in the safety of their refuge but, in a strange way, she felt an almost sympathetic connection with the ferocious storm. She couldn't be sure if it was simply her fatigue, her suppressed fear for Liath Luachra or a belated emotional response to the terrifying events of the previous days, but its fury seemed an apt expression of her own internal disarray.

Brushing such thoughts aside, she turned her attention to the Seiscenn Uarbhaoil man. Fiacail had dropped to one knee by the fire and was absorbed in his preparation of the stew. She watched with interest as he stirred the little pot with slow precision. Following the morning's disconcerting admission, she'd anticipated a period of discomfort and awkwardness but in fact, the warrior had been his usual irrepressible self.

46

Shrugging his embarrassment off like a worn-out cloak, he'd spent the day laughing loudly at his own jokes and telling bawdy stories to pass the time.

And yet, despite his apparent insouciance, she knew he'd spoken from the heart. Fiacail still had strong feelings for her and because of the fondness she bore him that distressed her. The cycle of their union had long completed its turn and she did not wish him to suffer any illusions in that regard.

Oblivious to her scrutiny, Fiacail lifted the pot from the fire and poured some of its steaming contents into their single bowl. Leaving it to cool for a moment or two, he used a wooden spoon to taste the stew, smacking his lips in delight at the result. 'Aaah!'

He beamed across the fire at Bodhmhall and Demne. 'Food of flavour in a sheltered nook with pleasant company. Such are treasures for a man to relish. Is that not so, wolf-cub?' He directed the latter to the young boy, who nodded vigorously in response.

'Yes, Fiacail.'

Bodhmhall fought the temptation to roll her eyes.

My nephew finds a new role-model in Liath Luachra's absence

Chuckling in satisfaction at this gem of wisdom, Fiacail lifted his right leg and released a loud fart, audible even above the noise of the storm. A startled silence hung about the fire then Demne started to giggle.

Another fart followed: a longer, more powerful discharge that extended effortlessly upon itself to build up to an explosive climax. This time Demne clapped his hands and laughed out loud in delight.

That was it, of course. With an appreciative audience there was no stopping the Seiscenn Uarbhaoil man. Over the course of the meal, he released an endless stream of farts, a veritable cacophony of noises that varied dramatically in terms of strength, pitch, duration and odour. Weary and in pain, Bodhmhall was in no mood to appreciate the childish, if well-intentioned, humour, even if it did leave her nephew rolling on the ground in laughter. She endured the noises with stoic forbearance however, until one particularly impressive eruption that made Fiacail stiffen and stare bleakly across the flames. Noting the warrior's sudden rigidity, the *bandraoi* felt a stab of alarm. 'What? What is it, Fiacail?'

An expression of distress spread across the Seiscenn Uarbhaoil warrior's face.

'What?'

'That last fart ...' Fiacail stared at her dismally. 'It ...'

'What?' she demanded.

'It wasn't a fart.'

47

Bodhmhall gaped at him in bewilderment. As her expression of dread slowly melted into one of repugnance, Fiacail barked with laughter.

'*Amadán!*' You idiot! She glanced to her left where her nephew was also doubled over in mirth. '*Is amadáin an bheirt agaibh!*' You're both idiots!

Furious, the *bandraoi* got to her feet and stalked off towards the spring, propelled from behind by a fresh gale of laughter. The shallow pool was located just beyond the protective overhang and as she crouched alongside, a spray of frigid raindrops spattered her hair and face. Cursing, she pulled the hood of her cloak up over her head, dipped her hands into the bubbling water and started to wash.

Amadáin!

She'd never really understood what it was about grown men, young boys and farting sounds although, with Fiacail at least, she'd come to accept it. The Seiscenn Uarbhaoil warrior had exhibited an unquenchable fascination with every basic bodily function for as long as she'd known him although, for some unfathomable reason, he'd seemed to derive particular amusement from fart noises. Possibly – and this was a suspicion she'd harboured in secret for several years – that enjoyment derived not from the sound itself so much as the reaction it provoked from her.

She clicked her tongue in irritation. As an infant, Demne too had displayed immense enjoyment when Liath Luachra, despite her initial vexation at the prospect of raising Muirne's son, blew on his stomach to make fart sounds.

She paused and bit her lip. That rare expression of the woman warrior's softness, mingled with the infectious giggling of the infant, produced an ache in her stomach every time she thought of it.

Which made her absence all that much harder to bear.

She immediately shut off that line of thought. Out in the perilous expanse of the Great Wild, it was not uncommon for people to simply disappear, never to be seen or heard of again. She didn't have the strength to face that possibility at present.

You could find her. You could use the imbas ritual.

She stiffened at that, the prospect triggering an immediate and involuntary rush of panic. Without thinking, she stepped forward, out of the shelter of the overhang to where the storm struck her with what felt like almost personal vehemence. A gust of hail stung her face. Stunned, she stood in the flurry of the gale, gazing into the darkness as the screaming wind snapped the hood from her head, whipped her hair free and sent it streaming out behind her.

'Bodhmhall!'

Fiacail's voice was barely audible above the howl of the wind but it was enough to draw the *bandraoi's* attention. Twisting about, she looked back towards the campfire, a firm bubble of light in the blustery darkness.

'Bodhmhall! Your nephew falls asleep at the fire.'

It was true. Demne had slumped forwards off the low rock where, only moments before, he'd been roaring with laughter. Despite that earlier gaiety, he now remained upright only because of Fiacail's mighty hand on his shoulder, holding him in place.

Hurrying back into shelter, Bodhmhall grasped the toppling child, and with the warrior's assistance, carried him to his bedroll. As she lay him down and tucked him in, the *bandraoi* regarded the limp little figure with affection. Demne had been pushed hard for weeks and had never complained, not once in all the time they'd been travelling. At night, desperate to partake in the grown-up discussions, he'd always insisted on staying up until he'd, literally, collapsed.

And with the resilience of youth, he'll leap from his bedroll completely refreshed tomorrow.

Bodhmhall and Fiacail returned to the fire and took a seat on opposite sides of the little blaze, she on a smooth stone, he on a mossy log hauled in from the forest. Finding themselves alone, neither spoke and all of a sudden it seemed as though the awkwardness, entirely absent over the course of the day, had finally asserted itself.

Fiacail leaned forward and silently poked at the ashes with a green sapling. Tossing the stick aside, he reached into his basket of supplies to extract a leather flask. Pulling the stopper loose with his teeth, he took a swig, shuddered and released a mighty belch.

Bodhmhall eyed the flask with curiosity. 'Does that hold *uisce beatha*?'

Fiacail glanced down at the container then up at her again. 'Yes. A little cache hidden among the belongings of the Bald Brotherhood. Do you seek its burn upon your tongue?'

'Perhaps.' She shrugged. 'I am tired of thinking. I understand it helps with that.'

His eyebrows rose in surprise at that. 'I do not believe it a taste you'd find to your liking.'

She pulled a face and gestured for him to pass it over. 'Let me be the judge of that.'

Fiacail chewed on his lower lip as he considered the *bandraoi's* request then – without warning –tossed the flask across the flames. Bodhmhall reacted with impressive swiftness, catching the container adroitly in her good hand. With a tired smile of victory, she raised it to her lips and gulped a mouthful down.

The corrosiveness of the liquid caught her by surprise, provoking a fit of coughing as it burned a raw trail down the back of her throat. She managed to keep it down but, like Fiacail, shuddered at the strength of it. Clearing her throat, she took another, more cautious swig.

'Be wary, *Cailleach*. That liquid has the punch of a spear thrust.'

Replacing the stopper, Bodhmhall gave the flask a shake, enjoying the feel and the sound of the liquid sloshing around inside. She tossed it back across the fire.

While Fiacail took his turn to sip, an extended silence settled between them. Bodhmhall watched the flames dance, feeling the comfortable heat of the alcohol simmering in her stomach. Now that the initial caustic taste had faded, the aftertaste was more bearable. She sniffed and rubbed her nose. 'That was a poor trick, Fiacail.'

The Seiscenn Uarbhaoil man regarded her in surprise. 'What do you mean?'

'With Futh. Back at the canyon. You could have told me your plan.'

'No.' He shook his head. 'Futh was a competent foe. He wouldn't have stepped into the trap if he'd sensed cunning and had I told you the plan, you'd have revealed it despite yourself. As it is, Futh now feeds the earth while you and I draw breath and sip the fire of *uisce beatha*.'

A sudden thunderclap exploded off to the north. Both glanced up in time to catch the flash of lighting carve a ragged line of fire across the sky. The *bandraoi* looked over to where Demne was sleeping but the boy had not stirred.

Fiacail chuckled softly. 'Father Sun and the Great Mother clash with rare passion tonight. Who do you think will win the quarrel?'

'Neither. They will talk, they will make amends. The cycle of life will continue.' Her mood softening, Bodhmhall found she was able to offer him a teasing smile. 'Perhaps this is your fault. Perhaps Father Sun was dissatisfied with your greeting this morning or maybe he simply doesn't like you anymore.'

'No, no. We get on well.'

'You get on well?'

'Yes. Father Sun likes me.'

The *bandraoi* hid her amusement at the assured response. Even after all these years, Fiacail still had the ability to surprise her. Of course, the Seiscenn Uarbhaoil man had always been something of an unconventional figure. She'd marked that quirkiness the very first time she'd encountered him in the mountains near the Dún Baoiscne stronghold. Searching for herbs that grew only around the heights, she'd been startled to find the handsome youth standing by the edge of a cliff, projecting his voice out into the valley below and laughing uproariously when the echo came back to repeat his words. Spotting her, he'd unashamedly pointed at the valley and cried, 'Look, Beautiful One! See how I fill the world with my voice!'

She wondered briefly if her nephew would grow up to be like that, another brash warrior convinced that the world at his feet was his own personal plaything.

If the Adversary has his way, Demne may not grow up at all.

Her jaw tightened at that, her earlier anxieties flooding back to submerge her good humour. As though sensing her change in mood, Fiacail wordlessly passed her the flask. She accepted it with a nod, took a little sip and closed her eyes, anticipating the sting of the alcohol. Already her head was feeling slightly woozy.

This is my last drop.

Opening her eyes again, she saw that she wasn't the only one experiencing the effects of the *uisce beatha*. Fiacail's right leg was tapping an unconscious cadence on the hard rock, an old habit of his when jagged from drink. Sensing her scrutiny, the warrior sat back on the moss-coated log and looked at her directly. 'A different person regards me from behind those dark eyes.'

The *bandraoi* was rolling her neck to loosen the stiffness in her shoulders. The movement produced a series of gristly pops and crackles but when she was done she looked at him in curiosity. 'What do you say?'

'I see a new hardness in you, dear one.'

'What do you mean?'

He paused, struggling to combat the muddying effect of the alcohol as he worked through what he wanted to say. 'I've always known you for a smart woman, Bodhmhall. A compassionate woman.' He sniffed and wiped his nose with the sleeve of his tunic. 'But you have changed. I see a different intensity in your eyes: less compassion, more steel.'

The *bandraoi* shrugged. 'I've borne the weight of leadership at Ráth Bládhma for more than eight years Fiacail. Through times of peril and despair. Such a burden would harden any person.' A thoughtful frown creased her brow. 'Cairbre tried to warn me of that many years ago but I didn't understand what he meant at the time.'

Fiacail sighed then leaned across the flames to retrieve the flask once more. 'Ah, Cairbre! He was no fool, that one. For someone who spent the better part of his life a slave, he had an astonishing understanding of the

51

qualities of leadership.' He looked down and poked the embers at the edge of the fire with the tip of his moccasin. 'Given the trials and disasters that beset *Clann Baoiscne* in recent times, the quality of our leaders cannot be said to have surpassed those of other tribes. Would we had leaders uncorrupted by lust for power or ego.'

Bodhmhall raised one sardonic eyebrow at that, a gesture not lost on the warrior.

'Yes, yes! I'm hardly well placed to lecture on leadership but I recognise my failings, at least. You may recall I withdrew my own candidacy for *tánaiste*.'

Bodhmhall nodded in acknowledgement but kept her own counsel. Despite the death of her brother, Cumhal – the previous *tánaiste* of *Clann Baoiscne* – some years earlier, she'd heard the elders had yet to choose a successor to lead the tribe once Tréanmór's rule had run its course. The Seiscenn Uarbhaoil man had at one point considered putting himself forward for the role and although she appreciated his abilities, in many ways that intention had been deluded. Fiacail had a well-earned reputation for 'ploughing every field'. This had led not only to the crumbling of their relationship but the erosion of his own status within the tribe as well. She'd always doubted that the Council of Elders would have accepted a candidate so driven by his *slat* to lead the tribe. 'Did Tréanmór know of your intention to submit candidacy for *tánaiste*?' she asked.

'Yes. He was not pleased at the possibility of a new rival.' Fiacail gave a rueful grin. 'Yet another reason for your father's enmity. He – and my own father – have never borne me tenderness for obliterating the union between you and I. They went to great lengths to arrange that union and although I know it's a poor excuse, in truth, its ruin had more to do with my own opposition to their plans than any dissatisfaction with you.' He paused. 'But I'm sure you must know that.'

'I know that now.' She bit back the bitterness. 'At the time I did not.'

Fiacail exhaled heavily. 'The elders say that time swallows our misdeeds. I would like to think that was true.'

Unwilling to discuss the matter further, Bodhmhall made no reply.

Another angry flash of lightning split the sky, much closer this time. For one frozen moment their view of the world was expanded in a flare of blue fire that abruptly reduced once more to the little pool of yellow illumination around the fire. The Seiscenn Uarbhaoil man looked up and chuckled to himself. 'Perhaps I should wait a day or two before seeking another boon of Father Sun.'

'I have a boon.' Bodhmhall bit her lip. 'But it is one I seek of you.'

The big man's forehead creased and the left side of his lower lip turned down as he drew back to examine her with a more critical eye. 'You know me as a man who'd grant you any reasonable boon. The fact that you'd slip your request in such a sideways fashion suggests one not only unreasonable but unpleasant to boot.'

The *bandraoi* sighed with weary resignation. It never paid to underestimate the Seiscenn Uarbhaoil man's perspicacity, even when he was in his cups. 'This boon is not one I'd consider unpleasant but...' She paused then abruptly tossed her hands in exasperation. 'Very well, Fiacail. I will not layer my words with sweet untruths. I speak of my nephew. I fear his presence at Dún Baoiscne will be used against me, will divert me from my goal.'

The warrior's forehead furrowed. 'I had understood the sole reason we travelled to Dún Baoiscne was to seek refuge.'

'That is one reason.'

'And the other?'

She hesitated then nervously licked her lips. 'The Adversary has always known far too much of our relationships within *Clann Baoiscne*, of secrets and histories only my family or someone very close could know. He has a watcher within the stronghold, that much is clear. If I can identify that watcher I'm sure I can garner the Adversary's identity from him.' Her brow furrowed. 'But the threads of evidence leading me to the stronghold form a complex knot. One I'd struggle to unravel if distracted by fears for my nephew.'

Evidently, this was not the clarification Fiacail had been anticipating for he maintained an expression of curious anticipation. 'And the boon ...' he prompted when she showed no signs of continuing.

She sighed. 'I would have you take Demne far from Dún Baoiscne.'

The warrior stroked his chin, considering her request with a kind of perplexed bemusement. 'I don't understand. Where do you wish me to bring the boy? Should we conceal ourselves in the nearby forest?'

She shook her head. 'As far from Dún Baoiscne as circumstances allow. Back to Seiscenn Uarbhaoil would be best. When my task is complete, I can come and reclaim him there.'

This time, the warrior stared at her, his countenance a grimace of bewildered outrage. 'You wish to leave a ... a child in my care? Hand back that drink, woman! Your head is addled.' He scowled, making no attempt to hide his displeasure. 'I'm no keeper of children. I am a warrior. Children are ... weak and whiney. And you would have me place such a yoke on my shoulders?'

Holding little sympathy for his arguments, the *bandraoi* simply ignored them. 'It's too dangerous for the boy to accompany me, Fiacail. And I don't have the luxury of shielding Demne from my father's machinations while I attempt to draw the Adversary's dark tick from its shadowed cranny.'

'And if I'm not present who will shield *you* from your father's machinations? You cannot seriously plan to face Tréanmór, his Whispers and his Five Friends alone?'

'I am not the nervous girl who left Dún Baoiscne eight years ago. I am a leader in my own right now.'

'Who you are or who you were has no bearing. Tréanmór is not a man to be trifled with. Even I would hesitate to confront that old bull.'

Bodhmhall paused. 'You did so once,' she said softly. 'To protect me.'

'Only because of Dub Tíre.' He blinked. 'Given events, I could hardly have done otherwise. As I cannot do otherwise on this occasion.'

'The *draoi* is dead. My father no longer holds sway over me.'

Fiacail snorted. 'Our fathers always hold sway over us,' he said simply. 'Even when they lie in their graves.'

Bodhmhall bit her lip, frustrated by the big man's obstinacy. Recognising this was an argument she wasn't going to win through points of vindication or a simple exchange of views, she settled for a tactical withdrawal, deftly manoeuvring the conversation to other topics.

'Tell me then of my father's three advisors. Apart from Tréanmór, they're the only ones who would have the opportunity and the knowledge to set the ambush at An Gleann Teann. What of Cathal Bog? Does he still serve as *conradh* [military champion]?'

The warrior considered her stonily at first, his suspicion at her uncharacteristic backdown evident in his features. Perhaps he was simply tired or the *uisce beatha* had finally softened his resolve but, after a moment, the *bandraoi* thought to see the tension ease from his features.

'Cathal Bog still serves as *conradh*,' he confirmed grudgingly. 'As long as there is Tréanmór, there will be Cathal Bog at his heels. One could not exist without the other for there is no force to the river without banks.' He turned his head and spat into the darkness. 'Besides, where else could that pig-fucker go? There isn't a single thought in that man's head your father didn't supply.'

He threw the flask back across the fire to her, possibly with more force than was necessary.

Toying with the stopper, Bodhmhall considered the harshness of his reaction with some sympathy. As her father's strong right hand, the

54

cynically named Cathal Bog – Soft Cathal – had been a figure of fear in Dún Baoiscne throughout her childhood. An ugly, intellectually dull man, the warrior had nevertheless held responsibility for upholding the rule as Tréanmór dictated, doling out admonishment to those who did not adhere. For the most part, such punishments had been rare and generally accepted as necessary by the tribal community, but it hadn't prevented Cathal Bog from acquiring a reputation as a violent and dangerous enforcer.

Secure in their status as children of the *rí*, Bodhmhall and her brothers had never had any real cause to fear the brutal warrior. Others, like Fiacail, had not been so fortunate. As a youth, he'd received at least three heavy beatings for romantic liaisons involving the women of other men in the tribe and, in one notable case, the wife of one of the elders. Even now, after all these years, the Seiscenn Uarbhaoil man hadn't forgotten – or forgiven – the violence of the pounding he'd received at Cathal Bog's hands.

'And yet …' Fiacail sat up straight, placing a palm on each knee to steady himself. 'I struggle to believe that Cathal Bog could be the traitor. He doesn't have the mind for treachery. His head is a shell. There is nothing between those ears but the lonely sound of the sea.'

Gripping the container of *uisce beatha*, Bodhmhall said nothing. She was of a similar opinion.

The Seiscenn Uarbhaoil man coughed and hacked to clear his throat. 'You should also know that since your departure Tréanmór has chosen a new *rechtaire.*'

The *bandraoi* nodded without surprise. It was only to be expected that Cairbre would be replaced. In a settlement the size of Dún Baoiscne, a *rí* needed his *rechtaire* to handle the day-to-day administrative duties that held the community together.

'Three men attempted to fill Cairbre's old role before your father declared himself satisfied. The current *rechtaire* is Lonán Ballach. Are you familiar with the man?'

She nodded. The younger son of a leader from one of the *Clann Baoiscne* subtribes, Lonán Ballach was a strikingly pompous man who'd risen to remarkable heights due to a rare ability to assess a situation rapidly and respond unerringly in a manner that benefited himself. To his credit, despite his overbearing arrogance, Lonán had invariably treated her with courtesy, although Bodhmhall had always sensed an underlying falseness to his polite demeanour. Her instincts cautioned her that he was something of a self-serving sycophant, a man who knew when to bow and scrape to the right people while concealing his own selfish ambitions.

I could believe such ambition of Lonán. And certainly a degree of ruthlessness. But would he truly betray his own tribe? It's hard to credit such treachery.

Particularly when it's not clear how he might benefit from it personally.

Fiacail retrieved the flask once more and took another swig, screwing up his face at the burn of the alcohol. 'Lonán has always been the man to talk loudest in company and yet he's always struck me as a stiff kind of man. His face bears a certain ... tightness. He spine is too rigid and his smile too strained. He does not drink, he doesn't curse and he doesn't fuck.' The big man shook his head incredulously at this last, perplexing shortcoming. 'I tell you no word of a lie. I've observed Lonán during the rituals and social gatherings. He always stands with his legs spread wide, as though he's got a blackthorn branch rammed up between the cheeks of his arse and fears to move for shifting it.'

Bodhmhall found herself laughing at the warrior's unkind – but not wholly inaccurate – description. Fiacail, meanwhile, reached down to scratch a loose scab from his right thigh. 'And then, of course, there's Becal.' He cast the *bandraoi* a shrewd sideways glance. 'Your fellow acolyte with Dub Tíre.'

She made no response but stared down at her feet. Fiacail nodded, belched and momentarily swayed, despite the fact he was still seated. Noting this, Bodhmhall judged the moment opportune to return to her original proposal.

'Your appraisal of those at Dún Baoiscne is helpful, Fiacail.' She hesitated. 'But not as helpful as the certainty of my nephew's safety.'

The warrior's eyes flicked up to fix on her, his gaze full of lucid reflection. He made no attempt to answer, deflecting this fresh attempt at persuasion with a wall of silence. Bodhmhall realised she'd misjudged the extent of his inebriation.

'You know I would not ask this of you if I did not judge it necessary.'

The warrior continued to regard her stiffly.

'Fiacail,' she pleaded. 'My nephew is more dear to me than my own life. I wou-'

'Not to me, Bodhmhall. Not to me, he isn't.'

She reached out with pleading hands. '*A chara*, would you really have me beg?'

'You do not know what you ask.'

'My life is in no danger at *Dún Baoiscne*. It is my childhood home. The people are my ...' She paused then for she had been about to say 'people' but even as her lips had formed about the word, she realised this was no longer the case. In reality, since her expulsion from *Dún Baoiscne* she was essentially *éclann* – clanless – and all that that status entailed. It was true she now led *Muinntir Bládhma* – the People of Bládhma – but such a ragtag assembly would hardly be recognised by a tribe as established as *Clann Baoiscne* or its contemporaries.

Close to desperation, she directed the full force of her appeal at the warrior but he did not flinch. 'If ever you have felt anything for who I am, for what I believe in … If you ever loved me Fiacail, I beg you to trust me in this matter.'

The latter was a low blow, a resort of desperation and one she regretted even as the words slid off her tongue. She opened her mouth to apologise but the retraction was abruptly forsaken as her *Gift* suddenly, involuntarily, kicked in. One moment, she was looking directly at the Seiscenn Uarbhaoil man, the next he'd disappeared from sight, completely consumed by a yellow blur of explosive intensity.

The *bandraoi*'s jaw dropped and, blinded, she was about to twist her head away from the glare when, just as abruptly as it'd appeared, it flickered and faded. Bodhmhall stared. Fiacail was back, his lifelight receded, once more shrouded by his corporeal form. From the lack of expression on his features it was evident the warrior had noticed nothing amiss, was oblivious to what she'd just experienced.

Stunned and struggling to comprehend the extraordinary expression of her *Gift*, she listened as he spoke, striving to concentrate and make sense of what he was saying. Apparently, he'd taken her plea to heart for, even as she strove to regain her composure, he was slowly – if unenthusiastically – nodding his head. 'Very well.' His voice sounded decisive if somewhat reluctant. 'I will bring Demne to Seiscenn Uarbhaoil but I warn you, I have little experience with children.'

Bodhmhall choked as she tried to form an appropriate response. 'Thank you,' she managed, somehow keeping her voice clear and even.

'Humph,' he grunted, not moving his gaze from the flames.

The *bandraoi* pushed herself off the stone and unsteadily circled the fire. Dropping onto the moss-coated log beside the warrior, she placed a hand on his shoulder and squeezed. 'Fiacail. Truly, I am very grateful. Words cannot …' She paused. For words couldn't.

Despite an air of sad resentment, the big man managed a half-smile. 'Do not fret, Bodhmhall. My instincts cry out at the folly of your request but I've made my choice. I will support you.'

She grasped his hand in gratitude.

In an obvious, if half-hearted, effort to change the subject, he gestured out at the surrounding darkness. 'Listen! The storm is weakening, the winds grow calmer. It is a good sign. Father Sun regains his contentment.'

'And what of you Fiacail?' she asked softly. 'What of your contentment?'

He gave her a startled look, surprised by the question. 'I am alive. I have a full belly. I don't hurt.'

'I speak of more than immediate sensation, as you know only too well. I would like to know your life holds the joy you so truly deserve.'

He opened his mouth as though to make a scornful remark but then something in his eyes seemed to change, a brief shadow sapping that characteristically devilish gleam. 'These past days, walking the land with you and Demne – despite the danger – these days have been, well … pleasant. Sometimes I even forget myself and imagine we were a happy family out for a stroll.'

He made a chuckling noise but it had a tight edge to it.

'And then of course, I remember the truth of our circumstances and the *brón* drops its leaden melancholy on me.' He shrugged then and made a self-mockingly dismissive gesture. 'I am no fool, Bodhmhall. I've seen the flicker of joy in other men's eyes when they return from the hunt or the fight, the snatch of a smile at the greeting of their woman and children.'

He picked a wooden splinter from the log, used it to pry a gobbet of meat from his teeth and spat it out into the darkness.

'As a youth I tasted happiness through the exhilaration of battle, the friendship of companions, the widening of a woman's thighs. As I grow older, that mantle of foolishness slips from these shoulders. I understand these are transitory pleasures, not genuine contentment. True happiness is less intense but more enduring. It is watching your offspring grow and prosper, it is a warm bed and the soft shoulder of a loved one to lay your head on. And you, Bodhmhall, you have the softest shoulder I have ever known.'

With that, Fiacail dipped his gaze back into the heat of the fire and his features took on the aspect of ancient stone. Bodhmhall could only stare dumbfounded. In all their time together, Fiacail had never once spoken so openly, so articulately with her on his feelings. 'What … of your woman?' she managed weakly, although there was an embarrassing catch to her voice. 'She brings you no happiness?'

Fiacail laughed at that, although not in an unkindly manner. It took her a moment to realise that this was also his answer.

'You are no longer bonded?'

He shook his head.

She made to speak again but he raised his hand, placing his fingertips against her lips. 'No more. Such talk serves only to raise ghosts of those who we once were. You have another in your life. I accept that.'

He laughed loudly then, too loudly, as though to banish the silent despondency that threatened to smother them both. 'We should sleep. We have another day's march ahead of us tomorrow.'

Unable to respond, Bodhmhall nodded dumbly.

They rose as one but, as she did so, the *bandraoi* felt as though some essential part of herself had torn away and remained attached to the mossy log. Standing, they faced one another, so close they were almost touching. Staring at the warrior's handsome brooding features, Bodhmhall was suddenly conscious of their physical proximity and the throb of her heartbeat, pounding in her ears. Even as she tried to make sense of these sensations, she saw Fiacail's heart begin to glow, burning incandescently inside his torso then swelling hot, orange and staggeringly beautiful.

What's happening?

Roused, her *Gift* was now stimulating her perception, fuelling an intensified awareness of both physical and emotional sensation that threatened to overwhelm her. At that precise moment, it felt as though her nerve-endings, her emotional receptors were swollen and over-loaded. She could see everything, hear everything, smell everything and each individual sensation was magnified a thousand-fold. Her breath was thick and warm, laden with moisture. The brush of air against her skin was soft as a lover's caress. Fiacail's scent was thick and musky and exuded a heady rawness that made her groan aloud. The warrior's lifelight blazed brilliantly, radiating colourful waves of desire that ignited and amplified her own.

Suddenly he was kissing her full on the lips and her body shivered at the hot probe of his tongue in her mouth, the firmness of his hand where it cupped her jaw. She responded without thought, reaching up to grasp his shoulders and somehow, despite his bulk, hauling him closer. Their hips connected and she could feel the hardness of him press against her belly. Sliding both hands about his buttocks, she drew him even harder against her.

Fiacail was already tugging at her clothing, brushing the cloak back from her shoulders, one hand grasping her left breast through the thin material of her dress while the other feverishly worked to unfasten the belt about her waist. She barely felt the looseness as the leather circle fell away, the folds of her dress dropping free.

Slipping one hand down inside the warrior's leggings, she clutched the growing stiffness of his *bod* and felt it swell. Bizarrely, despite his physical proximity, she couldn't actually see him for her *Gift* was flaring madly. Her vision was eclipsed not only by the crackling blaze of Fiacail's internal fire but the multitude of other lifelights surrounding them: insects, birds and small animals, all contributing their innumerable but individual flames to saturate the night with fire.

Bodhmhall was vaguely aware that they were on the ground, naked and entangled although she had no memory of falling. She felt him slipping in easily, filling her completely. At that point, all physical and emotional sensations merged and the only thing she could truly distinguish was the rhythm of movement. Consumed in the flood of sensations, she relished each wave of pulsing pleasure.

Chapter Four

Although the general mood around the campfire that evening was lifted by Fintán's return, Liath Luachra's despondency, the precariousness of their situation and the meagreness of the meal meant that mood never lifted beyond subdued relief. Consumed in her own grief, Liath Luachra initially remained in the shadows of the trees, maintaining an impenetrable distance between herself and the discussion at the fireside. For their part, the *Lamraighe* paid her no heed although Fintán occasionally threw a troubled glance in her direction.

Turning her face from the flicker of flames, she ignored them too, brooding instead over the discovery of Bodhmhall's cloak and picking at the details like the scab of a wound that wouldn't heal.

It was the smell of cooking meat that finally roused her from her desolation, the mouth-watering scent provoking an involuntary shift in her stomach. The interruption was enough for her to recognise the pointlessness of such dismal introspection. The scenarios running ceaselessly through her head had achieved nothing except to drag her deeper into a downward spiral.

With fresh purpose, she rose to her feet, returning to the fire where Fintán had taken responsibility for preparing the food. The hare and the fish had been successfully roasted on a makeshift spit, the mushrooms and watercress separated into four equal portions on a flat rock beside the little blaze. Shifting to one side, the *óglach* made room for her to sit. When she did, the others' conversation ceased as they considered her uneasily.

Liath Luachra was pleased to see that Gleor Red Hand's gaze looked clearer and that his spirits were boosted with the return of his son. His posture still exuded resentment but he had at least relented from glaring at her with his earlier hostility.

Muirne, too, had recovered some of the mettle that had been temporarily dampened by the woman warrior's interrogation. Although she said nothing, she now regarded the Grey One across the flames with a quiet loathing. When Liath Luachra raised her eyes to confront that gaze, the other woman did not flinch.

The meal was shared in awkward silence. Fortunately, due to the small size of the portions, it was not long before they'd finished. Liath Luachra remained ever silent, waiting until the last of the food had been put aside before plunging ahead with her usual directness.

'We must put our enmity to one side.'

The three *Lamraighe* considered her in silence with varying levels of curiosity and surprise. Gleor was the first to respond, although his reticence was evident. 'What are you saying, Grey One?'

'I am saying we must work together, strive for a common purpose over the forthcoming days.'

The *Lamraighe* leader made no response to that. In fact, he looked somewhat startled. Liath Luachra took the ensuing silence as a sign to continue.

'As I see it, we have two goals: locating Bodhmhall and Demne and working our way clear of this valley before our enemies find us.'

She looked at her companions, studying each of them in turn. All three appeared hesitant, even downright sceptical. In hindsight, she realised it might have been better to broach the subject with a little less bluntness. Bodhmhall, of course, would have handled the situation with much greater tact. Subtle and skilful, she'd have raised the topic with her usual diplomatic finesse. But then ...

She refused to continue that line of thought.

'Do you disagree?' she asked, impatient to have the issue addressed one way or the other.

Fintán looked from the woman warrior to Gleor and back again, dutifully deferring to his father's lead despite his poor history in that regard. Muirne raised the last sliver of fish in her hand, eying the woman warrior coldly while nipping at the white flesh with her teeth. In the end, it was Gleor alone who provided a response. Tossing a greasy hare bone aside, he sniffed and took a deep breath before speaking.

'The goals seem correct, Grey One but I would add one other. We must proceed to Dún Baoiscne, not only for the clothing and supplies we'll require but to warn *Clann Baoiscne* of the traitor in their midst.'

Liath Luachra considered that for a moment. 'At Dún Baoiscne ...' Her voice trailed off. 'Will you continue to lay claim on Demne?'

The *Lamraighe* leader exhaled heavily. 'There seems little point now. We were lured on this path with false promises for the boy's future. Besides, if Demne is dead the issue is moot.'

A sudden, sob of distress from Muirne Muncháem took them all by surprise. The others looked at the dark-haired woman but she'd already turned away, smothering her grief and refusing to meet their eyes.

Pulling her gaze away, Liath Luachra looked down at the ground. Although she hid it well, the Almhu woman's unexpected reaction had shaken her for it seemed disturbingly close to her own suppressed feelings of grief. 'He is not dead. Neither is Bodhmhall.'

Gleor said nothing but his expression left little doubt as to his true thoughts on the matter. 'We shall see,' he said simply.

With that, Liath Luachra grunted and made to stand but found the old man's hand on her arm, holding her in place with surprising firmness. Her face was stone as she turned her stare upon him. He released his grip.

'There are other matters between us, Grey One.' He paused momentarily, as though thinking the words through before saying them but never once taking his eyes from hers. 'We are in your debt.' The admission was grudging, expressed though gritted teeth. 'You have provided us with food and shelter for two days.'

'Yes,' she said simply.

'Although we are beholden to you, those actions do not balance the injury and insult received at your hand.'

She looked at him without expression, prompting his eyes to flare with fresh antagonism. 'You thrust my family and myself from the cliff at An Gleann Teann. You mishandled my woman at a time when she is with child. You belittled my own experience, treated it with open contempt.' His eyes took on a shaded glint. 'There is need of a reckoning between us.'

The woman warrior was unimpressed. 'Your family would be carrion had I not pushed you from the falls. Your woman is untrustworthy. If you want to be treated with respect, work to earn it. Do not assume you deserve it because of a position you occupy.'

Somehow, Gleor managed to keep his face impassive but she sensed the anger churning inside him.

'I raise this to give you fair warning,' he continued at last, a perceptible tremor to his voice. 'Our current circumstances prevent a resolution for now but at Dún Baoiscne … there will be a reckoning.'

Liath Luachra shrugged. 'At Dún Baoiscne, then.' Dismissing the threat with evident disdain, she reached forward suddenly, grabbing the last of the roast hare from the rock where Fintán had placed it. Raising it to her mouth, she bit off a stringy piece of meat and started to chew. 'Here, then, is what I propose for the morrow. It seems clear to me that our friends are on the far side of the river.'

She paused for both Gleor and Muirne were glaring at her, infuriated by her abrupt dismissal. 'If they live,' Gleor managed at last.

'They are on the far side of the river,' she repeated, paying him no heed. 'At dawn, we will start to work our way downstream. When we locate a suitable ford, we will cross to the northern bank.' She paused and redirected her gaze across to Gleor. 'Can you keep up?' she asked.

'I can keep up,' he answered stiffly.

The Grey One continued to regard him in silence but then abruptly nodded her head a single time. 'When we achieve the far bank, we'll leave the river valley and turn as it continues east towards *Clann Baoiscne* territory. I will travel ahead, scout for sign of Bodhmhall and Demne. If I find their trail, I will leave and Fintán will occupy himself with your care. From that point on, your son can keep you safe.'

Getting to her feet, the Grey One turned and, without another word, walked into the darkness of the trees.

***

They departed the campsite just after dawn the following day. Throughout the morning, Liath Luachra led them on the rough bank path between the river and the treeline of the adjoining woods. The breadth of that natural trail varied considerably, at times measuring little more than one or two paces when it became almost completely obstructed, then at other times stretching right back to the base of the mountains.

To reduce the risk of ambush, the Grey One travelled ahead, scouring the trail before them while Fintán and the others followed at a distance of about fifty paces. Glancing back, she was pleased to see that the youth took his responsibility seriously, remaining alert as he guided his two charges, ready to shift them into the cover of the trees at a signal from her.

Relieved to be free of their repressive company, Liath Luachra advanced with her habitual vigilance but found her gaze repeatedly drift towards the waterway alongside, as though by some miracle Bodhmhall and Demne might suddenly emerge to embrace her. Each time this happened, she swallowed the inevitable disappointment, choking on it like a mouthful of gristle. As the morning progressed, her mood darkened even further with the knowledge of how little distance they were making. She'd already lost two days because of *Na Lamraighe* and was still travelling over ground she'd already covered twice the previous day.

Her frustration eased to some extant when they eventually reached the chaotic stand of tumbled pines where she'd retrieved Bodhmhall's cloak and encountered Fintán. From that point on at least, she could console herself with the knowledge they were finally covering new terrain, albeit at an infuriatingly slow pace.

Despite Gleor's previous reassurances, his injury impeded their progress considerably. Whatever the cause of the blow to his head, it had left him with severe dizziness that upset his sense of balance and, consequently, his ability to walk. The *rí* of *Na Lamraighe* was doing his best but he was visibly struggling, stumbling repeatedly and leaning on Muirne or his son for support. As a result, he was lagging further and further behind.

Furious, Liath Luachra increased her own pace until *Na Lamraighe* were out of sight. Although aware that splitting the group was unwise, removing all visual connection with the people she held responsible for Bodhmhall's absence was the only way she could cope without surrendering to the mindless fury that continued to simmer inside her.

At mid-day, she reluctantly drew to a halt beside a slow-moving tributary streaming down to the river from a cleft in the ridge. Waiting for *Na Lamraighe*, she searched the banks for watercress and roots and had amassed a respectable mound of edible vegetable matter by the time they finally appeared.

Fintán was first to edge into sight and the relief on his face when he saw her was visible even at that distance. A moment later, Gleor and Muirne stumbled into view, the older man sweating profusely and grasping Muirne Muncháem's shoulder so tightly it looked as though he might collapse if he released his grip.

When they made it to the grassy patch where she'd piled the food, the *Lamraighe* leader slumped to the ground and lay moaning softly, his head in his hands. Muirne sat beside him, stroking his forehead and encouraging him to eat. Fintán, ravenous, grabbed a handful of the tubers and started chewing ferociously.

Sitting apart by the bank of the stream, the Grey One used Gleor's knife to cut up the watercress and popped a wad into her mouth to suck on it quietly. Despite her antipathy towards the Flower of Almhu, she'd been impressed by her care of her sickly husband. And by her unexpected hardiness, given the advancing pregnancy. She watched as the Almhu woman pushed herself wearily off the ground and, to her surprise, started towards her. Drawing to a halt before the woman warrior, she stood stiffly, a hand on either hip.

'Gleor cannot maintain the pace you set.'

Liath Luachra considered her quietly but offered no response.

'If you push him too hard he will die.'

The Grey One absently poked the tip of the knife into the tree, levering a piece of bark loose from the trunk. 'If we don't find Bodhmhall and Demne,' she countered, 'it's possible they will die. Is the life of your son less important than that of your man?'

The younger woman's fortitude abruptly wavered and she regarded the woman warrior bleakly. 'I do not display my feelings as openly as some,

Liath Luachra. But you know I'd not willingly place my son in danger. His absence withers me from the inside.'

'You took Demne from the safety of his home. You dragged him into the dangers of the Great Wild. All for your own political ambitions.'

Muirne angrily shook her head. 'No. My sole ambition was to cement Demne's future as a leader of *Clann Baoiscne*. We were hardly to know the summons was a ploy.'

Liath Luachra cocked her head and eyed her silently. 'I do not like you, Muirne Muncháem. I do not trust you.'

Muirne waved her hand in frustration. 'Who are you to judge me? *Is créatúr seabhaideach thú, in aghaidh nádúir, gan fear no páiste duit féin'*. You're a wandering creature. An aberrant, with no man or child of your own. 'What could you possibly know of children?' Her eyes took on a knowing gleam. 'Besides, I've seen how you avoid my son. You struggle with Demne's presence unless you're shouting instructions at him.'

As usual, Liath Luachra's face displayed no emotion but vigilant eyes would have noticed her hands clench tightly into fists. She rose from her seat in one smooth movement, twisting up off the trunk with the menacing dexterity of a river eel lunging for its prey. Muirne involuntarily took two steps backwards but her chin remained high. 'Go, then!' she exclaimed. 'Strike me, if that's your intent. But I speak the truth.'

The woman warrior sighed. 'Go away, foul blossom. Your crow caw irritates me.'

Muirne responded with a scowl, then spinning furiously on one heel, she headed back to join her man.

The Grey One wordlessly watched her stalk away. The Flower of Almhu's unexpected show of defiance had surprised her, but then the woman was more resilient than she looked. Six years earlier, despite being even heavier with child, Muirne had traversed the Great Wild on her own to reach Ráth Bládhma, defeating a ravenous wolf along the way.

Liath Luachra spat out the watercress for it had formed a hardened, indigestible clot inside one cheek. Slowly she shook her head. Muirne Muncháem was ruthlessly ambitious and completely untrustworthy but there was no denying the woman had iron to her.

Which, of course, made her all the more dangerous.

***

There was a subdued but angry muttering when the Grey One called for the trail to be taken up once more. Legs trembling, Gleor Red Hand got to his feet and stood precariously with one hand against a tree to keep his balance. Despite his quivering legs however, he brushed Muirne's proffered arm away and was first to lead off down the narrow path beside the river.

He couldn't keep it up, of course. Fifty paces further down the trail he was already weaving unsteadily. Another twenty paces on from that and he was bypassed by the woman warrior. He squinted his eyes to ignore her as she strode by, focussing on putting one foot in front of the other.

Moving at her usual pace, the Grey One wasn't long in leaving the others behind. As soon as they were out of sight however, she slowed, maintaining a strict distance that kept them from view but within hailing distance should the need arise.

The afternoon dribbled by, slowly and uneventfully. The woman warrior finally called a halt and although it was far too early and they'd made less distance than she'd hoped, she knew Gleor was on his last legs. There was also the issue of gathering food for the evening meal.

Forcing her way through the heavy undergrowth around the treeline, Liath Luachra pushed her way deeper into the woods until she found a suitable site to set camp, a secluded hollow at the base of the steep ridge. Using her sword, she cut a number of saplings then created another rough lean-to by jamming a straight branch into the crooks of two separate trees and layering either side with saplings placed at an angle to the central strut.

Stepping back, she considered her work with satisfaction. It was small and would hold no more than two people but she was pleased by its blended camouflage. From a distance of more than six or seven paces, the little structure was practically invisible, blending into the faded background of the surrounding trunks and branches. Anyone who might happen on the hollow would be hard pressed to spot it, even if they were actively seeking it. By the time the construction was completed, she could hear the others making their way along the trail and, calling out, she guided them through the trees towards the little refuge.

When he stumbled to the hollow, Gleor was struggling to remain upright and had clearly reached the limits of his endurance. Liath Luachra gestured for Muirne Muncháem to lead him into the lean-to. Crawling inside the little shelter, the sweat-stained young woman dragged the white-faced *Lamraighe* leader in behind her. Slumping heavily onto the thick bed of leaves and fern, he almost immediately passed out.

While Gleor slept, Liath Luachra stripped the tops of two straight saplings she'd cut earlier, sharpening the tips with Gleor's knife to fashion a rude pair of slender spears. Fintán, for his part, collected dead wood and tree litter for the fire, returning with an armload of dusty-dry kindling which he dumped at the centre of the hollow. Muirne meanwhile constructed a pair of snares using bark fibers sliced carefully from the trunk of a nearby tree. When these were completed, she handed them to the *óglach* who took them further into the woods, searching for a suitable animal run where he could set them in place.

Liath Luachra returned to the river and stalked the shallows with her spears while Muirne remained behind to watch over the dozing Gleor. The woman warrior made a point of warning her not to set a fire until she'd returned.

The Grey One's fishing expedition proved more successful than she'd anticipated for she succeeded in spearing three trout. Returning to the hollow, she found that Fintán had little more than a single scrawny squirrel to show for his efforts, however Muirne's foraging had garnered several large mushrooms to supplement the meal.

It was dark when Liath Luachra finally allowed a fire to be lit. Concealed in the hollow at the inner section of the wood, she was confident there was little chance of the flames – or their reflection on the leaves of the trees – being visible from afar. While the meat and fish were roasting, Gleor woke and crawled out of the lean-to to join them and although he looked markedly better than when he'd first arrived, his face remained pinched and pale.

Huddling around the fire, they nibbled on the scanty collection of nuts and mushrooms, waiting eagerly for the fish and the skinned squirrel to roast on their makeshift, greenwood frames. Despite their sheltered campsite, Liath Luachra shivered at a sudden gust that managed to cut through the surrounding trees, for the air was perceptibly cooler. Across the fire, Gleor started to cough as though in response to the drop in temperature.

Rising from her seat of dead wood, the warrior woman tossed Bodhmhall's cloak towards the old man. Despite his injury, he reacted with a warrior's instinctive alertness, plucking the garment out of the air before it reached him. Holding it in both hands, he looked down at it then back at her. 'Why do you throw me this cloak?' he asked in confusion.

'You have need of it.'

His eyes narrowed. 'I have no need of your offerings, Grey One.'

'It's no offering. My intent is to find Bodhmhall and Demne. If you sicken, you will slow me down even further. I would avoid that.' With this, she sat again and stared fixedly into the flickering fire. Gleor made a half-hearted attempt to return the cloak but she ignored him, staring deeper into the flames until he accepted the gift and let her be. From the corner of her eye, she watched the old man crawl back into the lean-to, lie down and wrap the wool covering around himself and Muirne. Soon, the soft sound of snoring emanated from the little structure.

Liath Luachra remained by the fire, feeding it with sticks and fragments of deadwood. She avoided Fintán's eyes but, from his awkward composure and clumsy attempts at nonchalance, it was obvious he'd already anticipated what she was about to propose.

'Fintán.'

'Yes, Grey One.'

'We should share warmth tonight. The weather turns and we have no blankets.'

'Very well, Grey One.' Despite the casualness of his response, she noted his foot tapping a nervous cadence on the hollow's grassy floor.

Liath Luachra tried not to sigh as she lay down and curled as close to the fire as she dared. She heard Fintán cough then nervously clear his throat. A moment later there was a brief crackle of dead leaves as the youth lay down beside her. She felt him awkwardly sidle up behind, wrapping an arm about her waist to pull himself closer.

Sandwiched between the comfortable warmth of the fire and the *óglach's* body heat, Liath Luachra slowly felt herself succumb to fatigue. She was on the point of drifting off when a sudden hardness between her buttocks prodded her back to consciousness.

'Fintán.'

There was an embarrassed silence. 'Eh ... yes, Grey One?'

'Turn yourself about. I'll lie against your back.'

'Uh. Very well.'

There was a fresh rustle of leaves as both turned around, Fintán first, then Liath Luachra.

'And, Fintán ...'

'Yes?'

'I have need of a deep sleep. If you find your rest disturbed, go into the woods and rub sap from the stick till the stiffness is gone.'

There was a distinct silence but she could sense the tension in the youth as she curled into his body. 'And dream well,' she said.

***

She slid out of a light doze before dawn, instantly conscious not only of the edgy hunger in her belly but of the fact that she had nothing to assuage it. Stretched on her side, her stomach growled against the snug nodule of warmth radiating from Fintán's back.

Detaching herself from the youth, she rolled away to sit up and peer about the campsite. The fire had died during the night and in the pre-dawn shadow she could barely make out the darker shape of the lean-to. She shivered as the cool touch of a fresh breeze stroked her face and exposed skin. Her fingers felt cold and clumsy and when she felt the slimy sensation of dew on a piece of wild grass she knew the change of seasons was almost upon them.

Rising to her feet, she crawled into the undergrowth further along the base of the cliff where she peeled off her leggings and loincloth. Crouched against the trunk of an elder tree, she urinated silently before wiping herself clean with a fistful of the dew-soaked scrub grass.

Because of the darkness, she had to work her way back through the trees towards the river by touch and recall alone. When she emerged from the woods near the edge of the river, the dawn was a feeble grey smear in the eastern sky, the river a gurgling slab of solid black streaming forwards against a background that was only slightly less dark. Picking a small twig from the ground, she clamped it between her teeth and chewed on it in an attempt to alleviate the pangs of hunger. When it was brighter and the visibility had improved, she could fill her stomach with water. That would have to keep her going until she managed to find something else to eat.

After a time, the gloom had cleared to a point where she could work her way down the river bank and there she stripped off her clothing to slip into the inky shallows. She washed quickly, splashing water onto her body and scrubbing herself with gritty sand from the lower bank. In the poor light it was a relatively precarious bath. The flow of the current was a constant tug against her side and by probing with her feet, she knew she was situated on a sandy ledge that sloped sharply downwards just a pace or two further into the water.

She shivered at the chill touch of the river, feeling little bumps of goosepimples form on her skin. Finally, trembling from the cold, she scrambled out of the water and up the bank to retrieve her clothes, not waiting to dry before dressing again. Her nose wrinkled at the smell of dried sweat but she ignored it as she pulled them on.

Feeling somewhat cleaner and slightly warmer, she sat on the dark riverbank, arms wrapped tight about her knees as she stared towards the eastern sky. Soon it would be bright enough to search for edible roots, grubs or nuts, anything to reduce the hunger. If she found enough to eat, she could bring it back to camp, using the prospect of breakfast to rouse the others and get them on their feet to continue the trail. She was determined to find a suitable ford to traverse the river as soon as possible.

Gleor will slow us again.

Her forehead creased as she recalled the *Lamraighe* man's ponderous progress the day before and she sighed in frustration, already anticipating the struggle of getting him up and moving. Muirne, no doubt, would exacerbate the situation, delaying their departure further as she argued for them to take their time so Gleor could keep up. The skin around the woman warrior's eyes tightened as she thought of Muirne, her constant arguing, her attendance at her man's side, her refusal to leave him to his own devices at any time.

She fears that I will kill him.

Liath Luachra clamped her molars down, crushing the twig. The realisation, startling though it was, would probably have surprised her more if there hadn't been a degree of truth to it. She had mused on the possibility of dispatching the old man so that she could proceed with her search for Bodhmhall, however in reality that had been nothing more than a fancy. She had no great abhorrence of violence when there was cause but she did not have the capacity for unnecessary cruelty.

With a sigh, she rose to her feet. She had a more practical issue to attend to: food!

Following the thin strip of land between the treeline and the river, she searched the earth and tree roots for mushrooms or tubers, anything edible. Stepping over some footprints in the mud from their passage the previous day, she was about to continue on her way when some peculiarity in the shape of the prints prompted her to stop and examine them more closely. In the poor light, it took her a moment to work out what had bothered her.

They're pointed in the wrong direction.

Dropping to her knees, she brushed her hand over the shadowed earth, located another four footprints and then traced the impression of one with her fingers, confirming the location of the deeper heel shape from touch alone. The heel was definitely set at the eastward end of the four tracks she'd detected which meant that the people who'd left them had been walking upriver. The tracks had not been made by her party.

Sitting back up on her haunches, she used her tongue to roll the twig from one side of her mouth to the other. From the tracks on that patch of ground alone, she could tell there'd been at least two individuals. One of them was a big man. That much was clear from the depth of the indentations, even on the firmer section of ground.

Scouts.

From Gob An Teanga Gorm.

71

Making a soft clucking sound with her tongue, she raised her head and attempted to peer further up the trail but it was almost impossible to see anything through the swathe of shadow. Father Sun seemed in no rush to push through the drab cloud cover, a gloomy prospect offering little more than the possibly of mist or rain in addition to the cold pinch to the air.

The woman warrior sniffed and wiped her nose. Whoever these people were, they'd used the illumination of a full moon to walk past that section of wood containing the hidden campsite, apparently while the little group had been fast asleep.

Without a guard.

She felt a cold clutch in her belly at that. They were all exhausted from weeks of trekking, surviving the ambush at An Gleann Teann and their subsequent trials in the swift-flowing river. Liath Luachra had been pushing herself even harder than the others and accumulated fatigue was causing her to make careless mistakes.

Still ...

Once again, she scanned the upriver trail. Once again, there was nothing to see but shadow.

Slowly, she wormed her way backwards into the undergrowth just inside the treeline. Here, nestled in the comforting screen of fern and bramble, she sat on her heels, chewing on the twig as she worked through the ramifications of what she'd discovered. Musing over possible courses of action, she allowed her eyes to drift downriver with the current and she stiffened abruptly as they came to rest on a distant glow – a fire – barely visible downstream. Evidently, there was some obstruction close to the source of the fire that had prevented her from seeing it earlier when she'd been bathing but it was visible from this particular angle.

A lump caught in her throat as she stared at the distant red flicker. Someone had set up a camp – quite a large one given the size of the fire – on the only route out of the valley.

They were trapped.

***

Although the sky had brightened with the incoming dawn, the valley remained overcast and shrouded in gloom. Like their fire, the wind too had died overnight instilling in the valley an eerie stillness. Between the two ridges that marked either side of the river, a low lying grey cloud hung suspended and unmoving, an ominous portent of doom. A faint mist had also formed upriver, and although too fine to severely hamper visibility, the edges of everything it touched took on a faint, ghostlike blur.

Crouched in a clump of fern set two trees in from the open riverbank, Liath Luachra shivered, regretting her generosity in offering Bodhmhall's cloak to the weakened Gleor. With the absence of sunshine, the air was distinctly cool and the need for concealment prevented her from moving to keep herself warm.

Despite the dullness of the morning – the black ridges, the mist-shrouded cliffs, the faded grey-green vegetation – the valley resounded to the chatter of the morning chorus, the chaotic chirping and tweeting that heralded the incoming day.

From her hiding place, Liath Luachra regarded a pair of fat wood pigeons perched high in the neighbouring oak. Both were oblivious to her presence and her belly growled as she imagined the fleshy, tangy taste of them. The fingers of her right hand tightened unconsciously around the leather thong of the sling wrapped about her left wrist.

I could strike one. I could strike one easily at this distance.

She scowled and turned her eyes away to avoid the temptation. Hunger was making her hasty, even more careless than fatigue.

Resting her cheek against the rough bark of the oak tree just beside the clump of fern, she closed her eyes and lapsed into a daydream, a favourite memory from many years earlier when she'd still been bound to *Na Cinéaltaí*. At the time, she'd been travelling alone through the Great Wild, traversing rough hill country for a meeting at the distant coastline. The spring weather had been uncharacteristically mild and she'd been pushing herself hard. Weary from days of travel, she'd paused to rest in a deserted valley at the foothills of an isolated mountain range.

The valley was a lonely passage squeezed between two giant slabs of jagged black rock and it had a deep lake at its centre. Although it must have been a harsh place at the best of times, while she was there, the watery quality of the sunlight and the overhanging cloud had imbued it with a striking palette of contrasting blacks and greys that she'd never previously encountered. Sitting quietly, she'd tried to absorb the sight but the sheer gritty beauty of the landscape had seemed almost too much for her swollen soul to take in. Just when she thought the scene couldn't possibly grow more transcendent, two perfectly white swans had appeared, winging their way down the valley to alight on the lake's oil-like waters with graceful ease.

Rapt, she'd watched the elegant birds drifting, their white silhouettes forming perfect mirror images on the still, black surface. Despite a great internal longing to remain there, soaking up that soothing calm, she knew the moment couldn't be sustained. She had places to be, people who were depending on her.

With immense reluctance, she'd torn her eyes away, got to her feet and departed the valley without looking back.

But she'd never forgotten what she'd seen.

Years later, when travelling that region again, she'd criss-crossed the mountainous terrain for several days and although she located several similar valleys with similar lakes, none of them quite resembled the one she remembered. After many further fruitless and frustrating attempts, she'd finally understood she was never going to find what she was looking for. The valley she'd experienced was gone, an element of time, of circumstance and of nature, existing now only as a ghost of what had been. In a different light, at a different time, it would be just another desolate valley in another forsaken piece of land.

A sudden flutter of wings snapped her mind back to a more immediate focus. Three swallows shot out of the trees about two hundred paces upriver and she caught a glimpse of them through the trees as they flapped wildly across the river towards the opposite bank.

The scouts were returning. With the arrival of daylight, they'd finally spotted evidence of the little party's presence and were now feverishly tracking them back downriver, probably hoping to trap them against the main body of the *fian*. In their eagerness however, they'd moved too hastily, startling some of the native birdlife.

Without moving, the Grey One repeatedly clenched and relaxed the muscles in her arms and legs, warming them up for the moment when she would make her move. In the neighbouring pine, the two pigeons abruptly took to the air.

Not long now.

A few moments later, the woman warrior caught a glimpse of a grey mist-shrouded figure through the trees at the end of the trail, about fifty paces from where she was concealed. A big man, with an unkempt brown beard and hair tied up in a short double-braid, he was shuffling forward with a kind of hunched-over lope, eyes fixed firmly on the ground as he followed the spoor downriver. Exposed in the open ground between the treeline and the river, he made a tempting target. A veteran of many ambushes, the Grey One was quite certain that's what was intended, particularly as she knew there'd been at least one other man accompanying him.

Breathing deeply through her nostrils, she remained where she was, still and motionless as stone.

Sure enough, as the big scout drew level with her positon, she became aware of another presence, much closer but much more silent. Someone was approaching with great care through the woods to her left. Remaining perfectly still, she waited, watching as the bearded scout continued forward, intermittently hidden from her line of sight by the trunks of the other trees. Off to her left, the source of the muffled movement drew closer. A moment later, a dark shape peeled out from the shadows directly before her.

Although smaller in stature than his comrade, the second scout looked no less deadly. A wiry, dark-haired individual, he'd rubbed dark river mud over his face and the exposed skin of his arms and legs to make himself less visible in the shadows. High in his right hand, he carried a steel-tipped javelin, ready to cast at a moment's notice. Two others sat loose in a long leather sheath strapped to his back. The combination of dark hair and streaks of greasy mud gave him an inhumanly fearsome appearance and at that moment he resembled nothing so much as a malevolent shadow, slipping noiselessly through the trees in search of prey.

Her silent scrutiny seemed to trip some innate sixth sense however, for the scout suddenly froze in place and looked around. His eyes – eyeballs eerily white against the camouflage of his darkened skin – scanned the trees and undergrowth intently. The woman warrior held her breath as his gaze slid towards the clump of fern in which she was hidden and which now felt far too sparse. Like the scout, she too had coated herself with a masking layer of river mud some time earlier. She'd also attached fern fronds to her battle-harness and had even gone so far as to weave several around her forehead. Swathed in the dense substance of shadow, she was sure he wouldn't see her as long as she kept her nerve and remained immobile.

Despite that conviction, it was still terrifying to watch as his eyes came to rest directly on her position … Then abruptly move on.

She didn't breathe again until he'd advanced once more, moving past her to a point where a large tree trunk momentarily obscured him from view. When he reappeared again, several paces on, she rose soundlessly from the fern clump, a sprouting shadow that merged with the dark bark of the tree.

Stepping around the trunk, she padded silently towards the treeline and emerged onto the open space beside the bank. Unwrapping the leather sling, she allowed it to drop to its full extension, the pouch drawn down by the weight of the round river stone cushioned inside. She moved forward a pace or two then stepped back again, establishing a position that gave a rough view of both scouts at once. The bigger man was still moving forward with his slow huddle, back towards her, head down as he scanned the ground ahead. His skinny comrade continued to shadow him inside the treeline, moving parallel and about ten paces to the rear, javelin poised as he scanned the trees ahead.

Adjusting her stance, the Grey One slowly lifted the sling and started to swing it in a sedate vertical arc. Turning her body so her right side was perpendicular to the movement of the big scout, she increased the speed and intensity of the swing, the arcs becoming tighter and closer and fast enough to produce a low whirring noise. With that she knew she hadn't a moment to lose for the closer scout would undoubtedly register the sound. She called towards the big man.

'Hey!'

Taken by surprise, the big man spun about, reverting back to his full height just as Liath Luachra released the sling tab and the bullet shot from the pouch. Despite the distance between them, she imagined she heard the impact of the stone smash into the scout's upper sternum, the whoosh of air, the crack of bone and the muffled exclamation as he was bowled off his feet.

She didn't wait to see him fall. As soon as she saw the strike, she was off, slithering back into the shelter of the trees. Even as she slipped two trees deep into the wood, a javelin from the second scout whizzed past her ear. Glancing off the tree trunk behind her, the force of the cast was so powerful the missile continued on to smack sideways into a second tree before tumbling onto the ground with a woody clatter.

He's fast!

She remained immobile behind the trunk of the oak where she'd taken shelter, chest and right cheek pressed hard against the rough bark. The scout would have seen her disappear behind it but he'd also be expecting her to continue towards the shelter of the other, adjoining trees, an issue that would cause him some concern given the increasing proximity to his own position. She closed her eyes and visualized him scanning the trees in desperation, frantically trying to work out which direction she'd taken while at the same time resisting the urge to attend to his comrade, if he still lived.

Waiting for another moment, she suddenly took another three quick steps, darting into the lee of another tree.

This time there was no reaction from the scout. Either he'd missed her or he'd spotted her but was lining up his second javelin for when she made her next move.

Only one way to know.

This time, when she moved, she did so as a forward dive, hitting the ground and coming up into the shelter of the neighbouring tree. Just as she eased into safety, another javelin went whizzing past, slamming into the trunk of an elm some paces behind her. She looked at the quivering haft and bit her lip. If she'd taken that move at normal height the missile would have pierced her skull.

She carefully wrapped the sling around her lower arm, knotted it and removed Gleor's knife from her belt. Her sword would be useless at such a distance whereas the dagger allowed more freedom of movement, something that would be critical until she succeeded in getting past her opponent's final javelin cast. By now, she knew, he'd be growing increasingly anxious. His companion was dead or grievously injured. He was down to one javelin and Liath Luachra was slowly working her way towards him.

When the third missile struck the tree, she instinctively knew he'd made a run for it and that was confirmed by the rapid swish of footsteps stirring up leafy debris. She spotted him about twenty paces off to her left, hurdling a fallen beech, slipping briefly on a patch of mud on the other side before regaining his balance. She immediately took off in pursuit.

They raced through the woods, parallel to the roaring whitewater, speeding between the tree trunks and bushes. Occasionally, she saw him cast a panic-stricken glance over his shoulder but he never caught a clear glimpse of her because of the erratic movement and the persistent obstacles in their path. He was faster than her and most likely would have outrun her if he'd taken to the flat ground beside the river bank. Hemmed in by the trees however, obstructed by roots, fallen trunks and other debris, the woman warrior's natural agility gave her the advantage. Despite his initial head start, she clung doggedly to his heels, just keeping him in sight at first but then gradually gaining ground. After a relatively short period of time she'd reduced his lead to ten paces or so but was growing anxious at the proximity of the thin smoke column which drew closer with every gasping pant.

The scout too seemed to take courage from the closeness of the smoke for he surged ahead with a fresh burst of speed. Fortunately, he wasn't able to sustain it and although he managed to break free of the vegetation and onto the path, he began to falter. Knowing there wasn't a moment to lose, Liath Luachra drew on every last reserve. Closing to within three paces of the fleeing warrior, she lunged desperately, tackling him about the legs and tumbling them both to the ground.

They hit the earth hard but the scout took the brunt of the fall. Stunned, he tried to rise but Liath Luachra, reacting faster, threw a punch that smashed him in the side of the head. Through instinct rather than intent, the warrior fell backwards and managed to roll to his feet. He'd just succeeded in drawing the sword from his scabbard when Gleor's knife slammed him in the left side of his chest.

The scout stumbled backwards from the impact, staring down in disbelief at the hilt protruding from his chest and the spray of blood that spurted with every heartbeat. Raising his head, he looked at the woman warrior, and his lips parted several times but he did not speak. Slowly, his face went slack, his knees collapsed and he toppled sideways to the ground.

Lungs burning, Liath Luachra stared at the body, wheezing for breath and almost crying from relief. Weak from hunger and fighting, she was thankful for her victory but so utterly spent she was in no state to appreciate it.

Gods, I tire of running!

Rolling onto her belly, she stared further down the trail where the riverbank curved inwards towards the ridge and back out again to form a deep, semi-circular arc. Less than two hundred paces away, on the far end of the curve, the thick smoke column rising above the trees was now very distinct. Before the sight of it had truly registered, a flash of movement prompted her to flatten herself against the ground beside the rotting remnants of a fallen branch. On the bank, a stocky man appeared out of the bushes, followed by another and yet another until a group of five warriors was lined up along the river. As though on cue, they all tugged the front of their leggings down, pulled out their *bod* and started to urinate into the fast-flowing waters.

Despite an instinctive urge to flee, Liath Luachra didn't move. Although none of the men carried javelins, in her worn out state, they'd run her down easily enough if they gave chase. Watching, she noted that all were armed with an impressive array of swords, hand axes and long knives. Three wore the padded leather tunics she'd previously seen on others from Gob An Teanga Gorm's *fian*.

Laughing and slapping each other on the back, four of the warriors headed back into the trees in the direction of the smoke. One, wearing an unusual leather helmet, continued to piss with impressive staying power. As he stood, dangling a golden arc into the river, his eyes turned across the water to where Liath Luachra was lying. Sprawled beside the rotted remnants of the fallen branch, the warrior woman was relatively confident she couldn't be seen. As the distant warrior's gaze moved along the curving riverbank trail however, she hissed in alarm, belatedly realising that the dead scout's body lay crumpled completely out in the open.

The warrior's shimmering arc lost height and he peered more closely, his attention drawn to the unusual shape on the distant trail. Curious, he raised his hand as though to shadow his eyes, and continued to stare. Unable to bear the tension, Liath Luachra kept her head down and momentarily closed her eyes. When she eased them open and looked up again, the warrior was still staring but displaying no visible sign of concern, and with relief she realised he hadn't recognized the corpse as one of his comrades. Lying on its side, legs twisted and back turned towards him, it probably wasn't even identifiable as a human body from that angle.

Pulling up the front of his leggings, the warrior immediately lost interest, turned on his heels and wandered back in the direction his comrades had taken. As soon as he'd disappeared from sight, Liath Luachra crawled over to the body of the scout, grasped both feet by the ankles and proceeded to haul it into the wood.

In the shadows of the trees, she rummaged through the dead man's possessions, stripping the body of the sword belt with its scabbarded sword and knife. A leather bag inside the tunic turned out to contain not only a small fire-making kit and a chunk of bread but, more excitingly, a thick lump of soft, white cheese.

Ravenous, she devoured the cheese immediately, closing her eyes and almost squirming with pleasure as the milky fat swelled in her belly. When she'd scoffed down the last of the cheese, she started on the bread but only managed a third of the loaf before she had to stop, for her stomach felt completely bloated.

Sated, she sat back against a tree trunk with a purr of satisfaction. Staring at the dead man, she briefly considered stripping the leather tunic but, given the gash from the knife and the extensive blood stains, decided against it. Getting to her feet, she turned her attention back to the smoke column towering up above the distant trees.

Gob.

Her lips curled in a silent snarl.

Working her way through the trees to the steep cliffs of the ridge, the woman warrior veered left and dropped to her belly to crawl cautiously in the direction of the enemy camp. She estimated she was within a hundred paces of the fire when she caught her first sign of her enemy, a young warrior with a spear, gazing impassively in her direction. Bored – and probably daydreaming – he hadn't spotted her but she remained motionless, concealed by the thick undergrowth.

The campsite had been well chosen. At the point where the river curved inland, the space between the water and the cliffs was narrower than at any other section of the river valley. Lying in the dense network of fern, she studied the terrain and was trying to identify a route through the various obstacles when two men abruptly emerged from the trees closest to the source of the smoke. One of them, the stocky man she'd earlier seen urinate in the river, was moving with an unusually hunched gait, as though in deference to his companion. The latter, a tall and slender man with an unusually elongated jaw, she recognised immediately.

'Gob!'

She spat the name from her mouth like rotten venison, hatred curdling in the back of her throat. Her lips turned back in a snarl and although she continued to watch them, she made no further sound. When the two men finally disappeared from sight, she wriggled backwards on her stomach to a point where she could rise without being seen and slowly got to her feet.

Leaving the enemy camp behind, she returned to the site of her original ambush. There, scouring the undergrowth, she managed to retrieve two of the skinny scout's javelins. The haft of one was broken from its impact with the tree but she salvaged the metal head.

The second scout was still lying where she'd left him, spread-eagled on the ground with a stunned expression on his face. The dent in his upper chest revealed where the egg-sized stone had struck him before rolling off and onto the ground beside him. The earth immediately around his feet and hands was scuffed and torn where he'd kicked and scraped during his last convulsions. It couldn't have been a pleasant death, she realised. On his back, lungs wheezing, struggling to draw air in through that shattered chest.

Because of his size, it was a task to drag the big man into the shadow of the trees but she managed it and set to rifling his corpse as well. The haul on this occasion was less in terms of weapons – a second sword and a sharp-edged hand-axe – but to her delight there was a small leather satchel with a full day's worth of rations for both scouts: a bag of nuts, several strips of smoked meat and some bread.

Still sated from her earlier scavenging, she felt no need to eat again but quickly gathered the booty and headed downriver to join the others. They'd be thrilled with the food of course. Her bad tidings would be another thing altogether.

***

Despite the lateness of the hour, the others were still sleeping in the shaded hollow, shielded from the brightening sky by the thick forest canopy. She roused Fintán first, leaning over him and placing a hand over his mouth. Startled awake by her touch, he started to struggle but relaxed when he saw who'd woken him. Releasing him, she turned to the *Lamraighe* couple's shelter to wake them only to find Muirne already up, sitting at the triangular entrance with eyes full of suspicion.

'Rouse Gleor.'

The Flower of Almhu's forehead crinkled and she shook her head. With a curse, the Grey One moved around to the other end of the structure where the *Lamraighe* leader's head lay just inside the entrance, snoring softly. Muirne hurried to intercept her, mouth opening to protest but something in the Grey One's ferocious expression silenced her. Instinctively sensing that something was wrong, the younger woman's features tightened but she wisely held her tongue.

Gleor came awake quickly enough when the woman warrior tapped him on the shoulder although his eyes were glassy and full of confusion. He stared up at her without recognition at first but then the glazed expression faded. Whatever his true feelings however, he had the wit to keep them to himself, knowing she wouldn't have woken him needlessly.

With a grunt, he levered himself off the bed of leaves and wriggled laboriously out of the little shelter. Rising to his feet, he paused, head in his hands as he fought off the dizziness the movement caused. Finally, dropping his hands to his side, he regarded her with a face that looked strained and pinched. 'What is it?' he asked, the quietness of his voice belying his stricken features.

'Warriors,' she whispered back.

Despite the pain he must have been feeling, his lips formed a thin line. 'Those dogs from An Gleann Teann?'

She nodded. 'Gob An Teanga Gorm's men.' At the mention of their enemy's name, her eyes flicked towards Muirne Muncháem. The other woman did not react, but simply held her gaze and reached one hand out for her husband's shoulder.

'Two scouts passed up the riverbank trail during the night. We had the luck our fire died down before they passed.' Despite the significance of the event, her voice sounded detached and remote. 'Gob's main encampment is located downriver. There are at least fifteen to twenty warriors.'

She paused then, allowing the *Lamraighe* leader a moment to digest what she was telling him. In that regard she had nothing to worry about for the old man had absorbed the details and his shoulders appeared to droop from the weight of them. He cleared his throat. 'This is bad,' he summarised with impressive understatement.

She felt no need to affirm that truth.

With a sigh, Gleor brushed the leafy debris of his bed from his leggings. 'We should flee. Retreat back upriver.'

'You forget the two scouts, Father,' Fintán reminded the older man respectfully.

'The scouts are no longer a threat,' Liath Luachra corrected him. 'But retreating back upriver would be unwise for it would simply delay the inevitable. We would end up cornered in an even more restricted part of the valley.'

Gleor acknowledged her point with a reluctant dip of his head. 'Perhaps we can steal past their encampment.'

Liath Luachra's lips twisted into an expression of doubt. 'Difficult. Our enemy have positioned themselves at the narrowest point of the bank. They have men spread across what little space there is.'

The *rí* of *Na Lamraighe* regarded her sourly. 'Must you challenge my every suggestion, Grey One?'

'It's not my intent to challenge your proposals but they have no chance of success. We are in a perilous position. We have no supplies and little in terms of equipment. Of us four, only two are fit to fight.' Gleor opened his mouth to protest but she waved him down with an abrupt slash of her hand. 'We are but two able fighters. Do not argue the point.'

The *Lamraighe* leader eased back, folding his arms stiffly. 'Do you have an alternative proposal?'

The woman warrior paused and her eyes turned thoughtfully in the direction of the river. 'We could attempt the waters.'

The others looked at each other. Their expressions said it all. 'Leaping into this stretch of water seems to be your solution to every problem we encounter,' Gleor commented dryly.

'We did it before,' she retorted. 'And we...' A sudden image of Bodhmhall and Demne popped into her mind. 'Survived,' she finished hollowly.

'Some of us did not leap so willingly at the time,' Gleor reminded her with a growl. 'And I for one will not do so now. I have little hope of surviving a second rinse in that white water. If I am to die, I will go down fighting. I will remain here and create a diversion, draw the enemy towards me while the rest of you make your escape.'

At this, Muirne reached out to take the old man's hand in hers. 'You cast yourself to the wolves thoughtlessly, foolish man.' She lifted the gnarled fingers and placed them on her stomach. 'Would you take the Great Leap to your ancestors without first laying eyes on your unborn son?'

'If it would save my unborn son ...' He rested an affectionate hand on Fintán's slim shoulder. 'And that of my firstborn son, then yes. I would.'

Despite her cynicism of Muirne Muncháem's personal motives, Liath Luachra could see the woman was genuinely troubled by this declaration.

'I have no life without you, Gleor. No future. If you intend to cast yours away by remaining here then I too will stay.'

'And I,' added Fintán.

'No,' Gleor declared with unexpected firmness, his voice ringing with the authority of a long-time tribal leader. 'You will accompany the Grey One. She will protect you.'

Liath Luachra offered the *Lamraighe* leader a sardonic eye. 'You forget yourself, Gleor Red Hand. I have no mind to do your bidding.'

'There must be some alternative to the river, Grey One,' Fintán interjected, keen to steer the discussion away from his father's intended sacrifice.

'If there is, then I do not know it.'

'But you have always found alternatives. The songs of your adventures always have you travelling inventive paths to outwit the challenges that confront you.'

'Usually one that ends in that damned river,' Gleor muttered under his breath. He ignored the frosty glare the Grey One sent his way.

'We do not have the luxury of time to dispute.' Liath Luachra stood up. 'Daybreak settles on us and the enemy will be awaiting a report from their scouts.'

'I tell you I am not going in that water,' the *rí* of *Na Lamraighe* insisted. 'I will stand and fight. That will give you time to run, to use the sacrifice I offer you.'

'You have no weapons.' Liath Luachra's voice was tainted with exasperation. She hadn't yet told them of the weapons she'd recovered from the dead scouts. 'What are you going to do? Strike them with insults? Pierce them with sarcasm?'

'Then lend me your sword.'

Her contemptuous look told him everything he needed to know about her thoughts on that particular suggestion.

'My knife then. That, at least, is my weapon.'

She shook her head. 'I need it. Besides, in your current health, it would be wasted on you. If you truly wish to hold a weapon in a reckless dash to end your life, you can have this spear.'

There was a silence as Gleor regarded the coarse wooden weapon she offered him. Raising his eyes to hers, his lips turned up in a cynical grimace. 'You truly are a poisoned thorn, Grey One. Is there nothing else you can do to make our end more ignoble?'

The woman warrior looked at each of them in turn and shook her head in disbelief. Why fortune had seen fit to set her ashore on this side of the river she would never know. She paused then and regarded the three *Lamraighe* with a scowl. 'I think Gob will do that just fine,' she said.

Chapter Five

Despite her growing sense of awareness, Bodhmhall knew that what she was feeling wasn't normal. Physically, she could feel nothing, see nothing but darkness, hear nothing, not even the low draw and release of her own breath.

And yet, when she focussed, it was as though she could perceive everything, things she couldn't normally perceive, shouldn't normally perceive: the tepid warmth of the distant stars, the patter of field mice in pasture beyond the forest, the crash of individual water droplets as they tumbled from the trees to smash against the earth.

And then there were the visions. Flickering into life before her, always changing, sometimes fading almost too quickly for her to even register. She saw her father sitting before a fire, a human skull in his hand, stroking the smooth, bony curve of the forehead with his fingers. She saw Fiacail mac Codhna raising a goblet and roaring with laughter before pausing to quaff it back. She saw Muirne Muncháem in a wood, caressing Gleor Red Hand's sweating brow. She saw Morag in the *lis* of *Ráth Bládhma*, standing with her spine bent backwards, counteracting the weight of her swollen belly. She saw Liath Luachra lying on her back, eyes closed as a heavy body thrust between her thighs.

Or is that me?

But the image was gone. It was impossible to tell.

She saw Demne. But an older Demne, a fuzz of hair on his chin as he chatted to some unfamiliar bald man with a tattooed skull. And then Liath Luachra again, sprawled in a pool of blood in some dark and stony passage.

She had the unsettling feeling that something was amiss, that some faint ominous undercurrent was trying to alert her to the visions' importance. In truth however, they all felt too indistinct to touch her. They were odours from far-away lands, drifting in on an offshore breeze, briefly discerned and almost immediately forgotten.

After a time, the run of images faded and eventually she began to sense light, not 'see' it so much as 'feel' it. Soon, physical sensation tingled at the periphery of coherence.

And came rushing back.

***

She woke to the warm flutter of breath against her ear, the scrape of bristles against the nape of her neck, the weight of an arm draped across her hip. Despite the fuzzy ache in her forehead, she immediately knew something was wrong. The arm about her waist was too heavy, too hairy. The musky smell of stale sweat and semen, familiar but oddly out of place.

Fiacail!

She groaned softly. The low sound trailed off as she attempted to shift sideways to dislodge him but the warrior's grip tightened involuntarily. His breathing quickened briefly, then just as quickly, subsided. Twisting her neck, she looked back to where his tussled head lay wedged against her spine. In the dim light she saw his lips quiver briefly as though trapped in a bad dream. Prising his arm off her, she slid out from under its weight and sat upright on the cold rock.

It was still dark but the air was calm and clear. In the sliver of light between the promontory and the surrounding trees, stars glittered and a half-moon hung lopsided above the black. The storm had blown itself out. After his earlier frenzy, the Great Father's rage was spent.

Struggling to ignore the woolly ache behind her temple, Bodhmhall tried to think, to remember what had happened, but her head felt full of fog. In a physical and intellectual sense, she could comprehend what had occurred but her emotions were frozen, disconnected and, as a result, none of it felt real.

The sleeping warrior snored as she crawled about the hard rock searching for her clothing. Her loincloth, fortunately, lay just alongside but it took some time to find the dress which had been tossed carelessly onto the ground near the dying embers of the fire. There was no sign of her belt and with the thickness of the shadows, little real prospect of finding it till morning.

Rising to her feet, she pulled the dress on over her head and adjusted the folds as she stared at the sleeping warrior.

Fiacail.

Her loins ached slightly. She shook her head, as much from confusion as distress.

Come now, Cailleach Dubh. It's not difficult. A man, a woman. What did you expect?

But no. It wasn't as obvious as that, not as simple as that. She remembered the conversation by the campfire, she remembered fragments of the actual sex but it was the moments in between that left her confounded. She'd drunk *uisce beatha* of course but, hoping to soften the warrior and convince him to help with Demne, she'd been careful to limit herself to sips after the initial two mouthfuls and the taste of it had been a deterrent in itself. No. At no stage had she lost control of her faculties.

Until she had.

She stumbled towards the spring and, lifting the hem of her dress, began to wash. The water from the pool was startlingly cold to the touch. It had been a long time since she'd had to do this.

And a long time since you've had to worry about the consequences.

She frowned at that. Still close to the cusp of her moon cycle, there was little real risk of pregnancy but she couldn't afford to take chances. Now there were herbs she would need to seek out as a matter of urgency. That realisation caused her to curse under her breath. What had she been thinking? What had she *not* been thinking?

The uisce beatha!

It could only be the *uisce beatha*. Even as she thought it through, she instinctively sensed the rightness of it. Something about that substance had violently ignited her *Gift*, inflaming it like oil thrown on an open fire. The subsequent conflagration had swamped her sensory and emotional perceptions, spiralling her off to the Otherworld and submerging all reason.

Bodhmhall bit her lip then for she'd felt an involuntarily contraction at the memory, her body responding to phantom sensations of pleasure. She'd orgasmed several times and although she could hardly ignore her natural physical reactions, at an intellectual level she could, and did, regret them. Circumstances were now much more problematic. Her relationship with Fiacail, complex at the best of times, had been complicated even further.

And Liath Luachra?

Her frozen emotions thawed for an instant and she experienced a sudden, uncharacteristic urge to lash out, to break or smash something beyond repair. With nothing to hand, she resorted to slapping the cliff face with the palm of her hand, an action that felt pathetically unsatisfying.

Uisce beatha.

She recalled the foul taste of it with bitterness, cursing her own foolishness. Of all the times to experiment with …

She took a breath and tried to exhale the anger. In hindsight, it was easy to believe she should have known better. If she'd taken the time to reflect on the potential side-effects of the *uisce beatha* before swallowing it, she might have predicted such an outcome. Some years earlier when Ráth Bládhma had been under threat, there'd been a hint of the potential susceptibility of those with *an tíolacadh*. A Tainted One, a creature with the ability to read a person's thoughts, had been defeated when he'd tried to enter a mind inebriated with *uisce beatha*. That attempt had backfired, the resulting agitation distracting him sufficiently for Liath Luachra to get close and kill him.

As her thoughts turned to the woman warrior, Bodhmhall felt her shoulders tense and this time her stomach wrenched from remorse as much as nausea. Distressed, she looked about for distraction, her gaze coming to rest on her sleeping nephew. The boy hadn't moved during the night, lying in almost exactly the same position as when she'd put him to bed.

A soft snore drew her eyes back to Fiacail. Stretched naked beside the fire, even in his inebriated state he'd intuitively yanked his heavy cloak up to cover his buttocks and lower back. A long, silver scar running down his left thigh gleamed in the moonlight where it protruded from beneath the folds of the covering. The consequence of a hunting accident from a time when they'd lived together at Dún Baoiscne, her memory of dressing that wound remained distinct. Although in immense pain, Fiacail had been too proud to admit the true extent of his discomfort. Putting on a brave face, he'd laughed shakily as she'd filled the wound with moss and herbs, temporarily sewing the split skin closed. The blaze of agony behind his smiling eyes and the powerful stress-sweat across his forehead had told another story however.

But that was Fiacail's story. Not hers. She was no longer the dutiful daughter, the shy and obedient mate she'd once been.

The seed of bitterness in her stomach flowered into full-blown queasiness. Leaning against the cliff face, one hand on its rough surface to brace herself, she began to vomit.

'Blaaauuuuugh!'

She threw up three times before she was able to stand, her legs trembling as she wiped warm bile from her lips. The *uisce beatha* had tasted even fouler coming up then it had going down.

'You cannot hold your drink, dear one.'

Bodhmhall turned to glare at the Seiscenn Uarbhaoil man. Roused by the harsh sound of her retching, he was sitting up now, his weight propped on one arm. He had a grin on him like a happy buck goat.

'Fear not, Bodhmhall. The secret to competency is a simple one. Practice. Nothing but practice.'

Bodhmhall walked wordlessly towards the log by the previous night's fire and took a seat. Grabbing the nearby waterskin, she raised it to her lips. Taking a swig, she rinsed out her cheeks but in her mouth the liquid still tasted of *uisce beatha*. She spat the tainted water onto the ground.

Fiacail did not fail to mark the tension behind the *bandraoi*'s silence. His left eyebrow curved up in a curious arch. 'You have an anger on you?'

She shook her head. 'No.'

The warrior considered that quietly for a time. 'Then you've come to regret that which we shared.' Instead of a question, the words were offered as a statement, allowing her the chance to deny it.

Too distressed to answer, Bodhmhall turned her head away.

As the silence dragged on, Fiacail dragged himself upright. Wrapping his cloak about him, he came over to sit beside her and reached up to brush the hair from her face. Unthinking, she pushed his hand away, prompting an aggrieved grunt from the warrior.

'What ails you, Bodhmhall?'

'I did not want this.'

'Want what?' he asked but his eyes had grown dark in anticipation of her answer.

'This physical intimacy between us. The rutting last night. I was not myself.'

He remained quiet for a time. 'Dear one, you enjoyed it as much as I.'

'It doesn't mat-'

'I did not force the desire upon you.' He scowled blackly. 'Neither did I set out from Seiscenn Uarbhaoil to woo you. I stayed away, Bodhmhall. Leaving you at Ráth Bládhma hollowed me out like a rotten tree stump but I did as you asked. I kept my distance and left you to the life you wanted. I would not have touched you if your desire hadn't been the equal of my own.'

Conscious that every word he uttered was true, Bodhmhall had no response. An unbearable silence stretched out between them until she punctuated it with a jaded sigh. 'This night ... I was not myself. I had no grasp of my thoughts. My body acted of its own accord.'

'I've heard this story before'.

'I tell you no lie!'

'Well, if not you, perhaps it was the Gods. Perhaps they conspire to meld us back together.'

'I don't believe in the Gods. Neither do you. Not really.'

'I'd believe in anything that softened your heart towards me.'

'Unable to face him, the *bandraoi* directed her gaze straight down towards her toes. 'Fiacail, I cannot offer you what rests with someone else.'

'Liath Luachra.' The Seiscenn Uarbhaoil man was unable to conceal the bitterness in his voice.

'Liath Luachra,' she confirmed.

The big man sighed and got to his feet. 'And if the Grey One is ...'

She turned her head to glower up at him.

'I mean,' he continued with uncharacteristic diplomacy. 'It has been some time. She could be ...' He paused then, transfixed by the dark intensity of the *bandraoi's* stare, unaware that it wasn't him she was seeing but a recalled memory from the *uisce beatha* visions: Liath Luachra sprawled in a pool of blood in some darkened, rocky passage.

'She is not dead,' she snapped, thrusting the image from her mind. A soft growl formed on the final syllable.

'Of course, of course.' Despite his agreement, the warrior did not sound convinced. 'But if ... well ... You know I'm here for you, dear one. Always here.'

Reaching over, he clasped her hand but her fingers lay limp and unresponsive in his great fist.

'You will still take Demne?'

'What?' He looked at her, taken by surprise at the sudden change in topic.

'Demne. You said you would take him away.'

'I ... Of course. I gave my word.'

She nodded, satisfied.

The warrior meanwhile sat awkwardly beside her, twisting his hands and sitting straight with atypical rigidity. 'There is something I would know, Bodhmhall. Something I would have you disclose with your habitual candour.'

The *bandraoi* stared at him without expression, still too upset to feel any genuine sense of curiosity.

'Have you... My past deeds. Do they ... Do they colour your response towards me?'

Despite the sense of guilt that lay like a heavy cloak on her shoulders, her fears for Liath Luachra and her shame at her own lapse with Fiacial, Bodhmhall surprisingly found herself soften. 'Foolish man. Those misdeeds were forgiven and put to rest many years past, long before you even came to Ráth Bládhma. In this world, after Liath Luachra and Demne, you're the person most dear to me.'

The big man went very quiet and for a moment Bodhmhall wondered if he might be weeping. A quick snort of laughter put paid to that.

'Well that's ... nice.'

'Can I can offer you one consolation, Fiacail?'

'More sex?' he asked hopefully.

She stared, taken aback. 'No!'

Fiacail's lips turned down in a frown but then he shrugged. '*Ar ais le lámhfheis faoin blaincéad, mar sin.*' Back it is to hand festivals beneath the blankets, then.

Bodhmhall shook her head in bewilderment, at a complete loss how to respond to the warrior's fixation. 'I meant that you no longer have a need to trouble Father Sun.'

The Seiscenn Uarbhaoil looked at her blankly.

'The boon you sought of Father Sun. You can extend the pleasure of morning slumber now that there's no need to continue the ritual.'

Fiacail considered that for a moment. 'I still want that horse,' he said.

***

Dawn seeped in with a grey shower that blurred the shapes of two men on grassy flatland to the south-west. Concealed in the dense screen of trees that shielded their campsite, Bodhmhall and Fiacail watched the distant figures examine the ground then turn to stare towards the cluster of mounds at *Síd Na Thost*. There seemed little likelihood they could be anything other than scouts from Gob An Teanga Gorm.

Despite the obvious absence of hiding places in their immediate vicinity, the pair were taking no chances. One of them held a javelin ready to cast at all times while the other moved about on all fours, sniffing and poking at the grass.

The Seiscenn Uarbhaoil man clicked his tongue softly. Despite the lack of sleep and the lingering effects of the hangover, he looked alert and ready, his natural fighting instincts galvanised by the prospect of danger.

'I recognise that graceless carriage,' he said suddenly, pointing his index finger towards the figure on the ground. 'That's Talorc an Soc – Talorc the Snout – of *Uí Barraiche*. He's said to have a rare nose for tracking.' The warrior turned to consider Bodhmhall with an incongruously upbeat expression. 'His family claim to be descended from the bloodhounds of the Ancient Ones. That's why they're said to never lose a trail.'

'Is he Gifted?' The *bandraoi* nervously clasped her hands, resisting the urge to scratch her palms. 'Will he find our trail?'

'I'm sure he'd like to,' Fiacail chuckled. 'Alas, the truth is Talorc's abilities are weak farts in a westerly gale. Four years past, when we were on *fian* together, I spent a night tracking a fugitive through the forest under his guidance only to discover, when daylight came, that we'd been following a family of wild pigs. We'd been walking in their shit for the better part of the night.'

The warrior tapped his nose, screwing it up at the memory. 'No. We have little enough to fear. The storm's wiped all trace of our passage from the Great Mother's mantle. Talorc and his friend are desperate, hoping we made for the most dominant feature on the landscape because if we're in the forest …' He paused to gesture at the trees surrounding them. 'They have as much chance of finding us as a free sow nipple in a litter of suckling piglets.'

Fiacail chuckled softly. 'There are no tracks left to follow, no clear direction we would take except a general route towards Dún Baoiscne. And now we also have the advantage in that we can see them and not be seen in turn. We can wait and watch where they go then take a route to counter it.'

He pulled a tuber – a remnant from the previous night's meal – from his tunic, took a bite and offered it to her.

She shook her head. 'My stomach hurts.'

'My heart hurts.'

'You'll survive.'

'You are cruel, Bodhmhall ua Baoiscne. So very cruel.'

The *bandraoi* glanced at the sky. The rain clouds were dissipating but the daylight remained grim and grey. The scouts meanwhile were moving away, back in the direction they'd come from.

'They've given up.' Fiacail chuckled happily. 'Returning to their master, empty-handed. *Agus soc searbh orthu, an bheirt acu'*. And sour pusses on the pair of them.

Bodhmhall continued to watch the departing figures. 'We should return to camp. Demne will wonder where we've gone.'

They slowly got to their feet. Fiacail gathered up his javelins while the *bandraoi* stood, hesitant and awkward, beside him.

'What troubles you, Bodhmhall?'

A wrinkle of frustration formed on the bridge of the *bandraoi*'s nose, vexed that the Seiscenn Uarbhaoil man could read her so easily. 'This coming evening will be our last alone in the Great Wild. After last night, I … I need to know that things stand well between us, that we are still … friends.'

'We will always be friends, dear one. Always.' He sniffed and wiped his nose. 'I know you for a woman who knows her own mind but one day you'll come to your senses and realise what a wondrous catch, what a fine figure of a man, I truly am.' A broad grin cracked his face. 'And when you do, I will come running, wagging my tail before me.'

Choosing to ignore the warrior's directness, Bodhmhall bluntly changed the conversation. 'Do you believe you can take Demne to safety? That is more important to me than loud tales of uncaught fish.'

'Have I ever let you down before?'

'Many times. Many, many times.'

'And if we discount those particular times?'

She laughed quietly at that. 'In that case, no. Never.'

'Well there you go!' He chuckled loudly, his white teeth glinting even through the shadows beneath the trees. 'Although, you will need to prepare the boy.'

The *bandraoi*'s smile faded. 'What do you mean?'

'Demne will not take your leaving well. You've always been his guardian, always been there when he needed you.'

'I am still his guardian. I am still there for him.'

'You cannot be there if you're tackling Tréanmór's Whispers and his Five Friends,' he countered. 'Unearthing the maggot in Dún Baoiscne's meat will take your full concentration.'

She gave no answer as she thought through the ramifications of what he was telling her but the big man hadn't quite finished.

'More importantly, Bodhmhall, you cannot enter the wolf den without a scheme for making your way back out again.'

The *bandraoi* frowned. 'Therein lies the problem, Fiacail. I have nothing. No advantage to work with, no valuables to negotiate with, nothing but the clothes on my back.'

'You have your wits.' He patted her reassuringly on the shoulder. 'You've always been the smart one, Bodhmhall. You will fashion a scheme to your satisfaction. You always do.'

***

Demne was still sleeping when they returned to the campsite. Rousing the boy, Bodhmhall fed him a cold breakfast of tubers, leaving him to chew on them while she packed the wicker backpacks and worked to remove any trace of their campsite.

They left the cosy cleft as soon as Demne had finished eating and as they made their way deeper into the forest, she glanced back at the little refuge with mixed emotions. The site had served them well, providing a safe shelter when they'd needed it most, but her sense of appreciation was blemished by the memory of her blunder with Fiacail and the guilt that continued to weigh her down.

Continuing in a north-easterly direction, they worked their way through the forest, the *bandraoi* leaving it up to Fiacail to take the lead and beat the trail while she retreated into herself to consider possible approaches to her father, the fearsomely devious *rí* of Dún Baoiscne. Despite the fact that they were family, they'd never been particularly close and their relationship, such as it was, had ended fractiously with her departure from Dún Baoiscne. Presenting herself to him now, without forewarning or preparation of any kind, was hardly going to place her in an effective position to solicit assistance.

Preoccupied with such intrigues, she left all conversation to the warrior and her nephew, a constant murmur that formed a backdrop to her complex machinations.

'There is no one ideal weapon, little wolf-cub,' Fiacail was telling the boy. 'Although, I've always been partial to axes myself.' He flicked a thumb back over his shoulder to where the pair of twin axes protruded above the pack. 'The Two Sisters have never let me down but every weapon has merits of its own and every fighter his preference.'

The big man clicked his perfect teeth together as he gave the matter further consideration. 'Mind you, it's always good to have a weapon that bears a visible aspect of menace, one that gives your enemies cause for reflection. Men are fickle creatures and can be swayed if they see an opponent charging them with a gore-spattered blade. Some will not be cowed at tackling such an opponent but some will, and in the heat of battle those are the little deceits that give you the edge.'

Demne nodded with almost comical earnestness at the big man's words. 'Liath Luachra says it's best to come from the sides. To take your opponent unawares or to wear him down in small cuts.'

'Liath Luachra,' grunted Fiacail. He lapsed into silence for a moment. 'She has her ways,' he said at last. 'And I have mine.'

With this, he called a halt on an open area of ground set into the side of the hill they were descending. Approaching a flat rock with a small rain-filled hollow at its centre, he pulled a bone comb from inside his tunic. Peering at his reflection in the surface of the liquid, he began to comb his hair and moustache, whistling softly as he did so.

Demne stared at him in fascination. 'What are you doing, Fiacail?'

'I am maintaining my features, *a gharsúr*. It would not be seemly to take Father Sun's generosity in such matters lightly.'

'Fiacail sustains his vanity,' Demne's aunt clarified helpfully from behind.

'Vanity?' exclaimed the warrior. 'Is simple veneration to Father Sun's intent not a quality to be admired?' He used the comb to tickle the boy under his nose. 'Shall I do your moustache?'

Demne chortled with high-pitched childish laughter and slapped his knee in imitation of the big man's mannerisms. Bodhmhall rolled her eyes but said nothing.

They continued onwards through the forest, travelling without incident until early afternoon. As the glow of the evening sun dwindled, Fiacail called a halt at a small clearing beside a steep stream that tumbled down a series of staggered rocks to a lichen-coated pool at its base. Although surprised at his decision to set camp so early, Bodhmhall conceded that it was a pleasant place to stop and enjoy the last of the sunshine.

With Demne dispatched to gather firewood, she set to unpacking the cooking utensils and the last of the supplies. Once they were laid out at the spot she planned to set the fire, she moved over to join the Seiscenn Uarbhaoil man who'd taken up position on a flat rock where he was cautiously sharpening one of his axes by drawing a whetstone along the edge of the blade.

'Fiacail.'

'Yes, dear one?' Raising the axe in both hands, he brought the blade close to his lips and blew the grainy residue from the metal.

'In the days to come, I know Demne would be pleased to receive instruction on the *gaiscíoch* path but ...' She paused. 'You should know he has already learned much from Liath Luachra.'

Focussed on his examination of the sharpened blade, the warrior did not look up. 'I can offer much instruction that Liath Luachra lacks.'

'I do not believe his interests extend to rutting and drinking as yet, Fiacail.'

'It is the warrior way,' he declared with faux gravity. 'But I will reflect on what you say.' His smile faded as he considered her with more serious eyes. 'And you, Bodhmhall? Have you fashioned a scheme to tackle your father?'

The *bandraoi* shook her head. 'Not one worthy of the word.' Discouraged by this reminder of her failure, she turned and left the warrior, returning to the base of the fire and arriving just as Demne appeared with a supply of dry dead wood and kindling.

She lapsed into reflective silence as they stacked the kindling and got the fire started. When the flames had taken hold, she had Demne sit beside her, using a fan of twigs to disperse the smoke while they boiled up the last of the meat and tubers. Despite Fiacail's concern, she didn't believe that Gob would dare to trail them so deep into *Clann Baoiscne* territory but it still made sense to take precautions and restrict a visible cloud from forming.

The sun continued to descend while they ate their meal but the sky remained clear, illuminated by a bright crest of golden sunshine to the west. When they'd finished, Demne went to bathe in the pool. The Seiscenn Uarbhaoil man moved up close to sit alongside her on the log serving her as a seat. 'It is an early camp,' he said. 'And still bright.'

'Yes,' responded Bodhmhall warily, not sure where the warrior was trying to lead the conversation.

'And I am going to scout the trail ahead.'

Her left eyebrow arched in wry surprise. With evening closing in, he was unlikely to get very far.

'And, thus, you have the privacy you need to speak with your nephew, to prepare him for your departure tomorrow.' He grinned brightly, taking no heed of the *bandraoi*'s stiffening posture. 'I will return before dark.'

Gathering up his javelins, the warrior got to his feet and started for the edge of the clearing. There, he paused to cast her a meaningful look before stepping into the trees and out of sight.

Bodhmhall stifled a groan. Despite her resentment of the Seiscenn Uarbhaoil man's needling, she knew he had the right of it. Dreading the inevitable separation from her nephew, she had prevaricated, putting off the conversation until the very last moment when there was no longer any plausible excuse to avoid it.

Pursing her lips, she stared into the flames and tried to work out what she was going to say. By the time he'd finished bathing and returned from the pool however, she still hadn't arranged the words to her satisfaction. 'Demne!' she called out to him with a resigned acceptance. 'Come sit by me, *a gharsúr*.' She patted a free section of the mossy log. 'I would have words with you.'

Her nephew obediently changed course to join her. As he sat himself down alongside her, the *bandraoi* regarded him with affection. His damp blond hair was plastered flat against his skull and enhanced the brightness of his eyes, triggering memories of his father at a similar age.

Lifting her good hand to reach out and embrace him, some sudden instinct prompted her to hold it back. Her nephew had changed since leaving Ráth Bládhma and over the previous days she'd noticed a subtle difference to him, a perceptible gravity she'd not noticed before.

In some respects, that was to be expected. Traversing the Great Wild had pushed Demne to his physical and emotional limits. He'd experienced hunger and discomfort, had been exposed to the brutal reality of violence and death and had even spilled his first blood.

The *bandraoi* chewed softly on her upper lip. Her nephew's innocence, that fundamental aspect of his childhood, had been tarnished and now the world would always be a bleaker, darker place. More importantly, at that moment her instincts were telling her if she treated him as a child, despite his relative youth, he'd almost certainly resent her for it.

She opted instead to take his hand, folding her fingers around the cold moistness of his palm, surprised to discover how much bigger it felt in comparison to the delicate miniature of her memory.

My nephew is a babe no more.

'I have decided to travel to Dún Baoiscne alone, Demne. At first light tomorrow. It's safer that you do not accompany me.'

She paused in anticipation of his reaction but, to her surprise, he continued to regard her quietly, as though waiting to see if she had anything further to add.

'Fiacail will take you to Seiscenn Uarbhaoil to instruct you in the *gaiscíoch* path. When my task at Dún Baoiscne is accomplished, I will join you there.'

'Why is it safer?'

She pressed her tongue against her front teeth as she considered the question, a surprisingly astute enquiry from one so young. 'Your father was destined to take on the mantle of leading *Clann Baoiscne*. Tréanmór grows no younger with years and with a peace of sorts now negotiated with *Clann Morna*, others will be jostling for that role. Should you accompany me to Dún Baoiscne your grandfather will use you to counter those challenges. He'd name you as Cumhal's successor and set himself up as guardian until you're of age, essentially remaining as *rí* in all but name.'

'But I don't want to lead *Clann Baoiscne*.'

She smiled at that. 'And that's a response that makes me proud. True leaders of men are those who step up to accept the burden of authority at times of crisis. Such individuals recognise when no others have the courage or the desire and generally, they accept the role with reluctance. In peacetime, conversely, those men and women who seek leadership tend to do so for much more selfish ends.' She raised her palms in a gesture of resignation. 'Such is the nature of people.'

Noting the boy's furrowed brow, she realised that he didn't completely understand what she was telling him, that he lacked the context and experience to fully comprehend the political ramifications. He couldn't hide the fact that the news had upset him however. She caught the momentary quiver of his lower lip but, to her relief, he did not respond with tears or pleading.

'But will you be safe, *a Aintín?*'

Bodhmhall felt a softness in her heart at the boy's genuine concern. Reaching out to take his other hand, she held both close to her chest before releasing them. 'There is some danger,' she admitted. 'But I believe I will be safe. They were my people after all, even though I'm no longer entirely trusted, or even liked.'

She saw how that surprised him. Raised at Ráth Bládhma where his aunt was generally held in high regard, he'd automatically assumed that everyone liked her. 'But why?'

The *bandraoi* carefully plucked a loose thread from the hem of her dress as she worked out what to say. Dún Baoiscne had always been something of a forbidden topic in the conversations between them but it was inevitable that Demne would learn of her troubled history one day and it was probably better he heard the story from her directly.

Bodhmhall deliberately dropped her hands by her sides to prevent herself from scratching her palms. Looking Demne directly in the eye, she took a deep breath and exhaled slowly. 'I took the life of a man at Dún Baoiscne, a man with the name of Dub Tíre on him. He was a person of status at the stronghold, a *draoi* and advisor to my father. The people of *Clann Baoiscne* respected him and had little tolerance for my killing of him.'

Her nephew's jaw dropped at this revelation. 'Was he a bad man?'

A child's response. Once again to the heart of the matter.

She frowned thoughtfully at that, wondering how much she could reasonably tell him, how much he would truly comprehend with his limited interpretations of "good" and "bad".

'I thought so.'

The boy grunted in imitation of Fiacail, her simple response clearly considered sufficient. The *bandraoi* hid a wistful smile.

Would that everyone thought like that. It's the life of ease I'd have.

'That was over ten years ago and I still hold to my actions but … there was a price. Some felt I should be put to death for what I'd done. Others thought I should be delivered to the Druidic Order for justice which, ultimately, would have meant the same thing. I escaped with my life through the intervention of family and my friends but, even so, I was exiled, obliged to leave my home and all I knew.' She hesitated. 'That is how I came to establish a new life at Ráth Bládhma, with Liath Luachra and the others.'

Bodhmhall turned away and kicked irritably at the ashes of the fire. Talking of her old mentor was stirring up old memories and it turned out that the old feelings of bitterness and anxiety she'd believed exorcized many years ago still lingered beneath the surface after all.

A pressure on the back of her hand caused her to glance down to where Demne had rested his own hand. The boy might not have known what to say but his good nature had instinctively guided him with the appropriate gesture.

'You should go to bed,' she told him, more brusquely than she'd intended. 'Tiredness curls your eyelids and there'll be no jawing about the campfire tonight.'

The boy didn't move and in truth she felt no real compulsion to encourage him further.

'Liath Luachra is gone, a Aintín. And now you're leaving me too.'

'Only for a short time, Demne.' Despite the ache in her stomach, the *bandraoi* managed to inject a forced sense of enthusiasm into her voice. 'Besides, Fiacail will take care of you. He has a good heart and will be a good influ- ... A good teacher. You will learn much from him.'

The boy looked to that section of the trees where the big man had disappeared and frowned. The *bandraoi* noted his reaction with interest. Despite Demne's growing admiration, he clearly wasn't entirely enamoured at the prospect of remaining alone with the warrior over a prolonged period.

'Do you have to go? We could return to Ráth Bládhma where we'd be safe.'

'We'll never be safe until the identity of the Adversary is known to us.' The *bandraoi* grimaced as she considered the prospect of the challenge before her. 'The only way to get that is through his spy at Dún Baoiscne and he's unlikely to reveal himself unless I'm there to stir things up.'

'Perhaps he'll reveal himself unwillingly, the way you do in our games of *fidchell*.'

'What do you mean?' Bodhmhall's eyebrows arched, her curiosity piqued. 'I reveal no intent in *fidchell*.'

'Yes, you do. There are certain patterns, certain movements you prefer over others. You use them at different times and in different circumstances but you always repeat them so I know how you're going to play.'

Bodhmhall stared at the boy, struggling to understand what exactly he was saying but found herself stymied by a growing weariness. She shook her head to clear the blur of shadows. 'That will have to be a conversation for when we meet again, my beautiful boy.'

'But I -'

'Shush now, *a gharsúr.*'

The boy attempted another plaintive tack but having made her decision, Bodhmhall was not to be moved. 'Do not make this harder for us, Demne. Let us pass this last night with fondness.'

Hearing the determination in his aunt's voice, Demne seemed to deflate and he offered no resistance when she urged him up and escorted him to his bed of heather. There, tucking him in, she kissed him on the cheek, her lips resting on the soft skin far longer than she'd intended.

Do not cry, Cailleach. For the sake of your nephew, do not cry.

She could feel his eyes on her as she made her way back to the fire. Regaining her seat on the log, she shifted herself guiltily so that her back was facing him. Staring into the flames, she fed the fire a fresh supply of wood as she massaged the cold space under her heart and fought to suppress a mounting anger kindled by a ferocity that would give her no rest. She didn't want to leave her nephew. She had no desire to return to Dún Baoiscne, back to her father and ...

Dub Tíre.

She realised that she was scraping her palms again, sinking her nails into the soft flesh. With a snarl, she dropped them to her sides.

I would not be here were it not for you.

There were times she felt a hatred so ferocious it actually scared her. Hatred went against her nature and emotions of such enmity both confused and frightened her. And yet, even now, despite the run of years, she couldn't draw Dub Tíre's face to mind without a shiver of revulsion.

The irony of it all was that the *draoi* had actually been quite handsome, a man of such striking features the eligible *Clann Baoiscne* women had murmured about him like drowsy honey bees when he'd first arrived at the stronghold. Despite such attention however, the severity and stiffness of his personality had quickly deterred even the most willing. Within a year, that severity took on an even more visible manifestation when the *draoi* hacked his hair short, tattooed his cheeks with obscure symbols and applied a silver pin through his nose and ears.

Initially, this self-disfigurement was received with a combination of consternation and trepidation by the people of *Clann Baoiscne*. In the end however, it actually served to enhance his reputation for it seemed to confirm what everyone had always believed about those sacred few touched by the *Gift*: preoccupied with the matters of the arcane and the divine, they had no time for the mundanities of sex or personal grooming.

Bodhmhall recalled how she too had been impressed by the *draoi*'s radical physical transformation but then she'd never been in any doubt of his power. On the day of his arrival at Dún Baoiscne, she'd perceived that power for herself, the tell-tale flare of red against the orange glow of his lifelight. At the time, she'd had but eleven years on her and by then of course her own *Gift* hadn't entirely settled. Much later, when it did, she'd done nothing to disguise it and it wasn't long before Dub Tíre's predator-like eye had distinguished her from the others.

And he'd wanted what she had.

***

Darkness had fallen when Fiacail finally returned to the campsite. By then, the fire had shrunk to a few flickering flames and Demne was snoring softly despite his earlier reluctance.

Hunched beside the embers, the *bandraoi* continued to stare into the ruddy glow. Her palms stung from scratching. Her mouth was sour.

'Bodhmhall.'

The warrior's voice was little louder than a rustle in the night, nevertheless it startled her from her reverie. Raising her eyes, she saw the dim form of him silhouetted against the darker treeline.

The shadow moved forwards, tearing away from the darkness that clung to him but it was only when he was practically standing beside her that she could make out the outline of his features from the red haze of the fire.

'Have you spoken with your nephew?' he asked.

Bodhmhall nodded, reluctant to speak for she did not know what she would say or where the words would lead her. Unaware of the ghosts that troubled her, Fiacail gave a grunt of satisfaction.

'And you have a scheme?'

The *bandraoi* nodded once more. 'I have a scheme,' she answered at last. 'But you will not like it.'

Chapter Six

The Grey One watched the warriors while she chewed on a sliver of smoked beef retrieved from the body of the second scout. Four men, they were spread in an uneven line across the narrow section of forest between the river and the base of the cliffs. Although standing within calling distance of each other – about twenty paces apart – the density of the trees and the thickness of the undergrowth meant their line of sight was obscured and any kind of extended conversation between them, difficult.

The enemy camp was situated about forty paces beyond this defensive barrier. Again, due to the thickness of the scrub, the campfire wasn't actually visible but there was no mistaking the scent of freshly cooked meat drawn upriver on the prevailing breeze. This smell had not gone unnoticed by the four guards who were glancing back in that direction with increasingly frequency and an evident eagerness to be relieved. On this matter alone, the Grey One sympathised with them. Familiar with the tedious nature of watch duty from her years with *Na Cinéaltaí*, she was only too aware how the unrelenting monotony could dull the mind and reduce the flow of time to a trickle.

There were tricks, of course, tricks to maintain one's vigilance and hold the tempting lull of sleep at bay. However, she could tell these men had no interest in such mitigating techniques. Hungry, bored, and secure in their strength of numbers, the Great Wild's feral menace held little dread for them. They wanted nothing more than to be relieved from duty, to return to the fire for the meal awaiting them.

Laggards.

The Grey One bared her teeth in silent condemnation. Negligence was one of the few personal traits that could truly get under her skin.

Even when she intended to work it to her advantage.

She turned her eyes towards the sun, once again studying its painstakingly slow decline along the summit of the northern mountain range. Stretched on her belly in a thicket of fern, she'd positioned herself less than twenty paces from the guards, as close to the line as she'd dared. Unable to move for fear of stirring the green fronds and drawing attention to her position, she'd hardly budged since crawling to that position before dawn. Now, after almost a full day of concealment, her muscles ached for the want of movement.

As evening fell, the breeze grew stronger, stirring the trees and rustling the vegetation and with that the woman warrior finally felt secure enough to shift about a little more. Flexing her arms and legs, she carefully stretched each limb, working the tension from her muscles.

When the discomfort had faded, she turned her attention to her clothing. Raising the hem of the heavy tunic, she felt the welcome touch of air against her skin. Clad in her usual battle harness and leggings, she also bore the additional weight of the dead scout's buffer tunic and helmet and the unaccustomed layers were making her hot and sweaty. The lingering body odour of its previous owner didn't help.

Eventually, she removed the helmet and rubbed her shaven head, remarking at the sharpness of the stubble on her scalp. The previous evening she'd taken a knife to her hair so that the helmet would fit, slashing at her dark mane until it was cropped close to the skull. Afterwards, she'd held the severed strands between her fingers, studying them with mute disquiet. Ever since quitting the brutality of her previous existence with *Na Cinéaltaí*, she'd intentionally worn her hair long. The simple act of hacking it off had felt like a backward step. In a strange way, it was as though by cutting her hair, she was cutting away the person she'd grown into over the previous ten years, reverting once more to the broken creature she'd once been.

A soft shuffling sound drew her eyes to the fern thicket just alongside her. There, the *Lamraighe* youth was just visible among the green fronds, clad like her in one of the dead scouts' tunics and looking equally as uncomfortable. He was also looking directly at the bristles of her shaven skull, triggering an angry tightness in her belly.

'Do flat chests and short hair draw your eye now, Fintán?' she whispered with uncharacteristic sharpness. 'The men will whisper behind your back.'

Taken aback by her unexpected hostility, the *óglach* turned his head away, embarrassed and angry.

Good. Anger before battle burns the shiver of nervousness away.

They ignored each another in intimate, if ill-disposed, silence as the evening shadows condensed below the ridges. Finally, a call echoed out from the camp to signal the change of guard.

The four warriors responded immediately, each starting back towards the campsite, not even deigning to remain long enough for their replacements to take their place. Having awaited this opportunity for the better part of the afternoon, Liath Luachra didn't hesitate. Choosing her moment in the bustle of incoming and departing guards, she rose to her feet in the shadow of an adjacent oak tree and strode confidently forwards. Behind her, Fintán followed, head down, close on her heels.

The Grey One walked with a purpose to her stride that wasn't completely feigned for she'd already worked out her route. Cutting away towards the ridge at an angle from the intersecting warriors, she made for a thicket of trees with dense undergrowth that the guards had been using for their ablutions over the course of the day. Having studied the constant coming and goings, she was relatively confident that anyone seen headed in that direction wouldn't look too much out of place.

The acrid stench of several days' worth of shit hit her nostrils before she'd even reached the thicket but it didn't prevent her from thrusting forward into the comforting screen of vegetation that obscured her from view. With a quick glance around to assure herself that the site was, indeed, unoccupied, she hurriedly twisted about, peering back through a gap in the bushes for any sign that their incursion had been noticed.

Fortunately, thanks to the timing, the foliage and the darkening twilight, their luck held. Bored and hungry, the returning guards had been focussed entirely on their return to the campsite. The new warriors meanwhile, had been too engrossed in conversations of their own to pay attention to anyone else. With their shadowed features and stolen clothing, Liath Luachra and Fintán hadn't warranted a second glance.

Beside her, the *Lamraighe* youth gagged suddenly and stifled a dry retch.

'*Dún do chlab!*' she hissed from the side of her mouth. Shut your beak.

'The reek!' he moaned, clamping a hand over his face at the overpowering stench of shit. 'It burns my throat.'

She kicked him furiously in the side of the leg, continuing to watch as the replacement sentries took up position and formed a line similar to that of their predecessors. They seemed to take an age about it. Unlike their hungry comrades, they were in no particular rush and moved without urgency, chatting and laughing before reluctantly drawing apart to their assigned positions. As they slowly settled into place, the shouted conversations dwindled and they turned their eyes towards the deepening gloom of the upriver forest.

Away from the interlopers in the trees behind them.

Liath Luachra exhaled deeply and allowed herself a momentary flush of relief. She clenched and unclenched her fists, unconsciously flexing her shoulder blades as she worked to loosen the tightness. Traversing the open ground in full view of her enemies had been terrifying for the ruse had felt ludicrously transparent. At the time she'd barely suppressed the urge to break into a run and even now her heart was still beating a panicked tattoo.

She took a deep breath, exhaled slowly through her nose and tried to focus on the next stage of the plan. They'd overcome a major obstacle in bypassing the initial line of guards but any respite was temporary. They were not out of danger.

With characteristic single-mindedness, the woman warrior physically shrugged her fears from her shoulders, turned her gaze to the terrain ahead and studied it with renewed focus. Thirty to forty paces north-east of the thicket, the enemy campfire could now be distinguished, although an uneven screen of trees reduced the fire – and the men around it – to an orange and black collage of flickering shadow.

The woman warrior's right foot tapped an unconscious, nervous rhythm. Despite the negligence of the initial guards, she sensed a more competent consideration behind the setting of the campfire which, equidistant from the river and the cliffs, allowed effective scrutiny of anyone attempting to pass.

During the day.

In her head, she worked through two or three possible routes past the enemy camp but the safest path seemed obvious. If they made for the ridge and followed the base of the cliffs, the thickness of the vegetation and fading illumination would obscure them, allowing them to slip safely past without their enemy being any the wiser. Once they'd circumvented the central campfire and put some distance behind them, they could veer back to the more accessible path along the riverbank.

Tapping the *Lamraighe* youth on the shoulder, she got him to lean forwards until her lips were close to his ear then quietly whispered her plan. Pulling back, she waited for his nod to confirm he'd understood. Beneath the thick forest canopy, the youth was little more than a shadow in the fading light but she caught the dip of his chin clearly enough. Satisfied, she took a deep breath.

And stepped out of the trees.

They moved swiftly towards the cliffs, using the natural cover of the tree trunks and foliage as much as possible, bare feet silent on the mossy earth. As they advanced, the woman warrior glanced repeatedly to the rear, keeping one eye on the guards behind them, one on the enemy campfire. A burst of raucous laughter from the latter momentarily shattered the peace of the otherwise silent forest and it was probably this distraction that caused her to miss the presence of a second campsite, mid-way between the thicket and the base of the cliffs, until they'd walked right into it.

Liath Luachra froze. Taken by surprise, Fintán stumbled desperately to one side to avoid running into her. Both stared at the clearing, illuminated now by the flicker of a small fire which seemed to have appeared out of nowhere, concealed until the very last moment by a deep U-shaped section of impenetrable bush.

Recovering from her initial shock, Liath Luachra breathed a sigh of relief for their luck continued to hold. The campsite was deserted and the thick vegetation shielded them from the view of the main campsite and the line of guards.

Before them, the small fire crackled welcomingly, a delicious scent of stewed meat emanating from a metal pot settled in the outer embers. Beyond the fire, at the apex of the U-shaped curve, the warrior woman could make out a stretch of heather bedding, overlain with a heavy blanket. Sitting on the ground alongside it were a water bucket and a sturdy leather satchel.

The Grey One quickly assessed the situation. Whoever this campsite had been prepared for – and its seclusion suggested an individual of some importance – that person was absent. Which meant …

Scuttling forward into the little clearing, she crouched by the bedding and started to rummage through the satchel.

'What are you doing!' Fintán's aggrieved whisper was tight and high-pitched but the woman warrior ignored him as she emptied the contents onto the ground; two sheets of leather with strange symbols etched into them, a trio of crystals, a bear claw, the small, white skull of a rat and various other strange odds and ends. Taking up the leather sheets, she approached the fire and used them as a pair of makeshift gloves to lift the lid from the steaming pot. Tossing it to one side, she proceeded to pour the stew into the upright leather satchel, ignoring the cloud of meaty vapour that enveloped her face.

Off to the side, Fintán regarded her anxiously, his jaws working wordlessly as though chewing on something particularly tough and tasteless. Focussed on the task of filling the satchel without spilling the broth, she didn't have the luxury to remind him that penetrating the enemy encampment had only been part of the final plan the little group of refugees had agreed on. Hemmed in by the river and the cliffs of the ridge, there'd never been any realistic prospect of escaping or opposing the enemy's superior force. With Muirne and Gleor incapable of any kind of protracted flight, the only viable alternative was to draw Gob An Teanga Gorm's men away from the *Lamraighe* couple's location. Naturally, the only practical means of achieving this objective was to create a diversion on the opposite side of the enemy encampment.

Excellent runners, both Liath Luachra and Fintán had a chance of eluding their pursuers in the vastness of the Great Wild provided they made it through the camp and escaped the confines of the valley. The key limitation to that plan had been the refugees' lack of provisions for it put them at a significant disadvantage once the pursuit was underway. Now that the Gods had seen fit to place a ready supply of food into their hands, the Grey One had no intention of ignoring it.

The stew continued to bubble as it slopped, thick and viscous, into the satchel. The heady scent of it tickled the Grey One's taste buds but she ignored the temptation for the heat from the metal container was already burning her hands through the leather sheets and the broth inside was almost certainly too hot to taste.

With the satchel filled to the brim, the pot remained half-full. The woman warrior eyed it thoughtfully as she gestured for Fintán to pick up the stew's new, makeshift container. Despite its cumbersome weight, she was reluctant to leave it behind for it still held at least two days' worth of food, a reserve that'd be extremely welcome if they failed to shake off their pursuers.

Resting the pot against her chest, she got to her feet, the heat of the lip burning her skin even through the double layer of clothing. Glancing at the youth, she jerked her chin towards the gap in the surrounding bush. It was time to leave.

To her surprise, Fintán remained where he was, the steaming leather satchel in his hand as he glowered at her, clearly infuriated by her brusqueness towards him.

'Be angry, later,' she snapped. 'We have to go.'

Glaring at him for the poor timing of this newfound defiance, she stepped out of the clearing.

Into the path of the two incoming figures.

There was one terrible moment of stunned inactivity as both pairs of individuals stared at one another. The Grey One's attention latched almost immediately onto the tall man to her left for there was something startlingly compelling about him. Tall and wiry, with a distinctive hawk-nose, he exuded an unmistakeable aura of authority. His eyes, sinister and black as the dark spaces between the trees, flickered from her own eyes to the tattoo on her left cheek.

The second individual – a youth no older than Fintán – was sallow-skinned and handsome and had a short, blunt nose, a sensual mouth and glossy black hair that fell to his shoulders.

Conán mac Morna!

She recognised him immediately and even as mutual recognition flared in the *mac Morna* youth's murderous eye she was moving, already reacting on instinct. Without pausing to think, she hurled the metal pot at him and barged forwards to deal with his companion. She caught the brief flash of outrage across the tall man's face, a mere heartbeat before her elbow smashed into it. Taken completely by surprise, he went bowling over backwards like a freshly hewn tree trunk and from the sharp crack of bone, she knew she'd broken his nose.

Spinning about to face the second – and more deadly – opponent, the Grey One was drawing her sword when his blood-curdling scream struck her. Scrambling frantically backwards, she halted in shock, staring to where Conán mac Morna was writhing on the ground, frantically scraping at his hair and face. It took two heartbeats to understand what had happened, that when she'd flung the pot its contents had spilled out, plastering the youth's head and face with the blistering stew.

As the horrific shrieks ripped the forest's previously silent mantle, Liath Luachra gawped, struggling to pull herself away from the compellingly awful sight. Finally, twisting around to Fintán, she found the *Lamraighe* youth too was gaping, his mouth open and his eyes wide like those of a panicked horse. 'Run!' she roared.

Without waiting to see if he responded, the Grey One took to her heels, pounding north-west, parallel to the cliffs. Smashing through the undergrowth, she darted between the trees, avoiding those projecting branches that she could actually see in the fading light, scrambling over the moss-coated barriers of fallen trees in her path. Above the sound of screaming, she could make out the angry commotion of other men, bellows and barks, alarmed and fully alert.

Realising that the clamour of her own flight risked drawing them on her, the warrior woman stifled her panic and forced herself to slow, gradually reducing her speed until she'd come to an unsteady halt. Dropping to a crouch, she started forward with greater caution, only to stiffen in alarm at the sudden crash of movement in the undergrowth behind her. Grasping her sword, she twisted about, blade at the ready. A white-faced Fintán suddenly barged through the bushes off to her right. Her shoulders sagged in relief. The boy had managed to keep up.

Spotting her, Fintán veered desperately to join her, gasping for breath as he slid onto the ground beside her. Struggling to draw air in great, painful gasps, neither spoke for several moments but stared back in the direction of the enemy camp. Dusk had now faded almost completely to darkness and flaming torches could be seen flickering erratically in the shadows where Gob An Teanga Gorm's men shouted to each other in their search for the intruders.

Liath Luachra nudged the boy. '*Ar aghaigh linn.*' Let's go.

They made their way towards the river, homing in on it from the sound of rushing water. Keen to put some distance between themselves and the enemy camp, they started downriver, only to find themselves hindered by the darkness. It being an overcast night, any sliver of moonlight was effectively smothered and the riverbank as dark as the inside of a black pig's arse.

Forced to a halt by the precarious terrain and the real risk of tumbling into the water, they dropped to their hands and knees, advancing with agonizing slowness through touch alone.

To the rear, the flames from the torches gradually disappeared from sight although the calls of the warriors remained audible for much longer. Liath Luachra knew that the combination of the river valley's narrowness and the absence of wind made the calls sound much closer than they were, nevertheless she pushed onwards until these too had faded completely.

Finally, exhausted, she led the *Lamraighe* youth off the bank and into the trees. Unable to see where they were going, they ventured just two trees deep where, by chance, they happened on a patch of fern and moss that offered some softness to rest on. There, to her surprise, in spite of his obvious fatigue, Fintán argued that they continue their flight, cover as much ground as possible while they had the opportunity.

The Grey One simply shook her head. 'We'd cover little ground in the darkness and achieve little more than wearying ourselves and leaving a trail a blind man could follow. Gob An Teanga Gorm's an experienced battler. He won't waste time trying to hunt us tonight. He'll rest his men until first light then find our trail and run us down.'

'But if w-'

'If we make a successful escape,' she cut him off brusquely. 'There's no incentive for them to follow. Our goal was to draw the enemy away from Muirne and your father. If you truly think it best to leave them to their fate, I'll not argue against it.'

Sensing her complete sincerity, Fintán's initial response was a stunned silence. The woman warrior suspected his jaw was hanging open but the darkness prevented her from confirming this.

'You would leave my father and Muirne? But wh-' The youth paused and grew quiet but that silence proved temporary. 'Do you truly hate them so much?'

The Grey One thought about that. 'Yes,' she admitted.

'I don't understand. If you bear them such ill will, why do you help them? We all know you could have escaped this valley with ease had you chosen to do so. Instead, you stayed, supporting them, protecting them, even offering your cloak to my father when he was cold.'

Bodhmhall's cloak.

'Stop talking,' she snapped. 'Sleep. We move on again before dawn.'

To thwart any further discussion she turned away and lay on her side, curling up in a nest of moss and beaten fern. Fintán, sensing her anger, took the hint for he refrained from further comment and lay down alongside her, his back against hers.

Despite his silence, the woman warrior could feel the tension emanating from him but fatigue gradually wore him down. After a time, she heard his breathing regulate and he settled into a soft snoring pattern.

If you bear them such ill will, why did you help them?

Her lips compressed. It was a fair question. Particularly when she had no real answer. The antagonism between herself and Muirne had also created tension with Gleor Red Hand from the moment the *Lamraighe* had first set foot in Ráth Bládhma. Following their departure from the settlement, that tension had subsequently spread to Gleor's leash-hound, Marcán and the other *Lamraighe* warriors.

For that reason, her behaviour made little sense, even to herself. Intuitively, she suspected she might be acting out of some sense of displaced loyalty to Bodhmhall. Whatever the *Lamraighe* couple's faults, the *bandraoi* would never have deserted them or left them to die.

The woman warrior clenched her teeth. From her perspective, the last three days had been trying in ways she'd never have imagined possible. In the old days, although she wouldn't have slit their throats she'd almost certainly have deserted them without qualm.

So why am I still here? What has changed?

Surprisingly, the answer came to her with unanticipated ease and clarity.

Because when Fintán returned, Gleor cried.

She folded that realisation around in her mind, not entirely sure what to make of it but knowing it couldn't be so simple.

And yet, instinctively, she sensed she'd got to the heart of it, even if she didn't quite understand it herself. Somehow, the old man's reaction to the sight of his son had unlocked something deep inside her, something she couldn't easily articulate or put into words.

Foolish!

She snorted, almost sneered at her own self-delusion.

Too agitated to sleep, she turned her thoughts to more realistic issues, practical considerations that were easier to get her head around. Replaying the infiltration into and the flight from the enemy camp in her head, she wondered whether there was anything she could have done differently but, in the end, decided there wasn't. The actions and decisions she'd taken had been sound. Their discovery in the little clearing had just been pure misfortune.

She realised she was grinding her teeth.

The most galling part of all was that everything had gone perfectly, right up to the point where they'd left the second clearing, and had they managed to get clear just a few moments earlier, they'd have missed Conán mac Morna and his tall companion entirely. Leaving the camp undetected and with a supply of food, they'd have been in a much better position, free not only to get a good night's sleep but to scout out an effective escape route. Now, conversely, they'd be running for their lives: unprepared, unfamiliar with the terrain and unrested.

Still, Conán mac Morna won't be on our heels any time soon.

She shivered briefly at the memory of the *Clann Morna* warrior floundering on the ground. The youth's agonized screeches had genuinely unnerved her, despite her complete absence of sympathy for him. Conán mac Morna was an utterly callous killer, something she'd witnessed with her own eyes at An Glenn Teann. She had no doubt that if she hadn't taken him out, he'd have killed her and Fintán both without a second thought.

But his companion …

She chewed quietly on the inside of her cheek as she recalled the youth's companion. In the heat of the moment, there'd been no time to even think about him but now, in hindsight, she realised there'd been something disturbing and yet oddly familiar about that tall man. He was no warrior, that much was evident from the sluggishness of his physical reactions. Nevertheless, the expression of outrage and sheer disbelief she'd seen in his eyes before she'd hit him, told her that this was a man unaccustomed to the threat of physical violence, a man unaccustomed to opposition itself. This therefore, marked him as someone who was very powerful indeed.

Although not powerful enough to stop her breaking his nose.

And that, at least, was a pleasant enough thought to lull her off to sleep.

***

It was still dark when Liath Luachra woke, roused by an innate, unconscious sense of the incoming dawn. With a grunt, she sat up and wiped her eyes. Peering around at the encircling gloom of overhanging trees, she slowly got to her feet to sniff at the morning breeze. There was always a subtle difference to the Great Wild at this hour, a kind of hushed stillness as though the very land itself was poised, breathless at the prospect of the incoming day.

Shuffling out of the dead scout's tunic, she tossed the heavy garment onto the ground beside the trampled nest of ferns that had served for her bed. The air was cool where it touched her skin and although it briefly caused her to shiver, it didn't overly trouble her. The extra layer had been welcome during the night but in the furious flight to come any extra weight would sap her strength and slow her down. Discarding it out in the open where Gob's men would easily find it also had the benefit of providing an additional incentive for them to follow. Enraged at the infiltration of their campsite, the warriors would be doubly incensed at this evidence of their fallen comrades and hungry to avenge them.

Fintán was still sleeping soundly but he woke rapidly enough when she kicked his heels. Rattled by the rough wakening, he momentarily floundered about in panic before realising where he was, peering bleary-eyed at the shadow-shrouded form of the woman warrior. The Grey One dropped the heavy satchel onto the ground beside him. 'Eat. There'll be little enough chance later.'

The *Lamraighe* youth stared dumbly at the leather container. Sighing, she led by example, digging one hand into the satchel and scooping out a sticky handful. The stew had cooled overnight, congealing into a solid, gummy mess that was glued to the sides of the bag. Although cold, it still tasted delicious and she chomped the fatty paste with pleasure.

Inspired by her example, Fintán too began to eat.

While she chewed, the Grey One did a mental stocktake of their provisions and equipment, striving to identify anything they might discard, anything of weight she'd overlooked that might slow them down. In truth, there wasn't really much to work with. Apart from the clothes on their backs, a small tinder pouch and the satchel of stew, they carried nothing but their weapons and even these were restricted to a sword and knife apiece. It was true she had her sling and six stones tucked inside her battle harness but their combined weight was negligible and they provided at least one long-range alternative to compensate for the lack of the javelins left behind with Gleor and Muirne.

When Fintán indicated he was finished, Liath Luachra picked up the satchel and used the straps to affix it to her back, alongside the sword scabbard. Taking time to ensure it was properly balanced and wouldn't chafe, she completed the final securing and led the way out of the trees.

In the minimal light, the riverbank flat was a barely visible grey line against a black background. Taking a moment to sniff the air once more, the woman warrior was pleased to note that the wind had shifted and now blew downriver from the east. This was a good thing in that it would blow the scent of their enemy towards them, possibly giving them the advantage of a few moments' warning were they about to close in.

Not that she had any intention of letting that happen.

By her estimation, Gob An Teanga Gorm's warriors would already be up by now, finalising their preparations while a number of the fleetest were almost certainly working their way along the riverbank by touch in an effort to outflank the fugitives.

It was time to go.

Despite the feeble light, the woman warrior started downriver with Fintán in tow. Although they forced to move at a crawl, the first gleam of dawn slid in much earlier than expected and within a short period of time they were able to get to their feet and gradually increase their speed from a wary jog to a careful lope. As the first glow of daylight spilled over from behind the eastern hills, they broke into a full-fledged run.

Leading the *Lamraighe* youth, the woman warrior set a gruelling pace. By now, Gob's forward scouts would also be moving at speed and she was damned if she was going to let them eat away at the slim lead they'd managed to achieve. If she and Fintán could maintain – or increase – the distance between them, the pursuing warriors' outflanking manoeuvre would fail, forcing them to slow to a more sustainable pace and consider alternative courses of action.

And this was what worried her. She could anticipate the more obvious tricks that might be employed but she couldn't predict what other stratagems they might draw on. From what she'd seen of Gob An Teanga Gorm, she knew he was no fool. An experienced fighter like him would have several schemes or options to fall back on.

And any one of those might cost her and Fintán their lives.

***

By early-morning they were breathing hard, sweating profusely, leg muscles burning from the strain of the pace. Although reluctant to allow their pursuers any opportunity to reduce the gap between them, by noon the Grey One knew she'd have to call a brief halt to rest and replenish their bodies with food and water.

She led the *Lamraighe* youth off the path by a narrow stretch of shingle that sloped down to a gritty strand at the river's edge. There, the woman warrior waded in up to her waist and plunged her head and shoulders into the current, ignoring the shock of cold water as she held herself in place.

At last, breathless, she stood upright once more and returned to the strand, silver rivulets streaming down her face and neck. Crouching, she cupped some liquid in her hands, raised them to her mouth and drank, repeating the action until her thirst was quenched.

Beside her, the *Lamraighe* youth was lying flat on his stomach, also drinking his fill and intermittently splashing water onto his face and the back of his neck to cool himself. She was pleased to note he was smart enough to restrict his intake, avoiding the risk of stomach bloat.

Easing back onto her haunches, Liath Luachra loosened the straps on her back, reached her right arm over her left shoulder and pulled a fistful of gooey stew from the satchel. Offering the first handful to Fintán, she took a fresh scoop for herself, mechanically chewing the meaty paste as she scanned the trail to the rear then twisting about to study the lay of the terrain before them.

Over the latter part of the morning, she'd noticed the river had widened discernibly. The banks too had lowered in height and steepness, a definite indicator of a weakening current. The mountains, unfortunately, showed no such reduction. The steep cliffs persisted in an unbroken line, continuing to hem them in. Naturally, there'd be some routes that cut through their rocky bulk, gaps or gorges that provided egress from the valley to the Great Wild beyond. Unfortunately, ferreting out such routes in unknown territory generally involved a painstaking process of exploration, hunch work and back-tracking. With Gob's men hot on their heels, they didn't have the time to do that. For the moment at least, they were better off following the river and although that meant they were much easier to track it also meant they could more easily maintain their lead to escape into the wider wilderness when the ridges eventually petered out.

Swallowing the last of her stew, the Grey One got to her feet. Walking towards a broad boulder that obstructed a portion of the view downstream, she rounded the bulky obstacle to stare at the stretch of water flowing off to the east. The river, glistening in the early afternoon sun, continued in a rough straight line until it disappeared from sight. Straightening up, the woman warrior squinted and peered with fresh intensity. At the furthest point of her vision, just where it blurred to mere impression, she thought she could make out a stretch of flat water.

A ford?

The possibility triggered a flicker of excitement but she quickly repressed it, fearful of getting her hopes up. It was probably nothing more than a trick of the light, an illusion triggered by her desire to get to the other side of the river, a fugitive still but, potentially, closer to Bodhmhall.

With a frown, she peered again but the distance was just too great to be certain. Admittedly, given the current topography, it looked a possible location. As a general rule, fords tended to be found on straighter, wider sections of the river where the current was weakest.

Only one way to know for sure.

Turning on her heel, she started back to where Fintán lay sprawled on the shingle, happily sucking a morsel of meat between his fingers. She tapped his rump with the side of her foot.

114

'Ar aghaigh linn. Teas-'

She stiffened and went silent.

Fintán stared up at her. Observing the rigidity of her stance and the intense manner in which she was staring across the waterway, he hurriedly got to his feet.

'What is it?' His voice was high-pitched and breathless. 'What do you see?'

The Grey One didn't answer but continued to stare, her lips set in a tight line. The far bank was an unbroken wall of thick green bush and dense forest that spread almost directly along the waterway. There was no break in the trees, no feature that looked in any way out of the ordinary. To the far right a number of birds fluttered from treetop to treetop but the activity seemed natural and unhurried.

'What is it?' demanded Fintán.

Absorbed in her scrutiny, the woman warrior irritably shook her head to silence him. She had thought to see a flicker of movement in the lower vegetation from the corner of her eye, a movement that was different from the normal range of forest rustlings and shufflings. Now however, there was nothing. The far bank appeared completely serene and even the bird twitter sounded untroubled.Despite all this, the hairs at the back of her neck continued to stand on end.

Nervous, she clucked her tongue. It might have been nothing more than the wind in the trees, her imagination triggered by her heightened instincts. Nevertheless, she couldn't shake the feeling that something wasn't quite right.

'Ready yourself.' She spoke softly from the corner of her mouth. 'We're leaving.'

They made their preparations quickly, finishing off the last of their food and checking the fastenings of the weapons and the leather satchel. At no time did the Grey One's eyes leave the far bank.

Quitting the water's edge, they made their way back to the upper section of the bank. The woman warrior was just clambering onto the upper level, levering herself to her feet, when Fintán grasped her left ankle. 'Grey One!'

Liath Luachra looked back, immediately spotting what had alarmed the *Lamraighe* youth: a thin column of smoke rising above the trees across the water. She sucked air in through her teeth and stared, her expression grim. As far as she could tell, the source of the smoke was located less than one hundred paces beyond the tree line. Curious, she continued to observe as the column of smoke increased in height. As the woman warrior watched, it

115

abruptly took on a darker, blacker hue and she felt a sudden tightness in her stomach.

'Move,' she snarled.

'What?' Fintán looked at her in bewilderment.

Reaching down, she yanked the startled *Lamraighe* youth onto the upper bank.

'*Rith!*' Run!

Once again, she didn't wait for the youth to work it out but thrust past him, plunging into the shadows where the trees overhung the flat of the riverbank.

Fool! You fool!

To her rear, the swish of ferns and the rhythm of Fintán's pounding feet confirmed he'd caught her up but, consumed by what she'd seen, she was too overwrought, too furious at herself to really notice. The smoke had turned black because someone had tossed green leaves onto the flames. The only logical reason for doing that was to make the smoke visible from afar.

Evidently, Gob An Teanga Gorm had placed men on both sides of the river and, lolling about in the open, she'd allowed herself and Fintán to be seen. Whoever had spotted them had immediately set the fire to alert their comrades to the fugitives' location.

Too breathless to swear aloud, she did so in her head. Letting themselves be seen had been an unforgiveable lapse in judgment on her part but one potentially exacerbated one hundred-fold with the possibility of a ford downriver. If there truly was a ford, the enemy warriors on the far bank would already be making for it. If they succeeded in reaching it before their quarry, they could cross and cut off the only viable route out of the valley.

Propelled by a mounting sense of panic, the Grey One hurtled along the riverbank. Despite an entire morning of running, she now felt caught up in an altogether more desperate race, obliged to outrun not only the pursuers on their own side of the river but a new group of warriors on the opposite bank.

The strain of the frenzied pace quickly sapped what brief respite the halt had given. Within five hundred paces, she was already gasping once more, heart thumping as she pushed herself forwards, driven by the certainty that if they didn't reach the ford first, they were lost.

Forty paces further upstream, the already precarious situation took a turn for the worse when the ground between the riverbank and the treeline narrowed abruptly, the trees drawing closer and closer to the water's edge.

Tossing an exhausted glance ahead, the woman warrior saw how the route was growing increasingly precarious where the constricted flat section of bank had been badly eroded and the tangled root system of the forest left exposed and jutting into the river. The dangerous matrix they'd have to travel was rendered even more hazardous by a number of toppled tree trunks lying half-in, half-out of the water.

With a breathless curse, the woman warrior veered inland, cutting through a break in the treeline. The impassable obstruction had left them with no option but to work their way through the forest and hope to find a route that bypassed the immediate section of riverbank.

Their speed faltered as they struck the thicker bush and uneven ground between the trees, reducing their pace to a weary scramble. Barging her way through the lower fern and brambles, the Grey One ignored the scrape and tear of barbs against her skin, doing her best to resist the growing sense of hopelessness welling up inside her when the river disappeared from view. Deeper into the trees, it struck her with fresh dismay that it seemed to be getting harder to push forwards and that the effort wasn't due to fatigue alone. The slope of the land had steepened. They were moving uphill.

The Grey One felt a flicker of panic. With the river gone and all sight of the sun and the ridge obscured due to the thickness of the vegetation, there was a real risk they'd lose their bearings and circle back on themselves, potentially falling right into the hungry grasp of their pursuers. Snarling, she ploughed forward through the shadowed green with even greater vehemence, determined to follow her nose and regain the river bank.

Although it felt like an age, it couldn't have been long before she sensed the terrain levelling off. A flash of blue through the trees off to the left triggered a fresh flare of hope and then, suddenly, she was clear of the forest, out into the daylight, pounding down a steeply angled pasture that looked to be mid-way up the steeply sloping ridge.

As the gradient slid downwards to an almost vertical plane, the Grey One tried to halt her thundering momentum but, realising she wasn't going to be able to stop in time, she instinctively launched herself off the almost vertical slope instead. She landed hard on her buttocks several paces down the grassy incline, the force of her impetus increasing her downward momentum even further. Moving too fast to even react, the Grey One was powerless to slow her terrifying descent.

Hurtling down the slope, she had no time to regret the impulsive action to leap, no time to register anything but the frightening speed of her downwards plunge. Several paces from the base of the bank, an upward-curving elevation in the otherwise smooth slope upended her and sent her tumbling head over heels to land in a dense patch of fern at the edge of the flat river bank.

Stunned but miraculously unharmed, she stared numbly at the blue sky above her while the pinwheels in her head continued to spin themselves out. When the world finally began to settle, she groaned and rolled onto her belly just in time to catch Fintán appear from above and hurtle past, sliding down through the grass to her right to land smoothly on his back at the rough flat of the riverbank. His eyes were wild as he stared at her, clearly still struggling to work out whether he was exhilarated or terrified or both. Although still in shock herself, the Grey One shakily forced herself to her feet.

'Are you hurt?'

Dazed, the youth looked back at her but eventually managed to shake his head. He opened his mouth as though to speak then abruptly shut it again.

Still dizzy, the woman warrior stared back up the steep slope, marvelling at how they'd managed to survive such a drop without injury. Her body, trembling from the combined stress of exhaustion and adrenalin shock, retched several times although nothing came up. Nevertheless, feeling somewhat improved, she stumbled towards a slight rise in the bank overlooking the shimmering water.

To the left of the rise, a dried out watershed had created a natural path down onto a triangular-shaped beach directly below her. There, a shingle strand projected four or five paces from the bank before disappearing, only to reappear a few paces on from that. From her position on the rise, Liath Luachra could clearly make out the tell-tail stain of shallows stretching all the way across to the other side.

The ford!

And there was no sign of the enemy warriors.

Wheezing as though she'd never suck enough air into her lungs again, the Grey One sagged heavily against a rotting tree trunk that had at some time in the past slid down the same slope she had. Staring at the line of splashing patches of ground that stretched across the river, she knew she should feel some sense of relief but was still too shaken, still too overcome from shock to feel anything.

As her mind cleared, she assessed the shallows, briefly considering the possibility of crossing to the other side. Any such thought was abruptly thwarted however, by the sudden arrival of four men stumbling out of the shaking foliage and lurching down onto a shingle beach that was almost identical to the one on their own side of the river. Stumbling to a halt at the water's edge, they looked across the river, postures stiffening as they spotted the two fugitives. A brief moment of stunned silence punctuated the warriors' noisy appearance but then one – a bearded brute dressed in the familiar padded tunic – released a bellow of challenge that was immediately taken up and echoed by his comrades.

For a time, the four figures continued like that, hooting furiously, slamming the hafts of their spears against their chests and roaring insults that by the time they'd crossed the waters were already unintelligible, even if their intent was clear. Breathing heavily through her nostrils, the Grey One returned the baleful glares, her eyes dark, fingers unconsciously stroking the sling on her wrist. For all the vocal bluster, she knew they were in no immediate danger. The newcomers were visibly jaded, probably as jaded as she was herself and, besides, neither party could cross the narrow ford without leaving themselves vulnerable and exposed to attack from their enemies on the other side.

Unimpressed, she turned to consider the *Lamraighe* youth who was staring at the distant warriors, struggling to maintain his composure as a fresh set of roars rumbled towards them, although on this occasion, they sounded perceptibly more strained and faint.

'*Ná bac leo. Níl aon rud le dhéamamh anseo.*' Ignore them. They're full of wind. Take the time to catch your breath.

White-faced, Fintán nodded, even if he didn't look entirely convinced.

The Grey One turned her gaze back to the four warriors whose yells had faded as they realised the limitations of their situation. She was about to toss a derisive yell of her own back at them when, suddenly – and shockingly – the warrior's call was echoed by similar roars, originating some distance upriver on their own side of the river.

Liath Luachra felt a cold hand clutch her gut. Across the water meanwhile, encouraged by the sound of their call being returned, the enemy warriors rediscovered their earlier belligerence, stamping their feet in the shingle and the immediate shallows, making savage threatening gestures and grasping their crotches as they howled at the woman warrior. She hissed in response and glancing at Fintán, could tell from the dispirited expression on his face that he'd understood, that she didn't need to explain.

The chase was on once more.

Chapter Seven

The fortress of Dún Baoiscne squatted like a watchful, grey toad on a hill in the centre of the sprawling Cuirreach valley. Directly above it, a colourless, circular cloud created from the combined smoke columns of three separate fires hung like a distended halo, drifting listlessly to the east in the absence of a discernible breeze.

The starkness of the fortress was amplified by the barrenness of the surrounding terrain. After centuries of occupation, the hill had been stripped clear of all vegetation larger than tussock grass. At its base, the valley floor had also been entirely deforested, the fertile land now made up of ragged patterns of fenced or tilled fields and extensive green pastures. For the greater part of the year, those pastures would be teeming with grazing cattle. At present however, the tribal herd would be on the *buaile*, up in the higher mountain meadows for lush summer feeding. Those that remained after the *Clann Morna* attack at least.

Gazing up towards her old home, Bodhmhall ua Baoiscne was acutely aware of its formidable defences. The outer embankment, a high earthen mound, was topped with wooden palisades. What wasn't so visible however, was the ditch cut into the crown of the hill directly in front of it, a ditch so deep it would take two tall men and a massive physical effort to clamber out.

The *bandraoi* exhaled heavily and shook her hands in an attempt to quell the trembling, deep feelings of nostalgia and homesickness mingling uneasily with an unrequited sense of bitterness.

I'm back. I'm home.

Undoing her cloak, she draped the garment over her left shoulder for she was sweating from the walk and the unexpected heat of the midday sun. She'd been travelling since dawn, having separated from Fiacail and Demne as the sky cleared from black to grey. That parting had been even harder than she'd feared and walking away, she'd drawn deep to resist looking back at her tearful nephew.

Fixing her eyes resolutely towards the north-west, she'd headed grimly in that direction, marching with a single-minded determination for the better part of the day. She'd only stopped walking once, pausing at noon to chat with a farmer and his two sons working the land south-west of the Cuirreach valley. While they spoke, she'd regarded the skinny boys with a pang of regret; neither of them could have been much older than Demne.

The farmer had recognised her immediately for he was a distant cousin she'd always been on good terms with, a man who when confronted by Tréanmór's Whispers had chosen to ignore them. He graciously invited her to share their mid-day meal and, heartily sick of porridge and forest food, she'd readily accepted the offer.

The repast had been basic: cold meat and hard-grained griddle bread washed down with fresh milk. Nevertheless, it had tasted better than anything she'd eaten in a very long time. Chewing with relish on a crust of fresh bread, she'd listened quietly as her cousin updated her on the more important tribal events of the previous years, most of it confirming tit-bits she'd already gleaned from other sources. Although six years had passed since the disastrous ambush at Gamhra, *Clann Baoiscne* remained in a weakened state as a result of the slaughter of its fighting men and the dispersal of its herds. In spite of those hardships, the tribe was slowly recovering. Over the previous five years, the herd had been partially reassembled from the animals within the fortress when *Clann Morna* had attacked plus a number of recaptured strays.

A new wave of *óglaigh* had also trickled through to replace some of the murdered warriors. Although lighter in number and experience than might have been desired, the tribe could now at least establish a basic defence of the *Clann Baoiscne* heartland, the Cuirreach valley and its immediate surroundings.

The more extended territories were another question of course and as he described the situation, Bodhmhall's cousin sucked in through his lips with a whistling sound, clearly troubled.

For a tribe to retain dominion over its territory, it had to be able to hold that territory. If not, competing tribes would inevitably test the previously established borders and, potentially, annex sections of undefended terrain. 'Walking the land' was an essential component of demonstrating that dominion but the *Clann Baoiscne* patrols, unfortunately, were not yet sufficiently strong or numerous to protect the full extent of their previous territory. Much of it, fortunately, bordered the uninhabited Great Wild so this was not too much of an issue. Where it rubbed against the territories of other tribes however, the situation became somewhat more complex.

Naturally, her cousin had questions of his own and, where possible, Bodhmhall answered them honestly for she appreciated his thoughtfulness in not questioning her return. When the questions began to require more detailed or circuitous responses, the *bandraoi* apologised with grace and got to her feet, excusing herself on the pretext of a pressing need to continue her journey.

She'd left her cousin with a warm embrace and a genuine desire to come back and visit although, in truth, she suspected there'd be little opportunity to do so. The *bandraoi* had waved to the boys as she'd walked away, smiling wryly to herself in the knowledge that her visit would be the subject of much gossip in the area for days to come.

The remainder of the journey to the *Clann Baoiscne* fortress had proven uneventful. On three occasions, she'd passed areas with evidence of settled land but she hadn't seen a single person until she entered the Cuirreach valley proper. There, two figures cutting wood on a distant hill had spotted her and paused in their labour to stare in her direction but, too far away to identify, they'd given a perfunctory wave and returned to work.

When the trail finally brought her in sight of *Dún Baoiscne*, the *bandraoi* stepped off the beaten track at a point about seven hundred paces from the foot of the hill. There, climbing a small mound to the left of the track, she took a seat on a moss-coated stone in the shade of a solitary oak tree and made herself comfortable.

Dún Baoiscne hasn't changed.

That much was true. From this distance at least, the fortress looked no different from the last time she'd seen it, almost ten years earlier.

Ten years!

The full scale of time that had passed since her departure struck her then and she tapped the ground nervously with the sole of her foot, all confidence in her plan abruptly evaporated. That sudden apprehension was accompanied by an unusual sense of fatalism. In a bizarre way, it felt as though everything that had happened to her over the intervening years had been leading to this point, this inevitable return to the tribal fold.

And now that she was finally here, all she could do initially was sit passively back and allow events to follow their course.

The first person to register her presence was a grey-haired hunter who emerged unexpectedly from a cluster of trees west of her little mound. A surprisingly spry old man, he was staggering under the weight of a wild pig carcass draped across his shoulders, unceremoniously held in place with a length of flax-fibre. Spotting her, the old man gave a friendly wave and veered towards her, visibly relieved at the prospect of a pause and a chat before starting the ascent to the stronghold. As he drew closer however, his eyes widened in horrified recognition and the smile melted on his face. Mumbling a stifled oath under his breath, he abruptly turned back to his original trajectory, somehow finding the vigour to lift his load higher and increase his pace up the hill.

Although she'd been anticipating such a reaction, Bodhmhall couldn't help but feel the sting of disappointment. The old man was known to her for his daughters had been close playmates as children. She had warm memories of visits to their farmlet and the rejection cut deeper than she cared to admit.

After that, it didn't take long for news of her presence to spread. Shortly after the hunter disappeared through the gateway of the fortress, two figures emerged to stare down in her direction. A few moments later, they disappeared only to be replaced by a fresh group of curious individuals. As she watched the reaction her return was provoking, the *bandraoi* allowed herself a cynical smile.

Welcome home, Cailleach Dubh.

It took a surprisingly long time for a formal emissary to be organised but, eventually, a slight figure in a crumpled grey cloak stepped through the gateway and started down the slope towards her. Despite the sun, the cloaked individual had raised his hood to obscure his features but Bodhmhall recognised the gait without difficulty. Once again, she allowed herself a somewhat cynical smile.

The emissary reached the base of the hill, followed the trail to the mound and slowly climbed to where she was seated. Coming to a halt before her, he rolled the hood back to reveal a handsome face with a neat brown beard and deeply intelligent blue eyes.

'I see you, Becal.'

'I see you Bodhmhall.' The handsome man gave a hesitant smile, disappointed by her lack of surprise. 'You are far from Ráth Bládhma.'

'Yes.'

Becal's lips twitched briefly, a nervous tic that the *bandraoi* recalled from childhood.

'Then this is truly a wonder. Had anyone told me Bodhmhall ua Baoiscne would reappear outside the gates of Dún Baoiscne during my lifetime, I'd …' He gave an exaggerated shrug. 'Well, I'd have believed them deluded.' With this, he looked her directly in the eye. 'And yet here you are.'

'And here I am.'

A brief silence trailed those words. Becal made a graceful flourish with his right hand. 'It warms this heart to see you, Bodhmhall. Despite the dismal circumstances of your departure, my memories of you are fond ones. Your company has been … missed.'

Not an entirely honest sentiment, of course. Bodhmhall kept her face neutral, concealing her true feelings. Almost ten years earlier when she'd sought support against her expulsion from the tribe, this young man – her colleague and supposed friend – had completely forsaken her.

'Why are you here, Bodhmhall?'

'I would have words with my father. Words of consequence for *Clann Baoiscne*. I assume he's aware of my presence?'

'Of course. It was Tréanmór himself who directed me to speak with you.'

'And will he receive me?'

'He has left the burden of that decision to me.'

Bodhmhall nodded in silent appreciation.

Very shrewd, father. By placing the burden of decision with the draoi, you avert the ire of the Druidic Order.

She maintained a neutral expression while she considered her contemporary. In his seventeenth year, in imitation of Dub Tíre, he'd grown the beard to conceal the weakness of his chin and to give himself a more dignified, more venerable appearance, which to a degree it had. As a youth however, Becal had been something of a feeble, unimposing child. Shy and anxious, but undeniably intelligent, he'd envied the respect garnered by those of greater physical prowess. Over time, that envy would probably have developed into full-blown resentment had he not, like her and their fellow acolyte, Demmán, been chosen for tutoring under the famed druid, Dub Tíre.

Ironically, despite his role as *draoi* for Dún Baoiscne, Becal's talent with the *Gift* had actually proven disappointingly limited. In truth, that talent had been restricted to an odd ability to smell colours and, as far as Bodhmhall could recall, even that particular skill had been somewhat inconsistent in application. Despite Becal's weakness with the *Gift* however, Dub Tíre's choice was revealed to be a wise one for his new acolyte displayed a rare instinct for the manipulation of ritual and tradition, a cornerstone of increasing importance for the druidic authority.

A series of wrinkles formed along the Dún Baoiscne *draoi's* brow as he observed Bodhmhall's scrutiny. 'Are you attempting to read me, Bodhmhall? Using that *Gift* of yours to assess me while I mull on my decision?'

'I don't need to use my *Gift*, Becal. I already know the answer.'

He cast her a thoughtful look. 'Oh? And what do you consider that to be?'

'You will grant me access.'

'Indeed?' His left eyebrow rose in a sardonic arch.

'Do not pretend otherwise, Becal. I know you too well.' She cautiously clasped her hands together. Having divested herself of her sling to avoid the appearance of weakness, she was obliged to treat any movement of her right arm with care.

'Your preference would be to refuse access of course, but you fear the information I carry will reach my father's ears through other routes. If, as I claim, the tidings are urgent and Tréanmór learns you rejected an opportunity of forewarning, he will hold you responsible.'

And you have always feared my father.

Becal smiled but there was a discernible tightness to his lips. 'This is the sum of your assessment?'

'No. Your natural wariness of circumstances outside your control will also drive your insistence to be present when my news is revealed. That way, you'll feel you have at least some influence over any response.'

His expression darkened at that. 'You should not make an enemy of me, *Cailleach Dubh*. You do not have many friends here.'

'I marked my friends when I put out my call for support ten years ago, Becal. Those who answered were easily counted and you were not to be found amongst them.'

At this, the *draoi* had the grace to look embarrassed. He diverted his gaze to stare back at the fortress on the hill. 'My heart urged me to step forward,' he admitted quietly. 'And it shames me that I did not do so.' His gaze came up to lock onto her hers once more. 'But how could I support you, Bodhmhall? You killed Dub Tíre, our master and teacher. You desecrated all that we had learned, all the dictates of the Druidic Order.'

'Any desecration was not by my hands, Becal.' Bodhmhall's eyes had taken on an uncharacteristic chill and a singular intensity from which there was no easy evasion. The *draoi* shifted uneasily from one foot to the other.

'You could have alerted *An Ollabh* - the chief druid. The Druidic Order would have put things to right.'

'The Druidic Order would have put nothing to right. It was *An Ollabh* himself who had Dub Tíre placed at Dún Baoiscne and the Order had far too much to lose by censuring one of their own. Such an action would have corroded the people's faith for how can you revere a spiritual leader revealed as corrupt and fallible?' She shook her head with unassailable conviction. 'Believe me, Becal. They would never have done the right thing.'

He shrugged uncomfortably. 'Right thing, wrong thing. Such definitions blur depending on the perspective of the person who takes them as his own.'

125

'It's hardly as difficult as you make out. Doing the right thing generally involves doing something that benefits others more than it benefits yourself.'

The Dún Baoiscne *draoi*'s lips creased up into a smile, fuller and less contrived than his earlier attempts. 'I'd forgotten your dexterity at such discourse, Bodhmhall. I'd also forgotten how much I enjoyed our talks. Unfortunately, now is not the time. Let me bring you to your father.'

***

Marching up the path to the stronghold felt like marching towards the past and with every step, Bodhmhall felt an increasing need to reaffirm the urgency of her undertaking. She could ill afford the luxury of sinking into nostalgia. Her safety and the future safety of her nephew depended on her success at Dún Baoiscne and to sow the seeds required to achieve her goal she had to appear focussed and in control, to comport herself with confidence.

Feigning a nonchalance she didn't feel, the *bandraoi* squared her shoulders and set her chin, determined to respond assertively to whatever might transpire. The simulated boldness was tempered somewhat by the reality of her appearance. With her tattered clothing, a cloak soiled at the border by the peaty earth and her unruly hair, she looked more like a bedraggled refugee than a visitor of standing. The niggle of pain whenever she jogged her arm meanwhile, was a persistent reminder of her physical limitations.

That realisation prompted another frown. At Dún Baoiscne, she would be entirely dependent on the goodwill of her father, a currency of very uncertain value. She would have to argue very convincingly to be permitted to stay, particularly given that her sole commodity of consequence – the information she brought with her – would be surrendered on her arrival.

The gateway to the earthen embankment was guarded by a wiry, greasy-haired youth who stared with open curiosity as she followed Becal across the causeway of the external ditch. As they drew closer, he dropped his eyes, feigning indifference as he pretended to examine the metal head of his spear. Once they'd passed him and entered the gateway however, she could feel the weight of his gaze on her shoulders.

'Young', she thought to herself. Young and she hadn't recognised him, which meant he must have been a mere child at the time of her departure. This simple fact irked her for a moment until she thought about the reason behind it.

There were people here who did not know her.

Didn't know her because she'd been away so long.

Ten years! Almost a lifetime for some, it seems.

The passage through the embankment consisted of a wide tunnel layered with stone and broad enough to drive two cows side by side. Although the inner section was generally sealed at night by a pair of heavy wooden doors, these now hung open, providing access to the interior. Through the opening, a swathe of trampled grass was visible. This stretched for twenty paces before running up against the second fortification: a stone wall that stood three times the height of an average man.

Becal came to a halt at the end of the passage, giving Bodhmhall a moment to draw up alongside and absorb the sight before them. The *bandraoi* stared in silence, her eyes exposed to the present but very much coloured by the past. She placed one hand against the wall to steady herself, momentarily thrown by the rush of memories. Dún Baoiscne was just as she remembered: the huts, the walls, the narrow grass sections, the stone and timber, even the mingled smells of cooking food and body odour that lingered in the air. Nothing had changed.

It felt strange, almost surreal, to be back and after so many years in the isolation of the Great Wild, her perception of those once-familiar features had changed. The huts looked much smaller but ironically, now she was inside the fortress, the great walls – twice the height of the Ráth Bládhma's single embankment – felt far more oppressive than she recalled. She imagined her people crammed inside during the *Clann Morna* attack six years earlier. The enemy would have lacked the strength of numbers to launch a meaningful assault on the fortress but it must have been terrifying for those huddled in fear.

The grassy section beyond the passage veered off on either side, stretching in two wide curves between the bulky arcs of the embankment and the stone wall. Occupying much of the curve to the left were a number of small huts, leans-tos, storage areas, and livestock pens. Most of the latter stood empty but a number of the huts were visibly occupied, something which surprised the *bandraoi*. Despite the stronghold's size and its function as a hub for *Clann Baoiscne* tribal activities, there had rarely been more than twenty to twenty-five individuals residing there at any one time. As a general rule, most people occupied land in the Cuirreach Valley and beyond, land better suited for the raising of cattle and crops. Most returned to the fortress infrequently and then only for important tribal gatherings or social events such as weddings and funerals. On such occasions, the population could swell to a hundred and fifty or more. In times of danger however, that number could multiply two or three fold as tribal members flocked in with their belongings, seeking cramped refuge behind its sturdy walls.

Proceeding along the curve to the right, the *draoi* and the *bandraoi* found themselves confronted by a crowd of between fifteen to twenty individuals gathered around the entranceway to the stone wall. Most were women and children, although Bodhmhall also spotted one or two older men in amongst them. A number of faces were familiar and she was relieved to see that the overall mood appeared to be one of open curiosity as opposed to outright hostility.

The crowd stood quietly, observing her with interest but stepping calmly out of the way when Becal pushed his way through towards the gateway. Two women nodded to her in muted greeting but one of the older men spat a glob of white phlegm onto the ground as she passed in front of him.

A freckle-faced woman with red hair tied up in a single plait abruptly stepped through the little assembly, planting herself directly in the *bandraoi's* path and forcing her to stumble to an ungainly halt. Taken aback by the unexpected obstruction, she stared but then the expression of uncertainty on her face gave way to one of joyful recognition. With a soft cry, she stepped forward and embraced the other woman.

'Bé Bhinn!'

'Bodhmhall. I did not think … They said that …'

The red-haired woman started to cry and Bodhmhall found that the only way she could prevent the tears from welling up in her own eyes was to draw her old friend close and hold her tight.

'*Fuist, a chara.* I did not forget. It swells this heart sore to see you once more.'

She glanced up then, suddenly conscious of Becal and others watching the emotional reunion. Releasing her friend, she straightened herself to her full height and stared unblinkingly at the surrounding faces until, cowed, they began to disperse. Becal, demonstrating unexpected thoughtfulness, moved off to one side to offer them a modicum of privacy.

Satisfied, Bodhmhall turned to kiss the smaller woman's tear-stained cheeks. 'Bé Bhinn. When I left Dún Baoiscne, there was little enough to lament but the loss of your company. And Emmel's, of course.' She glanced about at the dissipating crowd. 'Where is he? Is he off on the hunt?'

Bé Bhinn regarded her in silence, her face bleak and still. Bodhmhall felt a queasy foreboding rise in her stomach.

'You did not hear?' The red-haired woman's voice was steady but thick with emotion. 'He died with your brother at Gabhra. Fighting the bastard *Morna*.'

Bodhmhall felt herself sway, her heart hurting as though someone had struck her a physical blow to the chest.

Emmel! Gods, not gentle Emmel! Another one gone.

She could practically feel the blood drain from her face as the distressing news soaked in. Like Bé Bhinn, Emmel had been one of her closest childhood companions, a loyal friend who'd come to her support when she'd made her call against expulsion. A year before leaving Dún Baoiscne, she'd attended his bonding with Bé Bhinn. Childhood sweethearts, on that day they'd seemed the happiest couple within the tribe and now ...

She swallowed, gripped her friend's hands tight in her own. 'Your words draw the joy from my heart, *a chara*. I hadn't heard. Forgive my clumsiness in causing you to relive such grief.'

'There's nothing to forgive, Bodhmhall. You could not have known and, besides, my grief and I have come to terms over the years.' Bé Bhinn attempted a smile but was unable to maintain it. As it slipped from her face, her true desolation briefly revealed itself until she managed to whip it out of sight again. 'Time erodes the ache. What the elders say is true, although I confess there are still days I turn about and expect to find him standing at my side, that gap-toothed grin across his face.'

Bodhmhall closed her eyes to more effectively focus on holding her sadness at bay. After a moment, regaining her composure, she opened them again.

'You say Emmel died with Cumhal?'

Bé Bhinn nodded and her eyes took on a haunted glaze. 'That was a black day, Bodhmhall. So few of them returned and those that did were broken or bleeding. The dead – our men and our sons – were left behind to feed the wolves for *Clann Morna* came to the very walls, taunting us with their severed heads. Their forces encircled the fortress for six days before they finally tired of their sport and left to return to their own territories, driving our herds before them.'

Bodhmhall shuddered at the mental images created from her friend's words. Bé Bhinn put a gentle hand on her shoulder. 'Why did you come back, Bodhmhall? There is nothing for you here anymore. Nothing but ...'

She paused in sudden, flustered silence. Reddening, she plucked wisps of grass from her dress. 'I'm sorry, *a chara*. Such words are no fitting welcome. Speaking of the dead serves no purpose but to open old wounds and stir anguish in our hearts. Let us turn to more pleasant topics. Perhaps you'll come sup with me and we can laugh and speak of happier times? I live here in the fortress nowadays, sharing a hut with Niall Tuirseach.'

'Niall Tuirseach?' Bodhmhall stared at her.

Although the *bandraoi* had kept her features blank, Bé Bhinn must have been able to read the disbelief in her eyes for she nodded in weary, heart-breaking resignation. 'He's a good man.' She shrugged. 'He's not Emmel but he treats me well and we've lived as one for three years. I have borne him a son, a good boy who'll grow to be a warrior and defend the Dún Baoiscne walls, like his father.'

Bodhmhall nodded mutely, not knowing quite what to say. She remembered Niall Tuirseach – Tired Niall – a man who'd gained his sobriquet as a result of his plodding disposition. Although a pleasant enough man he was quite dull and at twenty years her senior, he was hardly the match Bé Bhinn would have desired, particularly given the depth of the intimacy she'd shared with Emmel.

She regarded Bé Bhinn with sad affection, making sure to conceal the true dismay she felt at her friend's misfortune. Before she could deliver an appropriate response however, Becal was back at her arm, gently urging her onwards. 'Bodhmhall, we cannot dally.' He turned to her red-haired companion. 'Bé Bhinn, her father awaits.'

Bé Bhinn nodded with a subdued resignation Bodhmhall couldn't recall seeing in her as a young woman. 'Later then.' She pointed towards a hut further down the southern curve of the embankment. 'That's where I reside now. It's warm and comfortable.' She hesitated. 'Come when you can. If you wish, we can go visit Demmán's resting place together.'

Bodhmhall nodded. 'I would like that.' She took the woman's head gently in her hands and kissed her on both cheeks. 'We'll talk later, grieve and laugh and speak of better times.' Clasping the other woman's hand, she squeezed it tight before reluctantly releasing her and turning to follow Becal's lead.

***

The *bandraoi* was still struggling with the terrible news of Emmel's death as they entered the gateway of the second fortification, another stone passage almost identical to the one in the earth embankment.

So much grief. So much grief and pain.

Approaching the gateway, she glanced up at the guard on the wall above. Another sentry, an older man this time whom she recognised as a second cousin of her father. When she was a child, that old man had regularly snuck her pieces of wild honeycomb as a treat. Now, his eyes darted furtively towards Becal and she could tell the *draoi's* presence was stifling his natural inclination to welcome her. As they passed beneath him and into the stone passage, he flashed her a quick smile then hurriedly turned away before the gesture was observed.

If climbing up the trail to the fortress had been like marching towards the past, emerging at the far end of that passage and into the *lis* was like physically stepping into it. The heart of Dún Baoiscne and the centre of her existence for many years, the fortresses' circular inner courtyard was almost twice the size of the *lis* at Ráth Bládhma. As a result, despite a central fire-pit, four roundhouses that followed the curve of the eastern wall and *An Halla Mór* – a rectangular building with a sloping, thatched roof that took up most of the space on the western side of the enclosure, it didn't feel overly constricted.

Bodhmhall felt her chest tighten as she stared at the roundhouse facing the entrance to the passage. That had been her own home once, the dwelling she'd shared during her limited time with Fiacail mac Codhna all those years ago. Now it looked uninhabited although, from the sacks and jumbled odds and ends visible through the open doorway, it was still being used for storage purposes.

Once again, she found herself experiencing that baffling, heady sense of time having passed yet, conversely, standing still. A great wrench of sadness twisted through her, a deep ache for a life shed, a life unlived, a life that might have been.

Several paces to the right of her old home was the neighbouring roundhouse where her brother Cumhal had lived with his then new woman, Muirne Muncháem. Both of them were long gone, of course, and now the entrance was occupied by a muscular man with more than forty years on him.

Cathal Bog – Soft Cathal – the nickname bestowed upon the Dún Baoiscne warrior, was an ironic take on the actual man. A broad-shouldered block, two brawny arms protruded from his sleeveless tunic like the knotted boughs of an oak tree, both coated in numerous white scars. His face, where it wasn't obscured by dense black beard, was also scarred and wrinkled from years of exposure to the elements. Centred about a lumpy, broken nose, it rose to a wide forehead where a headband restrained a tangled mass of black hair to reveal yet another jagged scar just above the left eyebrow.

Propped comfortably on a one-legged stool, Cathal Bog had his eyes down, focussed on a short slab of softwood that he was whittling with a compact carving knife. Tréanmór's principal bodyguard had always been something of a compulsive whittler, albeit not a particularly talented one. In general, the product of his endeavours tended to be artless things, quickly created and just as quickly discarded. A distinct absence of imagination also meant that the final form of the carving rarely differed, generally variations on a basic horse theme. Strewn on the ground alongside him, a small herd of discarded animals lay frozen in a silent, distorted stampede.

Bodhmhall stepped forward and the crunching sound of her feet on the pebbles of the *lis* caused a pair of hard, brown eyes to flicker up and regard her without expression. Bodhmhall nodded in greeting.

'I see you, Cathal.'

'I see you, Bodhmhall.' The big man displayed no surprise, no emotion of any kind in fact. The *bandraoi* had expected that but the complete absence of any reaction to her return was still quite disconcerting. It gave her the oddest impression that she'd merely stepped out of the *lis* for a few moments rather than being absent for almost ten years.

The bearded man's gaze flickered swiftly towards Becal but, once again, displayed no emotion at the *draoi*'s presence. Returning to his whittling, he ignored them both.

Bodhmhall tugged absently at the waist of her dress as she studied the silent warrior. What Cathal Bog had lacked in wit he'd more than made up for in loyalty over the years, applying her father's orders with an unquestioning, if heavy-handed and literal, assiduousness. Deferring to his *rí* for every instruction, Cathal formed few opinions of his own. His rigid, inexorable nature and sheer brutal physicality made him a fearsome man but at no time had his fealty ever been in question. Even now as she regarded him, Bodhmhall found it difficult to believe he could be a traitor.

Best defer judgement on that, Cailleach. Only those close to you can truly betray you.

Chewing on her lower lip, she let her eyes drift towards Becal, surprised to find him observing her with a calm, if somewhat calculating, air.

And you, Becal. Was it you? And yet what could possibly tempt you to sacrifice the position of authority you hold at Dún Baoiscne?

Although it was hard to believe it now, there'd actually been a time when she and Becal had been close. As a young girl, she'd been drawn to his obvious intelligence and a sense of humour that was far sharper than that of many of their contemporaries even if, at times, it could be cruel. Becal had a brutal way of belittling people he considered less intelligent than himself, using his innate skill with words to mock them in such a way they were never completely sure if they were being ridiculed or not. He'd never treated her with such acidic disdain, fortunately. She liked to think that was because he respected her own intellect but acknowledged the possibility that he'd simply realised she'd give back as good as she got.

As the years slid by and the innocence of childhood slipped away, Bodhmhall had found herself increasingly troubled by her friend's caustic behaviour. When both had been selected for Dub Tíre's tutelage, she'd been temporarily relieved, believing such an honour would soothe the corrosive edges of his bitterness. That relief had been short-lived however. A key feature of Dub Tíre's instruction was to pit his acolytes against each other, pushing them to excel at the detriment of their personal relationships. Becal and Bodhmhall had found themselves in increasing competition for their teacher's good opinion and, from that point on, he'd slowly drawn away from her, the more selfish and self-promoting aspect of his nature gradually asserting itself. In the end, at the time when she'd needed him most, he'd betrayed her, cast their friendship aside for his own self-advancement. As a result, it wasn't hard to imagine him deceiving his tribe in a similar manner even if she found herself unable to identify any advantage sufficiently worthwhile to tempt him.

Becal frowned as though sensing the antipathy of her thoughts towards him. 'Your father. We should not tarry.' He gestured towards *An Halla Mór*. 'He awaits.'

With a curt nod, Bodhmhall took the lead on this occasion, preceding the *draoi* towards the entrance of the hall. Approaching the two heavy timber doors, she felt herself falter, her breath catching at the back of her throat and an embedded dread gnawing at her insides.

Compose yourself, Cailleach Dubh. You slip into the rut of childhood behaviour.

She recognised the reaction for what it was, a nervous response instilled from her childhood in *An Halla Mór*. She'd spent the better part of her early life there after all, acquiescent and yielding to her father's overbearing personality. Despite the familial environment, the building had never been one in which she'd felt truly comfortable. Beyond the partitioned domestic section reserved for Tréanmór, his family and whatever female minders he was sleeping with at the time, *An Halla Mór* had always been something of an oppressively formal space, a site of strict gatherings and grave discussion. Its timbers were steeped with the emotive words of speeches, battle plans, exclamations of anger or grave judgements. When she'd been bonded with Fiacail it had been something of a relief to escape *An Halla Mór* for the less salubrious but more informal accommodation of the roundhouse.

Taking a deep breath, the *bandraoi* rallied herself. Carefully placing her hands against the panelled doors, she pushed them open and stepped inside.

As always, the interior of *An Halla Mór* was dark and smelled of fish oil from the flickering lamps that never quite made up for the absence of windows. Combined with the light streaming in through the open doorway however, it was sufficient for Bodhmhall to make out the familiar rectangular stretch of the hall, the two central fire pits flanked by rows of poles that supported the heavy thatch roof. Despite the clement weather, the furthest fire pit was full of glowing embers and the air still and stuffy.

The floor of the building was timber boards strewn with fresh layers of dry rushes. Shields, wolf skins and pegs with cloaks lined the long southern wall while a set of long shelves ran the length of the northern side. These held equipment, weapons and a number of three-legged stools, up-turned on flat heads: seating for when there was a formal gathering.

Beyond the second fire, a leather sheet was stretched on poles across the breadth of the hall, separating the hall proper from the domestic section. When she'd lived there, that closed-off area had contained four separate sleeping platforms and some storage chests. She assumed they were still there, shared now only by her father and his most recent conquest.

With a frown, she turned her gaze to a low table sitting off to the left of the fire where five grinning skulls had been placed in a line, polished curves gleaming in the dim light, empty eye sockets staring sightlessly up the length of the hall.

Na Cúig Cairde. The Five Friends.

The darkened eye-sockets flickered chillingly in the glow from the fire, an effect accentuated by the contrasting whiteness of bone. Tréanmór had arranged this macabre spectacle many years earlier with the intention of unsettling visitors to his hall, thereby proffering the advantage to himself in any home ground negotiations. As a child, Bodhmhall had always feared their silent, menacing scrutiny. Observing them now, over the distance of years, she simply found them ghoulish.

The Five Friends were the skulls of her father's greatest enemies and dated from the twenty years of his leadership of *Clann Baoiscne*. Three of the skulls had originally belonged to *Clann Morna* warriors, a consequence of the long-standing feud between the two tribes. A fourth skull was that of a bandit leader who'd successfully rustled the *Clann Baoiscne* herd until Tréanmór had personally tracked him down and slain him in combat.

The last – and the oldest – was that of a *Clann Baoiscne* tribal member, a *derbfine* who'd taken up arms against Tréanmór in competition for the position of *tánaiste*.

And lost.

The fact that his skull remained to provide adornment in her father's home served not only as testimony to Tréanmór's martial skills but a subtle warning to any future contenders considering the possibility of a leadership challenge.

A faint movement in the shadows to the right of the furthest fire pit drew the *bandraoi*'s gaze and she tensed when she made out the familiar silhouette of the man who'd so totally dominated her childhood. Seated on a wooden stool beside the fire pit, Tréanmór, *rí* of *Clann Baoiscne*, was turned at an angle from her but there was no mistaking the darkened, upright profile staring fixedly into the fire.

The figure shifted and Bodhmhall realised he was stoking the coals for the flames suddenly took life and flared up once more. Rising slowly to his feet, he turned to face her, his features now illuminated clearly in the light of the yellow flames.

The *bandraoi* felt her pulse quicken. Her father did not look to have greatly changed in the years since she'd last seen him. Older, certainly, and the mane of deer-brown hair now bore visible streaks of grey but his eyes were just as she remembered: severe, alert, and piercing her with predator-like intensity. Despite his age, the colourful *léine* he wore bulged with barrel-chested muscle.

'I see you, Bodhmhall.'

The voice, deep and sonorous, resounded powerfully in the darkened hall.

Bodhmhall swallowed and cleared her throat. 'I see you, Father.'

Both advanced until they were they were about two paces apart then stopped, regarding one another. His features were composed, she noted. The strong face flanked by the complex grey braids and underset with a steel-grey beard, recently trimmed.

'Shall we embrace?' asked Tréanmór. 'I understand that is how the emptiness of long absences is filled.'

She leaned forward and they embraced stiffly. To her surprise, Tréanmór bent his head and planted a kiss on her forehead. Releasing one another, both stepped backwards in mutual apprehension, as though belatedly realising they'd left their guard down.

'You have grown more beautiful, Daughter.'

'And you retain your regal appearance, Father.'

Both chuckled, amused by the exchange of such unaccustomed compliments. The good humour waned momentarily as the *rí* of *Clann Baoiscne* examined her, shrewd eyes missing nothing as they took in the tattered clothing and even the protective manner in which she supported her left arm. Bodhmhall gave an involuntary wince.

I can hide nothing from him.

Their eyes reconnected and Tréanmór thoughtfully stroked his bearded chin. 'You have a tale to tell.'

'I have.'

'Is this a tale for which my other advisors should be summoned?' He turned his eyes towards the doorway where Becal stood at the lintel, watching intently.

Bodhmhall shook her head. 'My words are for you alone.'

Although she had her back to the Dún Baoiscne *draoi* and couldn't see his face, she practically felt the sudden flush of hot fury that radiated out from him.

'Are you sure? These men are loyal to me, loyal to *Clann Baoiscne*, men whose counsel I trust and respect.'

Tréanmór spoke firmly but there was something in his tone that told Bodhmhall his words were for Becal's benefit, that he would concede to her request.

'The words I have to share are for you alone,' she repeated.

Tréanmór grunted. 'Very well. Becal, you may leave us.'

'But Tréanmór, your daughter comes with tidings of significance. Would you not have me present to receive counsel on such matters?'

Tréanmór's eyes lingered on the *draoi*, his expression dispassionate but still fiercely intimidating. Age, Bodhmhall realised, had done nothing to diminish her father's natural air of authority, the strength and confidence of a man accustomed to certainty.

'I mean,' spluttered Becal. 'How can I offer advice if I am not present to hear what is said?'

'Should I have need of your advice I will send for you.'

The *draoi*'s voice lips parted as though to protest once more but noting the *rí*'s expression, he wisely decided against it. 'As you wish, Great Tréanmór. I am at your disposition, always at your disposition.'

With this, Becal bowed and turned to leave but not before sending a furious glare the *bandraoi*'s way.

He will not forget this slight.

Tréanmór waited for the door to close behind the departing *draoi* before turning to face his daughter. 'So Bodhmhall. I trust that what you have to say is important enough to warrant the exclusion of my key advisors, three men whose advice I trust explicitly.'

Bodhmhall stifled a smile. She didn't place much weight on such words. Despite such grandiose claims, like all men of power, Tréanmór trusted no man completely. 'It is important,' she confirmed in a low voice.

'Then let us sit by the fire.' He gestured towards his earlier position and with her eyes now adjusted to the gloom, Bodhmhall could see that an additional stool and a small table with two wooden goblets of water had been placed there in preparation.

Approaching the fire, the *rí* of *Clann Baoiscne* regained his earlier seat and waited for her to join him. When she too had made herself comfortable, he sat up straight, hands resting firmly on his knees.

'Much as it nourishes this heart to see you, Bodhmhall, I have an uncomfortable truth to share.'

'Then do not spare me, father. You know of my preference for honesty.'

There was a barb at the end of that sentence which she hadn't intended although her father interpreted it as such. His posture stiffened slightly and his voice bore a trace of severity when he spoke again.

'Your presence places me in a position of some awkwardness, Daughter. You are blood kin but you are also *éclann*. Our people have already suffered great tribulations so I must tread with caution. Ten years ago I spared you the shame of formal expulsion by dispatching you to Ráth Bládhma.' His eyes caressed her face, studying her closely before he continued. 'You do understand you were banished, do you not?'

Angered by the question, she made him wait for several heartbeats before dipping her head in acknowledgement.

'Had you not departed Dún Baoiscne of your own volition ...'

'Of my own volition!'

Tréanmór paused at the furious interjection. 'Had you not departed Dún Baoiscne of your own volition,' he repeated, 'the Druidic Order would have forced my hand. You'd have been cast out without resource or assistance. As it is, they'll not be pleased to learn of your return.'

Bodhmhall angrily clasped the creases of her skirt before releasing them and pulling her hands away. 'Even now? They still care after all this time?'

'What I told you ten years ago remains just as true today. You threatened the Order's legitimacy, a transgression they'll never forgive. They've also grown more powerful since your departure. *An Ollamh* has cemented his influence with the *Uí Cuaich* so the Order's authority has strengthened even further.'

Bodhmhall found herself intrigued by this scrap of information. Located far to the north of *Clann Baoiscne* territory, the *Uí Cuaich* was a tribal confederation that, after many years of consolidation, was generally considered a tribe in its own right, one of the largest in the region. If what her father said was true and *An Ollamh* had the ear of its *rí*, then his caution was very much warranted.

'Have you grown fearful of the Druidic Order?'

Tréanmór's heavy eyebrows lifted with almost ponderous lethargy but beneath them, his eyes glinted dangerously.

'Not fearful, so much as … wary. It's true they have a growing influence but it's also one without true cohesion. Their number includes too many individual *draoi*, all seeking to forward their own agendas and, as such, their power is blunted.' He paused. 'For now at least. Still …' He gave a slant-shouldered shrug. 'They have their uses. It was through their intercession, after all, that a peace was negotiated with *Clann Morna*.'

Despite the casualness of that comment, Bodhmhall sensed a stifled vehemence behind the words and, with sudden insight, realised how difficult those negotiations must have been for her father. Proud and defiant, he'd have struggled to negotiate from a position of weakness and obligatory concession, particularly with the very people who'd killed his son and massacred the greater part of his fighting men. The fact that he didn't speak with even greater bitterness was telling in that it suggested there was far more to the story than he was willing to share.

'But you fear Becal will inform them of my presence?'

The *rí* of *Clann Baoiscne* snorted at that. 'Becal plays his games of ritual but only as far as I allow. The people like what he says. They find him … reassuring.' He reached over to grasp one of the goblets and, raising it to his lips, took a great gulp. Wiping his mouth with the back of his hand, he replaced the vessel on the table.

'When it comes to matters of significance, Becal cowers beneath my heel. He'll tell the Order what I want them to hear.' He coughed, cleared his throat and spat a throat-full of phlegm into the fire where it hissed briefly and died. 'Nevertheless, we cannot receive you formally.'

Bodhmhall patiently folded her hands in her lap, waiting for him to explain.

'The issue,' Tréanmór continued, 'is that there are many here who respected Dub Tíre. Because of your great offence against him, word of your presence is almost certain to reach the Order's ears.'

Her face clouded at that. 'My great offence.'

'You killed the man.' He gave her a reproachful look. 'Stabbed him twice thorough the heart and then fully admitted to the action. The Druidic Order were baying like ravenous wolves at the time. Had I not intervened, the punishment would have been far more severe than exile.'

'Had you intervened sooner there would have been no … offence.'

She saw the sudden glow of anger in his eyes and with that it was as though she'd never even left Dún Baoiscne. Every memory of discussions with her father seemed, inevitably, to end with that same expression of anger.

She exhaled heavily, grinding the soles of her feet into the reed-strewn, timber floor. She was managing this reunion poorly, giving into emotion and coming into direct conflict with her father, thereby creating an animosity she simply couldn't afford. Closing her eyes, she inhaled deeply and, galling though it was, she knew she'd have no choice but to concede the point.

'Forgive me, father. I recognise that my return poses something of a … hindrance.'

The *rí* of *Clann Baoiscne* continued to scrutinise her, assessing the sincerity behind such uncharacteristic contrition.

'It was not my intent to goad you, father. You've seen fit to receive me and my gratitude for that is sincere. It's also my hope you'll forgive the disruption of my return once you learn the reasons behind it.'

Her father remained silent, regarding her with chary introspection but, slowly, the stiffness appeared to ease from his frame. 'You come to Dún Baoiscne alone?' he asked at last.

He was probing now, alert and keen to learn of her tidings. Bodhmhall felt her own apprehension grow, conscious that it was at such times her father was most dangerous. Instinctively political and a natural manipulator, he'd be appraising every comment, every gesture she made, from a perspective of potential advantage.

She nodded in confirmation, knowing that as soon as their conversation was over, scouts would almost certainly be dispatched to track her trail and test her story.

'And where then is that lean gristle of spoiled meat? Your … friend.'

Despite having prepared herself for such provocation, Bodhmhall's genuine fears for the warrior woman meant the words still cut deep, something her father had no doubt intended. 'Spoiled meat' was his favourite pejorative for Liath Luachra, although one he tended to use sparingly, usually on those rare occasions when he was truly furious. That fact that he'd inserted it so early into the conversation and with such clear

139

intent, confirmed that he was testing her, trying to throw her off balance so she'd spill whatever secrets she carried.

'I don't know,' she answered, the calm in her voice surprising even herself. 'We were travelling across the Great Wild together with *Na Lamraighe* but we were sep-'

'*Na Lamraighe*!' Tréanmór's lips turned up in distaste. 'You travelled with Gleor Red Hand?'

Bodhmhall confirmed this with a sharp dip of her head. 'They are allies of Ráth Bládhma.'

'Allies?' Her father's derisive chuckle echoed loudly in the empty hall. 'You'd be better off allying with the trees.' Calming himself, he held up a placatory hand and settled back on his stool. 'But, please. Continue your tale.'

Fuming, Bodhmhall sat in silence for the length of five heartbeats, struggling to keep her temper in check.

'Before the last full moon, we received a *techtaire* at Ráth Bládhma, a *techtaire* purporting to come from you and bearing a summons to Dún Baoiscne. The very next day, a party from *Na Lamraighe* also announced themselves at our gate. They too had received such a summons and were on their way here.'

She broke off to reach for the second goblet of water and, while she sipped, took the measure of her father from the corner of her eye. The *rí* of *Clann Baoiscne* was frowning now, intrigued and vexed by the claims of the mysterious *techtaire*. Leaning forward on his stool, she could tell he was eager to hear more.

She replaced the goblet.

'Believing the summons authentic, we left Glenn Ceoch and travelled together for Dún Baoiscne. The party included myself, Liath Luachra, Gleor Red Hand and his warriors and his new woman ...' She hesitated. 'Muirne Muncháem.'

'Muirne Muncháem!'

Although her father had always been a man of the utmost self-control, his reaction to this particular revelation was unexpectedly violent. 'Muirne Muncháem!' he bellowed again, surging up off his stool to glare at her. 'Muirne Muncháem!'

The *bandraoi* kept her head lowered submissively, eyes to the floor, as his anger washed over her. It seemed to take an age before the outburst subsided and she only dared to raise her head when he'd grown silent and the shadows on the floorboards confirmed that he'd seated himself once more. Looking up, she found him glowering quietly, his nostrils flaring.

'You should know, Daughter, that Muirne Muncháem ...' The name was spat out with disturbing animosity. 'She abused the generosity and hospitality offered to her by our family. More than seven years past, she absconded from Dún Baoiscne in the darkness of night. Given the conflict with *Clann Morna* at the time, we could ill afford to dispatch men to search for her. It's long been our assumption she was passed, had fallen prey to some passing wolf pack.'

Her father lapsed back into silence but the pulsating life-light revealed through the surreptitious use of her *Gift* told Bodhmhall his fury had not truly subsided. More importantly, his reaction had also confirmed his lack of awareness concerning Muirne's original bid for sanctuary at Ráth Bládhma, a fact she was only too happy to keep to herself. Given his earlier provocation, there was a certain smug satisfaction in having knowledge he was not privy to, in beating him at his own game.

'And now,' continued Tréanmór. 'You tell me that *stiúsaí* – that trollop – resides with *Na Lamraighe*.'

'With Gleor Red Hand. She's his woman.'

Tréanmór's eyes bulged but to her great surprise, rather than reverting to his earlier fury, he released an unexpected bark of laughter. 'Gleor Red Hand!' He shook his head in amused disbelief. 'That old buck goat mounts your brother's woman.'

'Cumhal's gone these six years past, father. They are no longer bonded.'

The *rí* of Dún Baoiscne's firm carriage suddenly appeared to founder. 'There are some sad facts, Bodhmhall, for which I need no reminder.'

The *bandraoi* hurriedly turned her gaze away, discomforted by her father's harrowed expression. Sadness and vulnerability were two characteristics she struggled to associate with the *rí* of *Clann Baoiscne* and their presence on his distressed features was something she simply couldn't reconcile.

'But,' continued Tréanmór, fresh acid in his voice. 'I am sure Muirne Muncháem has fond thoughts of your brother in the clamour of Gleor's pounding buttocks.'

'Such clamour has probably grown silent.'

'What do you mean?' The bleakness had left her father's features and he was regarding her now with wary curiosity.

'It is likely both now sleep deep in the Great Mother's mantle.'

Tréanmór's harsh gaze continued to chafe her, as though trying to gauge something – she wasn't quite sure what – from her expression. Finally, defeated in his efforts, he gestured for her to continue. Although troubled by a number of burning questions, he was shrewd enough to let her continue the story at her own pace.

Bodhmhall looked down and poked a clump of matted reeds with her toe. 'I told you of the *techtaire* sent to us.'

'Yes.'

'I was suspicious of him at first. His face was not one known to me and, besides, the prospect of you sending for me seemed … unlikely.' She glanced sideways at him to catch his response but his face remained as still as stone. Sighing, she folded her hands in her lap, unsure if she felt more disappointed by her father's lack of reaction or her own lack of expectation. 'For these reasons, I demanded *an t-urra* – the surety – the evidence that you had sent him.'

'And what was *an t-urra?*'

Bodhmhall closed her eyes as she focussed on drawing the exact wording from memory. 'You broke one of two at three. You broke one of only one at sixteen.'

Tréanmór understood the riddle immediately. 'The leg you broke when you had three years on you. And at sixteen …' He paused and frowned. 'The bond broken with Fiacail mac Codhna.'

'Yes,' she answered hurriedly, eager to brush past that particular subject. 'Few people of *Clann Baoiscne* would have familiarity with either of those incidents. Fewer still would have familiarity with both.'

There wasn't even a flicker of emotion across her father's face as he took that in but she knew he'd understood what she meant.

'You are suggesting …' He paused, almost absently, to pick at a scab on the back of his left hand. 'You are suggesting there's a traitor in our midst.'

'Yes. Cargal Uí Faigil, the *techtaire*, openly admitted as much but then …' She shrugged. 'Safe in the knowledge he was sending us to our deaths, that was a secret easily shared.'

Tréanmór continued to regard her, his expression giving nothing away. 'Your claim makes little sense. What kind of person would betray their own clan: their family, their friends, the people with whom they've spent their lives?'

Bodhmhall recalled her conversation with Fiacail out in the Great Wild. 'Someone who benefits from its fall. Someone who disagrees with its leadership.'

His lips hardened at that. 'Who is it, then? Tell me.'

'I don't know, father. But that's the reason for my presence here at Dún Baoiscne.'

Overcome by a sudden weariness, the *bandraoi* slumped on her stool. She had argued her case as best she could. Knowing her father as she did, she also knew that what happened next was almost entirely out of her hands. Any decision from this point on would be Tréanmór's alone.

The *rí* of Dún Baoiscne calmly rose to his feet and started to pace about the fire pit, the nonchalance of his facial expression at odds with his agitated step. Bodhmhall watched as he circled the fire pit, eyes internally focussed, weighing up everything she'd told him, working through the ramifications, the options, the different possibilities. Despite her fatigue and the precariousness of her situation, she experienced an odd pleasure in watching him ruminate in this manner, observing in practice how he deliberated and came to his conclusions. Despite their great differences, her father was the most intelligent person she'd ever known. She might despise his methods and motivations, but there was no denying the extent of his accomplishments and she couldn't help but appreciate the strategic cunning and ruthless intellect that had enabled him to achieve them.

Tréanmór circled the fire pit eight times before drawing to a halt and eyeing her with guarded deliberation. 'You have the right of it,' he said. 'Few people would have had the understanding of the false *techtaire's* surety. He could have obtained that knowledge only from a member of *Clann Baoiscne*.'

The *bandraoi* nodded. 'A member of our immediate family, our household or … One of your three advisors.'

Tréanmór frowned but then nodded hesitantly, as though reluctant to allow the consequences of that accusation to seep in. 'This is why you were reluctant for Becal to attend this conversation?'

'Yes.'

He started pacing again, hands clasped behind his back, fingers of his right hand unconsciously beating a strict cadence. This time he walked the full length of the hall in silence, pausing briefly by the door to stare stonily at the wooden barrier, no doubt thinking of the anonymous traitor beyond. With a soft grunt, he turned on his heel and made his way back, bypassing the seated *bandraoi* to approach the table to the left of the fire.

Bodhmhall watched with distaste as her father halted before it and reached down to retrieve the nearest skull, raising the macabre trophy to settle it against his chest and then gently cradle it like a babe into the nook of his elbow. Oblivious or indifferent to her discomfort, he stroked the smooth cranium with almost reverential affection as he returned to his stool.

'Of our immediate family ...' he began but then hesitated briefly. 'Cumhal is gone, Crimall is gone, your mother is gone ... which leaves but you and I.' He reflected on that for a moment. 'But what then of our household? Cairbre or his woman – that silent one. Both of them could have answered the riddle of *an t-urra*.'

Bodhmhall shook her head. 'You know that Cairbre was loyal. Besides, he and Conchenn are passed, gone to join the ancestors.'

That news genuinely seemed to shock her father for he lapsed into startled silence. 'Yes,' he conceded at last, his expression softening. 'Yes, I suppose I clutch at straws. Cairbre was ever loyal to Dún Baoiscne.' He sighed and shook his head slowly. 'A shame. That old man had a mind to find paths through complex challenges that no-one else would ever dream of.'

He suddenly looked at her sideways.

'How did he die?'

'He was killed during an assault on Ráth Bládhma.' Her voice was flat. 'Prompted by the same person who whispers in the traitor's ear.'

Tréanmór's eyes darkened. 'There is another presence behind our traitor?'

'Yes.'

'Who?'

'I don't know,' she answered at last. 'I have considered that same question on countless occasions but an answer has yet to come within my grasp.'

Despite this fresh revelation, her father's reaction was muted, his thoughts cycling internally as he worked through the ramifications. After a moment or two, he considered her once more. 'Tell me of the attack, the attack on your party travelling to Dún Baoiscne.'

The *bandraoi* felt her shoulders droop at the prospect of recounting the events of that ordeal again. 'There's little enough to tell. Through the traitorous summons we were led to a trap at An Bearna Garbh. A *fian* lay concealed within the valley and th-'

'What *fian*? Was it a *Clann Morna fian*?'

She shook her head. 'There were one or two *Clann Morna* members but no, it was composed of warriors from many different tribes.' She paused, sympathising with the confusion she saw in her father's eyes. As a general rule, *fianna* – war parties – were tribal-based and to have one made up of members from different tribes was an anomaly, an occurrence observed only once before with Liath Luachra's mercenary group, *Na Cinéaltaí*.

'This was no *díberg* – bandit group,' she said, pre-empting his next question. 'These men were gathered for the sole purpose of carrying out this ambush. More importantly, they were directed by the same warrior who led the attack on Ráth Bládhma, one with the name Gob An Teanga Gorm on him. Is this man known to you?'

Tréanmór shook his head. 'This Gob An Teanga Gorm. Who is he? What drives his intent?'

The *bandraoi* gave a helpless shrug. 'That remains to be seen. I know only that, like the traitor, he walks in the footprints of another, directed on the path the Adversary sets him.'

Bodhmhall clenched her fists, feeling drawn and strained from the violence of those memories. 'Liath Luachra learned of the trap but despite the defences we prepared, our party was overwhelmed. Demne and I were separated from the others and escaped with our lives only to endure further hardships in the Great Wild. My own death would have been certain had it not been for the intervention of Fiacail mac Codhna and h-'

'Fiacail mac Codhna!' A hiss of shock from Tréanmór. 'Truly, Daughter! Your tale casts thunderbolt upon thunderbolt, consternation upon confusion. What connection does that prancing cockerel have with this tale?'

'No connection but circumstance.'

Her father regarded her cynically.

'I do not ignore the quirk of such timely appearance, father. But I know Fiacail better than any other. He has no motive in that regard.'

Tréanmór grunted, not even bothering to disguise his complete lack of conviction although he refrained, at least, from arguing the matter further. 'And who is this Demne?'

This time it was Bodhmhall who paused. 'Demne ...' she said at last, 'is Fiacail's son.'

Before her father could pursue that particular line of inquiry, she rose to her feet, obfuscating the subject in a flurry of movement and the distraction of a direct address.

'You have a traitor in your house, father. A traitor linked to the shadow-figure in the background who threatens us both. Should we not discuss how to counter that threat?'

Her father did not immediately jump to the lure. Instead, he stood watching her evenly, absently stroking the skull's smooth cranium. 'Why?'

The *bandraoi* paused, a chill fear enveloping her. 'Why, what?' she asked carefully.

'Why would this … this Adversary go to such lengths? I might anticipate an enemy utilising such tactics to depose a tribal leader like myself, but this? A *fian* dispatched to attack a minor settlement, a complicated plot involving a false emissary and an ambush by yet another *fian*. These are complex intrigues, Bodhmhall. Of a kind I'd struggle to implement against my own enemies.' He held both hands up in an exaggerated expression of incomprehension. 'And yet, you claim such machinations arraigned against you?'

Although her heart was beating furiously, Bodhmhall maintained a blank expression to deflect his piercing scrutiny. She recalled the advice Cairbre had once offered her with respect to telling lies.

If you're obliged to deviate from the path of truth, linger as close to it as possible to cloak your untruths.

'I've seen battles and blood enough, father. I've seen my friends and people die as a result of those intrigues.'

'But why? Why is this mysterious Adversary set in such extremes against you? Or rather …' And here her father's scepticism took on an altogether more calculating edge. 'What do you possess that this Adversary so desires?'

Demne.

'I don't know,' she said at last, conscious even as she did of how poor a response it sounded.

Vexed, her father dropped his eyes, rubbing the ridge of his nose between thumb and forefinger, a sure sign of deep contemplation. Without warning, his eyes flicked back at her.

'Let us speak plainly, Bodhmhall. I shall summarise my understanding of what you've told me and should I err, you may correct me.' He coughed and cleared his throat in melodramatic preparation.

'My daughter, my exiled daughter, returns unannounced, unwelcomed and in evident distress. Seeking refuge and hospitality, her sole offering in exchange is an improbable tale of a mysteriously determined and secret enemy.'

Tréanmór paused, watching her to see if she intended to refute this interpretation of events but Bodhmhall, sitting stiffly, avoided his gaze. When it became clear that no response would be forthcoming, he continued.

'This enemy is one so furtive my daughter remains ignorant of both his identity and motivation. This, despite the fact that he hounds her with a battle resource and a doggedness that would cause even the fiercest of *fianna* to waver.'

He sat back on his stool and regarded her without expression. 'Have I summarised the situation correctly?

The *bandraoi* regarded him in silence, her lips a tight line.

'Bodhmhall, you are my daughter. A father's instinct is to offer you sanctuary but you must know the fanciful ring your tale chimes in these ears. *Clann Baoiscne* can ill afford to be sucked into sordid machinations. As a result, I can offer you little more than a simple reprovisioning, a cloak to cover your back and a safe escort from our territory. You cannot remain here unless …' He paused and leaned forward to study her and, here, his true intent became clear. 'Unless, there's other knowledge you would share that might convince me otherwise.'

Bodhmhall's shoulders sagged, a woman at the end of her tether. 'There is more, father. But knowledge that's more suspicion than verity' She grew quiet for a moment as though to rearrange her thoughts but when she spoke again she was looking him directly in the eye.

'It's my belief that the traitor who aids the Adversary against Ráth Bládhma is the same traitor who facilitated the attack by *Clann Morna* six years ago, the same traitor who aided the rustling of the *Clann Baoiscne* herds …' She hesitated briefly. 'The same traitor who organised the assassination of my brother Cumhal.'

Chapter Eight

Through the remainder of the afternoon, Liath Luachra and Fintán ran without pause, an increasingly ragged lope that followed the flat parallel to the river and slowed only when the rugged terrain drove them back into the trees.

By late afternoon, both were struggling, haggard and spent from the grind of being hunted. Encouraging the flagging *Lamraighe* youth with a vigour that disguised her own exhaustion, the Grey One could only comfort herself with the knowledge that however badly they hurt, the warriors on their heels would be hurting just as much.

Soon the land changed again, the valley contracting as the mountains grew closer, the river narrower, the current faster. With the bleak illumination of an overcast sky, the high ridges had taken on a sombre, colourless quality. By contrast, the vegetation had grown even more colourful, the dominant evergreens yielding to autumnal deciduous trees, vibrant patterns of reds and golds and a forest floor that was clear of thick undergrowth and easier to negotiate.

As the afternoon shadow pressed in, they struck a stretch of forest where a storm had created a barrier of smashed trees and inter-tangled branches that was almost impossible to penetrate. The destruction extended all the way to the riverbank where the root systems were exposed, gouged out by erosion and too hazardous to negotiate at speed. Once again, they were forced to a crawl, assuaging their fears with the knowledge their pursuers would gain no advantage. They too would have to traverse that ground with care.

Pausing to catch her breath, the Grey One looked to the back trail. They'd heard no further ululations since fleeing the ford but at no time had she let up the pace. Twice, on elevated sections of riverbank, she'd seen columns of smoke upriver and although unsure what purpose they served, it seemed reasonable to assume their immediate pursuers were marking the way for their comrades to the rear.

And that prompted an interesting question. How many warriors were actually dogging their heels? Gob An Teanga Gorm would have sent his fastest runners, of course – four to seven men at a guess – but within any group there were bound to be mixed abilities. And, of course, there were the warriors from the other side of the ford who would have joined them.

The Grey One used her hands to smear the sweat from her cheeks and forehead as she considered the problem. Because of the brutal pace, she was confident that at least a number of the warriors would have dropped out. There was also a good chance they'd managed to extend the lead over their pursuers but she couldn't count on that. Even if they had managed to gain an advantage, they'd be unable to sustain it indefinitely.

Fortunately, she'd noticed that the mountain range across the river had been falling away over the latter part of the afternoon. That meant the barriers confining them to the valley were finally receding and a range of alternative paths would soon open up, making them all the more difficult to follow. If they succeeded in evading the enemy warriors until nightfall they'd have a chance to rest during the darkness hours and by morning, the circumstances of the hunt would have changed in their favour.

Manoeuvring their way out of the last of the tangled root systems, the fugitives pushed their way through a dense thicket of ash and undergrowth, emerging on a small promontory where the waterway made a dramatic turn to the south. Arcing in from the promontory, it curved sharply towards the base of the nearest mountain in the northern range before it rounded back on itself, in effect creating a tight, almost perfectly semi-circular lake.

Five hundred paces across the water from where they were standing, although on the same bank, the river narrowed once more, the current increasing speed to flush rapidly into the shadows between two distant rocky outcrops where it disappeared from sight.

Breathing hard, Liath Luachra studied this unexpected disruption to the pattern of the landscape, immediately noting the logjam of trees, sticks and other debris that had formed at the centre of the watery semicircle, nearest the northern hills. Beyond that, the ground was marshland, a quagmire devoid of trees or any other substantial vegetation.

A break! A gap in the mountains!

The woman warrior stared. From their position on the promontory, she could see right through, could almost make out the dense green of forest on the far side.

At last!

Beside her, also focussed on the gap, Fintán must have been having similar thoughts.

'Grey One! We can escape the valley.'

The woman warrior made no response. Her gaze had alighted on the marshy terrain past the logjam. She frowned as she took in the soggy flatness of it, the clumps of reed and slimy marsh grass interspersed with pools of black, stagnant water. Tempting though the route was, it was also a precarious one, crossing terrain that was almost certainly littered with sink holes, quicksand and other hidden dangers.

She turned her eyes downriver, trying to judge how far they'd have to travel before the southern mountains fell away. Unfortunately, the high outcrop at the far side of the waterway completely obscured that view. Biting her lip, she considered Fintán, now slumped to his knees, clearly near the limits of his endurance.

Growing increasingly anxious, the woman warrior studied the ground to the left of the logjam where the riverbank curled back, diverting the current to the shadowed gap between the outcrops. There, a shingle bank lifted directly onto a thickly forested hill rising at a sharp angle to a long slumping saddle connecting the nearest of the southern mountains with the outcrop on their side of the river.

'*Ar aghaidh linn.*'

The youth stifled a groan as he got to his feet but he staggered after her: stumbling, clumsy steps that followed the curving riverbank to where the log jam started. As they drew closer, that distinctive smell of marshland grew stronger, a powerful stench of decaying vegetable matter and rotting wood.

They came to a halt in the mud alongside the woody detritus. There, the warrior woman dropped to a squat and hauled a slim length of wood from the water, a broken branch worn smooth from immersion and constant abrasion. Raising her catch in both hands, she wiped the residual mud from it and stood to measure its length against herself. She grunted softly, satisfied to find it reached just above her jawline.

'Follow me,' she instructed Fintán as she started into the marsh. 'Step only where I step.'

At first, they travelled by using the visibly solid slivers of terrain, weaving a circuitous route that, nonetheless, took them in the general direction of the gap in the cliffs. Within twenty paces or so however, the softness of the earth prompted the warrior woman to start using her makeshift staff, testing the ground and poking muddy surfaces that appeared solid enough but which, potentially, contained sinkholes underneath.

Advancing deeper into the marsh, the solid ground grew increasingly scarce, the pools of brackish water increasing in size and number. The two fugitives soon found themselves obliged to leap from one little island of marsh grass to the next, a risky action due to the slimy vegetation.

At a point about forty-five paces from where they'd first entered the marsh, the Grey One halted abruptly and peered at the short stretch of ground separating them from the next tussock of marsh grass, a distance of about four paces. It looked stable enough but when the Grey One probed it with her makeshift staff, the pole sank easily beneath the surface without any resistance. By the time three quarters of it had submerged, she still hadn't hit bottom.

Sinkhole.

She yanked the pole free with a hollow, sucking sound that left its lower surface coated in a thick and gritty slime. Behind her, Fintán watched anxiously, doing his best to keep out of the way, for the tussock on which they were standing was barely wide enough to hold the two of them.

Liath Luachra jammed the pole into the mud directly alongside the tussock, where it protruded upwards like a lonely sapling. Grasping the *Lamraighe* youth's arm, she edged out over the edge of the grass and using the purchase of her grip, stretched her right foot over the sinkhole to a point almost mid-way between the tussocks. Extended to her limit, she placed her sole on the sticky surface and, muscles straining, pressed down lightly to create a shallow imprint of her foot.

Hauling herself back to safety, the woman warrior felt the quiver of tension in her muscles drain away as she regarded the footprint, now filling with water but still clearly visible. With the toes pointed towards the ridge, it left the impression that they'd continued onwards in the direction of the gap. Nevertheless, the Grey One remained unsatisfied.

Pulling Gleor's knife free from its scabbard, she took aim and then flung it at the tussock just beyond the one immediately in front of them. It was a good throw. The weapon struck the grass and although for a moment it looked as though it was going to sink out of sight, the guard snagged on the fibrous material and the hilt remained protruding upwards.

Liath Luachra looked squarely at the *Lamraighe* youth. 'Now,' she told him. 'We go back the way we came.'

Backtracking should have been an easy task given their recent familiarity with the more secure areas of footing. Instead, because of the Grey One's insistence on moving in a backwards motion, stepping into the very footsteps they'd created just moments earlier, it proved substantially more laborious. The task was complicated further by their efforts to avoid placing pressure on the heel of the footprints, something that would have revealed the ruse to any decent tracker.

Back on solid ground, they hurriedly continued the exercise, conscious that Gob An Teanga Gorm's warriors could appear at any moment. Throwing one last critical eye over the false trail, Liath Luachra tried to see it from the perspective of the pursuing approaching warriors, hopeful that the limited space and the effects of fatigue meant they wouldn't regard it too closely.

Working their way back to the log jam, the woman warrior glanced repeatedly towards the promontory at the far bend in the river where Gob An Teanga Gorm's men would inevitably appear. Advancing towards the woody debris, her eyes alighted on a jumble of flat rocks protruding out into the water just a few paces beyond. 'There,' she pointed for Fintán's benefit. 'We'll use that rock to take to the water. The surface will leave no imprint of our passing.'

The youth looked at the water, unable to disguise his nervousness.

'It's not the surge it was,' she reassured him. 'The current's slower here, much weaker. It'll help carry us past the logjam. Hurry, now.'

With this she moved swiftly along the curve of the bank, avoiding any area of soft ground. Reaching the rocks, she wiped all trace of grit from her feet, hauled herself onto the hard surface and slid forward into the water.

The shock of cold liquid made her gasp aloud but she ignored it as she kicked off from shore. Powerful strokes took her swiftly across the water even as Fintán lowered himself into the lake behind her.

Despite what she'd told the *Lamraighe* youth, the current was actually far stronger than she'd anticipated and she felt the pull almost immediately as it drew her towards the centre of the river. Fearful of finding herself back in the tow of the current and swept between the two outcrops, she cut towards the bank at a sharper angle, swimming strongly until she struck solid ground twenty paces on the other side of the logjam. Clambering onto the rocky shore, she grasped a boulder to lever herself to her feet and looking back for Fintán, caught sight of the youth splashing feebly offshore.

Wading back into the lake, up to the level of her chest, she reached out to grab his outstretched hand, pulling him to shore and onto the bank where he collapsed in a shivering, saturated heap. Unfortunately, she couldn't allow the exhausted youth any respite. Out on the shingle, they were still totally exposed to anyone emerging at the promontory so, kicking and cajoling him in equal measure, she rallied him onto his feet and into the trees.

It was only when the shadows of the tree canopy enveloped them, that Liath Luachra allowed herself to feel a measure of relief. Now, at least, they were out of immediate danger and had a passable chance of surviving the remainder of the afternoon. Had the enemy warriors appeared at any moment prior to that, all their efforts would have been in vain.

Nevertheless, the woman warrior knew they couldn't afford to stop. Despite the false trail and a narrow body of water that was more of a perceived barrier than a material one, they were still far too close to the pursuing warriors, particularly now that they'd sacrificed their lead. Ignoring her own exhaustion, she drove the youth onwards, forcing him to clamber up the steep slope, shoving him from behind when he stumbled, threatening him if he showed the slightest sign of flagging. Somehow they achieved the saddle and there, in a cluster of ash on a flat ledge overlooking the lake, they collapsed, utterly spent.

For a time, they lay in silence, the Grey One half-senseless, head throbbing, gasping for breath as she rode the rhythm of a pounding heart that threatened to erupt from her chest. When her head finally cleared, she remained on her side, unable to move, too tired to do anything but listen to the rustle of leaves overhead, the creak of boughs in the breeze, the distant twitter of tits and sparrows.

They'd been remarkably lucky. Despite the time taken to set the false trail, swim across the lake and clamber up the hill, they'd managed to achieve it all before their pursuers came into sight. Her earlier hopes had been correct, it seemed. Propelled by desperation, they'd managed to extend their lead over the course of the day.

With a great effort, Liath Luachra sat up. Undoing the straps of the leather satchel that now felt glued to her back, she yanked it free, dropped it to one side and plucked with distaste at her battle harness. It seemed ironic. A little earlier, she could have squeezed river water from her clothing yet now they appeared sodden with perspiration once more. Despite the swim, her skin was slick with sweat from the climb. It trickled along the nape of her neck, down her back and dripped into the nook where the waistband of her ragged leggings met her buttocks.

With a great effort, she managed to wriggle out of the leather battle harness and wearily hung it on a low branch to dry, shivering a little where the breeze licked her exposed skin. Although tempted to remove her leggings as well, she held off because of Fintán's presence, mindful of the disturbing infatuation he'd borne for her prior to leaving Ráth Bládhma. Subsequent events had served to curb those desires, nevertheless an awkwardness remained between them.

She considered the *óglach* splayed out alongside her, his face pale and strained, and wondered where all that original brashness had gone. 'Fintán?' she poked him, suddenly concerned at the lack of movement.

The youth managed to twist his head slightly and nod but he said nothing, which she interpreted as a sign he was still too breathless to speak.

Satisfied, she reached for the satchel, dragged it close and undid the sodden thong with trembling fingers. As expected, the contents were swimming in water, nevertheless she scooped out a handful and raised it to her mouth. Liquefied now, the stew was cold and tasteless but it was better than nothing.

With a sigh, she peered out at the sky through the hole in the canopy. Black cloud was congealing above the southern ridges, a sure sign of rain or, more likely, a storm. A bad storm.

She pursed her lips in thought. Generally, the prospect of such a storm out in the Great Wild was not one that would have pleased her but on this occasion there was a certain timeliness to be grateful for. Storm clouds would expedite the coming of darkness, the gush and scutter of its rain would wash their trail away. It might, indeed, save their lives.

Beside her, Fintán finally shuffled upright. Sitting cross-legged, he stared bleakly at her exposed chest, the flat breasts and midriff, before turning his dull gaze down towards the lake below. As he studied the terrain, he unshuffled the sword scabbard that was fixed to his back, unsheathed the weapon and ran a smooth finger along its blade.

'I named this sword, *Goineog Gearr,* Sharp Thrust.'

Liath Luachra regarded him without expression, too tired to encourage conversation.

The youth however had a need to speak, to expel whatever nerves still twisted his insides. He gestured at the woman warrior's weapon, lying on the ground alongside the leather satchel. 'What name does your sword carry?'

For a moment she wasn't going to reply, but seeing the boy didn't intend to let the topic slide, she consented to answer. '*Gleas Gan Ainm.*' Weapon Without a Name.

The boy considered her with a surprised expression. 'That's a stupid name.'

Liath Luachra shrugged.

'My father named his sword *Cantaire na Caointe* - Chanter of Death Songs. Back in the *Lamraighe* tribal lands, my uncle wields an axe by the name of *An Gaoth Garbh* – the Rough Wind.'

'That must terrify their adversaries,' the woman warrior said at last.

Fintán's countenance darkened in response and he looked at her with displeasure, believing he was being mocked although that hadn't been her intention. To her surprise, that ire faded abruptly and he stroked the weapon again.

'I named this *Goineog Gearr*. I thought that naming the weapon would make me brave. But it didn't. I still ran.'

The Grey One stared at him, confused. 'What do you mean?'

'I ran. At An Glenn Teann. I ran for my life. I left everyone dear to me behind.'

The woman warrior shrugged. 'What of it?'

'I deserted my father, my friends.'

154

'We all ran.'

'Marcán didn't. Marcán stayed and fought like the warrior he was.'

'Marcán's dead. He should have run too. You know what the Old Ones say; *Is fear rith maith na drochsheamh*. A good run is better than a bad stand. And An Glenn Teann was a bad stand.'

'I was a coward.'

'True,' she agreed. 'But sometimes cowardice is a good thing.'

His eyes turned from confusion to anger. 'A good thing?' he growled at the woman warrior with surprising menace, prompting a sardonic arch to her eyebrows.

'What's this? Is this the coward of An Glenn Teann who threatens me? One I'd kill as easily as I'd flick a fly?'

That seemed to lance the bubble of anger within him. The youth looked at her helplessly, lost for a response.

'Fear is a strong emotion, Fintán. But so is shame and, if you use it to balance your fear, it can serve a powerful motivation. When you're next in battle, draw up the memory of how miserable, how wretched that shame made you feel. Use that feeling to rally yourself and you'll find you've grown too angry for flight.'

With that, the woman warrior turned away to discourage any further discussion and started to untie the sling from around her arm. Loosening it, she unravelled the two lengths of sinewed cord, grasped the ends and yanked them to test their tautness. Both stretched slightly but, to her relief, appeared undamaged from their immersion in the water. The leather pouch, too, appeared unaffected.

Clicking her tongue in satisfaction, she began to wrap the weapon around her arm once more, conscious of the fact that Fintán was still watching her in silence.

'Does your sling have a name?'

Liath Luachra was about to snap an angry response but bit her tongue when she saw the haunted expression in his eyes. The youth looked utterly vulnerable, scared and forlorn. He had the exact same cast to his face as Bearach just before his terrible wounds took him away.

Disconcerted, she quickly turned her eyes away and cleared her throat, securing the last twist of the sling with an unnecessarily harsh yank.

'This sling isn't ...' She caught herself. When she spoke, her voice was uncharacteristically soft. 'This sling isn't the weapon it was when I first fashioned it. I've replaced the pouch twice, the two cords on at least three separate occasions. You cannot name a weapon that no longer exists. Besides, it's not the sling that kills your opponent but the bullet it casts.

The youth nodded gravely. More out of habit she suspected, than any true conviction.

He's soul sick.

The insight struck her with surprising intensity. This was, she realised, how he coped with the trauma of the violence at An Gleann Teann, the fear of death, the guilt of leaving his father. Unlike her, withdrawn and repressed, Fintán had a need to vocalise everything, articulate everything he felt inside.

She tossed him one of the sling stones which he adroitly caught in one hand. He studied it with interest, admiring the twists and curls of the rough wolf shape carved into the surface.

'To earn its name,' she explained, 'a weapon must be blooded. It must have physically spilled or at least drawn the blood of an opponent to retain a portion of his ghost.' She gestured at his sword. 'If it's not blooded, it's just a blade.'

Liath Luachra hesitated then, struck by the sheer volume of words she'd voiced. This was the most she'd spoken in several days. With that realisation, she felt herself pull back, retreating into the silence where she felt more at ease.

'It's th-'

'Whist!'

Fintán stared at her, too surprised by the urgent shushing to react. The Grey One however, had already turned away, raising her jaw with one ear to the wind as she stared down at the promontory. She had thought to hear a distant tinkle of metal on metal but given the distance and the breeze she couldn't be certain.

Both stared. There was no sign of movement from the thicket of ash saplings, no sign of anything out of the ordinary. After an extended period of time, the woman warrior slowly allowed herself to relax.

Nerves.

She opened her mouth to reassure Fintán but then her jaw stiffened in a grim rictus. Down at the promontory, a man with a sword strapped to his back had surged out of the ash trees. Coming to a halt, he looked about in surprise as another warrior stumbled into the open, followed by another and then another and others again until there was a small column of six men standing along the edge.

Although she knew she couldn't be distinguished in the trees from that distance, Liath Luachra instinctively pressed herself flat, an action the *Lamraighe* youth immediately replicated. Both watched as the enemy warriors looked around, evidently taken by surprise by the abrupt swerve of the river and the unexpected presence of the lake. Like their quarry, Gob An Teanga Gorm's men used the moment to catch their breath and the Grey One could tell from their drooping postures that they too were physically exhausted. Three of the men had already collapsed and one looked as though he was retching. Two others, more resilient, had spread out and were carefully observing the nearby bush, watchful for any sign of ambush.

The last of them, a muscular, dark-bearded man with a round face, stood alone at the very tip of the promontory, staring towards the logjam and the marshland that awaited them.

Cargal Uí Faigil.

She growled softly to herself. The deceiving *techtaire*, purveyor of false messages. In hindsight, she supposed, she shouldn't have been too surprised. To play the part of a *techtaire*, Cargal must have been one of Gob's best runners and therefore, a logical choice to lead the chase.

The warrior abruptly adjusted his stance to face the hill, his regard moving up towards the saddle and, for one terrifying moment, it seemed as though he was staring directly at them. Shivering, the woman warrior averted her own gaze and looked straight down at her hands, convinced that if she laid eyes on him he'd sense it and know where she was concealed. The reaction, of course, was irrational but although she knew this she couldn't help it. Naturally, when she finally managed to raise her head, the warrior had moved on again and was rousing his men to their feet.

Her eyes followed them as they made their way along the bank towards the logjam, noting how one of them, a bald, stringy man, hung back. One of the two fitter ones who'd been watching the forest, he was moving at a slow trot, studying the ground just ahead of him.

They have a tracker.

She felt her shoulders tense. This man was clearly competent for he was moving more carefully than the others, clearly seeing some story in the footprints that had peaked his interest.

By the time the others had reached the logjam, the tracker had already fallen twenty paces behind. As they followed the tracks into the marsh, he was bypassing the rock where she and Fintán had slid into the lake, only to pause a few paces further on, dropping to one knee to examine the ground more closely.

Damnú ort!

Her gaze darted ahead to where Cargal Uí Faigil was leading his men deeper into the marsh, jumping now from tussock to tussock just as she and Fintan had done earlier. The tracker meanwhile was on his feet again, looking back over the ground he'd already covered, eyes sliding inexorably towards the flat rocks. Although too far away to make out his facial expression, she saw how his body stiffened, pre-empted the moment when he swivelled about to yell in warning.

By then however, the other warriors had reached the end of the false trail, Cargal and one of his men poised on the tussock before the sinkhole. As the tracker's shrill warning pierced the limpid air, Cargal paused to look back. His companion however continued forward, stepping off the tussock and onto the surface bearing Liath Luachra's footprint.

It all happened so swiftly the warrior barely had time to cry out and the shocking abruptness of his disappearance took even the Grey One by surprise. One moment he was there, the next he was gone, swallowed up seamlessly by the muddy mire. Cargal Uí Faigil spun around and stared at the empty spot his comrade had occupied just a moment earlier. Even at that distance, Liath Luachra could see his stature stiffen, could imagine the expression of disbelief upon his face.

She turned to Fintán. 'We should move,' she said.

***

The rain rolled in with the darkness, preceded by a whooping gale from the west that shook the forest canopy like a throttled rat. By then, Fintán and the Grey One had already worked their way across the saddle only to find themselves once again confronted by an impenetrable cliff on the southern range. Frustrated, they retreated down the densely wooded northern slope of the saddle, finding refuge beneath an overhang just as the storm truly hit.

Shielded from the worst of the weather by a boulder that lay to the left of the overhang, the shelter was nevertheless assailed by a constant stream of gusts, something they tried to stop with a hastily made screen of leafy scrub chopped from the surrounding undergrowth. Retreating to the innermost section of the overhang, they found the ground littered with soft layers of desiccated leaf debris although there was little else of comfort.

With the enemy so close at hand, they didn't dare risk a fire although Liath Luachra didn't think the danger too serious. The daylight was as good as spent and she'd seen the slumped shoulders, heard the dismayed cries of their pursuers. Exhausted from the chase and stunned by the loss of yet another comrade, their morale would be broken. Overnight, that would gnaw at them, of course. By morning the simmering anger would be transformed to a bloodlust for vengeance but for the moment at least, they were comparatively safe.

The two fugitives huddled morosely together, feasting on the watery stew while they watched wave after wave of grey showers lash the forest beyond their shelter. When her hunger was sated, Liath Luachra regarded the dwindling contents of the satchel with thoughtful eyes, knowing that without it, they'd have been enfeebled by now. She felt a fresh surge of gratitude to whatever ancestor had been watching over them, relieved that she'd taken the chance of grabbing the stew when she could, despite the ensuing events.

She frowned then, her thoughts turning to the screaming *Mac Morna* youth and the tall man with the smouldering eyes.

'Fintán.'

The *Lamraighe* youth looked up. Despite the food, he looked completely done in.

'Do you remember the tall man?'

He regarded her in confusion. 'The tall man?'

'Back at the enemy camp. Where we stole the stew.'

A muddled comprehension flickered as he wiped his weary eyes. 'Yes,' he said uncertainly.

'Describe him.'

'Well, … he was … tall.'

Liath Luachra bit down her temper. 'Describe how he looked to you. His features. Exactly as you remember them.'

Fintán thought about it for a moment. 'He had deep eyes. Very red lips. Brown eyes. And his beard hid a strong chin.'

'Yes. Good. Did his features strike you in any way familiar?'

'I …' The youth wavered. 'I don't think so. Perhaps. Is it important?'

Frustrated, the Grey One exhaled heavily. 'I don't know.'

They both lapsed into a silence punctuated by the undulating howl of the wind. Liath Luachra shivered. It would be a cold night.

The ensuing silence proved too much for Fintán to endure. 'Do we move on tonight, Grey One?' he asked, casting an unenthusiastic glance at the storm outside.

'No. Tonight, you can sleep.' The woman warrior considered the pelting rain, barely visible now in the last eddies of shifting light. 'Tomorrow, we head north-east at first light. I caught a glimpse of a mountain in the distance before the storm hit, a mountain I recognised from my time in *Uí Barraiche* territory.' She gestured loosely towards the mouth of the overhang. 'This hill marks the limit of the mountain range that keeps us to the valley and the foothills beyond are no obstacle. When we're ready we can travel to seek help from *Uí Barraiche.*'

A flare of excitement burned through the dullness in Fintán's eyes. 'We've succeeded then! We're clear.'

The Grey One shook her head. 'No.'

'No! But you said we'd reached the limits of the mountains, that tomorrow we cou-'

'They have a tracker. I have to kill him.'

Fintán regarded her blankly, thrown by this new and unexpected complication. 'Why?'

'Because he's good and has a nose for our trail. If Gob's men continue the chase, he'll make escape more difficult. Besides…' And here she shrugged as though the point was obvious. 'There's Cargal Uí Faigil.'

She said nothing more, her meaning entirely clear. Fintán swallowed.

'But, Grey One. Perhaps we should seek such vengeance when we're better prepared to deal it out.'

'It's not just a matter of vengeance, Fintán. Cargal Uí Faigil is Gob An Teanga Gorm's trusted man and will most likely know the identity of the Adversary. I too would have that name.' She picked up the sword that was lying unscabbarded beside her, wiped the blade clean with an angry gesture. 'We've harried to his game for far too long, always reacting and at a disadvantage.' 'This time I intend to take the fight back to him. This time I am going to war.'

***

While Fintán struggled to find the least draughty corner in which to lay himself down, Liath Luachra approached the outer edge of the overhang. She was hobbling slightly, a dull ache in her knees and hips and her leg muscles burning. She couldn't remember having ever felt so depleted, so physically worn, and she dreaded the inevitable stiffness that would stifle her movements the following day. Even now, her entire body felt like dead weight.

Then ignore it. You know what you have to do.

A sudden thunderclap left her ears ringing. It was almost immediately followed by a great flash of lighting that illuminated the forest in flickering blue before the world was, once again, engulfed in shadow. *Thit an tóin as an spéir.* The arse fell out of the sky. A deluge of knife-blade rain pummelled the forest, striking the canopy so hard it drowned out the shriek of the wind. Wisps of black mist whipped past the mouth of the overhang.

Liath Luachra shivered and absently massaged her heart. She could feel the old fury bubbling up inside, nurtured by a growing sense of grief and the yearning for vengeance against the one person responsible for it all: the Adversary.

Giving into that fury, that hatred, could lead to only one place, she knew.

But she no longer cared.

If it hadn't been for Bodhmhall that fury would have consumed her many years earlier, reducing her to a burnt out husk and a horribly violent death in a circle of blood and entrails, of screaming women and children. The *bandraoi* had taught her how to control her fury by diverting its flame. Her kindness and affection had softened the woman warrior during the days when she was most stiff with hatred and close to breaking inside.

But now, of course, Bodhmhall was gone.

And Liath Luachra no longer knew where to go.

'What are you looking at, Grey One?'

The woman warrior started. Absorbed in her thoughts, she'd completely missed the *Lamraighe* youth's approach as he sidled up beside her. Furious, she responded with the first thing that came to mind.

'The end.'

'The end of what?'

'The end of … of everything.'

Perplexed by the ambiguous response, the youth still sensed the emotion underlying it.

'Why do you weep?'

Liath Luachra turned a feverishly dangerous eye towards him. 'I do not weep,' she snapped. 'Why would you say that?'

Cowed by the heat of her response, the youth backed away, saying nothing as he silently pointed to her face. Raising a hand to her cheeks, the warrior woman was shocked to find them wet to the touch and was suddenly aware of the tangy taste of salt seeping between her lips.

Hurling the youth a terrifying glare, she turned and stalked out from the overhang without another word, into the full force of the storm.

Chapter Nine

Lulled by the unaccustomed luxury of a sleeping platform and fur blankets, Bodhmhall slept far later than usual. It was almost noon before she finally roused, stirred by the repeated slap of a hand against the lintel of the roundhouse doorway.

Curled in a snug cocoon of comfort, the *bandraoi* forced her eyes open and peered at the entrance. Bé Bhinn stood hunched at the doorway, her head poking into the gloomy interior. Tangled in the threads of aftersleep, Bodhmhall struggled to separate past from present but the smiling Dún Baoiscne woman was, at least, consistent with both.

'Raise your bones, Bodhmhall. Father Sun sits high and directs us to Poll na mBan.'

With an effort the *bandraoi* slipped free from the furs although the whiff of body odour from the bubble of air beneath the layers caused her nose to wrinkle. Following the prolonged discussions with her father the previous evening, she'd made a half-hearted attempt to wash the sweat of her travels away but had been thwarted by a head-numbing fatigue. Succumbing to bed, she'd drifted off to sleep, feeling grimy but satisfied that she'd achieved what she'd initially set out to do. Her father had granted her the hospitality of the fortress for a period of ten days. Ten days in which to recover. Ten days in which to recuperate from her injuries. Ten days to identify and expose the traitor.

Although if all went to plan, it would take far less than that.

She pushed such thoughts aside as she dropped her feet to the floor. The reed-strewn clay was cold against her soles but, yawning, she got to her feet and stumbled outside. The late morning sun was much brighter, much warmer than she'd anticipated and she raised one hand to shield her eyes from the dazzle. Standing to the right of the doorway, Bé Bhinn beamed, a heavy basket in her hands that looked as though it'd taken the better part of the morning to pack. She grinned at her friend's beleaguered state. 'Shall we turn our faces north?'

Although still ill-prepared for the challenge of conversation, the *bandraoi* grudgingly mumbled assent and gestured for the red-haired woman to lead the way.

Ten days.

And by oversleeping she'd already wasted half a day.

She rubbed her eyes as she considered her next steps. At Poll na mBan she could make her plans and discreetly question Bé Bhinn. And then of course, there was that matter of a bath to consider.

Situated in the hills just north of Dún Baoiscne, Poll na mBan – Hole of the Women – was a swimming hole of great beauty within a secure distance of the fortress. An ancient gathering place for the *Clann Baoiscne* women, it was theoretically off-limits to the male members of the tribe although Bodhmhall knew for a fact that her brother Cumhal had snuck in there on at least one occasion. Driven by boyish curiosity when he'd had less than ten years on him, she recalled only that he'd been unimpressed by what he'd seen, summarising the experience as '*nothing but women talking and swimming!*'

To his credit, there'd been some veracity to that description. It was true the site served as a place to celebrate the important milestones in the women's lives but, most days, it was just a pleasant spot to swim and talk without the distraction of the opposite sex.

Leaving the fortress, the two women descended the gentle slope and travelled north across the fields to a series of low hills fronted by overlapping cliffs of solid granite. A well-trodden path wove a circuitous route along the base of the solid grey walls to terminate at Bruinn Danann – the Great Mother's womb – a narrow passage providing access to the sacred site.

Little more than a crack in the imposing rock face, the passage's high walls were smooth from endless cycles of erosion. A tall standing stone to one side of the entrance bore some of the Ancient One's characteristic carvings on its surface: a long-haired, big-bellied figure obviously meant to represent the Great Mother, Danu.

Following Bé Bhinn into the sunless passage, Bodhmhall shivered at the sudden drop in temperature. She'd forgotten how dark and oppressive the narrow space could be, and the odd sense of weightlessness created by a subtle – but sharp – descent as it carved its way deeper into the rock.

Fortunately, the path through the cliffs was a short one and, as they negotiated its final curve, the walls expanded dramatically into a large canyon densely packed with oak and ash. A worn path continued into the wood and, following it, they meandered between the larger trees. Finally, it too opened out into a clearing that stretched to a curving black cliff face thirty paces away. Poll na mBan, a wide pool of dark, still water, ran from the centre of the clearing right up to the base of that cliff.

Bodhmhall stared, her heart-rate quickening at the memories stirred by the sight of the pool. As a child she'd spent countless days here with friends, chattering and laughing, swimming in the dark water or simply basking in the sun. Fed from some unidentified underground source, the pool could be bitterly cold, even in the heart of summer. Fortunately, the half-ring of flat rock immediately surrounding it acted as an effective suntrap. In summer, shielded from the wind by the encircling cliffs, the clearing could grow uncomfortably hot. On such occasions, people invariably retreated to the shelter of the trees where moss-coated bowers offered varying degrees of shade and privacy to chat.

Two of the bowers to the left of the pool had already been taken by the time Bodhmhall and Bé Bhinn arrived. A pair of teenage girls was seated in the nearest one, too engrossed in conversation to look up at their approach. A trio of naked old women occupied the second bower, wrinkled bodies exposed to the heat of the sun as they conversed amongst themselves and with a fourth woman in the water. The conversation faltered briefly when they saw the two young women and they stared openly at Bodhmhall before returning to their discussion.

'*Ná bac le na gobacháin sin,*' Bé Bhinn advised her lightly. Pay those busybodies no mind. 'We'll sit off to the side and have a comfortable time by ourselves.'

The fair-haired woman led the way around to the right side of the pool, continuing until she'd found a flat section of rock to her satisfaction. Dropping her basket, she sat and started to massage her left ankle. 'And old ache,' she explained. 'I twisted it three years ago but the pain comes back from time to time.' She gestured towards the pool. 'Go. I'll follow.'

Bodhmhall slipped out of her dress. Unwrapping her loincloth, she dropped it on the ground as she approached the edge of the pool then eased carefully onto the sloping lip of the rock and lowered herself into the water. The shock of the cold liquid against her skin after the heat of the sun triggered a fresh flash of memory and, for a moment, she was a child once again, hooting and splashing in the pool with her friends. For the first time in what seemed like years, she felt safe and at peace.

Using her feet, she pushed back off the rock, propelling herself to the centre of the pool. There, she lay floating on her back for a time, staring up at the encompassing cliffs and the deep blue cup of sky that they framed. Finally, twisting onto her front, she ducked her head underwater and dived, kicking deeper and deeper into the darkness until her instincts prompted her to flip about and kick back up towards the sunlight.

Surfacing in a spray of water, she whooped in a great lungful of air before slowly swimming back to the edge of the pool. Resting against the smooth grain of rock, she became aware of a throb in her arm and belatedly realised that she'd pushed the injured limb too far. For now, the discomfort was dulled by the coldness of the water but as she warmed up, the pain would return in full force to admonish her carelessness.

Irritated, she transferred her gaze across the pool and saw that the woman who'd been swimming had now emerged from the water to join her comrades. All four were whispering closely together, but the relaxed postures suggested the *bandraoi* wasn't the subject of their conversation.

Clambering onto the rock ledge, she sat and dangled her feet in the water, enjoying the cold contrast of it with the heat of the sun against her head and shoulders. Father Sun hung directly overhead now, no doubt why Bé Bhinn had chosen that particular time to come and fetch her.

Rivulets of water streamed from her sodden hair, dripping onto the nape of her neck and back. Brushing a few loose strands from her eyes, she caught a flicker of movement as her friend rummaged in her basket, pulled something from it and then rose to come and join her. The *Clann Baoiscne* woman sat directly to Bodhmhall's rear, surprising the *bandraoi* by running fingers through her hair, assessing the worst of the knots and tangles.

'Your hair's a snarl of briars,' she decided aloud. 'I'll brush it out. I can tell your arm pains you.'

Taking a handful of the *bandraoi's* damp hair, she started to work on the knots with her fingers, loosening the worst of them then combing them out with some oil and a bone comb, the objects Bodhmhall had seen her retrieve from her basket.

Initially stiff and ill at ease, Bodhmhall gradually allowed herself to relax, enjoying the simple sensation of the comb sliding through her hair and along her scalp. Within a short time, she was feeling wonderfully unwound.

'It's pleasing to have you back, Bodhmhall. Losing you so closely after Demmán was a hardship.'

Bodhmhall said nothing but reached her right hand back to squeeze her friend's knee. She hadn't allowed herself to think of Demmán for a very long time but here, embedded once more in her old world, it was impossible to block memories of the freckled young man with hair as bright and red as his sister's. A shy and sensitive boy, he'd displayed rare potential with the *Gift* until his untimely death. His passing had been a great loss to them all in more ways than one.

Don't think about it. That does you no good now.

'Will you stay?'

Bé Bhinn's voice pulled her back to the present. 'What?'

'Will you stay and make Dún Baoiscne your home once more? Such news would be sweet to these ears.'

The sentiment was expressed with such earnest lack of guile, the *bandraoi* winced from a combination of affection and guilt. 'Alas, *a chara*. I cannot. When my tasks are done, I return to Ráth Bládhma. I have responsibilities there that cannot be put aside.'

'Oh.' A soft silence followed that single syllable yet some echo of the evident disappointment seemed to ring in the air for a very long time.

'Bé Bhinn, I … I truly regret my absence in your time of trouble. You've suffered cruel strikes and it's a sad thing to have no friend at hand to soften such blows.'

The fair-haired woman looked down and gathered the hem of her dress between her fingers. '*Fuist*, Bodhmhall. Don't fret. You've suffered equally, perhaps even more than I.'

She released the dress and patted down the creases.

'You know that I too have many regrets but the one thing I regret most of all was being too weak to prevent your expulsion from Dún Baoiscne. When you were gone, I feared for your safety. We had no news for it was forbidden to speak your name aloud. Only your brothers, Cumhal and Crimall, dared to talk openly of you and after the Gabhra massacre, even that was lost.'

Bodhmhall felt her heart sink. Her brothers, like Demmán, were a subject she'd struggled to face since learning of Cumhal's death at Gabhra. 'Then … There was no further news of Crimall?'

Bé Bhinn shook her head. 'His body was never found.' Her face took on a mournful hue and it was a moment before she spoke again. 'In truth, we found few bodies. In the days before we dared leave the fortress, the wolves feasted well. The few mutilated corpses we did recover were almost impossible to identify for *Clann Morna* had taken many heads.'

She grew quiet for a moment as her thoughts turned to the past, finally concluding that reflection with a sad sigh.

'Six years have passed, Bodhmhall. Had Crimall lived, he'd have returned to seek vengeance for Cumhal.'

Bodhmhall felt her heart sink for she knew her friend spoke the truth. There was no doubt then, no hope. She was last of Tréanmór's children, the last of her line.

Except for Demne.

She pursed her lips in thought. 'Was Cathal Bog present at the Gabhra ambush?'

'No. As always, he remained at Dún Baoiscne by your father's side.'

'And Becal?'

'Yes. Becal was there. He was one of the few survivors and even carried a badly wounded warrior back to the fortress on his shoulders.'

'And Lonán Ballach?'

Bé Bhinn looked surprised. 'The *rechtaire*? What cause would he have to go out with the warriors?'

Bodhmhall dismissed the subject with a shrug. 'I don't understand why *Clann Morna* suddenly attacked like they did. There'd been no spilling of blood between the tribes since I was a child. Even my father's bloodlust diminished over those years.'

Bé Bhinn turned her head and spat. 'Who can tell with *Clann Morna*. They're twisted sprites. Predators. Killers. They'd slice your throat as soon as look at you.'

Bodhmhall hesitated, wondering whether she should press the subject further. Clearly, her friend knew little of the attack beyond the fact that it had killed the one person she most cared for. The *bandraoi* was loathe to press her or upset her further.

Considering her old friend's reflection in the pool, Bodhmhall felt a sudden yearning to share her suspicions, to unburden herself of heavy secrets. As a child, Bé Bhinn had been nothing but discreet with confidences shared and yet the *bandraoi* couldn't help but think of the suffering she'd endured over the intervening years. Bodhmhall had seen many good people broken through grief and traumatic circumstance. She herself had changed as a consequence of her experiences since leaving Dún Baoiscne, growing ... How had Fiacail put it?

Less compassion, more steel.

The warrior's observation had rankled at the time, even as she'd recognised the truth to it. The years had made her less trusting, more callous, and although she despaired at harbouring such reservations with Bé Bhinn, she knew she couldn't risk revealing her thoughts to anyone.

'And your heart remains ever with the warrior woman: the Grey One?'

Bodhmhall's lightened mood abruptly darkened. Behind her, oblivious, Bé Bhinn continued to chatter.

'In truth, I never got a knowing of the woman warrior but I admired her mettle. She was strong, took nonsense from no-one.'

Bodhmhall silently fingered the polished, black stone pendant that hung from a leather cord about her neck, a gift from the Grey One shortly after they'd made a pairing.

A sudden chortle escaped Bé Bhinn's lips. 'Do you remember how she took Cathal Bog's sword from him? Gods! The look on his face.'

And although her heart was aching, Bodhmhall did remember, recalled it with perfect clarity in fact for that was the very day she'd first set eyes on the woman warrior. Summoned to Dún Baoiscne with her mercenary band for a possible service, the Grey One had been unimpressed by her father's brazen attempts to reduce her price by questioning her ability. Angry, she'd challenged her father's hulking bodyguard to prove the point.

And she'd proven it. Much to everyone's surprise – including Cathal Bog's – she'd initiated an attack of such sinuous ferocity that the *conradh* had been pressed backwards. Stumbling on a loose piece of stone, he'd momentarily lost his balance but that moment had been long enough for the Grey One to slide a blade beneath his jaw, drawing a bead of blood from his chin and forcing him to drop his weapon.

And there, suddenly, was something to snag her thoughts, a potential motivation for Cathal Bog's treachery that she'd never even considered until that very moment. The big warrior had displayed no obvious rancour following his combat with Liath Luachra. Concealed behind that blank stoicism however, she'd always sensed he'd not forgiven the woman warrior for embarrassing him in full view of his own people.

But then what motivation to betray his rí and those people? Simple vengeance against a single éclann seems wholly excessive.

Perhaps ... Perhaps ...

She bit her lip, suddenly feeling very weary.

There are times I wish I did not think so much.

Conscious that her friend would be expecting some kind of response, she gave a non-committal grunt. Absorbed in a battle of her own with a particularly unruly knot however, Bé Bhinn appeared to have missed her discomfort.

The Dún Baoiscne woman continued to groom the *bandraoí*'s hair in silence while Father Sun continued his path across the blue pastures above them. Finally, getting to her feet, she took two steps back and cocked her head at an angle to better admire her handiwork. 'You have beautiful hair, Bodhmhall. Dark and sleek as a night of rain. And here is the perfect clothing to go with it.'

Reaching for her basket, she rummaged through the contents, finally withdrawing a folded, faded-blue garment. Standing, she shook it free and held it up to display its full length.

'Do not take this as an insult, *a chara*, but your clothing smells like something a corpse was laid to rest in. Please honour us both by accepting a *léine* of mine.'

Taken by surprise, Bodhmhall clumsily accepted the proffered clothing and stuttered her thanks. She studied it for a moment, appreciating the fine needlework before pulling it on over her head. The garment was warm and dry, the material surprisingly soft and ... deliciously clean.

Bé Bhinn nodded in approval. 'Good. Perhaps even good enough to soften the hearts of *Clann Baoiscne* men towards you.' She gave a mischievous grin. 'Maybe they will take your hand and try to kiss you.'

Bodhmhall's lips gave a cynical twist. 'Of course.'

'But, yes! Yes! They'll set gentle whispers to your ear.' Bé Bhinn deepened her voice, producing a reasonable impression of a gruff male. 'Oh, beautiful Bodhmhall! First spring blossom, bright ray from the sun.'

'Sweetest berry of the mountain,' laughed the *bandraoi*, her heart lightening in response to the game.

'Flavour in the fruit.'

'Silver in the moonbeam.'

Both started to chuckle. 'It's true,' said Bodhmhall. 'Such declarations from the mouths of *Clann Baoiscne* men are daisies in a sick bull's puss.'

Sniggering, Bé Bhinn raised her two hands in an exaggerated, faux-romantic embrace. 'Oh, Bodhmhall ua Baoiscne!' she intoned. 'You are the sweetness in the honey. And, ooooh! How lovely is this pale hand, this slender waist ...'

'And the soft legs spread wide beneath.'

On the far side of the pool, the four old women broke off from their conversation, startled by the howl of laughter rippling across the water towards them. Concealing smiles behind knowing hands, they slowly shook their heads and returned to their discussions.

***

The two women took an indirect route back to Dún Baoiscne, following a gentle path to a sheltered glade west of the fortress where the tribal burial ground – and Demmán's resting place – was located. Approaching one of the grass-covered mounds in the shade of a sprawling ash tree, Bodhmhall paid her respects to the charming youth who'd been one of her earliest friends and a brother acolyte under Dub Tíre's instruction.

As she regarded the grave, Bodhmhall felt a rush of emotion clog her throat, a phlegmy lump that made it difficult to breathe. She hadn't been to this spot since ... Well, since ...

Do not think of that.

The *bandraoi* flinched.

She dragged her focus to the little bouquet of wildflowers held together with a flax tie that lay atop the mound. On the forest floor, just inside the treeline, a number of older, decomposing bouquets were also visible, prompting a twist of sadness in the *bandraoi*'s heart. Clearly, Bé Bhinn came here to tend the grave on a regular basis.

She glanced carefully to her left where the red-haired woman was wiping a tear from her cheek. 'It does not please Niall that I come here.'

Bodhmhall considered her in surprise. 'To your own brother's grave?'

'Because of the manner in which he died. Niall says it was ... unmanly.' Her lips compressed and she seemed to regard the grave with greater intensity. 'Do you think he's at peace, Bodhmhall?'

Bodhmhall bit her lip before responding. 'Demmán faced a dark and lonely end, *a chara*. But I'm sure he rests easy with the ancestors. Nothing can touch him where he dwells now.'

Bé Bhinn nodded. 'Bodhmhall ...' The *bandraoi* waited for her to finish.

'I've always wanted to ask you. Did you ever ...' She paused again, clearly distressed but determined to finish her question. 'Do you ... With your *Gift*. Did Demmán ever talk to you?'

Eyes fixed firmly on the red-haired woman, Bodhmhall slowly shook her head.

'Not even after th- '

'The *Gift* offers no such abilities, *a chara*.' Reaching out, she touched the other woman's shoulder and pulled her close to embrace her. 'Those times are done, Bé Bhinn. Demmán has passed and we must live even more furiously for his sake or it was all for nothing.' With a sigh, she released the trembling woman. 'Come. We should return to the stronghold. Unfortunately, I suspect further poor tidings will await us there.'

***

Leaving the glade, they made their way back to the grassland that stretched across to Dún Baoiscne and began the long traverse back to the fortress. At the base of the hill, heading up the gentle incline, Bodhmhall spotted the grey-bearded Niall Tuirseach leaning against the post of the entranceway, talking quietly with yet another under-aged sentry. Bé Bhinn's man watched as the two women made their way up the slope, nodding in formal acknowledgement to the *bandraoi* when they drew up before him.

'I see you, Bodhmhall.'

'I see you, Niall.'

There was a brief silence while Niall Tuirseach tugged a ponderous lower lip with his fingers, struggling to draw up the words he'd been instructed to pass on. 'Your father … Tréanmór. He desires your company at *An Halla Mór*. Knowing of your connection with Bé Bhinn, he asked me to seek you out.'

This time it was the *bandraoi*'s turn to offer a formal nod. 'My thanks, Niall.' Turning to her friend, Bodhmhall reached over to squeeze her shoulder. 'And my thanks to you too, *a chara*. For your company, for the *léine* but most of all for your unfaltering friendship.'

Bé Bhinn smiled but said nothing, the presence of her husband stifling some of the old zest she'd displayed at Poll na mBan.

Bodhmhall made no attempt to address Niall Tuirseach as she left the pair behind and entered the passage. Despite the formal courtesy of the old warrior's words, the stiffness in his stance left little doubt that he bore her no affection and resented her interaction with his woman.

Nursing her aching arm, she proceeded into the fortress, followed the grassy inner corridor to the second gateway and entered the passageway to emerge onto the central *lis*. At first, she thought the enclosure deserted for the central fire-pit was cold and there was no one to be seen apart from a single, unfamiliar sentry on the upper ramparts. Both doors of *An Halla Mór* stood open but its shadowed interior meant she could see nothing against the glare of the afternoon sun.

Stepping over the threshold of the meeting house, Bodhmhall paused to allow her eyes to adjust to the gloom then started when she noticed Cathal Bog sitting on a stool right next to her, just inside the doorway. The numerous horse-like carvings at his feet indicated that he'd been there for some time.

The surly-eyed warrior raised his head to regard her dispassionately, silently massaging the smashed gristle of his nose as she passed him by. Proceeding inside, she found Tréanmór sitting by the fire, occupying a posture almost identical to the one in which she'd left him the previous evening. Hearing the tread of her feet, he twisted about on his stool. With displeasure, she noted that he held one of the Five Friends nuzzled close to his chest in the manner of a child holding a favourite puppy.

Her father's eyes flickered over her, taking in the new *léine* and enhanced presentation. Wordlessly, he gestured at the two free stools beside the fire and Bodhmhall sat, placing her hands primly on her knees as she prepared herself for whatever was to come.

For several moments, Tréanmór said nothing, then suddenly he straightened up and reached both hands forward to rub his thighs. 'I may not have your *Gift* Daughter, but these bones sense the coming of winter with far greater accuracy than they ever used to.'

Bodhmhall nodded non-committedly, waiting for him to get to the point. Never a man for small-talk, she knew he wouldn't keep her waiting long.

'I have reflected on your tidings,' he informed her, absently shifting the skull from one arm to the other. 'Deep into the shadowed hours.' He paused to allow a melodramatic silence to build between them. Bodhmhall bit back an impatient retort.

Always he plays these games.

'I also had you come here to let you know that I've summoned those warriors living closest to the Cuirreach valley. It'll take them a day to assemble but by dawn tomorrow they'll be on the path for An Glenn Teann to search the land and escort those of your comrades who still survive to Dún Baoiscne.'

Bodhmhall felt something give inside her, a tightness in her chest that she hadn't noticed until that moment. 'Thank you, father.' She bowed her head, her gratitude entirely genuine. 'Thank you.'

'You are my daughter,' said Tréanmór in an offhand manner, as though this explained everything. 'What did you expect?'

Not so much.

'Meanwhile, I'd have you commence your search for the shadowed rot concealed within this fortress.' He coughed and wiped his lips with his hands. 'Becal has retired to your old haunt at Pluais na mBlaoisc – Cave of Skulls.' His gaze tightened in on her then, scrutinizing her for any reaction to the mention of Dub Tíre's old training site. His efforts at unsettling her however were completely in vain. The *bandraoi* maintained her implacable expression. Finally, with a sullen grunt, the *rí* of *Clann Baoiscne* conceded defeat.

'Lonán Ballach will also be returning from a visit with his people. I've left word for both to assist you on the pretext of improved relations and future trade with Ráth Bládhma so you have some latitude with the questions you wish to pose.' Her father paused then and offered her a sideways glance. 'You are certain you can identify the traitor?'

She nodded with exaggerated conviction 'I've come to understand the workings of the Adversary better than most. I can sense the trace of a pattern behind his actions. Together with the *Gift*, I believe I'll recognise the traitor.'

'Good.' Tréanmór stroked his beard, pleased. 'The Five Friends yearn fresh company and whisper that need to me at night. They assure me the presence of another would satisfy their yearning.'

Bodhmhall regarded him warily, unsure if he was being serious or not. Although she retained her composure, the mere possibility that her father now slept with those skulls was enough to fill her with alarm. Taking a deep breath, she massaged her brow as though from fatigue to disguise her unease.

'You've spoken of Becal and Lonán Ballach but ...' She inclined her head subtly in the direction of the doorway where Cathal Bog was still focussed on his whittling. Although he was out of earshot and appeared oblivious to their conversation, she'd kept her voice lowered throughout the discussion.

'You will not question Cathal Bog.'

The *bandraoi* stared, unable to conceal her surprise.

'He is not the traitor you seek.'

Again, Bodhmhall said nothing but her disapproval must have been plain to see.

'He cannot be the traitor,' her father insisted. 'There is nothing that would tempt him. Here at Dún Baoiscne, he has everything to satisfy him.'

Bodhmhall quietly considered that explanation. When she spoke again her voice was strictly neutral. 'In my experience, most men or women desire more than they possess. In one form or another.'

Tréanmór shook his head. 'Not Cathal. As long as he has his carving, a roof over his head, a warm bed and an occasional woman encouraged to share it ...' He shrugged.

Bodhmhall winced internally at the thought of any woman being 'encouraged' to share the gruesome warrior's bed but didn't try to argue the point further. Despite his intelligence, her father could be completely obdurate at times and there was no value in trying to change his mind once it was made up.

'Very well, father.' She rose to her feet. 'I will leave to seek out Lonán Ballach.'

'No. Seek Becal first for he's the one I'd trust last. And take care when you venture to Pluais na mBlaoisc. It's some distance from the fortress and you are not so loved here as you once were.'

Bodhmhall considered her father, the firm, bearded jaw, the eyes sharp and flickering from the glint of the fire. She nodded and made to go but he reached up to grasp her arm.

'There is one other matter to discuss before you leave. I would like to speak of your future.'

The *bandraoi* regarded him uncertainly. 'My future?'

'When your task at Dún Baoiscne is done. When the traitor's head drips scarlet above the fortress gates.'

Bodhmhall felt her own jaw tense. 'That will depend on what we learn. And then there's Liath Luachra and Ráth Bládhma to consider.'

'Mmm.' Tréanmór grunted and stroked his bearded chin. He looked displeased. 'You understand you are the last of my line.'

Bodhmhall felt a tremor of foreboding and wondered where the conversation was leading. 'Yes,' she answered warily.

'And you have learned of the hard days endured at Dún Baoiscne since you left? The sacrifices made, the indignities suffered?'

Once again, she nodded, feeling increasingly nervous.

'Much of our territory has been lost to the bastard *Morna*. Other tribes have followed their lead, nibbling at our lands, snatching the choicest ground. We even struggle to defend what ground remains.'

The fire in his eyes flared as he yielded to the anger that had been bubbling within him. Without warning, he lashed out with his foot and sent the spare stool tumbling into the fire pit.

Shaken by this unexpected violence, Bodhmhall stared at the stool, smouldering now in the heat of the flames. Her father made no move to retrieve it but instead turned to burden her with the full weight of his stare.

'*Clann Baoiscne* must reclaim the land lost to us, Daughter. And that will take time. Time to recover our strength, time for new *óglaigh* to fill the spaces left by their predecessors.' He paused. 'But time is a luxury I do not have.'

Grasping a stick from a nearby pile of kindling, he reached forward and stoked the fire, ignoring the stool now ablaze at its centre.

'But you, Bodhmhall. You have time. You have the youth to re-establish leadership of our lineage. Now is the moment to step up and assist your people, to have that empty belly of yours finally bear fruit.'

The *bandraoi* looked at her father in horror but, consumed in the rhetoric of his own agenda, he didn't seem to notice. She swallowed, her mouth suddenly dry. 'I was expelled from Dún Baoiscne. By those same people.'

Tréanmór flapped his hand in a dismissive gesture. 'That was politics, divisionary tactics to assuage the Druidic Order. Nothing more. Kinfolk and tribe is of greater consequence. Your brothers are no more but you can take their place to produce an heir.'

He'd started to play with the skull again and despite everything, Bodhmhall found herself transfixed by the sight. She stared helplessly as the fingers stroking the smooth sides of the cranium before she finally managed to pull her eyes away from the macabre sight. Fists clenched, she glared at her father with blazing eyes.

'My gratitude for your hospitality has been sincere, Father. But I have no wish to be drawn into your schemes, no desire to serve as brood mare for your political ends.'

Tréanmór was unimpressed, almost indignant. 'You were ever defiant, Daughter. Headstrong and airy. I've shown patience while you made a mockery of our family through your association with that wasted gristle but it's time to put such weakness of character aside. You have a responsibility, a duty to continue our line.'

'I lead my own life now. And my own settlement. That is where my responsibility lies.'

'Hah! You are *éclann*, Daughter. You have no tribe to protect you. Your settlement has how many warriors? Three? Four?' He gave a derisive snort. 'A determined *díberg* of any size would be enough to wipe you out. Any neighbouring tribe could make a claim on that land and you'd be powerless to prevent it.'

'It is the Great Wild, Father.' Bodhmhall could hear the heat in her own voice now. 'There are no neighbouring tribes. And you forget, we've already defeated one larger force sent against us.'

Tréanmór grew quiet then, regarding her silently through smouldering, lidded eyes. 'I see the fault now,' he said at last, his voice a barely audible croak. 'The lack of a mother and my own absence leading the people … There has been no-one to reign in your headstrong nature.'

He snorted then, his face a mask of complete disgust. 'Go!' He turned away so as not to face her. 'You are a disgrace to our line. Leave now.'

Needing no further encouragement, Bodhmhall turned and fled the hall.

***

The *bandraoi* was still trembling with anger when she reached the valley floor and started east across the fields in the direction of Pluais na mBlaoisc. Barely able to contain her rage, she cast a furious glare back at the fortress on the hilltop behind her, resisting the almost overwhelming urge to scream.

The unexpected turn to the conversation with her father had completely thrown her. Clearly, her earlier impressions of her father had been entirely erroneous. Tréanmór *had* changed, his habitual icy restraint eroded by the perfidious influence of the Five Friends, grief for his sons and the frustrations to his own political ambitions.

175

She kicked furiously at a loose sod, experiencing a surge of satisfaction at seeing it fly through the air and break apart on the ground several paces ahead of her. The previous evening, she'd been taken aback by the rare glimpse of her father losing his temper. This afternoon however, that anger seemed to have diminished, transformed into something altogether more vitriolic and savage.

And he was all the more dangerous for that.

The *bandraoi* stalked onwards, replaying segments of the conversation in her head, becoming so absorbed in her thoughts that when she finally looked up again, she was surprised to find she'd almost reached the eastern forest.

Drawing to a halt before the treeline, she inhaled deeply, using an old breathing technique to calm and focus her mind. Soothed, she started forwards once more, following the run of the treeline north towards a rough trail that cut directly into the trees.

The trail followed a circuitous route towards the foothills, weaving its way between large strands of giant oak and beech. Overhead, the autumn canopy had already faded to a golden brown and the *bandraoi* knew it wouldn't be long before that whole section of forest was stark and denuded.

After what seemed a much longer walk than she recalled from her youth, the trees finally cleared and she caught sight of the distinctive shape of Pluais na mBlaoisc – the Skull Cave – poking out from the vegetation. A large bare-stone mound, its likeness to a human skull was reinforced by its similar shape and two oval shaped apertures – the 'eye sockets' – that provided access to the inner caverns. These curved into the rock at opposing angles, connecting deeper inside to form a rough U-shaped passage.

The *bandraoi* pressed her tongue against her teeth, struggling with mixed feelings of nostalgia and revulsion. This strange rock formation and its immediate environs had been the home she'd shared with Dub Tíre, Becal and later, Demmán, for the better part of three years. An intense and fearful time, she'd probably have stayed longer if it hadn't been for the bonding with Fiacail mac Codhna organised by her father. At the time, the obligatory departure had actually been a huge relief for Bodhmhall. By then, any intellectual joy of learning had long since faded, quashed and corroded by Dub Tíre's mercurial temperament and the strict ban on visiting family and friends that he'd imposed on his acolytes. The *draoi* had been greatly displeased to lose the skills of his most promising student and had complained bitterly, but there'd been little he could do to oppose the *rí* of *Clann Baoiscne's* decision.

She bit her lip.

And this is Becal's now.

Looking down at her hands, Bodhmhall realised they were shaking. Angered by this expression of weakness, she clenched them repeatedly until the trembling ceased, ignoring the pain it caused her injured arm, now resting once more in its sling. When she felt ready, she advanced towards the cave, entered though the right 'eye socket' and followed the curving passage around to its apex. There, it intersected with another, much shorter, passage that cut deeper into the rock for four or five paces and led into a wide cavern. Roughly triangular in shape, this narrowed to a tight gap that had been curtained off with a leather flap.

Illuminated by a pair of flickering torches and a low fire smouldering in a central fire pit, the cavern had a surprisingly cosy appearance, appropriate given that when Bodhmhall inhabited it, the area had served as the main living quarters.

'Becal?'

Her voice rang hollowly off the stone walls. There was no reply but the fire suggested the *draoi* wasn't far away.

Repressing her nervousness, the *bandraoi* looked around, struck by how little the place had changed. The ancient hand paintings on the western wall, the crude wooden shelving, the dried herbs, mortar and pestle and the bowls of crushed ingredients were all exactly as she remembered. Even the stones of the fire pit looked as though they hadn't been replaced in all the years she'd been away.

The one difference that did leap out at her however was the absence of three of the four sleeping platforms that used to occupy the area just inside the entrance. Now a single sleeping platform remained and the empty space around it was a stark reminder of times past.

Moving across to the leather flap, the *bandraoi* brushed it to one side but even with the light of the torches it was too dark to see into the next cavern. She recalled that it was circular in shape and had a wooden door set into the rock at a point directly opposite where she was now standing. Presumably that door was sealed for it led into a draughty fissure that penetrated down into the earth for over twenty paces, terminating in An Brocach – The Burrow – a tiny space that could only be reached by crawling on one's hands and knees.

Dub Tíre had been singularly obsessed with An Brocach during her time at Pluais na mBlaoisc, convinced that the sensory deprivation it induced had the ability to augment the effectiveness of the *imbas forosnai* ritual. The *draoi* would retreat there on a regular basis in his efforts to commune with the Great Mother or to seek guidance from the ancestors. At such times, his acolytes were usually glad to see him go although that relief was tempered by the inevitable consequence of his return. For the first day or two following those reappearances, Dub Tíre was usually raving, seeing malevolent spirits in every moonbeam, portents in every breath of wind or sudden bird movement. Sometimes he'd suffer violent fits that left him thrashing on the ground, spitting and foaming at the mouth while they struggled to hold him down.

The first time this happened, Bodhmhall had noticed an odd tang to the *draoi*'s breath, something she also noticed on every subsequent occasion. Over time, she'd come to learn that the smell was that of *beacán scammalach* – dream mushroom – an intoxicant used by the *draoi* to promote dreamlike states and visions. Dub Tíre had generally explained the fits away as successful manifestations of the Great Mother's touch. Bodhmhall had never spoken up to contradict but she'd known this couldn't be true, only because she too had performed the *imbas forosnai* ritual and had succeeded on the first attempt.

An action she'd never repeated since.

The sound of footsteps in the exterior passage drew her back from the past and she stepped guiltily away from the leather flap. It had barely dropped back into place when Becal entered the cavern, starting awkwardly when he spotted her.

'Bodhmhall!'

Once he'd got over his initial surprise, she noted how quickly he accepted her presence. Her visit had been expected.

'I see you, Becal,' the *bandraoi* answered, completing the traditional formality. She shifted her weight awkwardly from one foot to the other. 'I understand Pluais na mBlaoisc serves as your home now.'

The *Clann Baoiscne draoi* shrugged. 'I've little enough say in the matter. Your father prefers that I remain outside the fortress and although they're content to attend my rituals, the people also favour a safe distance from the *draoi* at most other times.'

Bodhmhall had to nod in sympathy. She too had suffered the fickle nature of the *Clann Baoiscne* people's superstitions.

'Tréanmór sent word that you would come.' He hesitated and regarded her with suspicion. 'But he was vague as to why.'

The *bandraoi* eyed him thoughtfully. Although she'd prepared a set of questions to disguise the true intent of the interrogation, her instincts now urged her to take a less circumspect approach.

'I seek information.'

'Oh,' said Becal simply. 'Very well.' He took a seat on a log by the fire and gestured for her to take the single stool beside it. Settling down, Bodhmhall considered the *Clann Baoiscne draoi*. She'd expected some degree of bitterness as a result of his dismissal from An Halla Mór but there'd been no bite to his words, no smouldering resentment at his treatment. If anything, he seemed oddly acquiescent and sat with his shoulders hanging, slumped like a beaten dog.

Placing a pot on the metal rack above the fire, he quietly stoked the ashes, tossing on a few slivers of wood and peat to build up the flames.

'What is it you wish to know?'

Facing him directly, Bodhmhall slowly applied the *Gift*, watching as the glow of the *draoi*'s lifelight bloomed into prominence. 'I wish to know how my brothers died.'

Becal seemed to grimace at that but she ignored the facial gesture, concentrating instead on the yellow flame now visible against the deepening gloom of the chamber. With practice, any facial expression could be manufactured. The lifelight, constant and relatively unwavering, was far more difficult to read but anything it did reveal would almost certainly be true.

'Your brothers died in battle. You already know this.'

'I know nothing of the details. You were there. Tell me what happened.'

The *draoi* released a wheezing sigh, covering his discomfort by reaching over to stir the contents of the pot. 'It's not an experience I like to dwell on. I'm uncertain what you wish to hear.'

'Tell me how it started. Why were so many of our warriors at Gabhra?'

'It was a *fian*.' He looked at her and although focussed on the lifelight she sensed that he'd blinked in surprise. 'I thought you knew.'

Bodhmhall shook her head.

'Huh.' Although he sounded surprised at her lack of knowledge, Becal continued. 'There were strange sightings to the north in the days leading up to the attack. A hunter had come to Dún Baoiscne speaking of two campfires in areas of rough terrain where no-one dwelled. That same day, a farmer came seeking help to search for his son. They too had seen smoke from fires. Fearful of rustlers, his son had ventured out to investigate but never returned.

Suspecting a *díberg* in the area, Cumhal assembled a *fian*, a band of thirty men, seasoned warriors and a handful of the elder *óglaigh* deemed ready for blooding. We departed the fortress at first light the following morning.'

'Why d- ' the *bandraoi* began but Becal had already anticipated the question.

'I'd already planned to travel north to replenish my supply of *gaméis*. You know...' He made some gesture with his hand but with her full attention on the lifelight, Bodhmhall couldn't make it out. 'The plot in the Gabhra woods that Dub Tíre showed us. It made sense to travel together.'

Bodhmhall made no reply but pursed her lips in thought. *Gaméis*, a herb greatly valued for its medicinal properties, was exceptionally rare and *draoi* often spent an inordinate amount of time seeking it out. The plot discovered by Dub Tíre was the only location within two days march of Dún Baoiscne with a relatively consistent, if variable, supply during the late summer months.

'We separated at the Gabhra marsh. The *fian* continued their northern path while I started up the hill to Dub Tíre's plot. I'd not travelled far when I heard a strange sound, a great whirring or humming, like the song of a thousand flies.'

Having heard that sound once herself, Bodhmhall knew immediately what he was referring to. 'Javelins.'

'Yes. Javelins.' Becal's voice was hoarse. 'I scrambled back in the direction the *fian* had taken, following the ridge to try and find a path down to intercept them. By then the screams had already started.' He had to pause for a moment and when he spoke again his voice was choked with emotion.

'I broke out of the trees, onto a bare section of slope and looked down to see our men pinned to the earth. War-painted *Clann Morna* warriors were swarming from the trees beyond the trail, their bellows and war cries shaking the very air.'

Once again, she heard the *draoi* pause as though to recover his breath.

'I saw your brother, Cumhal. He was one of the few spared from the javelin volley. He led a spirited defence with the men remaining to him and for a time they rallied, defiant in a great clash of spears. Several *Morna* men went down but their numbers were overwhelming.

Your brother took a cowardly stab to the back from some stripling. He fell but pierced as he was, he still had a sting to him. Goll mac Morna moved in for the killing stroke but took Cumhal's sword point in the eye. To this day, they say he bears an eyepatch to hide the hardened scar tissue.'

The agitation in his voice faded as he drew to the end of his tale. 'The last I saw of Cumhal, he was being crushed beneath a tide of warriors, then a hail of stabbing, red-pointed spears.'

The *draoi* lapsed into silence and although Bodhmhall had to swallow the sob of emotion building up in her own throat, she forced herself to continue, studying Becal's lifelight for any sign of falsehood. She could see nothing to suggest his dismay was anything but genuine.

'You saw all this?'

'Yes.'

'With your own eyes?'

'Yes.'

'But how …? How did you survive?'

'The slope on which I was standing stretched far to either side. Its height prevented me from descending but it also prevented the *Clann Morna* warriors from reaching me. Knowing they'd find a path soon enough, I fled. I came across a single wounded straggler on my flight to the Cuirreach valley. We were the only survivors.'

Bodhmhall could feel a tightness constrict her heart. 'And Crimall? What of Crimall?'

'Crimall was leading the vanguard with two *óglaigh*. They would have been the first to enter the thicket of trees from where the *Mac Morna* warriors emerged. They couldn't have survived.' He wiped his eye and sighed. 'A few days later, we were finally able to return and retrieve what remained of the bodies. We found the tattooed leg of one *óglach* but nothing more. We also found what was left of Cumhal but …' His voice trailed off.

Overcome with emotion, Bodhmhall's grip on the *Gift* loosened and the cavern immediately grew brighter. Becal's lifelight was absorbed into the light.

The *bandraoi* turned away, determined not to let him see her weep. Despite this, the *draoi* reached over to place one tentative hand on her shoulder. 'I'm sorry, Bodhmhall. I can see how my report wounds you and I … I know we've had our differences but I'd not willingly place the burden of such tales upon you.'

Refusing to acknowledge that statement of sentiment, Bodhmhall regained control of her emotions and swung about to face the *Clann Baoiscne draoi*. Her heart, numbed by his story, ensured her expression offered nothing but an impassive blankness.

'It is strange.'

181

'Wh- what?' Becal was hesitant, unable to read her, yet disturbed by her rejection of his attempt at sympathy.

'The *Clann Morna* attack. Coming in such a manner without warning or provocation. Was there trouble, some bad blood between the tribes before the assault?'

Becal considered her question but then slowly shook his head.

'So then, why would the *Clann Morna* suddenly break the peace like that? In all the years since that fateful day has no-one ever sought to discover the reasoning behind it?'

Again, Becal shook his head. 'There's been no interaction between the tribes since the attack, no communication of any kind. Peace was established only through the intervention of the Druidic Order who negotiated for both tribes. Tréanmór had to cede land and an annual tribute of cattle to avoid the recommencement of hostilities but I doubt he or any other member of *Clann Baoiscne* would deign to speak directly with the killers of their husbands and sons.

They're twisted sprites. Predators. Killers. They'd slice your throat as soon as look at you.

Recalling Bé Bhinn's passionate reaction, Bodhmhall had to acknowledge the truth to that observation. With a sigh, she wearily rose to her feet. 'You have my gratitude, Becal. For your forthrightness, I thank you.'

'You're leaving?' Becal too, hurriedly got to his feet. 'So soon? I thought we might speak of other matters.'

'I have no heart for discussion, Becal. There's nothing more to be said. Besides, I leave Dún Baoiscne as soon as possible for I'm needed back at Ráth Bládhma.'

'But I wished to talk of the old days, to rekindle our friendship.' The *draoi* looked panic-stricken. 'Bodhmhall, I understand your anger towards me but what could I do? Dub Tíre terrified me. Your father too.'

The *bandraoi*'s expression hardened. 'Becal - '

'You must speak to your father for me.' The *draoi* pressed ahead, ignoring the expression of surprise on her face at the abrupt shift in the conversation. 'Tréanmór bears a grudge against me. He blames me for the death of your brothers and has me isolated here.'

'Becal, my father simply despises you. He has little other than contempt for you.'

The *draoi* staggered backwards as though he'd been physically struck. Pale and flustered, he stared at her, speechless. As she coolly returned that regard, the *bandraoi* wondered whether anyone else had ever told him that to his face. Overcome with disgust, she gathered up her cloak and prepared to leave.

'Wait!' Becal reached out, grasping both her shoulders as though to physically prevent her from departing. Seeing the flare of anger in her eyes, he suddenly dropped his hands and backed away again. 'Bodhmhall, please! You must speak to him. I never thought my life would lead to this, this ... living in isolation like Dub Tíre. Here at Pluais na mBlaoisc, I am hollowed out from loneliness.'

'Becal, I'm leaving now.'

As she walked towards the passage, he followed closely behind, pleading and desperate. 'You were always Dub Tíre's favourite, his 'talented one'. By rights ... '

'Leave me, Becal.'

'By rights, it's you who should be serving as *draoi* of *Clann Baoiscne*. Not I. If you could b-'

He stopped talking.

Bodhmhall ua Baoiscne had entered the narrow passage and departed the cavern.

Chapter Ten

Liath Luachra was already drenched by the time she'd made ten paces from the cave mouth. Rain was pummelling the forest canopy, the sheer force of it driving the branches downwards. Water pooled on every flat surface, filled every depression and overflowed in leaking rivulets too numerous to count.

Consumed by her own internal seething, the woman warrior was oblivious to the storm's true severity and pounded unthinkingly uphill towards the saddle. As she crested the hill however, she found herself confronted by a gale with such a high-pitched, piercing whine it drowned out every other sound and made it almost impossible to think. Rainwater flushed through the forest canopy, streaming down onto her head and shoulders, her arms, and even down the inside of the leather battle harness.

Gazing down the steep, shadowy slope to the lake, the woman warrior's determination momentarily wavered and fearing deflection from her purpose, she acted on instinct, impulsively launching herself from the edge.

The descent was far more terrifying than she'd anticipated. Loosened by the deluge, the soil was treacherously unstable so her feet repeatedly slid out from under her and the woman warrior ended up mostly slithering on her back and buttocks, counteracting that downward momentum by grasping at bushes and tree trunks to slow her fall. It wasn't long before she tumbled to a halt on the flat ground at the base of the hill, her rear caked with muck and grime. Levering herself off the sticky earth, she got to her feet and stumbled forwards, arms raised in front of her face to protect herself from the branches being whipped by the blustering squalls.

Careering through the undergrowth, she emerged onto the shingle bank, exposed to the full force of the storm. There a sudden gust took her by surprise, striking with such power it knocked her off her feet and sent her scuttling back into the relative shelter of the treeline.

Clambering back to her feet, she clutched the mildewed trunk of an oak tree and stared out at the lake, a frothy layer of spume churned up by the pounding rain. Captivated by the sight, it took her a moment to realise how far the water level had risen since the last time she'd seen it. Short wavelets now lapped the upper edge of the shingle shore and threatened to drive all the way up to the treeline itself. Given the force of the downpour, she knew it wouldn't take long for the water to flush down through the mountain tributaries and into the main waterway. It was only a matter of time before the lake levels rose still further and made the crossing even more difficult.

There was no time to waste.

Shoulders hunched, she ran forwards onto the shingle beach, pushing through the wall of grey rain until she could feel cold splashes against her upper shins. Wading waist deep into the turbulent foam, she plunged headfirst into the water and kicked furiously to drive herself from shore. Swimming underwater at first, she surfaced about ten paces from where she'd first dived. Almost immediately, it was a struggle to breathe, her mouth and nose obstructed by spray whipped up from the wind and the extraordinary ricocheting effect of rain hitting the water. Twisting her head, she managed to suck in a lungful of wet air then settled into a powerful stroke, ploughing forward through the churning waters in a rough line for the easternmost point of the logjam.

The extreme conditions meant the crossing was far more difficult than earlier that afternoon. Swimming against the wind and current made it seem she was covering twice the distance. Focused on her stroke and regular gasps for air, she didn't dare break the pattern to see how much distance remained. Feeling her body start to flag, she was greatly relieved when her hand finally struck the rough shale of the opposite shore.

Scrabbling for purchase, she hauled herself into waist-deep water below a raised section of the bank and sat exhausted and wheezing for breath. Rain continued to drum painfully against her head. Disoriented by the muddying effect of the downpour and the growing darkness, it took a moment to work out that she'd made it to a point several paces beyond the logjam.

Too tired to feel any elation, she continued to sit struggling for breath, flinching when a snap of blue lighting lit up the riverbank and revealed the logjam already unravelling, breaking apart as a result of the rising water levels. Pulling close to the bank, the Grey One tentatively raised her eyes above the lip and peered around. A fresh lightning bolt momentarily blinded her but confirmed the absence of any enemy warriors.

Hauling herself onto the bank, she staggered for the nearest trees, her leg muscles heavy and soft from the swim, her battle harness waterlogged and chaffing, the woollen leggings hanging in loose sodden folds. Pausing to catch her breath, she scanned the terrain stretching off to the high promontory at the river bend, a mere three hundred paces from where she crouched yet barely visible through the rain. There was still no evidence of any enemy warriors which, given the storm's ferocity, she'd expected. The loss of their comrade to the marshland would have discouraged them from any further advance towards the ridge. Their scout would have alerted them to the tracks of the fugitives leading into the water but they'd obviously decided not to cross the lake either. With the storm bearing down on them, they'd really had but one option for shelter: back the way they'd come.

With a groan, she lurched out of the trees and started for the distant bend but after just a few steps she knew she was in trouble. Reducing her to a clumsy shuffle, her lower joints were aching from the day's manic run and after the swim both legs felt as though they might give way beneath her at any moment.

Stumbling to a halt, she started rubbing them furiously, feeling the clench of the muscles even through the sodden material of her leggings. She grimaced, recalling how during her time with *Na Cinéaltaí* there'd been many times like this, times when she'd had to push herself to her physical limits, fighting pain and fatigue through sheer bloody-mindedness.

And it had always hurt. One way or the other it had always hurt. That seemed the one true constant between those days and the present. The pain never stopped.

She managed another twenty or so paces towards the bend before accepting the fact that she had to change her plans. Her body was seizing up and on the point of failing her. To make matters worse, she had no idea where the enemy camp might be located. Despite having passed through this territory, the physical stress of the run meant her memory of the landscape was hazy. She could barely recall what was around the bend not to mind any potential areas where they might have sought shelter. With the imminent onset of total darkness, any hope of locating the enemy campsite was now completely impractical.

Meanwhile, she too had to get out of the storm or she'd almost certainly end up dying from exposure. Tiredness sucked at her ability to think but, ignoring the physical discomfort of rain and wind, she looked towards the trees. The only place she was likely to find shelter was somewhere along the cliffs. Fronted by forest, the worst of the rain would have been deflected and there were bound to be cracks and crannies in the cliff face big enough to crawl into, hopefully small enough to help retain some of her body heat.

Stop wasting time.

Once again, she shambled back towards the trees, relieved to be out of the worst of the wind which was now actively sucking heat from her body through the wet clothing. Pushing through the scrub and the rapidly thickening darkness, it didn't take long to reach the base of the cliffs where she staggered to a halt and looked up at the darkness looming ominously above her.

She followed the cliffs east, stumbling through patches of undergrowth and tangled thorn, barely able to see her way in the dark. She was shivering uncontrollably by now, her skin chilled, her vision muddied from fatigue and she feared she wasn't going to last much longer. Just at the point where she'd almost given up hope, she came across a series of craggy, waist-height fissures in the lower cliff face that offered at least some possibility of shelter. A few paces further on from that she could just make out several flat moss-coated slabs that had broken away from the upper section of the cliff and landed at an angle to create a kind of tent-like shelter that concealed yet another of the many fissures in the base of the cliff.

Entering the rude shelter, the woman warrior immediately felt warmer although she suspected the effect was illusionary, a side-effect of her weakening body. Knees creaking, she crouched to see how far the crack penetrated the rock but struggled to see anything with the light now almost completely gone. She frowned, gnawing at her lip but knew she had no choice. It was too dark and she was just too tired to go any further.

Squeezing into the tunnel-like crack, she started crawling, following the curve of the crack by touch alone and surprised to find it coated with thick layers of desiccated leaves and woody debris, presumably blown inside over the years. After four or five paces, the crack seemed to curve sharply and then opened out dramatically. Pausing, she stretched out a hand on either side but was no longer able to touch the walls.

Scooping some of the dead leaves into a pile, she used the flints from her tinder pouch to light it, the sparks taking hold of the desiccated leaves almost immediately. As her little fire flared up, the resulting flames cast a soft yellow glow that allowed her to make out her surroundings: a surprisingly large cave high enough to stand up in and measuring roughly five paces by six. What interested her most of all however was the even larger pile of dry leaves and debris she spotted just off to the left of her fire.

Hurrying towards it, the Grey One quickly stripped out of her clothing and bent down to rearrange the debris into a thick, nest-like bed. Climbing into the middle of the pile, she lay back and scooped the layers over her legs and lower body, then her stomach and chest. Just before the fire flickered out she had time to drag her sodden clothing on top to act as another layer.

With the light gone, the Grey One lay shivering incessantly, staring up into the darkness. Slowly, very slowly, the nest captured what little heat her body was still able to generate and she began to feel the first sensations of warmth. Comforted by the knowledge she was going to survive, her internal tension finally begin to unravel and her heartbeat slowed. Free of the need to focus on her immediate survival, her thoughts inevitably drifted back to Bodhmhall.

Although the discovery of the *bandraoi's* cloak still left a hollow in her heart, there was also a perverse sense of justification, a kind of sneering 'I told you so' confirmation that happiness was a delusion. Over their ten year relationship, Bodhmhall's intimacy and affection had calmed the woman warrior, the *bandraoi's* personal magic preventing her from slipping back into dark shadows of the manic creature she'd once been. But now Bodhmhall was gone.

Since the moment she'd found the cloak, she could actually sense the regression taking place inside, her senses hardening, the slow return of old traits and habits of a lifetime. She'd always been aware of that capacity for violence lingering beneath the surface, latent but deadly, ready to poke through the thin veneer of domesticity.

She felt a sudden desire to spit.

Now that her path had come full circle she had no choice but to acknowledge the killer she'd once been, to embrace it. Now was the time for vengeance and although Liath Luachra the domesticated *conradh* of Ráth Bládhma might not have achieved it, Liath Luachra the crazed mercenary of *Na Cinéaltaí* most certainly could.

Beneath the leaves, she fingered the knife she'd taken from Fintán, using the pain of its point against her finger to kindle a more lucid hate for Gob An Teanga Gorm. She imagined plunging the blade into the hatchet-faced warrior's neck, a quick thrust followed by a deft twist of the wrist to intensify the damage.

And then withdrawing it, the slick suck of moist tissue, the crimson spurt of arterial blood, the unmistakeable tang of wet metal in the air.

Bloodsucker. A good name for the knife.

That thought made her pause. She had no idea if the knife in her hand was a named weapon, if it had already been blooded or not.

I'll ask Fintán.

The sudden absurdity of that notion was enough to make her wince. In the end, the *Lamraighe* youth had proven himself a competent and loyal, if slightly annoying, companion. She felt some guilt at deserting him in the manner she had but there was nothing she could do about that now.

The simple truth was that she would not see him again. She had made her decision. She had nothing worth living for but vengeance. She would take the battle directly to those who'd taken the only thing she cared about, give them a fight to end all fights.

And she would die on her own terms.

***

'Grey One.'

'Uh?'

'Grey One. Rouse yourself. We must speak.'

Liath Luachra's eyes flickered open at the sound of the *bandraoi*'s voice. For a moment she sat silent, flustered and confused for she was crouched by a standing stone on the crest of a high hill. All around her, the ground was bare of vegetation, the earth a barren brown that looked as though as it had been scorched by fire in the recent past.

A soft breeze ruffled her hair but the air wasn't particularly cold. Sunlight warmed her back and caused spirals of moisture to uncoil into the air from the frosted surface of the standing stone and the metal blades of her javelins.

'Bodhmhall?'

She looked around but could see no sign of the *bandraoi*. At a loss, she raised one hand to brush the thick strands of hair from her eyes. For some reason this struck her as unnatural or wrong.

Suddenly frustrated, she pulled a javelin free and struck the blade against the stone. The vibration of the blow travelled up the length of her arm.

'What are you doing?' Bodhmhall's voice startled her, more because of its gentle reproach then for the fact that it seemed to unfurl out of the air.

'I battle the world.'

'Why?'

She tried to speak but the words caught in her throat and she had to struggle to get them out. 'Because I despise it.'

She heard a quiet sigh and then the *bandraoi* was sitting beside her, one hand warm and soft over her own. Looking at those beautiful features, the long dark hair flowing in the breeze, the woman warrior suddenly felt like crying.

'What's happening? I don't understand.'

The *bandraoi* pointed into the distance. 'There's something you need to know.'

Somehow, even as she turned to look, the woman warrior knew she wasn't going to like what she saw. Sure enough, her heart sank when her gaze fell on the tall column of smoke far away in the distance, its source concealed from view by the shoulder of a second hill.

Liath Luachra tried to groan but for some reason found herself unable to do so. As she struggled to make a sound, the *bandraoi* took her face in her hands and stared deep into her eyes.

'Wake up, Grey One. He's here. Wake up!'

189

She woke with a bone rattling thump, as though she'd fallen from a height before striking the earth. As always when roused in the Great Wild, she did so without noise or movement, still and unmoving, senses absorbing the sensations of the world about until she was physically ready to sit upright.

She blinked, confused. The stony refuge had taken on an eerie green glow, a kind of sickly phosphorescence that softened the edge of the darkness and allowed her to make out some of her shadowy surroundings.

There's someone here.

Beneath the leaves, her fingers grasped the hilt of the knife. She didn't know how she could possibly know but her instincts were screaming at her, in total contrast to what her senses were saying. She could see nothing, hear nothing, smell nothing.

To the right of her makeshift nest, a shadow suddenly detached itself from the wall, a tall man-shaped figure that moved soundlessly to loom over her. The Grey One stared, completely rigid with terror. The figure had no face, no facial features of any kind, nothing but an unnatural black smoothness where the eyes and mouth should normally have been. Breathless, she watched as the *Fear Dubh* – the Black Man – bent down to crouch over her, drawing its head low until less than a finger's breadth separated it from her face.

Trembling, the woman warrior found she could do nothing but stare back in horror. The figure had no breath, no smell, nothing but a black emptiness.

Her hand exploded from the leafy detritus, thrusting upwards with the knife to target the hollow in the neck between the *Fear Dubh*'s jaw and chest. To her horror, the knife sank directly into the blackness, the complete absence of friction causing her fist to be swallowed up as well. Wide-eyed, she stared while the '*Fear Dubh*'s' shoulders shook with what she took for mirth.

Slowly, the terrifying shape moved one hand down over the pile of leaves, hovering momentarily over the spot where her groin was located. Before she had time to even guess at its intentions, she saw the hand plunge deep into the leaves, wincing at the anticipation of contact.

I feel nothing!

It was true. Despite the fact that the *Fear Dubh*'s hand and wrist should have been wedged deep inside her crotch, she could feel nothing, absolutely nothing apart from a rising anger at the clearly calculated, sexual affront.

She slashed up wildly with the knife again but with each swipe, the blade passed harmlessly through the '*Fear Dubh*'s' frictionless form. Sensing its growing amusement at her increasing bewilderment and frustration, the woman warrior tried to snarl but just as in the dream, found herself incapable of producing any kind of sound.

Summoning every ounce of strength, the Grey One lunged from the leafy bed and opened her mouth to scream and ....

***

Startled, she sat up, layers of soil and leaves and clothing falling away from her chest.

Too terrified to move, she stared around in hushed, heart-shaking dread.

The cave was silent and although there was a vague grey smear where the crack in the rock led outside, it was otherwise completely dark. There was no phosphorescence, no *Fear Dubh* and her instincts no longer tingled.

A dream. It was a dream.

Baffled and shaken, she tried to roll onto her side but found her neck had kinked overnight and her left arm was asleep where she'd lain on it. A deep stiffness had also settled into her joints and there wasn't a part of her that didn't ache.

Rising to her knees, she wasn't entirely sure how she felt. Physically battered, of course. And somewhat bewildered and disturbed by the strangeness of the dream. She shook her head in distaste. The dream hadn't felt like a dream. Meanwhile, the memory of the spectre's sexual slight filled her with sick fury and she had no-one to vent it on.

It was still dark when the woman warrior wriggled out of her shelter. Rising to her feet in the hollow of the leaning boulders, she stared out at the grey of the incoming dawn and scratched absently at those areas where grit had worked its way inside her clothing. She was pleased to see the storm had passed but its moisture still hung heavy in the air, dripping liberally from trees and bushes. Breathing in through her nostrils, she absorbed the Great Wild's damp silence, the fresh, earthy odour of a new day.

The Grey One sensed a strange kind of jaded exhaustion to the forest's rhythm that morning. With the cessation of the storm and the passing of danger, she had the intuitive impression of revival. Birds and other forest creatures were timidly venturing forth from their nests and burrows, familiar behaviours and patterns being resumed as life's cycles continued.

The Grey One knew all this instinctively. She'd always had a kind of intimate connection with the Great Wild, an intrinsic relationship that in some ways surpassed her relationships with people. Intimately familiar with its sights, its sounds, its smells and its textures, she understood the unstated rules and the complexities, the sheer physicality of existence, the violence,

191

the ongoing competition for survival. She could lose herself in the Great Wild's immensity, become part of it, whereas with people she felt exposed. She struggled to make sense of their motivations and often misunderstood their intentions or social norms.

Cold and brittle, the woman warrior stumbled through the semi-darkness in the direction of the river. Emerging onto the slightly brighter expanse of the river, it was still difficult to distinguish much in the pre-dawn glimmer. The land was grey, a series of contrasting shades that seemed more form that substance. The river was a dark smudge against a mildly lighter backdrop, the far bank little more than a ghostly impression, half seen or imagined through the gloom.

Moving painfully, the Grey One started towards the promontory, pausing only to quench her thirst and rummage for food by some rotting logs, overturning them to feed on the grubs and beetles underneath. The insects were crunchy, tasteless and provided less than a fistful of sustenance but chewing them kept the worst of her hunger at bay.

Reaching the promontory, she followed the curve of the river bend to the dense thicket of ash, working her way through it until she hit the chaotic stretch of mangled trees and root systems that had been so hard to negotiate the previous day. Ironically, the storm seemed to have gouged many of the obstacles free. With the subsequent drop in the river level, the bank – admittedly much narrower – was now relatively clear of obstruction, although areas remained where she had to crawl through the muck on her hands and knees.

Clambering back onto more solid ground, Liath Luachra got to her feet and considered the landscape ahead. Despite having passed through here the previous day, none of it looked familiar. As the open river bank was too exposed for her liking, the woman warrior squelched though the saturated grass towards the treeline. From there she started south, quietly working her way through the scrub just inside the treeline, studying the ground ahead for any sign of movement.

Less than six hundred paces from where she'd left the river, a sudden prickle set her hackles on end and caused her to freeze in mid-step.

She wasn't alone.

Dropping to the ground in the shadow of a broad oak, the Grey One made no movement as she let the scents and sounds of the Great Wild wash over her. In the forest, stillness and shadows were your allies, a motley grey cloak that absorbed you into the background. Movement and noise were what tended to draw the eye.

Overhead, the forest birds continued their noisy chitter, apparently relieved to have survived the storm. The leafy boughs of the evergreens creaked gently in the wind. She could hear or see nothing out of the ordinary but she trusted her instincts, instincts which had never yet misled her.

When she finally judged it safe to move again, the Grey One did so at a crawl, snaking painfully slowly through the grass and undergrowth on her stomach. Experience had taught her to approach forest battles without haste. Nothing killed a person faster in such battle situations than impatience.

At a small patch of earth between two flax plants, she found the first indication that her caution was justified. A footprint. She considered it quietly, chewing on the inside of her cheek. Flat and well-formed, it was deep and looked to be the print of a male foot, a big one at that. Raising her head, she carefully looked around and now she'd found one, other clues to someone's passing became apparent as well. Two small patches of flattened grass mere steps from where she lay. A few steps further on, beside a large thorn bush, was a broken twig that would have taken some substantial weight to cause the woody material to compress and snap the way it had.

She poked the imprint with her forefinger then ran it around the inside rim. The sides were relatively firm and didn't crumble or fall apart at her touch.

Recent, then.

It had to be. Certainly after the rain had stopped. If it'd been created during the downpour the print would have been a lot looser or, given the strength of the downpour, quite possibly washed away.

And probably nearby.

That made sense. No normal person would have willingly ventured out in such a storm – and here she unconsciously overlooked her own actions in that regard. Whoever had left the footprint therefore, would only have done so after the worst of the storm had passed. And they were unlikely to have strayed far from their refuge.

Keeping her head low, she scrutinised the surrounding forest, seeking a likely location for the enemy campsite. Her own experience suggested it'd be somewhere along the cliffs, a crevice or a cave like the one she'd discovered. The forest itself would certainly have provided insufficient shelter. Unfortunately, there was no indication, no tell-tale clue. She could detect no smoke from a campfire, no sound of movement or the normal bustle of a camp, not even the whiff of smoke on the breeze.

The woman warrior found herself nodding at that. She was clearly dealing with capable opponents and in a strange way she'd always approved of competent enemies.

Moving at a crawl, she retreated the way she'd come, working away from the river in a curving movement that brought her circling around to approach that same area from a much denser section of forest. Obliged to move slowly, the process took longer than she'd hoped and although it remained dark below the forest canopy, those sections of sky glimpsed through the breaks had already started to take on a piss-weak half-light.

She was still slithering forward when the sound of a hacking cough made her freeze. Breathless, she waited, tense and ready to run although she knew the thick clumps of reddening fern effectively concealed her from view. Peering carefully through a gap in the fronds, she caught an unexpected flash of white within the gloom less than twenty paces from where she was lying. Intrigued, she continued to watch and was eventually rewarded with another, this time it lasted long enough for her to make out what it was: a pale face peering around a tree trunk in the direction of the river. The Grey One shuddered. In the deep shadow of those trees she knew she'd never have noticed the hidden warrior if her instincts and his coughing fit hadn't alerted her.

She studied the warrior's location for a time and was still working out the best route to come up on him from behind when he abruptly emerged from his hiding place and started back in the direction of the cliffs. Rising swiftly, the Grey One followed at a crouch, struggling to keep the shadowy figure in sight for he moved with that loose, flexible pace of one very much at home in the forest. It was only when he stepped into a bright spot caused by a gap in the canopy that she recognised him as the scout she'd seen by the logjam the previous afternoon.

Approaching the cliffs, the scout entered a small clearing where he continued towards the entrance of what looked like a surprisingly large cave. A second man, with a faceful of elaborate tattoos, stood by that dark entrance watching his approach with a stern expression. Staying within the trees, the Grey One dropped to her haunches and watched.

The tattooed man wiped beads of moisture from his face while greeting the scout then both spoke in low voices, suggesting that they were either being excessively cautious or their comrades were still asleep within the cave. Liath Luachra wiped a smear of forest moisture from her own forehead. Normally, she'd have assumed the latter for despite their losses, this group still had far superior numbers and such advantages tended to make people careless. In this case however, because of her earlier intrusion into their main camp and the recent loss of a comrade to her bog trap, she suspected they'd have learned their lesson. They wouldn't be taking any chances.

The men's shoulders shook and a trickle of mean laughter reached her ears but she wasn't able to make out what they were saying. She clicked her tongue in annoyance. She'd have liked to have learned a little more about them and their intentions to help her decide on her next course of action. As it was, both were two far away to give her any chance at taking them by surprise. To reach them, she'd first have to cross the clearing that led up to the cave, an exposed stretch of grass that would put her in plain sight for a distance of over fifteen paces. The grassy patch also extended north and south of the cavemouth for another twenty or thirty paces so there was little chance of weaselling her way inside by stealth.

To complicate matters further, she had no long-ranged weapons such as a javelin or spear. There was the sling of course but, still damp from the lake crossing, she doubted it was dry enough to use with accuracy and was unwilling to test it under such dangerous conditions.

The woman warrior sighed. Once again, it would be all about watching and waiting, learning her enemies' weaknesses and placing herself in the best position to make use of those weaknesses when the moment was right.

With this in mind, the woman warrior started around to the west of the clearing on her hands and knees, working her way to a dense thicket of closely-packed oaks choked with heavy undergrowth. Right at the edge of the treeline, it seemed the best place to take watch or take advantage of any distraction or opportunity that might present itself.

Arriving at the thicket, she settled against the moss-encrusted bulk of the tallest tree, resting her cheek against the crusty bark. A soft breeze brushed through the forest, stirring up a sea of rustling black and grey shadows.

As the two warriors continued to talk, a third man emerged from the cave holding hunks of what looked like bread or cheese and passed them to his comrades. The Grey One stared enviously, her gut contracting to a shrivelled knot. All three seemed to be enjoying what they were eating for they chomped happily between the more animated pieces of conversation.

Exasperated, she reached over to grasp a nearby fern frond, twisted a number of the unfurled heads free and popped them into her mouth. The reddish-green material was hard and bitter, splintering into little pieces when she crushed them between her molars. She chewed unenthusiastically, working hard to produce some saliva, trying to convince herself she was eating even if there was no actual nourishment involved. At last, no longer able to bear the taste, she spat the gooey mess from her mouth, flicking the unused heads away with disgust.

Frustrated, she stretched on her back against a buttress of the tree, half-listening to the warriors' distant mumbles and distracting herself from hunger by considering various options to reach the cave mouth unseen. She was still in the middle of these thoughts when she realised the warriors' soft talk had petered out and, even more alarmingly, a heavy set of footsteps seemed to be coming in her direction.

Hurriedly, she rose to a crouch, drawing her knife free while positioning herself to keep the tree trunk between her and the approaching warrior, now so close she could actually hear him muttering loudly to himself. Alarmed, she rose to her feet, clinging as tightly as possible to the trunk of the tree, preparing to move in a contrary direction to his approach. Thinking to hear the shuffle of footsteps on the right, she slid around to the left only to stop in shock when he appeared around the trunk and stopped directly in front of her. Separated by a distance of not more than two paces, she stood rigid, staring in consternation when he pulled the front of his leggings down and hauled out his *bod*.

With a lick of clarity, she understood.

He hasn't seen me.

Stepping into the shadowed forest from the stale light of the clearing, the warrior's eyes hadn't yet adjusted to the change in brightness. Liath Luachra was just one more grey shadow against a whole swathe of background shadows.

The woman warrior gripped the knife hilt even more tightly, barely daring to breathe as she took in the closeness of him, the forehead glistening in sweat, the broken hook nose and the distinctive smell of decaying teeth. Silver piss spattered the earth in front of her feet and the warrior released a long sigh. Liath Luachra decided to remain motionless. There was still a chance he'd finish up without seeing her, return to the cave none the wiser.

With a quick shake and a grunt, the warrior returned his *bod* inside his trousers and seemed about to go when his eyes suddenly narrowed. Forehead creasing, he bent forwards and as his mind cleared the background clutter, he saw her, actually saw her for the first time. His jaw dropped.

And she stabbed him through his open mouth.

The knife thrust was applied with such panicked vigour, the blade penetrated deep into the warrior's skull. Death was instantaneous, soundless, the dead weight of him collapsing so abruptly it yanked the weapon and her arm to the ground.

'Gamall?'

Struggling to free the blade, the Grey One was only vaguely aware of the call from the clearing but immediately understood that she was in trouble. Somehow, despite the silence of the kill, one of the dead man's comrades had noticed something amiss, probably the unnatural movement of the warrior as he'd fallen forwards into the trees.

'Gamall?'

The woman warrior finally manged to work the knife free and grimaced as she looked toward the clearing. The tattooed man had drawn his sword and was cautiously approaching the thicket. Behind him, the scout had also drawn his sword but was using his to pound the stone at the mouth of the cave, the metallic clatter of it echoing deep inside.

'*Dúisigí!*' Alarm!

Cursing her ill fortune, Liath Luachra slipped back deeper into the trees, stiffly negotiating the circuitous route that led back towards the river. Now that they were aware of her presence, her plans for vengeance were thwarted for she no longer had any advantage. Outnumbered and in poor physical condition, she couldn't hope to challenge them in any head-on combat.

Forty or fifty strides brought her through the thickest part of the vegetation but from behind she heard a fresh flurry of shouts. They'd found the hapless Gamall's body.

The calls became more frequent after that and she could hear the four remaining warriors hard on her tail, beating the bush and calling out to each other to make sure she didn't bypass them. Struggling to push her exhausted body onwards, she knew she must be leaving a trail any half-competent warrior could find, not to mind someone as skilled as their tracker. Unfortunately, because of that tracker, concealment wasn't an option so she had no choice but to run, to push herself as fast and as far as she could and hopefully lose them before returning at a later stage to finish what she'd started.

Weaving through a particularly dense section of ash trees, her ankles suddenly folded under her and she fell, striking her head a glancing blow off one of the nearby trunks. Fortunately, it wasn't a bad fall and she was almost immediately back up on her feet, pushing out of the trees and onto the open riverbank.

Veering left, she started south, doing her best to ignore the growing discomfort. Her left hip was starting to hamper her, the tightness of the connecting muscles constraining her reach so that she was forced to compensate by overstretching with her right foot. After less than a few hundred paces, she knew she'd made a mistake for she was struggling badly and their tracker would eventually notice the odd shape to her prints. It wouldn't take him long to work out that she was in difficulty, that they could simply run her down at their leisure.

Through sheer determination, she managed to maintain a relatively fast pace for a time, following the river to a point where it turned inland then folded back out on itself again to create a broad and graceful curve. By the time she'd reached the far end of the curve however, she was wheezing badly, her gait increasingly ungainly. Slowing to approach a break in the riverside growth that looked back along the curve, she barely had time to catch her breath before she saw a flurry of movement at the opposite end of the arc. Three of the remaining warriors came into view, bunched up in a close pack, however several hundred paces ahead and emerging onto a clear patch at the centre of the curve, she spotted a younger, slimmer warrior pounding along at great speed.

A sprinter.

Her heart sank.

Dispatched ahead to harry her and slow her down until the other warriors caught them up, it seemed a surprising move given her ineffective gait and she could only assume the tracker hadn't yet noticed how truly incapacitated she was.

Although her legs protested, she veered south, away from the river and up into the thickly forested foothills below the ridge, sloshing through clogged mud and puddles that slowed her even further until she gained the slightly drier high ground. While she ran, she assessed the terrain ahead for some opportunity to deal with the sprinter. Dogging her heels now, he would soon be on her. Unfortunately, any action she did take would have to be fast and final for the other warriors would only be a few hundred paces behind him.

She continued to clamber uphill, following a steep deer trail that ran parallel to a deep gorge stretching down from the ridge. Choked with trees, gorse and high fern, the dense green screen obscured its true size but from the sharp drop-off, the woman warrior could tell it was steep, quite possibly a sheer cliff. Any misstep would end in a very long fall that would almost certainly be fatal.

It was about another seven hundred paces before she finally came across a workable site for ambush and even then she almost killed herself in the process. Moving along a section of the deer trail where the land had flattened out, she took a sharp bend at speed before spotting a slimy patch of mud at the very last moment. With her natural reactions blunted from fatigue, she wasn't able to avoid it in time and slipped, hit the ground hard and rolled off the side of the trail. Desperately grabbing a clump of fern, she barely managed to stop herself tumbling into the faux-benign green chasm waiting below.

Heart pounding, she hauled herself over the lip of a rain-slickened rock and back onto the trail, grunting at the effort of struggling to her feet. Although shaken, she was about to move on again when she paused, struck by the site's potential. Quietly, her eyes took in the sharpness of the bend, the muddy patch where the skid marks from her almost terminal tumble were in clear evidence.

It was possible. But she'd have to time it perfectly.

Still trembling from the scare of the fall, she withdrew her sword and moved close to the treeline at the bend opposite the gully and the muddy patch. By then, she could already hear the distant sound of the sprinter, moving impressively fast and drawing irrevocably closer. A shiver of fear ran through the woman warrior and she could feel the nauseous build-up of panic in her stomach.

Patience. Hold fast.

From the solid pound of his feet, she could tell the sprinter was on the flat section, then moving even faster along the trail towards her.

Patience.

He was almost on her, the heavy thud of footsteps echoing loudly now as he drew close to the bend. Bracing herself on her back foot, the Grey One held the sword out with both hands and …

Now

She lunged forward, driving the sword before her just as the warrior thundered around the bend. Like her, he too caught sight of the muddy patch but was still fresh enough to change course to avoid it, instinctively veering his momentum to the side and driving himself completely onto the blade.

Even with her preparations, the sprinter's momentum was enough to send the two of them floundering back onto the muddy ground. Instinctively, the Grey One rolled onto her feet, conscious that there was no time to spare, that even if she'd disabled the enemy warrior, she had to go. Glancing down at him however, she was struck by the disbelief and shock in his eyes. He was unexpectedly young, little more than a boy and probably not even as old as Fintán.

Somehow, he managed to sit up, despite the weapon piercing his body. Staring down at the sword hilt and the length of blade embedded in his stomach, he seemed to shiver and then raised his head to look at her with desperate eyes, pleading with her to confirm that this wasn't actually happening, that it was all some kind of horrible mistake. For one terrible moment, the Grey One felt an overwhelming sense of shame, of embarrassment, of complete and utter pointlessness. She had to turn away to avoid the boy's gaze.

Through the guts.

A long death, painful death.

Knowing she had no choice, she eased around behind the young warrior, wrapping her left hand around his forehead. Pulling his head back, she drew the knife across his open neck in one short and simple movement.

'I'm sorry,' she said and realised she was crying.

Her survival instincts overrode every other emotion however. The sprinter's body had barely even hit the ground when she was up, pulling the sword free. Warm blood dripped down the blade and onto her hands as she slid it into the scabbard attached to her back. She tried to start running again but her chest was wheezing like a punctured bellows. Her body, stiff and aching all over, could move at little more than a clumsy hobble.

The shadows were starting to deepen but she'd barely made fifty paces when she heard a cry of anger from down the trail and realised her remaining pursuers were almost on her. With mounting despair, she attempted to drive herself forward but her body, pushed too far, was just unable to give any more. A sick feeling blossomed in her belly and she realised she wasn't going to make it, that all her plans had been for nothing. This was it. She could go no further.

Staggering to a halt, she leaned against a tree, wheezing for breath as she eyed the trail to her rear. She had never felt so worn in her life, so battered or so beaten, so completely at the end of her tether.

Further down the trial, she caught a glimpse of movement in the distance and her hands began to tremble. She couldn't expect an easy death. Too weak to fight, they'd disarm her quickly then she'd be entirely at their mercy.

And, given what she'd cost them, they wouldn't be gentle.

Leaning back against the tree for support, she raised her hand to her sword hilt and prepared herself for death. Exhaling deeply, she was about to draw her weapon when her eyes fell on the thick wall of vegetation of the gorge alongside the trail and a sudden thought struck her.

Death on my own terms.

Stepping back as far as she was able, she took a deep breath then lunged forward. In complete silence, she launched herself off the flat section of trail.

Into the green abyss.

Chapter Eleven

The afternoon sky had lost its glow by the time Bodhmhall made her way back through the forest but in some respects the darkening clouds better suited her mood. The intensity of her interactions with Becal and her father had left her emotionally bruised and although she'd always known the return to Dún Baoiscne would try her, she now wondered at the wisdom of confronting the past in such a head-on manner.

Becal's desperation in particular had caught her unawares, especially as she hadn't discerned any hint of it during their initial conversation outside the fortress. Despite his standing in the community, the strain of his social isolation had taken a heavy toll and after so many years she could tell his mind was beginning to fray.

Perhaps like Dub Tíre.

The *bandraoi* shuddered and drew her arm close to distract herself with the pain. She felt a certain degree of sympathy for his plight but she had no intention of letting his pleas touch her. Becal had made his choice ten years earlier when he'd decided to forsake her. In spite of their deep childhood friendship, their years as competing acolytes had strained that relationship, a situation the *draoi* had compromised even further when he'd betrayed her, aligning himself with her father for his own advancement. Now, like bad milk, what remained had soured beyond the point of salvage.

To avoid thinking of Becal, she turned her mind instead to what she'd learned from the conversation. The account of her brothers' deaths had been distressing but worth it to finally learn the truth behind the hearsay and glean some information relevant to her own inquiries.

Even if the results were less than satisfying.

Deep in her heart, she'd always suspected Becal as the traitor. As a result, she'd been surprised when everything he'd told her aligned with what she knew from other sources. The study of his lifelight meanwhile, had revealed no tell-tale sign of the anticipated deceit over the course of the conversation.

So his innocence, at least with respect to the death of my brothers, seems genuine.

She was still mulling over that conclusion when she emerged from the forest and started across the flatland in the direction of Dún Baoiscne. As she drew closer to her destination however, those thoughts were discarded for she caught sight of a large number of people converging at the bottom of the hill in preparation to take the path up towards the fortress. Curious and a little uneasy at such uncharacteristic activity, she increased her pace, continuing to study the distant figures until she managed to work out who they were likely to be: the *Clann Baoiscne* men summoned by her father, the warriors destined for An Gleann Teann the following morning.

By the time she too reached the bottom of the hill, darkness was falling and the area was deserted, the warriors having already disappeared inside the fortress. Hurrying up the path towards the entranceway, she hastened inside, making her way to the *lis* just in time to see the last of the warriors shoving their way into a visibly crowded and boisterous Halla Mór.

Breathless, she halted, wondering whether she should follow them inside or retreat to her roundhouse to avoid her father's wrath. She was still standing there, striving to make out individual snippets from the jumbled patchwork of conversations when a sturdy, thick-necked figure emerged from the roundhouse to the right of the gateway.

'Bodhmhall ua Baoiscne!'

The gruff voice startled the *bandraoi* away from the mumbled discussions. Turning, she faced the newcomer, momentarily struggling to align the familiar voice with the figure before her.

'Lonán Ballach?' It was difficult to conceal her surprise. The *rechtaire* of Dún Baoiscne had aged markedly since the last time she'd seen him, the full head of grey hair reduced to a balding pate offset by a tufted outcrop of matching white sideburns. The tight, aquiline face was also far more wrinkled then she remembered. Respectfully, she inclined her head. 'I see you.'

Lonán Ballach had never been a man renowned for his humour so she was surprised when a creaky smile cracked though the habitually stony features. 'Ah, Bodhmhall. It's good to see you, good to have you back within these walls.'

The *bandraoi* returned the smile with a weak smile of her own. Although Lonán had never openly criticised her, neither could she recall his being particularly vocal in her defence during the dark period of her expulsion. 'It's pleasant to see the old home.' Somehow, she managed a smile. 'Although …' she gestured towards the crowded hall. 'It looks to be a tumultuous night.'

Lonán nodded with extravagant sagacity. 'Of course. The warriors called in by your father. To seek out your friends at An Gleann Teann.'

He's well informed.

She stared intently towards An Halla Mór as she gathered her thoughts, aware that Lonán was regarding her, as though awaiting further comment on the subject. She decided to let the silence speak for itself and after a moment the older man cleared his throat. 'Your father suggested I approach you to discuss future relations with Ráth Bládhma.' He glanced toward the hall. 'Perhaps now is an apt moment. This business of the mission to An Gleann Teann will allow us to speak freely.'

'Of course.' The *bandraoi* winced internally at the prospect of yet another exhausting conversation but quickly rallied with the realisation that this was the ideal opportunity to question the *rechtaire* without interruption.

'Very good! Come then, daughter of Tréanmór. I can at least offer appropriate hosting for such an honoured guest.'

Without waiting for a response, the older man turned, gesturing grandly for her to follow as he made his way back to the roundhouse from which he'd originally emerged. Plunging through the narrow entrance with the ease of practiced repetition, he disappeared from sight as a heavy fur fell down behind him.

Bodhmhall however, had remained where she was, staring stiffly at the shadowed rectangle of the doorway. A moment passed and then another before she finally clamped her lips and advanced hesitantly towards the dwelling.

The interior of the roundhouse was snug and comfortable, warmed by a low fire and insulated with layers of thick pelts coating the walls. By the time she entered, Lonán had already taken a stool at a high wooden table and was pouring a steaming green liquid into two wooden drinking bowls. He handed one across the table to her with restrained hospitality as she sat to join him. Awkwardly accepting the drink, Bodhmhall held it in both hands, staring at the bubbling contents while studiously avoiding any sight of the empty space to the left of the dwelling beside the sleeping platform.

'This is a sup of my own concoction,' the *rechtaire* informed her. 'As a fellow herbalist, I would value your judgement.'

Bodhmhall raised the bowl to her mouth, noting a slightly bitter scent somewhere beneath the liquid's otherwise flowery perfume. Dipping her lips, she pretended to swallow for since her experience with the *uisce beatha* she had no intention of ever drinking anything unfamiliar again. 'Pleasant,' she lied.

Lonán nodded, accepting the compliment as though it was his due. Sitting back on his stool, he rested both hands on the soft girth of his stomach.

Bodhmhall instinctively drew up the *Gift*, noting the solid gleam of his lifelight against the dim illumination of the roundhouse. To her great surprise, the *rechtaire's* yellow flame sputtered unexpectedly, settled for a moment then sputtered again.

He's excited.

The *bandraoi* hid her bemusement. Normally, such twitches of the lifelight were associated with sexual arousal but it was hard to believe that physical attraction was the trigger on this occasion. It seemed unlikely that a political animal like Lonán harboured any carnal desire for her, particularly given the minute period of time they'd spent together. No. It had to be something else about her presence that excited him.

Releasing the *Gift*, she was about to turn her study to the *rechtaire's* face but instead found her eyes drawn to the colourful pattern of a *fidchell* board sitting upright on a bench beside the table. Following her gaze, Lonán gave a quiet grunt.

'I see you've spotted my one weakness.' Reaching over to grasp the *fidchell* board, he placed it carefully on the table between them. Plucking one of the small bone pins free, he rolled it delicately between his fingers. 'Do you like to play?'

Bodhmhall shook her head. 'The game was a passion for Cairbre, but not so much for me. He did his best to instruct but I was a poor pupil.'

The *Clann Baoiscne rechtaire* gave a haughty nod of sympathy. 'It's true. *Fidchell* is not a game for everyone. It requires a sharp mind and rare nimbleness of intellect, attributes found in a select few.'

The *bandraoi* stifled a grin at the arrogance of that statement, imagining Fiacail's irreverent response had he been present. Oblivious to her veiled amusement, Lonán made a brushing motion with one hand as he moved the board aside with the other.

'But let us move to more immediate matters. Tréanmór tells me that potential now exists for the closing of ties between Dún Baoiscne and Ráth Bládhma. After all these years, that comes as something of a surprise.'

Bodhmhall nodded, preparing to deliver the story she'd practiced in advance.

'Given the great distances involved.'

The *rechtaire's* expression did not change and his voice remained just as affable, nevertheless an underlying scepticism to the words caused the *bandraoi* to consider him more closely. Lonán returned that scrutiny with an ambiguous expression and despite his air of almost tangible pomposity, she reminded herself to tread with caution. For all his puffed-up conceit, Lonán Ballach was nobody's fool, a fact amply evidenced by his enduring existence in her father's household.

'Yes,' she said, taking the decision to continue as though she hadn't noticed. 'Ráth Bládhma has dairy in abundance but lacks the skills of metal-working required to replenish our needs. Dún Baoiscne meanwhile, seeks to expand its herds so ...' She waved a hand to indicate the obvious conclusion. 'Yes. I believe there's ample possibility for trade discuss-'

'I think not. Not for the moment at least.'

Bodhmhall pursed her lips and frowned, taken aback by the interjection, a behaviour completely at odds with Lonán Ballach's habitual tactfulness. 'You are uncommonly direct.'

Lonán gave an indifferent shrug. 'There are times for subtlety and then there are times for a more forthright approach. Trade with Ráth Bládhma is not a matter of urgency so I consider this an opportune occasion to discuss an alternative proposition.'

'An alternative proposition.' She repeated the words but even aloud they made little sense.

Lonán made a steeple of his fingers and pressed the tips to his lips. 'Given your extended absence, you're probably unaware of the growing discontent with your father's leadership.'

He hesitated to see if she had anything to add but Bodhmhall remained silent, surprised and confused by such uncharacteristic bluntness. A conservative and cautious man by nature, the *rechtaire* must have truly felt secure to risk the wrath of her father by speaking out in such a manner.

'Some say your father has proven a poor leader and should no longer hold that role. Some say it was his behaviour that drew the *Clann Morna* attack on us.'

'Some might say that relating such opinions to his daughter was ... unwise.'

Lonán acknowledged that reality with a brisk dip of the head. 'Perhaps. But it's my reckoning you'll not run to share what I tell you. Your father's fury towards you is well known. As is his intention to force you to continue his line.'

Bodhmhall stared, gobsmacked by the extent of the *rechtaire*'s knowledge and his unexpected confirmation of her own suspicions. The reaction prompted a smug smile from her host.

'Your father shouts loudly when angered. And the guards on the internal ramparts are nephews of mine, placed there over time and loyal to me.' He smiled. 'But with respect to your father, since Cumhal and Crimall's demise, he's bedded several women yet produced no further progeny. It was only a matter of time before he sought you out to try and convince you to revive his line. Your unexpected arrival at Dún Baoiscne must have seemed a sign of approval from the Ancestors themselves.'

Bodhmhall raised the wooden bowl and blew steam from its contents while she assembled her thoughts then replaced it untouched on the table.

Once again, a Dún Baoiscne conversation had taken a completely unexpected turn to leave her floundering in its wake. Angered, she turned an eye towards the *rechtaire*.

'Lonán Ballach, you drive your tale like you'd drive a sick pig. Why don't you come to the point and tell me what you want?'

Once again, Lonán's face adopted that increasingly off-putting smirk. 'I share these secrets to demonstrate our mutual interest in countering your father's authority. If Tréanmór is removed as *rí*, he cannot compel you to act against your wishes.'

But if you were rí, you could.

Keeping her face expressionless, the *bandraoi* applied the *Gift* once more. 'Continue.'

'It is my intent to summon a Tribal Council and argue for the selection of a new leader for Dún Baoiscne.'

His lifelight sputtered again and sudden comprehension struck the *bandraoi*.

He's been planning this for a very long time.

She bit her lip. It was no wonder the *rechtaire* was excited. He'd probably been scheming and arranging this challenge to her father for years. Now, with the bulk of those warriors loyal to Tréanmór dispersed to An Gleann Teann, he finally felt safe enough to step forward and bring his plan to fruition.

'And you will be Dún Baoiscne's new leader.' Bodhmhall made no attempt to disguise the disdain in her voice.

'And why not? Tréanmór has had his day and you know he walks increasingly in dark shadows. He spends more time talking with the Five Friends than with his advisors.'

'Perhaps. But my loyalties might more plausibly swing towards my father.'

'They might but I sincerely doubt it. I've known you since you were a child, Bodhmhall. I know you have no desire to serve as receptacle for some stranger's love honey just to secure your father's ambitions. All the whispers to reach my ears of late confirm this is so.'

Sensing that he had her attention, he continued to press his case.

'As Tréanmór's daughter, your presence would serve as passive support for my leadership but, more importantly, as silent disapproval of your father. If the tribal elders see Tréanmór's own daughter doesn't support him they'll question his suitability, thereby strengthening my appeal.'

He must have read her thoughts then for he slapped the table with his palm to add unnecessary emphasis. 'Yes, Bodhmhall. Even with your history it will be enough. You are his daughter and only remaining progeny. And do not forget, with my success come further benefits. Forgiveness from the Druidic Order might be negotiated. You might once more be welcomed back into the tribal fold.'

Which just goes to show you don't know me half as well as you think.

Bodhmhall made no comment as she considered the *rechtaire's* words. It was difficult to believe she was sitting there, coolly amicable while this treacherous toad openly planned her father's removal and her own exploitation. The situation left her feeling oddly giddy and dislocated. Playing for time, she pretended to drink.

'It's a bold move to challenge my father. You're familiar with the Five Friends. You've seen what happened to others who raised a challenge and failed.'

Lonán calmly rested his hands on the table. 'I've bided my time and held my peace for a long time, Bodhmhall. It's taken much consideration in the choice of this moment. Your father's warriors depart at dawn, my own supporters are in place and word has already been sent to gather the elders in.' His lips parted to reveal a set of uneven teeth that shone yellow from the reflection of the fire. 'The elders are set to arrive two mornings hence. Once he sees the people are against him in sufficient numbers, Tréanmór will have no choice but to concede. The change of leadership will happen peacefully.'

Bodhmhall said nothing to reveal her scepticism. One way or another, her father would fight.

But this is a fight that doesn't concern me.

With this in mind, she slowly applied the *Gift* once more. 'What are your intentions towards Ráth Bládhma?'

'I have none. Ráth Bládhma is too distant to be of consequence. Should you prefer to remain there and trade with Dún Baoiscne that could prove fortuitous for us all.' He beamed. 'You see? With your father out of the way, new possibilities already present themselves.'

She pressed her tongue against her front teeth as she worked through the ramifications of Lonán's offer while maintaining her attention on his lifelight. 'To offer any demonstration of support I'd need to satisfy myself you harbour no ill intent towards the settlement.'

'I've already told you. Ráth Bládhma and its people have nothing to fear from me or my supporters. My sole interest is the leadership of Dún Baoiscne.'

And that, she suspected, was almost entirely true. Lonán's lifelight had not so much as quivered while he'd been speaking. Consumed by his own political agenda, her settlement and its people held absolutely no importance for him.

And probably never had.

He's not the Adversary's man.

Her instincts told her that much. As did the admittedly erratic lifelight. Was the *rechtaire* trustworthy? Absolutely not, within the context of *Clann Baoiscne* power struggles, but neither was he the person she was looking for.

Just to make sure, she decided to test that conclusion a little further.

'There is no other party offering you support? No-one from outside the tribe?'

'I have more than enough support within the tribe. Why would I need the help of outsiders?' Lonán sounded aggrieved by the suggestion and the irritation in his voice was mirrored by a fresh quiver of his lifelight.

It's not him.

'Enough!' he declared abruptly. 'I have been forthright. Do we have agreement between us or not?'

Bodhmhall wavered on how to respond as she let *an tíolacadh* fade. This new intrigue had the potential to unravel her own plans and she had to tread very carefully.

'The political manoeuvrings between you and my father mean little to me, Lonán.' She sighed. 'I'll not oppose you but neither will I support you. I'll attend the tribal council but will not speak and people can make of that what they will. Afterwards, I'll ...'

She paused, distracted by a growing clamour of voices from outside and the heavy tread of many feet in the *lis*. Glancing at the *rechtaire* she saw that he too was looking uneasily towards the doorway. The meeting with the warriors, it seemed, had taken nowhere near as long as anticipated.

'Afterwards,' she continued, 'I'll leave Dún Baoiscne for the *Uí Cuaich* territories. I have business there with *An Ollamh*, urgent tasks to complete before I return to Ráth Bládhma.'

Lonán was still staring at the doorway but he relaxed visibly as it became clear from the noise that the warriors were departing the *lis* through the stone passage, bound for the outer ring of the fortress. Returning his attention towards her he gave a grudging nod of acknowledgment.

'Your full support would have pleased me more but ...' He allowed a faint trace of disappointment to dull his eyes, his smile to droop ever so slightly with unspoken disapproval. 'Very well. Your silent attendance at the tribal council will satisfy me for I can work my words around that.' He considered her then with renewed munificence and raised the *fidchell* board in both hands.

209

'Let this board game be an offering of the goodwill between us, Bodhmhall. Perhaps in time, should you apply yourself, you'll attain a sufficient level of skill to offer some basis of a challenge.' His smile suggested there was little chance of this occurring.

Fighting the urge to slap him, the *bandraoi* silently dropped her eyes to the table.

'I'll wrap this board in flax for you to take away. Alas, my limbs are not as flexible as once they were. Perhaps you could fetch that leather satchel to carry it. There, on the floor. By the bed.'

He continued to smile agreeably but that smile faded as Bodhmhall continued to stare down at the wooden surface without response.

'If you could just fetch me the satchel,' he repeated. 'Over there.' This time he also pointed helpfully towards the satchel but, once again, the *bandraoi* refused to turn her head in the direction he was indicating.

'I don't understand.' Bodhmhall could almost hear the frown twist his voice. 'Why do you ...' His voice caught and she heard the stifled gasp of comprehension. 'Oh! Oh, of course! This was where it happened.'

Bodhmhall remained silent.

'This dwelling ... It was used by Dub Tíre. This was where you killed your master.'

For a single moment, the present was lost. Bodhmhall was a frightened young woman again, standing alongside the sleeping platform, a bone-handled knife gripped tight between her fingers. Warm blood was spurting over the back of her wrist and the sensation of bloodied spittle was damp on her face where the *draoi* had coughed his last breath.

'Forgive me.' The *rechtaire* sounded genuinely contrite, worried no doubt that his blunder might impact on her decision. 'I didn't think.' He lifted his hands, palms raised upwards in a helpless gesture. 'It was all so long ago.'

This time Bodhmhall raised her eyes and considered him evenly. 'Not so long for me.'

The older man swallowed but even then, even in that moment of awkwardness, she could see the shrewdness in his eyes as he calculated how he might best use this apparent weakness for his own ends.

He's just like my father. Another old bull vying to lead the herd.

The slap of a heavy hand against the outer lintel of the doorway made them both jump.

'Bodhmhall ua Baoiscne!'

The voice from outside was unfamiliar but firm. Fortunately, it bore no detectable trace of menace or hostility. 'Are you within? Your father requires your presence and I've been tasked with escorting you.'

Glancing at Lonán Ballach, the *bandraoi* saw his face take on a stricken look. His eyes widened at the realisation that with Tréanmór's warriors still present at Dún Baoiscne, he'd potentially revealed his hand too early. In his eagerness to obtain Bodhmhall's support, he'd placed her in an optimal position to expose his schemes should she choose to do so.

It was tempting to let him sweat it out but Bodhmhall decided the risks were too great. 'One moment,' she called as she rose from her stool. Brushing the hem of her *léine*, she considered the nervous *rechtaire* who still had the *fidchell* board in one hand. In the other, he'd taken one of the pins and was twiddling it anxiously between his forefinger and thumb. Realising the agitated picture he must present, he quickly replaced the board on the table, slotted the pin into one of the free holes and dropped his hands by his side.

'I'll report nothing of this conversation,' Bodhmhall told him in a low voice. 'But you should tread warily, Lonán. Very warily.'

She pointed at the white pin he'd misplaced in that section of board reserved for the darker pins. 'Because of the moves you've now committed yourself to make.'

***

The escort sent by her father turned out to have a surprisingly deceptive voice. From the deep tenor she'd heard through the doorway of the roundhouse, Bodhmhall had expected a seasoned warrior but it was a gangly, straw-haired youth with no more than sixteen years on him who stood awaiting her.

The youth nodded briefly in acknowledgement as she emerged from the dwelling then turned on his heel and started towards An Halla Mór. Following him, the *bandraoi* glanced about the shadowed *lis*, noting the two darkened figures lounging by the neighbouring roundhouse.

Ah!

Lonán hadn't taken any chances then. If she'd refused to help him he'd made his preparations to ensure she didn't alert her father. It would have been a major risk to accost her within the *lis* but a risk they'd apparently been willing to take to silence her.

A shiver ran down her spine as she hurried after the youth. Before them, the doorway of the great hall flared with warm, yellow light, promising sanctuary against the dangers of the darkness tumbling down in the air around them.

The youth made no attempt to engage her in conversation which was something of a blessing. The *bandraoi's* mind still reeled from the *rechtaire's* revelations and the realisation of how close to death she'd really been. She'd always suspected Lonán's arrogant exterior of concealing a more devious nature but the true depths of his ruthlessness had caught her by surprise and left a foul taste in her mouth.

She fought the sudden urge to spit. The timing of Lonán's machinations posed a serious hindrance. Fortunately, now she was aware of his intentions, there was still a chance to sidestep them if she worked quickly enough.

Approaching the hall entrance, the youth stood aside and gestured for her to continue through the open doors. Taking a deep breath, the *bandraoi* consigned her concerns to a dark space for later consideration and, steeling herself, stepped across the threshold.

The interior of the hall was still stuffy and thick from the body odour of the twenty or so warriors who'd so recently occupied it. Both fires and the torches on the walls added to the fusty atmosphere.

Three figures were gathered by the innermost fire pit. Two of them, her father and a youthful, bearded warrior, were seated on stools while the third, Cathal Bog, stood off to the side, leaning casually against one of the vertical posts.

Studying the seated warrior, Bodhmhall realised she recognised his face from her earlier years at the fortress. Uargal mac Camal, a youth from one of the lesser *Clann Baoiscne* sub-tribes, she'd encountered him at various tribal gatherings, although they'd never exchanged more than the occasional pleasantry. On reflection, she supposed his presence was hardly a surprise. With the dearth of *Clann Baoiscne* warriors it made sense for her father to reach out to the wider sub-tribes for replacements. For warriors such as Uargal, the opportunity for advancement would have been too great to refuse.

As Uargal turned to watch her approach, she noted how much he'd changed since she'd last seen him. Back then, he'd been a handsome youth, well-formed but slim with smooth facial features. Now, he looked muscled and markedly more menacing, his handsome features marred by a red scar that stretched down his chin and cut a furrow through the thick growth of his beard.

'Daughter. Welcome.' Tréanmór's greeting was muffled by a mouthful of half-chewed meat. 'Come join us.' He hooked one foot around the leg of the nearest free stool and drew it closer. Bodhmhall slowly sank onto the rough wooden surface.

Her father gestured at Uargal with a half-eaten pork chop. 'You remember Uargal, perhaps?'

'Yes.' The *bandraoi* turned to the young warrior. 'I see you, Uargal.'

The warrior respectfully inclined his head. 'I see you, Bodhmhall'

'Uargal leads the *fian* to An Gleann Teann at dawn tomorrow. There, he'll not only seek out your companions but cleanse the territory of any who trespass on *Clann Baoiscne* land. It's well time we sent a message to those who think we've lost our bite.'

Bodhmhall nodded with controlled politeness. Despite her father's easy manner she could sense an underlying tension to him and she noted the drink by his side remained untouched, a sure sign of agitation. To her dismay, she also noticed he was cradling one of the Five Friends, caressing the skull, sliding fingertips over the smooth curves of bone. She wondered briefly if the action was premeditated, to unsettle her. It would be like her father to play such tricks, knowing how she'd feared the grinning skulls as a child.

'You've spoken with Lonán?'

It seemed an innocent enough enquiry. Knowing her father however, she couldn't be entirely sure. It was possible Tréanmór was already aware of his *rechtaire*'s disloyalty and using the question as a trap to test if she could be trusted.

'Yes.'

'And Becal?'

Not a trap, then.

'Earlier this afternoon.' She paused and glanced uneasily at the two silent warriors on either side. 'You wish to discuss this now?'

Tréanmór shook his head. 'Later. First, there are more pressing matters to address. Our patrols have discovered some … less threatening trespassers on *Clann Baoiscne* territory and brought them here to share the hospitality of Dún Baoiscne.' He took another bite from the pork chop but then looked up to regard her with a chilling intensity that caused her heart to miss a beat. 'Can you guess who it might be?'

'Liath Luachra?' she asked hopefully, causing her father to scowl. Choosing to ignore his daughter's response, the *rí* of *Clann Baoiscne* turned to shout at the pimple-faced youth who'd remained standing at the hall entrance. 'Congal. Fetch our guests. Have them brought here now.'

The youth acknowledged the order with a nod and promptly disappeared into the night. Following his departure, Tréanmór's eyes turned inwards as he chewed quietly on his chop. The two warriors, following his lead, also remained silent and the resulting hush seemed oddly emphasised by the crackling of the fires and the sound of tearing meat.

From the corner of her right eye, Bodhmhall caught Cathal Bog openly watching her as he slouched against the pole, thumbs tucked into his sword belt. To her left Uargal hawked and spat a mouthful of phlegm into the flames to produce a gruesome sizzle. Looking up, he caught her eye and smiled thinly, his fingers probing the line of damaged tissue that cut into his beard.

'Ah.' Her father tossed the pork bone aside. Wiping his fingers on the knees of his woollen trousers, he rose to his feet. 'They come.'

Despite the pressing weight of her father's scrutiny, Bodhmhall turned to watch as a party of five shadowy figures emerged from the darkness to step across the threshold, into the light of An Halla Mór. Led by the gangly youth, they crossed the wooden boards towards the fire, the two central figures – a man and a child – flanked on either side by a battle-hardened warrior.

Bodhmhall surged to her feet with such force, her stool went tumbling onto the floor.

'Demne!'

The scared expression on the child's face transformed to one of surprise then of joy, mingled with relief.

'Bodhmhall!'

The boy made to rush towards her but a swift manoeuvre of the spear haft by the guard beside him forced him to remain in place as they drew up before the assembled company. He looked pleadingly to his aunt who'd torn her eyes to the subdued presence of Fiacail mac Codhna. The Seiscenn Uarbhaoil man's clothing was far dirtier and unkempt then when she'd last seen him and he nursed an impressive blue-black bruise on the side of his face.

'Fiacail! What are you doing here?'

The big warrior's eyes found hers then narrowed as though exposed to a contrary wind. 'I see you Bodhmhall,' he said with quiet formality. 'Alas, your father's hospitality is not of a nature to be refused.'

Her gaze flicked up to his shoulders where the heads of his axes – the Two Sisters – were usually to be seen. This time however, there was no sign of them. The Seiscenn Uarbhaoil man's gaze meanwhile, had drifted around to study the hall's other occupants, finally coming to rest on Tréanmór's sullen bodyguard.

'Cathal Bog!' To everyone's great surprise, Fiacail's face split into a broad grin. 'It gives such joy to see you again.'

Cathal regarded him with an unstated hostility that would have subdued most other men. But not Fiacail, it seemed. Resting his weight on one leg, the big warrior leaned back and folded his arms with apparent satisfaction. 'It's reassuring to find stability in such tumultuous times,' he declared. 'Despite the passing of years, the fires of Dún Baoiscne continue to burn in the Cuirreach valley, Tréanmór's reign endures, and Cathal Bog's tongue remains as still as his langer.'

The *Clann Baoiscne* conradh surged upright from the post in one swift, menacing movement but remained in place as Uargal waved him down. 'Tread lightly, Fiacail mac Codhna,' the younger warrior growled. 'You're not in Seiscenn Uarbhaoil now.'

'Come, come, Uargal. Let it not be said we offer cautions to our honoured guests.'

Her father's voice pulled Bodhmhall from her rattled thoughts, the reasonable and affable tone putting her immediately on her guard.

'Our Seiscenn Uarbhaoil kin have travelled far,' Tréanmór continued. 'The least we can do is offer the hospitality of warmth and feasting. The bonds between us must be maintained in such perilous times. After all, it's only through unity that we remain strong. Is that not so, Seiscenn Uarbhaoil man?'

Bodhmhall could see the defiant glint in Fiacail's eye as he considered her father. 'You forget I used to dwell in this fortress, great Tréanmór. The flavour of the feasting here was always one to leave a sickness in my belly.'

The warmth faded from the *rí* of *Clann Baoiscne's* face and he regarded Fiacail with much more visible coldness. 'I remember you well enough, son of Codhna. And it seems there's truth in what the elders say. The old dog always returns to his vomit.'

Bodhmhall felt a tightness in her chest.

'Father ...'

She turned to face the *rí* but Tréanmór no longer had eyes for her. His gaze was locked firmly on Demne, his face strained and pale. In the yellow light from the flames, her nephew's blond hair had taken on an even more golden hue and, at that particular moment, he looked more like his father than ever.

Tréanmór's face swung back on her with such violence that she actually stumbled backwards. Nostrils flaring, he stared at her with unbridled fury and it took several terrifying heartbeats before he appeared to regain control. Eyes still locked on her, he slowly reclaimed his seat. Turning to the child, he gestured for him to approach. 'You, boy.' He slapped the free stool beside him. 'Come close. Sit here where I can see you.'

Demne looked uncertainly at Bodhmhall but under her father's hostile scrutiny, the *bandraoi* didn't dare react. Upset, the boy turned to Fiacail instead, the big warrior responding with a stiff nod of assent.

With obvious misgivings, Demne timidly approached the *Clann Baoiscne ri* and sat on the stool beside him.

'So, you must be Demne.'

Her nephew hesitated. 'Yes.' His voice was low and quavered slightly.

'And Fiacail, over there. He is your father?'

The boy looked to the warrior who nodded encouragingly.

'Yes.'

'I see.' Uncensored scepticism stained Tréanmór's voice. 'You have no brothers? No sisters?'

'No.' Demne's voice had dropped so low it was difficult to hear him above the noise of the hissing and sputtering logs.

'What was that? Speak up, boy.'

'No.' This time the answer was louder, clearer.

'Demne? It's not such a common name, is it?'

Too frightened to speak, the boy simply shook his head.

'So, then you must also be the same Demne who jumped from the cliffs at An Gleann Teann. With Bodhmhall, there. Is that not so?'

'Y-yes.'

Tréanmór thoughtfully stroked his beard. 'Which, by her own reckoning, occurred before she'd even encountered your father. That seems odd, does it not?'

This time, Demne was too scared to respond and a terrible, prolonged silence spread through the hall. Without warning, Tréanmór reached forwards and grasped the boy's shoulders, staring directly into his face. Trembling, Bodhmhall fought the urge to rush towards him.

Several moments passed before her father released the boy and when he turned to her again his eyes bored into her. 'This is my grandchild. Cumhal's son. There can be no doubt. He's the very image of his father.'

He glared at her, challenging her to deny it but she turned her eyes down to the reed-coated floorboards. Already she'd seen the plots, the plans forming in the space behind his eyes. Demne offered everything her father desired: an heir, a future leader for the tribe, a rallying point for *Clann Baoiscne* and its allies.

His accusations corroborated, Tréanmór jubilantly returned his attention to the boy. 'So tell me true, young Demne! Who is your mother?'

'Muirne Muncháem.'

216

The *rí* of Dún Baoiscne stiffened as though someone had struck him a blow. His forehead creased into a series of deep furrows and he lapsed into silence for a moment before raising his right hand, palm outwards.

'Go.' Her father's eyes flickered around at everyone else in the hall. 'All of you but Bodhmhall, leave us now. Uargal ...' He turned to address the younger warrior. 'Take our guest from Seiscenn Uarbhaoil to his old quarters. He can relive happy memories of his days amongst us. As for you, Demne ...'

Lifting her eyes, Bodhmhall saw that the child was cowering away from her father. She watched as his expression softened and he reached out to offer a reassuring pat on the shoulder. 'You have nothing to fear from me, boy. You're of my flesh and are destined for great things.'

With a gesture of his hand, he directed the boy's gaze towards a gap in the leather sheet across the inner hall which provided access to the domestic section of An Halla Mór. 'Fatigue sits heavy on your features. Pass through there and you'll find a place to lay your head. Come morning, we can start to know one another.'

Tentatively, the boy got to his feet and moved towards the leather sheet, Tréanmór's eyes following him until he'd passed through the gap and out of sight.

By the time, the *rí* of *Clann Baoiscne* returned his attention to the hall, the warriors were thrusting Fiacail roughly through the doorway. For one instant, just before he was swallowed up into the darkness, he looked back at Bodhmhall and grinned.

And then he was gone. And the hall was silent, empty except for herself, her father and Cathal Bog, once more returned to his post on a stool by the doorway. The *bandraoi* regarded him uneasily.

Tréanmór stared wordlessly into the flames of the fire, the skull now sitting on a stool to his side. His face appeared calm, almost contemplative although Bodhmhall knew it could switch to severity with striking abruptness.

'Muirne.' He gave a bitter laugh. 'I should have guessed. That is why she left, why she wandered off into the night all those years ago.' His eyes flickered up, piercing her with their intensity. 'Tell me,' he said simply.

The *bandraoi* swallowed. 'He is my nephew,' she said at last. 'Cumhal and Muirne's son. The Flower of Almhu came to Ráth Bládhma seeking sanctuary and I could not turn her away. She ha- '

'Did you truly believe you could deceive me, daughter?'

She stumbled, caught by the sudden interruption. 'In truth, no. But I had to try.'

'Is any of what you told me true?'

'Everything I told you was true. Except where it related to Demne. I had to protect him for it's the boy the Adversary seeks. I couldn't risk revealing his existence because of the traitor here at the fortress.' She glanced at Cathal Bog but he had his head back, resting against the door jamb as though he was dozing.

'And so, the truth shines bright at last.' A cynical chuckle from her father. 'And what of Fiacail mac Codhna. What's his role in all this?'

'It's as I told you. We encountered Fiacail after the ambush. He offered his assistance and claimed parenthood of Demne in an effort to protect him.'

'If Fiacail mac Codhna offered assistance,' her father scoffed. 'It would be the assistance of the bee seeking nectar between your petals.'

Looking at her, he somehow caught the shadow of guilt in her eyes.

'Hah! A busy bee, then. I thought as much.' He shook his head and grunted. 'Truly, Bodhmhall, daughter or not, if you hadn't delivered my grandson into my lap, this betrayal would have meant your life was forfeit.'

He sighed and reached, almost unconsciously, to grasp the gleaming skull once more. Taking it in his right arm, he settled it into the nook of his elbow and regarded her with chilling calm.

'But then you've always been a disappointment. Your quest for vengeance left the tribe without a competent *draoi*. Despite my attempts at arranging a bonding with Fiacail mac Codhna, you end up slapping buttocks with him only once the bond is annulled and there's no advantage to be gained. And finally, the single task I seek of you, the simple duty of delivering a grandson, you fail by aligning yourself instead with that twisted gristle, Liath Luachra.' He shook his head with demonstrable disenchantment. 'Truly a disappointment.'

'It grieves me to cause such dissatisfaction, father. The *bandraoi's* voice was full of bitterness. 'Unlike Cumhal, Crimall and I were always set to fail for we could not compete with such perfect unions as the one he shared with Muirne.'

'Perfect?' Tréanmór snorted.

The *bandraoi* stared at him, wondering at the unexpected venom in his voice. Raising her hand, she gestured towards the leather sheet. 'I will not strain your patience with my presence any longer. I'll fetch Demne and - '

'My grandson,' he interrupted with brutal candour, 'remains here with me tonight. And for all future nights. It is I who'll protect him against any threat, given how ineffectual you've proven against this … Adversary. Should you choose to leave Dún Baoiscne once you've completed your search for the traitor, you're free to do so but you'll leave without him. Should you prefer to remain here that possibility too is acceptable but only on the condition you obey my bidding and provide me with grandchildren. Either way the boy stays here.'

Chapter Twelve

At first there was weightlessness. And then there was falling, plummeting through a blurred smear of trees, vines and scrub. Branches and brambles snagged her clothing, tore her skin as she whipped by. Some vegetative net caught her, yanked her brutally to the side where she smashed against a tree trunk, slamming it hard with her left hip and ribcage. Almost immediately, she was flipped head over heels, some other solid object hit her in the face and then she was spinning, too disorientated to know what was happening.

She landed in a shallow stream clogged with undergrowth, striking the water and the spongy growth hard. Submerged, her instincts kicked in and pushing herself up with her hands, she found she was sitting in a stagnant brown pool dark with shadows, no deeper than her kneecap and clogged with slimy green weed. The water was freezing and her clothes sodden, plastered in a slick muck that clung to her flushed and sweating frame.

Too dazed to move, she sat still, jaw clenched to prevent herself from hissing at the pain in her side. White spots danced before her eyes as she struggled to calm a thundering heartbeat. Breathing hard, she fought the urgent urge to vomit as her body surrendered to shock, barely conscious of her pursuers' faint voices floating down from above.

'Those are her tracks, right there. I heard her fall.'

A brief silence.

'I'm not scrambling down there. That's a sheer drop through those bushes.'

A sudden movement in the water between her legs would have made her shudder if she hadn't been so numb from shock. She watched a black eel slither across her inner right thigh, sniffing at her bloodied knees before wriggling back into the water and out of sight.

The appearance of the eel was enough of a stimulus to get her moving again although trying to stand was pointless. Overhanging branches from the willow trees and tangled woody debris on either side of the stream had intertwined to create a thick lattice. Admittedly, this had softened her fall and probably saved her life but it also prevented her from getting to her feet. All in all, that didn't overly bother her. Her body was still too shaken to stand upright in any case.

She started downstream at a half-crawl, wriggling through the tangled network of vines and debris, fists sinking into the muddy bed as she followed the barely visible flow of current. Eventually, she realised the voices had disappeared but she knew she hadn't lost them. They'd be out there somewhere, working their way to either end of the gully to intercept her when she finally emerged.

And she'd never felt less like fighting in her life.

Despite her laborious progress, the foliage choking the stream gradually began to clear, the tangled trees and plants replaced by clumps of reed as she got closer to the river. By then, the adrenaline had worn off and the damage to her body was making itself known. Her left side, where she'd hit the tree, was stiff and extremely painful when she moved. The left leg of her leggings had been sliced open to and revealed an extremely bad gash down to the knee. The entire right side of her face was swollen and tender to the touch while the rest of her body had too many cuts and bruises to even count.

As the narrow channel expanded, she emerged into daylight. Grey and gloomy though it was, it was still something of a relief to know that at least she'd die out in the open, her body exposed to the elements rather than rotting away in some obscure waterway. Continuing her slow crawl, she was surprised to find that much of the water had drained away on the flatter land while the bed of the stream had widened considerably. Individual clumps of reeds had merged to broad swathes of muddy green that bordered her on either side to form a wide muddy channel interspersed with smaller clumps of reed.

Pausing to rest, the Grey One lay on her right side, inhaling the pungent air. Her fear had a duller edge to it now, the constant undercurrent of anxiety worn away by the sheer physical toll of exhaustion. She recognised this effect, had seen it once or twice before with comrades in *Na Cinéaltaí* who were no longer alive. There was a point of sustained endurance where exhaustion or injury finally doused all the fire in a person's eyes and left a deadened kind of resignation. At this point, people generally stopped fighting and accepted the inevitability of death.

Having made her decision when she left Fintán, Liath Luachra too had accepted the inevitability of death, although she knew she was going to continue scrambling about in the filth, eking the last few lungfuls of life. Having fought fear, pain and discomfort her entire life, she honestly didn't know how to do anything else.

Rolling back onto her stomach, the Grey One was about to start moving again when a flicker of movement on the far side of the shallow channel pulled her eye. Turning her head slowly, her gaze came to rest on a section of solid ground protruding from the reeds to create a low promontory overlooking the mud flat. On it, three men stood staring silently across at her: Cargal Uí Faigil, the scout and the tattooed man from the cave mouth. All three were holding swords. As she watched, the latter removed his tunic and used the flat of his blade to proudly slap the hard muscle of his upper body, it too bristling with impressive flame tattoos. Turning her focus to the dark-bearded leader, Liath Luachra recalled the last time she'd seen him back at the lake, on another promontory, staring across the water to where she'd been hidden.

But this time there'd be no hiding.

Despite the distance that separated them, little more than twenty-five paces, she could feel the *techtaire's* cold loathing. To his credit, when he finally spoke he spared her any heartfelt homily on his intended vengeance for lost comrades, any self-serving justifications.

'Finish her.'

The scout and the tattooed man didn't waste any time, slipping down off the lip of the promontory and starting across the mud flat to kill her. To everyone's surprise, including Liath Luachra's, that didn't go as planned.

The centre of the muddy channel, the area where the main flow of the storm waters emptied out overnight, was still completely sodden and far less solid than it appeared. By the time they'd made five paces from the promontory, both warriors were up to their knees in thick, clinging mud. Reduced to a crawl, they floundered painfully though the mud, making slow but inexorable progress towards her.

Up on the promontory, Cargal Uí Faigil was unimpressed by the delay, calling angrily at his men to get up off their arses and kill her. Slumped on the opposite side of the channel, too battered to even contemplate running, Liath Luachra felt a weak surge of hope. Sitting up, she studied the area the two men would have to cross to reach her and spotted a half-drowned clump of reed less than five paces away. She started crawling towards it while the warriors, continuing their laborious struggle through the brown mush, eyed her carefully but appeared otherwise unconcerned.

The two men were still a good ten paces from her by the time she reached the clump, really little more than a decaying stump with a thin selection of short reeds protruding above the surface mud. Nevertheless, the fibrous roots that spread out underneath stabilized the immediate area and offered a small but relatively solid platform.

Climbing onto the centre of the clump, the Grey One unsheathed her sword and used it as a support to get upright, tentatively probing the edges of the clump with her foot to test how far it spread before it began to sink. Planting her feet wide enough to ensure a firm purchase and a decent balance, she gripped the sword and waited for her enemies.

The tattooed man warrior was first to reach her. Several falls meant that his colourfully elaborate tattoos were now coated in several layers of slime and although she'd expected the difficult crossing to have enraged him, he surprised her by approaching with striking calm. She felt a moment of fear when she saw the lethal determination in his eyes, the hardened competence of his stance. This man intended to kill her. Quickly, efficiently and without hesitation.

When he was less than five paces away, the Grey One melodramatically stabbed the tip of her sword into the stump and grinned manically at him. 'They're unusual tattoos,' she said, almost conversationally.

Momentarily unnerved, the warrior paused in mid-step. Satisfying himself that there was nothing he'd missed, he started forwards again.

'Did a little girl paint them?'

Despite the warrior's obvious pride in his body adornment, the clumsy taunt shouldn't have worked, couldn't have worked … and yet it did. The man must have had some long-held, pent-up anger for her comment somehow enraged him to the point where, despite the ankle-deep mud, he lunged forward to kill her.

Attacking with a powerful downwards swipe, he swung the blade wide but because of the solid platform the Grey One was able to draw back and dodge the blade with relative ease. The treacherous surface however meant the warrior miscalculated the strength of his swing and his feet slithered out from under him. Unbalanced, he toppled and hit the mud with a wet slap.

The Grey One was on him like a rapacious eel. Releasing the knife she'd held in concealment behind her wrist, she stabbed it down with all her force, right through his heart.

The big warrior kicked and wriggled beneath her weight and succeeded in bucking her off but as she rolled back onto her feet, bloody knife in hand, she could tell he was done. Weak, rasping gasps came from his lungs but he was already choking in his own blood. As she retreated to her little island of stable ground he attempted to get up but collapsed again, blood spurting from the wound in his chest to form a crimson pool in the muck slime beneath him.

A yell of anger brought her attention back to the next threat – the scout – who'd drawn to a halt and was wisely keeping his distance as he reassessed the situation. From the way his eyes lingered on her feet, she could tell that he was on to her, that he'd understood the positions were reversed. On her small but stable platform, she now had an advantage in any one-on-one combat against an opponent on the slippery mud. Making sure to keep a safe distance, the scout looked furiously back over his shoulder. Tossing a quick glance in that direction, the woman warrior saw that Cargal Uí Faigil had entered the mud flat to join the fray.

By the time he'd made it half-way across, the *techtaire* too was plastered in sludge, struggling through the wet, exhausting suck of it. It took him a time to join his comrade but when he did, both immediately veered off from one another as though in unspoken agreement. With that, the Grey One understood. They intended to nullify her advantage by outmanoeuvring her, by coming at her from two different directions. Unable to relinquish the stable ground, she'd have no choice but to engage one of her opponents head on while the other attacked her exposed side.

Clearing her throat, she hefted her sword, tossed it from her left hand to her right as her body swung clumsily to face one, and then the other, of the approaching warriors. Breathing deeply to maintain her calm, she waited until they were four paces away. Glaring intensely at Cargal Uí Faigil, she suddenly spun on one foot and flung Fintán's knife at the scout.

He was fast, she'd give him that. Despite concealing her intentions, some instinct had alerted him and by the time she was raising her hand to throw, he was already moving backwards. Hampered by the mucky surface, he also attempted to dodge but anticipating that reaction, she'd intentionally thrown low, more interested in eliminating him from the fight than ensuring a kill. The knife took him in the left thigh, the blade sinking deep into the flesh below his hip.

She had no time to verify the effectiveness of her throw as Cargal Uí Faigil had already taken the offensive. Too close for her to position herself to best effect, she barely had time to turn and fend off the sword thrust, bringing her own weapon up to deflect it before it pierced her side. The two blades clashed with a metallic crack, rasping as they slid off one another. The *techtaire* immediately retaliated with a second attack, slyly using the smoothness of the mud to spin around and hit her with another attack from an unexpected angle. Again, although she managed to counter it, she was unbalanced by the awkward angle and the force of the blow and driven backwards off the reed clump. With a sick feeling, she watched Cargal Uí Faigil step onto the solid ground. Now she had no choice but to retreat onto the flat, taking three hesitant steps backwards as he caught his breath, silently eyeing her as he worked his next move.

She screamed then at the sudden burn in her left hip, belatedly realising that she'd backed up on the fallen scout. Injured though he was, he was still game for he'd slashed at her with his sword, a weak thrust but one strong enough to carve a deep gash through the flesh. With a roar, she instinctively jammed her own weapon backwards, using both hands on the hilt to drive the blade straight though his forehead.

By then of course, Cargal Uí Faigil was on her again. Lunging forwards at speed, he thrust directly at her. Forced to relinquish her own weapon – now lodged firmly in the scout's shattered skull – the Grey One attempted to dodge to one side but her exhausted body meant she was simply too slow. The blade took a slice out of her shoulder.

Knocked off balance by the blow, the Grey One toppled but the *techtaire* too lost his footing and fell forward onto this face. Both struggled to get upright, he attempting to find his feet while she clambered over the dead scout, trying to find his fallen sword, now lying somewhere in the watery mud. Panicked, she groped desperately as the *techtaire* got to his feet, ignoring the pain in her shoulder as she sank her hands in up to their wrists.

Where is it?

Just as the *techtaire* came at her again, her right hand found the hilt of the weapon and she levered it up just in time to block the incoming downward stroke. Unfortunately, the strength of the attack was such that the sword was knocked right out of her hands, her wrist ringing painfully at the vibration of the blow. She caught a last glimpse of the sword spinning into the air then something crashed on her stomach, completely knocking the breath out of her.

Betrayed by the treacherous footing, the *techtaire* had slipped once more, the full bulk of him crashing onto her. Breathless, she tried to get to her feet but a fist smashed into the side of her head, knocking her flat again. Dazed and half-blinded, she felt her arms forced down by the *techtaire*'s knees, the full weight of his body now resting on her chest and arms. A thick pair of hands clamped about her neck and began to squeeze.

The sudden compression around her throat truly terrified her and her mouth gasped like a landed fish, unable to get air to her lungs. The Grey One's right hand flapped about manically, frantically seeking something to use as a weapon, finding nothing but mud, reeds, the dead scout's leg.

The knife!

Her sight was fading when she somehow found the knife in the scout's leg, somehow managed to yank it free. Doing her best to twist it around, she jabbed it into the *techtaire*'s unseen bulk, again and again, unsure if she was hitting anything or if she was simply stabbing herself.

Ironically the pressure around her throat only seemed to increase and she was on the point of blacking out when it suddenly eased. She was distantly aware of the great weight rolling off her, a firm hand holding her around the shoulders, helping to lift her from the mud. A familiar voice sounded in her ears but it seemed vague and very far away.

'Calm, Grey One! Calm!'

Fintán's voice!

'It's done, Grey One! It's done.'

***

She spent that night shivering in the shelter of the trees, holding the *Lamraighe* youth close to draw warmth from his body. Sleep was elusive, thwarted by aches of all types and severities and in the end it was exhaustion alone that allowed her to slip into the respite of unconsciousness. She slept until well past dawn on the following day.

She woke empty and emotionally hollowed, as though a thief had stolen her substance during the dark hours. Fintán had already risen by then, leaving two heavy cloaks draped over her body to keep her warm. Emotionally fragile, the thoughtfulness of that simple gesture was enough to cause a lump in her throat.

Physically, she was in a bad way too, of course. Battered and slashed, her pounded body protested when she finally sat up. Her feet, grazed and blistered, also hurt but she forced herself to stumble stiffly from the shelter of the trees, out onto the bank of the mud flat. She saw that the mucky layer was wet again, dampened by an overnight shower that had coated it with a fresh film of moisture. A few pools of cloudy water mirrored the dull sky overhead. The bodies of the warriors also remained out there, lying where they'd fallen and already being picked at by the birds and other animals.

She sighed, swaying weakly as she regarded the scene before her. There was a barrenness to the mud flat that she was unfamiliar with, a starkness that didn't sit well with her. Once again, she'd somehow survived outlandish odds and yet such victory or accomplishment did nothing to quell her loneliness, the despair she felt at losing Bodhmhall. Even now, her heart hurt like the bloodburn of fingertips after coming in from the winter cold.

The sound of someone pushing unhurriedly through the reeds made her turn and she saw Fintán emerge from a head-height clump further down to her right. As he approached her, the *Lamraighe* youth looked subdued, almost a bit scared. Looking down at her hands and the front of her battle harness, she realised that both were still caked with dried blood.

As was often the case when trying to speak with people, the Grey One had no idea how to start the conversation. She cleared her throat and immediately regretted it for it was still raw, the black and purple marks only part of the damage from the throttling she'd received at Cargal Uí Faigil's hands.

'How did you carry me here?'

The *Lamraighe* youth looked at her curiously. 'I didn't. You managed to walk. Do you not remember?'

Annoyed, because she didn't remember – had no memory of it at all, in fact – the Grey One said nothing. She resisted the urge to respond with a sharp shake of her head, conscious that the movement would only serve to hurt and make her dizzy. Fintán waited in silence for a moment then turned, to gut the two eels he'd been carrying. The Grey One understood that he wasn't anticipating a response from her, had been with her so long in fact that he no longer expected anything from her. The realisation prompted unfamiliar feelings of remorse.

'No,' she admitted at last, shifting her weight awkwardly from one foot to another. 'But I remember that Cargal Uí Faigil was killing me, that you saved me from death.'

She attempted a smile but it hurt and she wasn't entirely sure if this was as a result of her injuries or simply because her facial muscles were unused to such movements.

'Thank you, Fintán. I did not expect to see you again. Or even imagine you'd want to come and help me. I ... You did well.'

Fintán stared at her, his eyes wide. He appeared stunned by the rare words of praise.

Leaving him, she wandered along the edge of the mud flat until she found a pool where the water looked relatively clear. There, she painfully peeled off her leggings. Because of her injuries, removing the tight battle harness proved a more substantial challenge. Her fingers, numb from fatigue, fumbled on the straps and, in the end, unable to manoeuvre her arms or shoulders, she resigned herself to leaving it on and washing underneath as best she could.

It took a while to scour the worst of the sweat and blood away, even using the grubby sand to scrub it off but the cold bite of the water helped to provide some clarity of mind. As she washed, she was surprised to discover a poultice bound around the injuries on her shoulder and her leg. Fintán must have applied them while she slept.

Returning to the bank, she accepted the youth's offer of a fresh poultice and sat quietly raking her fingers though the muddy soil, biting her tongue as he carefully worked around the gash. The wound itself burned excrutiatingly but, in an odd way, the pain was almost absorbed in the meshwork of other aches and pains: the broken ribs, the gash in her leg, the other injuries that made up the entirety of her aching existence.

Tasting blood in her mouth, she swallowed, immediately grimacing at the pain it caused. She scowled. Between that and the cut to her shoulder, Cargal Uí Faigil had certainly left his mark on her.

Her eyes drifted down the bank where the warrior himself was sprawled, up beyond the reeds where Fintán had dragged him. His hands and legs had been fastened tight with rude flax bindings for he wasn't dead as she'd originally believed, hoped for in fact. With his knees pressing her elbows down into the mud, her attempts at stabbing him had been ineffectual and done little more than make shallow gashes in the only part of his body she'd been able to reach: the side of his left leg. In the end, it had been Fintán who'd taken him out, clobbering him from behind with a hefty slab of oak wood.

She nodded at that. She'd always appreciated a decent rear attack.

Conscious now, the false *techtaire* was glancing at them nervously, no doubt in fear for his life.

'Let's go and talk to our enemy,' she said.

***

Having passed the night unable to move, Cargal Uí Faigil's hair and skull were still coated in grime, his body a veritable carapace of mud. Despite this, the sly expression was exactly as Liath Luachra remembered from when she'd first locked eyes with him at Ráth Bládhma, a strange brown colour, like sun-dried mud or shit. Although in visible discomfort, the *techtaire* greeted them with some bravado, his lips drawn into a smile over unwhite teeth.

'Do you come seeking your vengeance, Grey One?'

Liath Luachra stood regarding him in silence, Fintán to the rear of her right shoulder. Crafty one that he was, the *techtaire* assessed them both, glancing at Fintán briefly before discounting him and directing his full attention to her. He knew on whose decision his life would hang.

'You should spare me,' he said.

The woman warrior's lips twisted in a wry grimace. 'To have you come at me again?' She shook her head.

'I am not your enemy, Grey One. Release me and you have my word I'll slink home to my tribal land, never to bother you again.'

'You have a false tongue Cargal. I've known men like you. Even if you truly intended to leave as you say, someone would make you an offer and you'd discard your word. You'll return, with Gob An Teanga Gorm and that smiling friend with the knife until you or we are dead.'

'Conán mac Morna?' Cargal Uí Faigil's face assumed a distasteful expression. 'He is not my friend.'

The woman warrior shrugged. 'I'll still wipe the smile from his face.'

'In truth, I never liked that youth either,' the *techtaire* agreed. 'But as younger brother to Goll mac Morna, his place on the *fian* could never be refused.' He suddenly grinned up at her. 'Mind you, you'll struggle to wipe the smile from his face given that he no longer has one. That stew burned him to the bone. He'll be lucky to survive.'

228

She grunted. 'No-one will weep that loss.'

A sudden wave of weariness ran through her. Feeling faint and unsteady, she slumped against the trunk of a fallen tree for support, wincing when the rough bark hit her shoulder. Her frailty was not lost on the *techtaire*.

'Your wounds reveal themselves.' His voice rang smug with satisfaction. 'The thrust of my sword was true.'

'It was,' she admitted. 'But not as true as Fintán's blow to your head.'

This time, it was he who grunted, keen to change the topic. 'You cannot hope to overcome your enemies, Grey One. Not with the wounds you carry. That shoulder will fester and you'll fall to fever. You have no choice. Make an agreement with me and we can work together. I will not betray you.'

Liath Luachra said nothing but raised her fingers to her mouth, tenderly touching her swollen lips. The *techtaire* regarded her warily, striving to read her thoughts from her blank expression. The silence extended until Liath Luachra got to her feet and drew Fintán's knife – retrieved from the mud – from her scabbard. 'It seems there is nothing more to discuss between us.'

His eyes flickered warily to the blade and back to her again. 'What I tell you is true, Grey One. We can work together against your enemies. I have knowledge that will help you, insights you'll want to know.'

She laughed softly at that, raised the knife and scraped the tip of the blade against her leather harness to test its sharpness. 'There is nothing you can give me. The one thing I want, you do not have.'

'Wait, I…'

Ignoring him, she leaned in, bringing the blade to his throat.

'Tréanmór's daughter lives!'

Liath Luachra froze. She stared tersely at the *techtaire*, unsure if she'd heard him correctly. Sensing how close his life hung in the balance, the warrior suddenly couldn't speak fast enough.

'The *bandraoi* lives. She's alive! I tell you no lie. She's alive.'

The woman warrior continued to regard him, her gaze unreadable, her eyes cold as ice. Her grip on the knife tightened, the knuckles whitening as she struggled with the competing desire to hear him out and to silence him for good. Somehow, she managed to still her hand. 'Spill your secrets,' she snarled.

'Gob An Teanga Gorm! He …' Although he was speaking quickly, the Grey One still had the sense that Cargal Uí Faigil was choosing his words with care, eager not to give too much away but at the same time, wary of raising her ire. In which case, he had his work cut out for him.

'The Cailleach Dubh escaped Gob's men. She managed to reach the fortress of Dún Baoiscne.'

'That's arse-to-mouth talk.' Her voice dripped scorn. 'I don't believe you.'

'It's true!'

He was pleading now and as the Grey One scrutinised him, she could see the mounting alarm in his eyes. Unless he was truly skilled at falsehood and deception, it was hard not to credit his belief in what he was telling her. Fearing to give in to the possibility of hope when it was so likely to be dashed however, she was reluctant to accept it. 'Dún Baoiscne is still two or three days' travel. You could not possibly know whether she made it or not.'

The *techtaire's* face was ashen, straining from the effort to convince her. 'Our scouts followed sign of the Cailleach Dubh and the boy headed towards *Clann Baoiscne* tribe lands then lost their trail. But Gob has a lock of the woman's hair.' His eyes followed her nervously, fearful that she would disbelieve him. 'That way, her resting place at night can be known.'

The woman warrior's face screwed up in anger. 'What *ráiméis* are you spouting now?'

'That's what I was told! Gob An Teanga Gorm is *rígfénnid*. I do what he tells me and that's what he told me. He says that if they have a lock of the *bandraoi's* hair they can tell where she'd been sleeping. That's why such a small number of warriors was sent in your pursuit while Gob took ten warriors to the north.'

The woman warrior considered him suspiciously, fighting to suppress the pulse of anger now rising up inside her. The *techtaire* would say anything to make her hold her blade but ... Gods! Could it be possible? She was terrified to hope it could be true but was it possible? Could Bodhmhall still breathe the air of life?

'How can they know where she is simply from a lock of hair?'

'*Sin é mar dhraíocht!*' The *techtaire* tried to shrug but was hindered by his bonds. 'That's *draoi* knowings. I've seen the *draoi* at night when he explores the dreams of the person he seeks but I'd not claim to understand the powers of the Gifted Ones.' He paused then and his eyes took on a sly look. 'And what of you, Grey One? Have you no visitors at night? They also have a lock of your hair.'

A cold sensation rippled down the woman warrior's spine as she recalled the blank-faced *Fear Dubh* from her dreams. It seemed too much of a coincidence for the *techtaire* to make such a far-fetched claim but she was loathe to believe him and decided to keep her thoughts to herself.

'Your talk bores a hole in my head with its emptiness. How could they get a lock of my hair?'

'I don't know. I've already told you my *rígfénnid* doesn't tell me everything.'

She frowned at that. 'You don't know much, do you?' She paused then, momentarily distracted by the pain in her left side. Shifting her weight to take the pressure off the wound, she considered her prisoner once more. 'Tell me of your leader. Who is he?'

'Gob An Teanga Gorm.'

She shook her head. 'As *rígfénnid*, Gob An Teanga Gorm may lead the *fian* but he doesn't set its purpose. He receives those commands from someone else.' She sniffed, wiped her nose and regarded him keenly. 'It's that tall man, isn't it? The wiry one whose nose I broke. He's behind all this.'

The *techtaire*, previously so vocal, suddenly seemed less keen to speak.

'Who is he?' pressed the Grey One. She locked him with a gaze of chilling intensity and although the threat was unstated it was also unmistakable.

It took a moment for his response to come and when it did, it sounded lukewarm and reluctant, almost resentful. 'He's a *draoi*. A powerful *draoi* from the north.'

Liath Luachra nodded to herself. Even from her limited interaction with the tall man, she'd sensed the power within him. She should probably have guessed he was a Gifted One. 'Go on, then. This *draoi*. He must have a name. Who is he?'

Cargal Uí Faigil looked down at his feet, his earlier bluster now all but dissipated. 'I can't tell you. He'd know if I spoke his name aloud. I've seen how he works in the darkness of night. He has no mercy, no remorse. Mine would be a cruel and protracted death.'

The Grey One regarded the *techtaire* with fresh interest, struck by the depth of his transformation. With his clotted, crusted hair and mud-streaked face, he suddenly seemed reduced or shrunken. There was no doubt as to the veracity of his fear. He was genuinely terrified of the *draoi*, even more terrified than he was of her.

And she no longer had patience for that.

Drawing closer, she grasped his chin with her left hand and raised it so that she could stare into his eyes.

'Tell me.'

He shook his head.

She jabbed him just below the knee with the point of the knife, pushing the tip of the blade so that it penetrated the depth of a fingertip into his flesh. Cargal screamed, not so much from pain as from anticipation of pain. But he told her.

***

Leaving the shaken *techtaire*, Liath Luachra and Fintán withdrew to the trees to speak more freely. As usual, the woman warrior was brusque and to the point.

'You heard what he said. Bodhmhall's alive and in *Clann Baoiscne* territory. And possibly Demne as well.'

Fintán didn't say anything and she realised he was probably thinking of his wounded father and the pregnant Muirne, stranded out in the wilderness with no-one to help them.

'I cannot make it alone, Fintán. At least, not in time to be of any help.'

The youth looked away and Liath Luachra breathed deeply. Unaccustomed to asking for help, it galled her to be in a position where she was obliged to do so, particularly from someone she felt bound to protect. The unfortunate truth however was that she was simply too weak to travel alone. Even travelling with the youth's assistance, she knew the journey would be arduous and extremely demanding.

Worried, she studied the youth with more attention than she had at any point over the previous days. He'd lost much of the brazen manner that had marked their first encounter and the romantic notions he'd held towards her had been irrevocably quashed since then. She felt a degree of regret in that regard. She'd been somewhat brutal when dealing with his bombast although, to be fair, the youth's resemblance to Bearach had always caused her great discomfort.

Finally, Fintán turned back to face her. 'And what of my father and Muirne?'

'Gleor and Muirne are in no immediate danger. They're alone but they have weapons and food. Cargal Uí Faigil said that Gob and his men travel to seek Bodhmhall and Demne. They need our help first.'

'I heard him say that but I also heard him tell you Gob travelled with at least ten warriors. Even if we get to *Clann Baoiscne* territory and find our comrades, we can't tackle that many warriors. You barely survived this last combat and you can hardly stand.'

'I will think of something.'

232

He surprised her by chuckling. 'You have the hardiness of stone, Grey One. The odds seem impossible but yes, I will come with you. On the condition that, afterwards, you help my father.'

'Our deal is made.' Liath Luachra turned and looked to the north. A strong wind was rising in over the mud flat from that direction and it had the chill of late autumn.

'What of Cargal Uí Faigil? What shall we do with him?'

'I shall occupy myself with Cargal Uí Faigil.'

'Will you kill him?'

She paused and looked at the stricken figure, still hunched down by his bindings. 'I don't know. Sometimes the people we detest most can be more useful than those we trust.' She shrugged. 'But then of course, sometimes people can only be what their weakness of character allows.'

Fintán considered that for a moment. 'How do you know so much about people?'

'Because,' she said, pulling her cloak tighter around her. 'I used to be one.'

Leaning into the gust, she started back to the mud flat.

Chapter Thirteen

Dawn seeped through the sky like blood through an oozing bandage. From the ramparts of Dún Baoiscne's inner wall, Bodhmhall watched the arrival of the eastern blood sun with muted apprehension. Although not one to take much heed of portents, the ruddy clouds augured little good and did little to quell her growing disquiet at the challenges that lay ahead.

Earlier, from that same vantage point, she'd watched Uargal lead fifteen warriors away from the fortress, their hazy forms almost indistinguishable against the pre-dawn shadow. Soon after the warriors' departure, a strong wind had rolled in from the north-east, dragging a series of vicious showers in its wake. The grey downpour had quickly driven the people of Dún Baoiscne indoors and rinsed all trace of red from the sky.

Despite the weather, the *bandraoi* had remained on the ramparts, enjoying the solitude she'd found in the lee of a wicker shelter that protected her from the worst of the elements. The muffled sound of rain slapping against the fortress had also proved an unexpected balm, a damp solace to her internal fretting. Concern for her nephew meant she'd slept poorly and her slumber had been further disturbed by the worrying crunch of heavy footsteps in the *lis*. Several times the footsteps had circled the roundhouse. On one occasion, they'd stopped directly outside the entrance and although the midnight walker hadn't entered, the menace in that sudden silence had left the *bandraoi* trembling. Finally, the footsteps had started up again and thankfully moved away, fading into the distance.

Cathal Bog.

With her distrust of Becal and Lonán now partially quelled, her suspicions had transferred fully to the silent warrior, a particular concern given her father had assigned him to keep watch on her activities. Even now, although she couldn't actually see him, she could feel the predatory weight of his gaze as he watched and waited to see what she'd do next.

The threat of Cathal Bog wasn't the only concern that lay heavy on the *bandraoi*'s shoulders. Much of the early morning had been taken up with thinking about how best to deal with Lonán Ballach's grab for power and the imminent arrival of the *Clann Baoiscne* elders. She did not have much time before the calm of the fortress was rent asunder.

A shuffle of movement drew the *bandraoi*'s eyes to where a female figure was climbing the stone steps that led up to the rampart. Clambering onto the wooden platform, the figure turned, head hunched against the rain and started towards her.

Bé Bhinn!

Brightening at the sight of a friendly face, Bodhmhall waved and waited for her to reach the shelter.

'*A chara!* You're about early.'

The *Clann Baoiscne* woman pulled under the awning with some relief. The rain had turned her red hair dark brown and the freckles that stained her nose and cheeks seemed more prominent in the dull light. 'Niall travels with the *fian*. I had to help him prepare.' She raised her hand to brush a smatter of raindrops from her face. 'I was back to feeding the pigs when I saw you atop the wall and thought you'd like some company.'

'With you, of course. Although at Dún Baoiscne I must dance to my father's tune.'

'Yes, I'd heard.' Her friend's forehead furrowed in sudden concern. 'I overheard some whispers this morning, Bodhmhall. Before Niall's departure. They said you intend to remain at Dún Baoiscne, to reclaim Fiacail mac Codhna as husband.'

Bodhmhall's lips parted in a wry smile, tipped with an icy bitterness. 'Fresh Whispers spread by my father. You know how he likes to utilise his Whispers.'

'I thought as much but …' Bé Bhinn hesitated. 'There is something else … Something I felt you should know.' She regarded the *bandraoi* uncertainly then nervously licked her lips. 'One of the warriors leaving for An Gleann Teann was on guard duty in the *lis* last night and …' She hesitated. 'He told me he'd seen Fiacail alone with your father in An Halla Mór, late in the night when everyone else was abed. He didn't hear what was said but he told me that much *uisce beatha* and laughter was shared within those walls.'

The *bandraoi* blinked at that. Whispers from her father, lamentably, were to be expected but this was a new twist.

'The Whispers also say you have a nephew, Cumhal's son.'

'That much is true.'

The red-haired woman mused over this fresh morsel of news then startled the *bandraoi* by leaning close in the confined space of the shelter and whispering urgently in her ear. 'Leave, Bodhmhall. Take your nephew and return to Ráth Bládhma. There's a growing tightness to the air here at Dún Baoiscne. I'd not have you entangled in whatever results.'

The *bandraoi* regarded her friend, impressed by her instincts with respect to the long-simmering political dynamic that was only now coming to the boil.

'That's my sweetest desire, Bé Bhinn. But I have obligations to fulfil before I can leave.'

Her friend considered that for a moment and although her gaze remained unsettled, she nodded her acceptance. Sighing, she turned away to look over the wall. The internal stone barrier was higher than the outer embankment and allowed a direct view down the valley. Even at this distance, wispy curtains of rain could be seen, driven west along the valley floor.

Neither woman spoke for a time. Concerned by the tension in her friend's stance, Bodhmhall continued to observe her from the corner of her eye.

'I sometimes wonder at the life you lead out there in the Great Wild,' the red-haired woman said at last. 'Niall describes Ráth Bládhma as a perilous place, a fragile island in the wilderness.'

'There's some truth to that,' the *bandraoi* admitted. 'Life at Glenn Ceoch's not an easy one and it has its dangers. That said, our *ráth* has stout walls and we've held the territory successfully these many years. Besides, it has its attractions. The valley's quite lovely and holds good grazing land. After years of rearing, we have an impressive dairy herd.'

The *bandraoi* could feel her mood lift as she spoke of home. She turned to face the other woman now perched with one elbow against the wall, listening with obvious interest.

'Come with me, *a chara.*'

'What?'

'Come to Ráth Bládhma with me. And do not let tribal loyalty cloud your decision. We both know the shallowness of its depths here, the ...' Bodhmhall felt her voice catch and swallowed to clear her throat before continuing again. 'Even now, after all these years, the bitterness eats at me. I know you must feel the same.'

The offer had taken her friend completely by surprise. Bodhmhall could tell that much from her stunned expression. Saying no more, she looked away to give her friend the space to work through the proposition. When the *Clann Baoiscne* woman's response finally came however, it was with a sad shake of the head.

'Your invitation is generous, Bodhmhall but I must decline. Despite everything's that happened I have a son here, a home and a husband. Besides, both Demmán and Emmel rest in the Cuirreach valley. T'would be a poor act to desert them, to leave them alone and untended.'

'Your son would be more than welcome, *a chara.* There are many children at the settlement and another would be joyously received.'

'And Niall?' The red-haired woman's face was unreadable.

Bodhmhall hesitated, ruefully regarding her friend. The question had caught her off guard. 'Niall doesn't like me,' she answered carefully. 'So I doubt he'd like Ráth Bládhma. Or that he'd accompany you there. But then … Is that such a loss? With your parents, Demmán and Emmel gone, do you not remain with Niall Tuirseach from necessity rather than true affection?'

Bé Bhinn's face crumpled and the *bandraoi* stopped, horrified at the realisation of how callously she'd overstepped the boundaries of friendship. 'Forgive me, *a chara.*' She held both hands out in apology. 'I spoke rashly. I …'

'You cast truths like hard stones, Bodhmhall.' Bé Bhinn's lower lip trembled but her voice remained surprisingly firm. 'I don't deny what you say but my reasons for staying surpass those arguments. The truth is I fear for my son's safety. Dún Baoiscne undoubtedly stifles the spirit and our history here breaks my heart but you can't argue that my son would be reared more safely out in the Great Wild.'

Bodhmhall looked away, biting down the urge to argue the point.

Meanwhile, the red-haired woman had pulled away from the wall and was gathering her cloak about her with quiet dignity. 'I know your words were shared with my interests at heart, Bodhmhall but your circumstances are different to mine. They always have been.' Her dark green eyes regarded the *bandraoi* with sad conviction. 'I am not the daughter of a *rí.* I do not have powerful friends or a courageous partner to support my decisions. It's been a sore challenge but for the sake of my son I've forced myself to make peace with what happened here. That is all I can do.'

Bé Bhinn turned and started back along the ramparts in the direction of the steps. With a sick feeling in her stomach, Bodhmhall watched her last friend in Dún Baoiscne walk away.

***

The rain had ceased when the *bandraoi* finally descended to the *lis*, still troubled from her conversation with Bé Bhinn. The air remained thick with moisture, the grey stone of the wall slick and glistening. The leather flaps of the roundhouse doors creaked against their bindings in the rising wind.

At the bottom of the western steps, Bodhmhall pulled her cloak tighter and started towards the roundhouse where Fiacail had been confined. No guards were visible at the entrance but she spotted two warriors inside the doorway of Cathal Bog's dwelling, poised to intercede if the Seiscenn Uarbhaoil man tried to leave. Of the big *conradh* himself, there was no sign and she was about to question her instincts when he appeared from behind

237

An Halla Mór. Increasing his pace, he reached the roundhouse before her and leaned nonchalantly against the wall, his heavy-lidded eyes watching as she approached.

Despite the knot of fear in her stomach, she scowled defiantly as she made to enter. Masticating apathetically on some unidentified morsel of food, the warrior made no acknowledgement.

'Bodhmhall!'

Inside the roundhouse, the Seiscenn Uarbhaoil man uncoiled fluidly from the sleeping platform. The interior was cold, the fire unlit but Fiacail, dressed in woollen trousers and *léine*, appeared untroubled by the cooler temperatures. With a broad grin, he rolled lightly onto the soles of his feet and advanced as though to embrace her. 'Aaah, Bodhmhall! You brighten an otherwise dismal morning.'

Unmoved by the greeting, the *bandraoi* remained just inside the doorway, feet slightly apart, arms stiff by her sides.

'The pox take you, Fiacail mac Codhna! One thing! One single thing I asked of you.'

The warrior drew to a halt, startled by the fury of her response.

'Come now, Bodhmhall. Those are harsh words to cast about.'

'You're as useless as buttocks on a fish! How could you let yourself be taken?'

'Buttocks on a fish?' Fiacail grinned, amused by the comparison. 'You might recall I was travelling with a child. A child who doesn't run very fast.' He raised both hands in an expression of helplessness. 'What did you expect of me?'

'Less than was requested but certainly more than was delivered.'

At that, the Seiscenn Uarbhaoil man placed one hand over his heart and flinched melodramatically, feigning a serious wound. 'Now that sharp tongue truly cuts deep. Dear one, I did my best to protect your nephew but the terrain was thick with *Clann Baoiscne* patrols. It was as though they knew we were out there. When they eventually discovered us and offered ungentle invitation I fought them but ...' He reached up to touch the bruise on his face and winced. 'That turned out as pleasant as a dose of the runs after a hard shit.'

'You spoke with my father again. After I was obliged to retire for the night.'

'That's true. Tréanmór bade me visit him at An Halla Mór. His tune had changed since our earlier discussion for this time he was all honeywords, soft as cream after my comfort, offering drink and seductive propositions.'

'Seductive propositions? What was offered? The horse you so enviously sought of Father Sun?'

This time Fiacail laughed openly. 'A mount of a different type, Bodhmhall.'

The *bandraoi* took a deep breath but there was no disguising the anger in her voice when she spoke again. 'What did my father propose?'

'That I reclaim you as my woman and have you bear my children. With that, he offered the best land in the Cuirreach valley and ten of his dairy cows. All in all,' he admitted. 'It was a tempting offer. Your father learned his lesson late and seeks to make up for lost time with further grandchildren. He'd have golden butter rubbed on your flanks and thighs each day were you to deliver what he desires.'

'I thought you were my friend.' This time there was an audible quaver in the *bandraoi*'s voice.

'I am your friend. I'm probably the only true friend you have in this fortress.'

'And yet, here's my nephew in Dún Baoiscne despite your promise and you sharing drinks and laughter with my father during the dark hours.' The *bandraoi* took a deep breath and exhaled heavily. 'I've always thought you a man of straight integrity, Fiacail. Not one to make a zig-zag of conscience. Now, I truly question the convenience of our encounter in the Great Wild.'

'For the first time, the warrior's face displayed displeasure, his eyes narrowing at the veiled accusation. 'Suspicion fouls your judgement, Bodhmhall. It was circumstance and nothing more that caused our paths to cross. Besides, you know me. I am a man who bares all –'

'Gods, yes!'

He ignored the jibe. 'And who conceals nothing. I am not a man for underhand dealings. That's why my answer to Tréanmór's proposition was that he kiss my freckled arse.'

'So you say.'

Fiacail's features darkened. 'Now you fall back on addled talk. There's no need for this. Accept my own proposition and accompany me back to Seiscenn Uarbhaoil. There you and Demne can both have my protection.'

Spine straight as a hazel rod, Bodhmhall shook her head.

Fiacail opened his mouth to speak but then abruptly seemed to change his mind. 'Well, scratch your ass, so.'

With this, he lay back on the sleeping platform, placed his hands gently on his chest and closed his eyes. 'My offer remains, Bodhmhall, should you choose to bite the biscuit of humility. Until then, it's a damp day. Make sure the flap hangs correct when you leave.'

***

Cathal Bog was still outside when Bodhmhall stormed from the roundhouse and although his expression didn't change, a certain tautness to his posture confirmed he'd heard every word of the discussion. Ignoring his blunt stare, the *bandraoi* stalked back to her own roundhouse, plunged through the doorway and stood rigidly in the centre of its Spartan comfort.

Free from scrutiny, she finally gave in to the stress that was bubbling up inside her, dropping the façade of strength she'd managed to maintain throughout the morning. Slumping to the ground, she sat clutching her injured arm and screamed silently into the layers of her cloak.

It took a time for the trembling to subside but the *bandraoi* gradually recovered herself. Fragile but determined, she stumbled to her feet and removed her *léine*. Retrieving the bowl of water and a loose rag, she started to wash.

As always, the simple ritual of bathing calmed her, the touch of the rough cloth against her skin a physical distraction from the anxieties crowding her head. Feeling more at ease, she put the cloth and bowl to one side and sat on the sleeping platform, rubbing her palms together as she worked through the next steps of her plan. In the hub of deception and intrigue that was Dún Baoiscne, the effort of achieving her own ends had taken its toll, however that effort had been worth it now that her goals had for the most part been achieved, her seeds all sown. From this point on she could shift her focus to more practical preparations and allow those seeds the time and space to germinate.

***

Bodhmhall finally emerged at mid-day. By then the rain had returned with a vengeance, heavy hail battering the roof of the roundhouses, forming deep puddles in a dip to the eastern side of the *lis*. Surveying the sky, she nodded to herself in silence. The torrential downpour looked set to continue for the remainder of the afternoon and well into the night.

From the refuge of her doorway, she examined the *lis*, noting that the guard who usually patrolled the ramparts had retreated to the passageway to avoid the rain. Despite being rugged in a heavy sheepskin cloak, he still looked miserable due to the chill draughts that howled down the stone-lined tunnel with the westerly wind.

In Cathal Bog's dwelling, the warriors she'd seen earlier that morning were still present, visible through the doorway. Of the big *conradh* himself, there was no sign although she felt safe to assume he was in there too, sheltering from the weather and waiting for her to step outside.

240

She swallowed then, her nerves suddenly raw. Four warriors in the internal *lis* alone.

Tréanmór takes no chances now he has a grandson close to hand.

Turning her attention to Lonán Ballach's roundhouse, she studied it for a time but the lack of activity or any flicker of light confirmed his absence. Cunning as ever, the *rechtaire* had most likely made himself scarce in preparation for the elders' forthcoming arrival the following morning, lining up his *fidchell* pins for the real game to commence.

Launching herself from the doorway and into the rain, the *bandraoi* scurried across the sodden *lis* to An Halla Mór. Forcing the doors open with her good hand, she slipped inside and quickly closed them behind her. As she shook the raindrops from her cloak, her gaze fell to the empty stool by the entrance and her lips twisted into a grimace.

No doubt he'll be along.

Drawing back her hood, the *bandraoi* made her way down the gloomy hall to the inner fire-pit where her nephew and her father were seated. Although engaged in conversation when she'd arrived, both now sat up, peering into the gloom towards her as they tried to make out who'd entered. Recognising his aunt, Demne sprang from his seat with a yelp of delight and rushed forwards to hug her about the waist.

'*A bhuachaillín.*' Bodhmhall stroked his head fondly but her eyes remained on her father. For his part, Tréanmór returned her gaze with an unexpected equanimity. Given his previous hostility towards her, the *bandraoi* was surprised by his composure, even more surprised to see the full set of the Five Friends back on their table, apparently forgotten.

'Father.'

He continued to scan her, his features shrewd and attentive but displaying none of the anger from the previous evening. She breathed deliberately to loosen the tension in her chest.

'Bodhmhall, I should warn you that if you come seeking to take my grandson from Dún Baoiscne, my decision remains unchanged.'

Bodhmhall bowed her head in a conciliatory manner. 'I'm aware of the futility of argument with you, Father. I'll not waste your time nor my own breath on circumstances I cannot alter. Besides, you were correct on one point at least. The boy is safer here than at Ráth Bládhma.'

Tréanmór graced her with an approving nod. 'You finally accept the reality of circumstance. That pleases me, Daughter.'

The *bandraoi* forced a compliant smile. He didn't mean a word of it of course. Knowing her as he did, he certainly wouldn't have believed her contrite acquiescence. She picked at the sleeve of her *léine*. There were

241

layers to her conversations with her father. Words exchanged and opinions articulated but for all of that, the most important details were often worked out through their mutual scrutiny of what remained unsaid and unrevealed.

The *rí* of *Clann Baoiscne* reached for a wooden jug and poured himself a goblet of some yellow-tinted liquid before turning to address his grandson. 'Demne, you will leave us now. We speak of issues not for your ears.'

Disgruntled by this abrupt dismissal, the boy made a point of getting up slowly, although not so slowly as to risk a rebuke from his grandfather. Making his way towards the gap in the leather screen, he looked plaintively back at his aunt before disappearing inside.

Satisfied, Tréanmór refocussed his attention on the *bandraoi*. 'For all our differences, Daughter, I have to commend you on your rearing. The boy has a keen mind, subtle too.' He sniffed then and wrinkled his nose as though confronted by an unpleasant odour. 'Mind you, it still galls me to consider that it was from Muirne Muncháem's thighs he was issued.'

Bodhmhall eyed him closely for his expression had become one of rare moodiness.

'It was with Muirne Muncháem alone that your brother ever defied me, Bodhmhall.' He shook his head in gloomy reflection. 'That woman had Cumhal beguiled, waving her piss flaps at him the way she did. She had him dangling like an eel on a hook. Razor sharp and yet …' He stared into the fire. 'Dangerously sweet. Sweet enough to steal honey from a swarming hive.'

Bodhmhall said nothing. As the target of Muirne's antagonism during her time at Dún Baoiscne, she needed no reminding of the Almhu woman's sting. It all came down to the desire for power, of course. With the benefit of hindsight and much reflection, she understood that now. Power had always been a draw for Muirne, the hunger she couldn't sate, the coveted food just out of reach on another's plate. Fearful of Bodhmhall's close relationship with the Dún Baoiscne *tánaiste* and the threat to her own influence, the Flower of Almhu had sought to undermine her at every opportunity.

Tréanmór rose to his feet and started his habitual pacing about the fire-pit. He must have felt in a rare place of security for his natural reservation momentarily slipped from his shoulders. 'Did you know, the Flower of Almhu came to us without a dowry?'

Bodhmhall stared. She hadn't known. For many years her brother's bonding to the Flower of Almhu had been the standard to which she'd been held to account and to learn of that flaw in what she'd thought a perfect union was truly a revelation.

'Without a dowry,' Tréanmór continued. 'Without a settled alliance, without benefit of any kind. Indeed, she came with little more than her father's enmity for, by all accounts, Tadg mac Nuadat opposed the union.' He came to a halt and regarded her, his face unreadable. 'To spare your brother's future reputation as leader, I accepted Muirne and spread the Whisper they'd received Tadg's blessing. Cumhal was forever grateful of course, but ...'

Tréanmór turned to look at her, his eyes still hot from the reflected glow of the fire. 'But Muirne Muncháem is not the reason for your visit. Why have you come, Daughter?'

The *bandraoi* parted her lips to speak but at that moment, the hall doors opened, the high-pitched creak underscored by the howl of the wind. Distracted, she twisted about to watch Cathal Bog slink in, close the door behind him and silently reclaim his stool.

With a frown, she turned back to her father, her head inclined. 'We agree that Demne's safer here at Dún Baoiscne but the traitor still poses a threat. Last night, with the ... disruption, the account you requested was forgotten.'

Tréanmór sat up straight, suddenly all interest. 'You know the traitor's identity?'

'No. But I know more. Yesterday, I spoke with Becal and questioned him at length.'

'And do you think he's the traitor?'

Although her father's features were composed, the *bandraoi* discerned an unexpected eagerness in the tone of his voice.

He wishes Becal to be the traitor. It aligns with his own distaste for the man.

'I don't believe so.'

The *rí* of *Clann Baoiscne* grunted unhappily. 'So not, Becal.' He frowned. 'More's the pity. I'd imagined the scent of treachery in that gnat's fart.'

'Oh, there's treachery in him for certain but then, you already knew that.'

Tréanmór held her gaze and a thin smile showed her he hadn't missed the jibe. He made no attempt to deny it. 'Lonán then.'

Bodhmhall shook her head, struck by the irony. A fortress-full of traitors yet none of them the one she was seeking.

'Lonán's not the traitor either?' There was a note of impatience in her father's voice. 'Are you certain? When he wants something hidden, Lonán's mouth can be as tight as a cow's arse in fly season.'

'He's not the Adversary's man.'

The response was not an outright lie but to her surprise, Bodhmhall experienced an unexpected moment of filial guilt at not alerting him to the *rechtaire*'s intended treachery.

'And you used your *Gift*?'

'Yes. On both. It seemed to confirm what they told me.'

Tréanmór's jaw tightened. 'Well, if not Becal or Lonán, then who is the traitor?' This time there was a detectable trace of exasperation to his words.

Instead of responding directly, *the bandraoi* sat back on her stool and jerked her head in the direction of the doors. She watched her father's eyes flicker towards Cathal Bog then back to her, observing how the comprehension sank in.

'No.' Tréanmór shook his head, the firm tone making it clear he brooked no such possibility. 'Not Cathal. You have erred. Dún Baoiscne is Cathal's home. No fox shits in his own den.'

'Cathal is no fox. And the same argument could be used for Becal or Lonán.'

Her father made no reply as he thought that over. After a moment or two, still unwilling to accept her allegation on the matter, he bluntly attempted to redirect the conversation by reaching for the jug. 'You will have some honeyed leaf? It is a smooth drink.'

Bodhmhall frowned, understanding that there would be no further discussion on the identity of the traitor. 'You offer no *uisce beatha*?' she asked cynically. 'As you did with Fiacail?'

With that, Tréanmór's eyes fixed on hers, surprised but also bearing the tiniest flicker of amusement. 'You know of Fiacail's visit?' A rough chuckle trickled from his lips. 'Well, it's no secret, Bodhmhall. The simple truth is that I like to hear men talk. Many words of wisdom have been spoken within these walls and that Fiacail, he's a windy speaker.'

'Fiacail's always claimed that any wisdom spoken here passed out through the roof with the smoke of the fire.'

Tréanmór's lips clamped into a tight line. 'Fiacail's breath does not decorate his mouth.'

The *bandraoi* shrugged. 'It hardly matters. It wasn't from Fiacail that I learned of your meeting. Your Whispers are not the only ones that travel through the fortress.'

An uncomfortable silence stretched between them.

Don't do this, the *bandraoi* warned herself. *Don't put everything at risk by stirring up the past.*

244

Tréanmór meanwhile had clasped his hands. He locked his fingers together before disentangling them again. He didn't say anything but there was no mistaking the warning in his posture.

It served only to provoke her further.

'Do you not agree?'

He gave a cynical smile. 'So, you wish to speak of the Whispers? He shook his head with faked regret. 'I suppose it was inevitable.'

'That depends,' she countered. 'Do you speak of the Whispers of your midnight meeting with Fiacail or ...' Despite the stretch of the intervening years, the words came out bitter and jagged. 'Or the whispers that Dub Tíre and I were lovers. And that I killed him in a jealous rage.'

A terrible anger stretched between them and she felt as though the silence of it might creak under the strain.

Fool! You fool!

It seemed to take two lifetimes before her father cleared his throat and spoke again.

'There were good reasons for introducing the Whispers all those years ago, Daughter. Just as there are good reasons today.'

Caught up in her own anger, Bodhmhall's response came out in a low snarl. 'Spoken with the zeal of practiced deceit. The only time you use the Whispers is when you seek political leverage or opportunities for tribal expansion.'

His features darkened but she continued to hold his eyes in challenge, suddenly conscious of how fast her heart was beating. 'I know of the secret agreement you made with the Druidic Order, of your offer to smother the reality of Dub Tíre's offence.'

Tréanmór had sat up straight to deliver his retort but those words caught him like a kick to the chest. Bodhmhall watched how he flinched in shock, relishing the rare satisfaction of seeing him caught for words.

'What did you expect, Father? The passing of years inevitably leads to the loosening of tongues. Even after my expulsion, I kept in contact with some of my older peers and over the years, I learned all about the outrage played out by the Order, how they knew the falseness of your Whispers but kept their silence to maintain their status among the people.'

Tréanmór somehow managed to rally himself. 'Accepting my offer meant the Order was beholden, indebted to me. To *Clann Baoiscne!*' His voice was hoarse but he swallowed to clear it. 'It was a debt repaid several times over after the *Clann Morna* assault for it was only through the Order's intervention that *Clann Morna* ceased their hostilities against us. The subsequent negotiations would never have happened without the agreements made between us. Besides …' He eased back on his stool, growing visibly more comfortable with his argument. 'Whispers or no, you killed one of their own. It would have gone worse for you if I hadn't spread that rumour. Introducing the element of passion gave greater acceptance to your deed and allowed the possibility of a lesser punishment.'

'No it didn't. The Druidic Order knew the truth of Dub Tíre all along. All the Whispers did was soften his guilt and transfer it to me.'

The *rí* of *Clann Baoiscne* drew himself up to his full height. 'If it troubles you so, perhaps you should have considered the consequences before you killed him.'

'Had you heeded my warnings there would have been no consequences. I told you of Dub Tíre's rotting of the soul many times, yet you did nothing.'

'I had you bonded to Fiacail. I had you removed from his influence.'

'You had me bonded to Fiacail to forge a link with Seiscenn Uarbhaoil. Any other reason was secondary. Do not attempt to claim otherwise.'

'You made no complaint at the time.'

This time, the *bandraoi* held back, literally biting her tongue to prevent the retort at its tip. She glared at her father, ignoring the incensed rhythm of her heart, the hot sweat of anger on her brow. Tréanmór's riposte was a poor one, a clumsy one, yet for all that a successful one for it effectively targeted her own feelings of remorse following the events prior to her expulsion.

Back then, in her desperation to escape the manic existence of Pluais na mBlaoisc, Bodhmhall had flung herself headlong into her new life as Fiacail mac Codhna's woman, intentionally cutting all contact with Dub Tíre and her fellow acolytes. Immersing herself completely in her new role, she'd done everything she could to void them from her thoughts. Unfortunately, her absence meant Dub Tíre's resentment at the loss of his most talented pupil had fallen squarely on the remaining acolytes.

Survivor that he was, Becal had managed to extricate himself by having himself dispatched to assist a *draoi* in a distant tribal area, leaving Demmán alone in the cave with their master. Isolated from all those who cared for him, Dub Tíre had been able to take advantage of the younger apprentice's vulnerability, using his own absolute authority to whittle at his confidence, groom him and eventually consume him.

One miserable morning, sometime after Bodhmhall's bond to Fiacail had descended to its demeaning and inevitable conclusion, Bé Bhinn had arrived at the fortress, distraught and almost incapable of speech. Fearing the worst, Bodhmhall had left her in Emmel's care, rushing back to the family's farmlet to find Demmán hanging from an oak tree to the rear of the *clochán*. His neck had been secured to the branch by his own belt.

Over the following days, Bé Bhinn had been inconsolable. She had been unable to speak or eat so the duty of preparing the body for burial had fallen to Bodhmhall. It was while she was washing down the corpse that she'd found the first marks, traces of physical and sexual abuse so brutal and so cruel it'd sickened her.

Driven by a level of fury she'd never experienced before, Bodhmhall had sought out her old master, to confront him and demand an explanation. Even then a part of her had still believed, still hoped that she'd somehow misunderstood, misinterpreted what her eyes were telling her. She'd found Dub Tíre, not at Pluais na mBlaoisc but back in the roundhouse he used when residing at the fortress, the one now inhabited by Lonán Ballach.

Entering through the little doorway, she'd discovered him poised on the edge of his sleeping platform, reeking of the sickly *beacán scammalach*. Intoxicated, belligerent and knowing she couldn't threaten him, the *draoi* had scoffed at her accusation, struck her and called her an ingrate. Spitting in her face, he'd openly admitted what he'd done, completely misjudging her intent and determination.

Until she'd lodged the knife in his heart.

Bodhmhall felt her shoulders slump.

Tréanmór was familiar with these events of course. Even after all these years, master manipulator that he was, he'd had no qualms in using them against her.

This is a waste of time.

Sighing, she looked at her father. He was standing before her, glowering, his body rigid with anger as he waited for her response. Ten years she'd been waiting for this moment, she realised. Ten years waiting for this opportunity to have it out with him, to express her true feelings at his – and Becal's – betrayal and now that the moment was upon her there was none of the satisfaction she'd hoped for, none of the resolution to the hole it'd left in her heart.

This is a waste of time.

She had been a fool, of course. She'd given in to her emotions and allowed herself to dredge up old grievances at a time she could least afford it. And, besides, Tréanmór would never change. He'd never acknowledge the injury he'd caused or accept responsibility for it. Any discussion with him would only ever revert back to this pointless, endless sparring between them.

247

She sighed.

Bé Bhinn had the right of it all along, she realised. All she could do was accept the reality of the betrayal, learn to live with it and get on with her life.

Wearily, she got to her feet. 'I should leave,' she said. 'But I'd say my farewells to Demne first if you'd allow that.'

Although taken aback by her sudden termination of the dispute, Tréanmór was still furious and continued to glare at her. Unable to speak, his answer was a dismissive gesture towards the screen, an angry instruction for her to go and do what she liked as long as she left him. Without waiting for any further confirmation, the *bandraoi* moved towards the gap in the leather sheet near the western wall.

Easing though the slim opening with little difficulty, she looked around the gloomy space that was illuminated solely by a flickering oil lamp on the floor beside one of the sleeping platforms. Her nephew was sitting, propped on the edge of the platform's wooden frame. He looked sad and forlorn and when she entered he glanced up at her but said nothing before dropping his eyes again. The *bandraoi* took a seat on the edge of the platform beside him.

'What is it, Demne? What troubles you? Was it your grandfather?'

The boy looked at her suspiciously, as though wondering whether she could read his thoughts. After a pause, he shook his head.

'Grandfather was trying to be nice.' He hesitated and when he spoke again there was a brittle edge to his voice. 'But he's not nice, is he *a Aintín*?'

The *bandraoi's* heart went cold at the uncharacteristic animosity in the boy's voice. She put her hand on his jaw, gently pulling it around so that his eyes and hers met. 'Tell me what happened, Demne.'

The boy took a moment to reply and it seemed to her that he was trying to prepare the right words. 'Last night … the sound of voices woke me. I looked through the crack.' Here he paused, to indicate a shallow crack in the leather sheet just beside the bed where he'd been sleeping. 'You were gone but grandfather was there, grandfather and the warrior with the beard.'

'Uargal?'

He confirmed that with a sharp dip of his head. 'They were speaking softly but I could hear them when I put my ear up to the crack.' He sniffed and rubbed his nose. 'Grandfather was talking about An Gleann Teann and the warriors going there. Uargal asked him what he should do if he encountered Liath Luachra and grandfather went very quiet.'

248

Demne lapsed into silence again and although tempted to prompt him, Bodhmhall held her tongue. The boy had to do this by himself.

'Grandfather said the Grey One needn't return'''. Her nephew swallowed and looked as though he was about to cry. 'I think he meant to harm her, *a Aintín.*'

Demne looked at his aunt with anxious eyes, as though seeking reassurance that everything was all right, that Liath Luachra was in no danger and that everything was well in the world. It was a sensation the *bandraoi* was familiar with, prompting painful recollections of the time she'd gone to confront Dub Tíre, hoping against hope he'd assure her that her world was safe and sane.

'I'm sorry, Demne. You've discovered your grandfather's true nature. And that the values we live by aren't always shared, even by those who should be closest to us.' She raised her hand to stroke his face again. Of late, he'd grown less tolerant of such 'motherly' demonstrations of affection but on this occasion he did not resist. 'It's a harsh lesson, *a bhuachaill.* But a necessary one.'

Somehow, she found the strength to force a smile. 'But I wouldn't worry for Liath Luachra. The Grey One's courageous and strong. You've seen how she never turns her back to strangers. Think on that when I leave you and then prepare for we leave Dún Baoiscne tonight.' She held his eyes then, making sure he understood the gravity of what she was telling him. 'But with discretion, yes? Do not let your grandfather know what we plan.'

Demne nodded enthusiastically. He was clearly more than ready to leave the forbidding fortress.

Satisfied, she reached inside her *léine* to withdraw the skin of *uisce beatha* she'd concealed since her arrival at Dún Baoiscne. 'But before you do, there is one thing I would ask of you.'

***

The *bandraoi*'s heart was cold when she left the sleeping quarters and returned to the main section of the hall. Consistent as ever, Tréanmór was seated at the fire, although on this occasion he'd moved from his usual seat, switching stools in a calculated snub so that his back was turned towards her when she emerged from the gap in the screen.

Bodhmhall paused to stare at the indomitable figure. Although conscious of her father's intent, the snub had all the impact of a raindrop on a wooden shield. Given her historical grievances, the more recent irreconcilable developments and the latest revelation of his orders for Liath Luachra, nothing Tréanmór did would ever touch her again.

Neither of them spoke as she walked past, giving the fire pit a wide berth. Nevertheless, just as she stepped outside the circle of light on her way up the length of the hall, something made her halt and look back. Tréanmór remained hunched over the fire, staring fiercely into the flames.

Bodhmhall shook her head. This then would be her last memory of her father, the last mental image to take away and draw on.

Chapter Fourteen

It took a time for Cathal Bog to approach the roundhouse of Fiacail mac Codhna but it was the cries of pleasure that eventually drew him in. Slipping through the door flap with soundless intent, the silent warrior paused, his eyes adjusting to the gloom but compellingly drawn to the two-person sleeping platform. There, in the flicker of a single oil lamp, smooth skin gleaming, Bodhmhall ua Baoiscne rhythmically ground the shadowed form beneath her thighs with formidable concentration.

Despite such preoccupations, the *bandraoi's* heightened senses immediately alerted her to the covert arrival. She'd grown increasingly sensitive to the *conradh's* relentless presence of late. Following her final conversation with Tréanmór, he'd continued his surveillance with ever increasing fastidiousness, displaying even more belligerence and self-righteousness hostility than she'd ever detected from him before.

Earlier, passing through the *lis*, he'd made a point of letting those heavy-lidded eyes linger on her breasts, a clear message that everything had changed. Despite her previous status as daughter of the *rí*, his authority was now the greater.

Concentrating on the rhythm of her movements, the *bandraoi* refused to look around, keeping her eyes firmly closed until she heard a hollow crack and the thud of a heavy weight hitting the ground. Only then did she cease, twisting about to reach for the oil lamp. Lifting it high, the dirty yellow flicker revealed Cathal Bog sprawled insensible on the wooden floor.

Fiacail mac Codhna stepped out of the shadows, a heavy piece of wood in his hands and a great smile across his features

'Forgive me, Dear One. Like Cathal, I found myself … distracted. So distracted, I forgot to hit him for a moment.'

Her response was a withering glare.

'Well!' The Seiscenn Uarbhaoil man shrugged helplessly. 'In truth, I did not believe your plan would work.' Looking down at the prostrate warrior, he gave Cathal's leg an arbitrary kick as though attempting to transfer the blame through physical contact.

Disengaging herself from the mound of furs she'd arranged in the approximate form of a horizontal figure, the *bandraoi* irritably pulled on her clothing. 'Cathal saw what he expected to see. The single light drew his eyes and with the last conversation we played out for him his natural assumption was to see two bickering lovers making up in the usual fashion.'

Fiacail grunted unhappily. Like her, he was conscious of the unstated layers of genuine dissension that had lain beneath that deceptive performance. 'And the Two Sisters?' he asked quickly, eager to change the subject.

'In his roundhouse. The guards were examining them as I passed this afternoon.'

Pulling the oiled hood of her cloak over her head, Bodhmhall didn't make pause for further discussion but headed directly for the doorway.

It was almost total darkness outside of course, a soupy murk with a consistency condensed by the pounding rain. The *bandraoi* regarded the downpour with mixed feelings, conscious that although it would make for unpleasant travelling it would also drive the fortress dwellers indoors and, more importantly, wash all trace of their tracks away.

With Fiacail in tow, she scurried towards Cathal Bog's dwelling, hastening through the doorway to find the two guards stretched on the floor, reeking of *uisce beatha*. The *bandraoi* watched wryly as Fiacail tested the leather skin that lay between them, with his toe. He grunted with surprise at the gurgle it produced for the container was still more than a quarter full.

Three days earlier when she'd proposed taking the skin, the Seiscenn Uarbhaoil man had objected strenuously. Now, he regarded her with visible admiration.

'How did you get them to drink it?'

'I had Demne deliver it as a gift from Tréanmór. They'd hardly have accepted such a gift from you or I directly.'

'*Cliste, a Cailleach Dubh. An chliste.*' Clever. Very clever. He turned his attention to the two warriors. 'And how long will they sleep?'

The *bandraoi* shrugged. Prior to passing the skin to Demne, she'd added a proportion of the same soporific herb she'd once used to conceal Muirne Muncháem from the Tainted One, a herb that rendered her so insensible the creature had failed to detect her. These two men were both physically bigger of course but …

'Time enough.'

Fiacail thoughtfully rubbed the bruise on his face, his eyes lingering on the closest warrior, a man Bodhmhall belatedly recognised as one of the guards who'd escorted him and her nephew into An Halla Mór two nights earlier. 'Tell me,' said Fiacail at last. 'Tell me, at least, that they'll have sore heads when they awake?'

'They'll have sore heads.'

He beamed gleefully at that, his distinctive teeth a white smear in the dimness of the roundhouse. 'But not as sore as Cathal Bog's.'

The satisfied smile faded just as suddenly as it'd appeared and the *bandraoi* found herself being scrutinised with far more focussed attention. 'And are you certain this is what you want, Bodhmhall? From this point onwards, there is no turning back.'

The *bandraoi's* jaw tightened. 'There was no turning back from the moment I entered the fortress, Fiacail.' She gestured urgently to where the warrior's axes stood propped against the wall beyond the roundhouse's single bed. 'Now, gather your weapons. Demne awaits.'

Once again, the pair ventured out into the deluge, this time taking a circuitous route towards An Halla Mór, keeping the buildings between them and the guard sheltered in the passageway. In truth, there was little chance of the warrior observing them for he'd lit one of the passageway's internal torches to carry out repairs on his spear. Night blind, he'd see nothing in the darkness beyond the end of the passage.

Demne was waiting anxiously in the shelter of the great hall's eaves but his lips parted into an excited grin when he saw them emerge from the sodden murk. The *bandraoi* felt a brief flush of pride for the boy had dressed competently in his heaviest clothing and, from the look of the satchel on his back, had even managed to secret a small supply of food to take with him.

Crouching alongside him, she ruffled his stubbly hair. 'You did well, Demne. So very well, *a gharsúr.*' Her eyes turned to the wooden doors of the hall where a thin crack was the only evidence they were slightly ajar. 'And your grandfather?'

'He sleeps.'

She nodded. 'Good. Then let us leave this place.'

In silence, they made their way across the darkness of the *lis* and up the northern stairway to the summit of the inner wall. There, ignoring the rain, Fiacail removed his cloak and lifted his tunic to unfurl the rough flax rope that he'd concealed by wrapping about his waist. Working quietly, he affixed the fibrous cord securely to the top of the wooden balustrade and dropped its full length down the outer side of the wall.

They took it in turns to descend to the grassy curve between the two embankments. Bodhmhall first, followed by Demne while Fiacail took up the rear. It was a slippery descent but the *bandraoi* made it to the ground without mishap, not overly hindered by the restriction of one good hand. Squatting at the base of the wall, she cautiously scrutinised her surroundings while Demne slid down to join her. With the weather and the darkness there was little enough to see but, critically, there was little likelihood of detection. Away from the main entrance and the optimal areas of sunlight, there were few huts at this section of the fortress, little more than a few empty stalls and pens where, in better days, dairy cows would have been calving.

They had no choice but to leave the rope where it hung although Fiacail cut a length to take with him before leading them quietly around to the main entrance to the fortress. There, as with the inner fortification, the sentry had retreated to the shelter of the passage. Unlike his more conscientious colleague however, this individual had settled down against the wall with a fur cloak and fallen fast asleep in the light of a single torch. Tiptoeing closer, Bodhmhall recognised the youth from her original arrival at the fortress.

Taking no chances, Fiacail subdued the young guard by walloping him over the head with the haft of one of his axes and then tying him securely with the rope he'd cut back at the wall. Keeping silent watch in a shallow alcove at the inner end of the passage, Bodhmhall was struck by the sudden, poignant realisation that this was the exact spot she'd been standing when she'd first caught sight of Liath Luachra all those many years earlier. As she recalled it, the woman warrior had been storming through the passage with typical intensity at the time, brows knitted, a scowl on her face and her cloak flapping madly behind her. Radiant and fierce in the afternoon sun, she'd stomped right past the *bandraoi* without a second glance.

Ten years.

The *bandraoi* felt a looseness inside her chest. Up to this point, her entire focus had been on her own – and Demne's – survival. Powerless to influence matters and fearful of losing heart, she'd intentionally pushed Liath Luachra to the back of her head. With her father's instructions to Uargal mac Camal however, the Grey One's safety was now once more foremost in her mind.

Be alive, Grey One. Stay alive.

And come back to me.

With the guard out of the way and the long passage muffling any sound, it wasn't difficult to disengage the latch that secured the gates in place, although it required all three of them to lift it. Pushing one of the gates ajar, they silently slipped outside, crossed the causeway and started down the trail at the front of the fortress.

After several paces, the *bandraoi* paused and turned to stare back at the bulk of the fortress, her old home now barely discernible through the curtain of rain and darkness.

'Do not tarry, Bodhmhall.' Fiacail's voice was a quiet hiss though the downpour.

Turning, she hurried after the warrior.

And pushed into the hard darkness.

***

Fiacail roused them at dawn, when the initial smudge of grey provided enough light for travelling. The rain had ceased overnight but the forest air still hung thick with the earthy smell of moisture and water dripped liberally from the trees.

Cold, stiff and still damp from the previous night's dousing, they rose without complaint, conscious that they remained perilously close to the fortress. It'd been Bodhmhall's suggestion to take shelter at the rocky overhang south of the Cuirreach valley. Familiar with the terrain, she'd decided the position not only offered shelter but a useful head-start for their subsequent journey and was sufficiently far from Dún Baoiscne to make the discovery of their tracks unlikely. It had been Fiacail however who'd managed to locate the site in the terrible conditions, based on her directions alone.

They moved out immediately, without even taking time to breakfast. Once again, the Seiscenn Uarbhaoil man took the lead with Bodhmhall and her nephew following as closely as they could, struggling to keep up as he moved ghost-like through the trees. An experienced woodsman, Fiacail had the skills to traverse the Great Wild with ease. More importantly, he also had the advantage of a full day's reconnaissance of the intended trail before his capture by the *Clann Baoiscne* warriors.

In daylight, the fugitives were able to travel more swiftly but it was still mid-day before they broke through the forest to a clearing where the trees gave way to waving grasses. Flushed and breathless, they stared up at the low, flat-topped mountain that was their destination.

As she stood panting for breath, Bodhmhall groaned internally at the prospect of further exertion. Intimately familiar with this region, she knew that the only approach to the summit was a steep climb up the western slope and her leg muscles were already burning. Glancing towards her wheezing nephew, she suspected that he too must be nearing the limits of his endurance.

Heedless of their beleaguered state, the Seiscenn Uarbhaoil man took off once more. Gritting her teeth, the *bandraoi* grabbed Demne's hand and forced herself to follow at an unsteady lope.

Crossing the clearing, the little party re-entered the forest and worked their way through the damp, green undergrowth to an area where the incline sharpened abruptly as grey rock thrust upwards through the skin of the earth. Locating the route to the summit, they scrambled uphill through clumps of fern and blackthorn, dense forest that was ankle deep in pine needles and the occasional stretch of bare rock.

By the time they reached the summit, the little party was sweating and soil-stained however, reinvigorated with fresh purpose, the *bandraoi* took the lead and guided them to the northern side of the plateau where a broad stone ledge protruded out above an extremely high cliff.

Collapsing onto the stone surface, the bedraggled entourage panted with relief as they considered a view that was, quite simply, spectacular. Stretching north to the Cuirreach valley, the distant fortress of Dún Baoiscne was visible as a dark lump beyond the lush spread of the green forest below.

Bodhmhall sighed and allowed herself the luxury of a rare moment's respite. She felt safe here for she knew the plateau well, having chosen the site specifically for its views to the north and over the flatlands of the south. It would be a cold place to camp given the high risks of setting a fire, however a series of caves further downhill would serve as a suitable shelter if the weather happened to turn again.

As Fiacail came to join her she shifted to one side, making room for him to sit alongside. 'This is the place?' the big warrior asked.

Too jaded to speak, she settled for a simple nod.

'And the bait was well-laid?'

This time, Bodhmhall took a deep breath before responding. 'As well as it could be, Fiacail. Using words of emphasis at the appropriate time is no easy task but Becal and Lonán Ballach should recall the destinations I mentioned once they learn of our escape. Cathal Bog overheard your proposal for Seiscenn Uarbhaoil so he'll assume we're making our way there.

'And we will see the pursuit from here.'

'We *should* see them from here. The plateau is the perfect place to watch all three southern routes.' The *bandraoi* pointed to the north-east where a rough track was discernible and swept her finger around in a wide curve to the south of the plateau. 'There is the Bearna track to Seiscenn Uarbhaoil. If we see the Adversary's forces anywhere on that track, we'll know Cathal Bog as the traitor.'

Her finger edged a little to the left.

'And there, the route to the *Uí Cuaich* territories.' If pursuit comes from that angle, then Lonán Ballach is our man.'

She sighed, her finger now pointing left. 'And finally, An Bearach Thiar, fastest path to Ráth Bládhma and, even now, the one that tugs most strongly at my heart. If the Adversary's warriors appear there, then Becal it is who's spoken false.'

'So the direction of pursuit will reveal the traitor?'

'Yes.'

Fiacail dubiously stroked the ends of this moustache. He'd never been entirely convinced of the *bandraoi*'s plan since she'd originally outlined it, considering it overly complex and subject to too many unpredictable circumstances. Bodhmhall had accepted those shortcomings but with her hand forced by Lonán's anticipated challenge, it had been the best she'd come up with under such trying circumstances. She wasn't amused therefore, when the warrior decided to relitigate the matter once more.

'Are we not more likely to see *Clann Baoiscne* warriors in our pursuit than the Adversary's men? Your father, after all, will be desperate to recover his grandson.'

'True, but from today my father will have his hands full countering Lonán Ballach's bid for power. The *Clann Baoiscne* elders will be arriving now, possibly as we speak. Tréanmór will gnash his teeth but to retain his grip on power, he has no choice but to remain and oppose his *rechtaire's* challenge.'

She brushed some dirt from the sole of her foot.

'For his part, Lonán will also be preoccupied. Unless, of course, he truly is the Adversary's man, in which case we'll see pursuit on the *Uí Cuaich* route.'

'But what then of Becal and Cathal? They could send *Clann Baoiscne* warriors independent of your father.'

Bodhmhall shook her head. 'Becal is not trusted by my father. *Clann Baoiscne* warriors would never be dispatched on his words alone. As for Cathal Bog, my father will keep him and all the other warriors close for his conflict with Lonán Ballach. The *rechtaire* now has far more supporters at the fortress and my father will need every man available to him. Like Becal and Lonán, even if Cathal's the traitor there's little else he can do but alert his master.'

She watched Fiacail silently work through the logic of her plan once more and bit down the snap of annoyance building up on the tip of her tongue. The warrior was a competent strategist in his own right and his opinion was worth heeding. When she'd first explained her plan to travel to

Dún Baoiscne he'd grudgingly agreed to the pretence of his capture only because he'd known she and Demne could only escape the fortress with his help. The decision to feign the growing animosity between them however, had been his idea and it'd been quite an effective one at that. With the *bandraoi*'s debilitating injury and a seeming absence of support, her father and his warriors had been lulled by her apparent helplessness and consequently, had dropped their guard.

'You should take me as your man, Cailleach Dubh.'

'What?'

'Give me your consent and I will abandon this life of constant hunger, of danger and discomfort and ...' He looked around until his eye alighted on a nearby clump of vegetation. 'And nettles.'

This provoked a tired smile from the *bandraoi*.

'Come! I make no jest. You've always desired a child. With your intelligence and my ... superior looks, imagine the progeny we could produce. Clever, handsome little warriors to rule the world.'

Despite her weariness, the *bandraoi* laughed softly at that. After the trials and the tension of the previous days it felt good to laugh and grateful for such small pleasures, she slapped him playfully on the shoulder. 'Your tongue's worn away from all your jabbering, Fiacail mac Codhna. You're full of weak notions.'

The big man laughed but to her ears his good humour sounded forced. 'Maybe I am and maybe I'm not. My notions may not be strong but at least they are many.'

***

They didn't anticipate any immediate sign of pursuit. It would take time after all, for their absence to be confirmed, time for the traitor to get word to the Adversary, time for the Adversary to organise the dispatch of warriors in pursuit. Nevertheless, unwilling to take any chances, Bodhmhall decided to watch the trails south of the Cuirreach valley for the remainder of the afternoon.

Sitting on the stone by the edge of the cliff, she was relieved to see the early moisture burned away for one of her plan's greatest weaknesses was that a heavy mist or rain might drift in to obscure their view.

Lulled by the sun, the caress of a gentle breeze and the soothing birdsong from the nearby trees, the *bandraoi* felt herself relax completely. Free from Dún Baoiscne, there was an immense relief in the absence of constant scrutiny, the disapproving stares from unforgiving tribal members, and the exhausting effort of sparring with her father. Weary from the day's travel and a lack of sleep, the *bandraoi* felt her eyelids flutter and her head nodding despite her best efforts to remain alert.

When she opened her eyes again, she was no longer sure if she was awake or asleep. Certainly, she was still on the plateau for the view north to Dún Baoiscne remained unchanged. What had changed however, was the view overhead where the sun had taken on an unnatural green colour that bathed the landscape in a sickly hue.

Confused, the *bandraoi* looked about, conscious of the complete absence of birdsong and the earlier soft whisper of the breeze. Unconcerned, she understood then that she was in a dream state and would probably have relaxed and allowed herself to drift even deeper into sleep if it hadn't been for an uncomfortable background sensation that grated at the edge of her consciousness. Although she could see nothing, she had the oddest, unsettling impression that she was being watched.

A loud snort of laughter startled her awake and she jerked upright in alarm. Blinking, she looked around in confusion. The sun was warm on her face, the breeze stirred her hair and at that very moment two wood pigeons fluttered past, wings taking them north towards Dún Baoiscne. Behind her, she could hear the voices of Fiacail and Demne – the origin of the laughter – conversing loudly on the subject of her nephew's birth and early days of infancy.

Exhaling slowly, Bodhmhall turned around to observe them, curious to see Demne's reaction. Like all children, she knew her nephew was fascinated by the concept of himself as a new-born.

'I was present when you were little more than a few hours from your mother's belly,' Fiacail was telling him. 'For days you squealed like an injured pig.'

'Like a pig?' The boy's eyes were wide.

'Like a pig. But do you know what I remember most?'

Fascinated, the boy shook his head.

'The shit you produced. In truth, I've never seen a child make such a mass of offal. You seemed to create a quantity of shit that weighed more than the weight of your own body. I don't know how that's possible.'

The conversation deteriorated into a bout of giggling.

'Shit or no, I've promised your aunt to initiate you in the *gaiscíoch* path. But know this.' And here the warrior's voice suddenly turned stern. 'I will drive you hard for the *gaiscíoch* path sets arduous trials and you must overcome each one.'

'Trials?' The boy's voice was thick, not so much with concern as intrigue.

'Indeed. Physical trials that would challenge the mettle of a hardened warrior. As it is, an *óglach* like you must leap a stave of your own height and run under another the height of your knee. While pursued though the forest you must pluck a thorn from your foot without breaking stride. Later, when buried up to your waist in the earth, you must defend that position from spear-wielding warriors while armed only with a staff and shield.'

There was a silence as the boy considered these gruelling challenges. 'Can you do all these?' he asked Fiacail at last.

The *bandraoi* was unable to smother her snort of laughter.

Fiacail cast her a withering look.

'Go now, boy. Return to your position above the trail and keep careful watch while I speak with your aunt.'

'Yes, Fiacail.' Demne leapt obligingly to his feet and ran off through the trees to the lookout spot he'd been assigned, eager to assume his new responsibility. Fiacail also got to his feet but instead of returning to the southern edge of the plateau, he moved only a few paces to take a seat beside Bodhmhall.

'Demne grows fond of you,' the *bandraoi* noted.

'Your words are daubed with disapproval.'

'No.' Bodhmhall shook her head. 'Not disapproval. You know the respect I hold for your battle prowess.' She paused. 'It's Liath Luachra. She taught Demne all that he knows of the *gaiscíoch* path. I'd always imagined she would complete his training.'

The Seiscenn Uarbhaoil man said nothing but then he didn't have to. Shuffling his feet awkwardly, he considered her with a sideways glance. 'I think,' he said at last. 'If the Grey One is alive, she'd recognize the need to have the boy trained, whether by my hand or by hers. Surely, she'd accept that we all have our roles to play. Our fates may not be to our liking but, in the end they're our fates and they are set.'

The *bandraoi* glanced at him uncomfortably. Fiacail clearly didn't know the woman warrior as well as he believed. Of all the people she'd ever encountered, Liath Luachra was the one least likely to bow to the dictates of fate. The warrior woman's innate resistance to anything she didn't believe in was a fundamental part of who she was.

'We have not spoken of Liath Luachra and what has passed between you and I.'

The *bandraoi* turned her head to consider him coolly. 'What do you mean?'

Fiacail sat forward, his elbows resting on his knees. 'I mean that if the Grey One is truly alive, I'd prefer not to have her biting at my heels in the manner of a cheated lover.'

Bodhmhall chewed on her lower lip for a time as she considered the warrior's words. 'She'll never love you for it, Fiacail,' she admitted at last. 'But she knows you saved my life – and Demne's – on more than one occasion. She'll respect you for what you did and that will colour her thinking.'

The Seiscenn Uarbhaoil looked at her in disbelief. 'You intend to tell her?'

'Yes.'

'But why?' The warrior's voice betrayed his incredulity. 'A rare flower may bloom from the bed of truth, I grant you, but most such growth yields thorn and bramble. Some subjects are best left undisturbed, like the graves of the Ancient Ones in the shadows of the dark woods.'

'I will tell her because I would know. I'd not have our bond tainted by falsehood.'

Fiacail chuckled, clearly amused by what he saw as naivety. 'She may not think the same.'

'Then that is something I will face. We have a bond based on truth, for good or bad, or we have nothing at all.'

The warrior frowned, his forehead creasing into a series of thin lines. 'You should reconsider, Bodhmhall. The Grey One is uncommonly troubled. You cannot know how she might react to your honesty.'

Angry now, the *bandraoi* twisted about to face him directly. 'You know nothing of Liath Luachra. You've a passing familiarity with the warrior but not the person beneath. The Grey One is someone who's endured much personal hardship, who's dragged herself above her past and above her history through sheer force of will. If there's anyone who deserves my honesty, it is her.'

'I know enough of her to fear she'll break your heart, dear one. Alive or dead, she'll bring you grief in the end.'

Bodhmhall cast him a baleful look. 'Then alive or dead, that's a price I'll pay.'

Bristling with anger, she got to her feet while Fiacail watched silently, taken aback by the depth of her anger.

But the *bandraoi* hadn't finished with him.

'You know, Fiacail. Long ago, I too believed our fates were set but it turned out I didn't have the right of it. Despite what the Druidic Order would have you believe, the Gods and the Ancestors don't choose our fate. We choose that ourselves and I have chosen Liath Luachra.'

She gestured roughly to the section of rock where she'd been sitting. 'There's a comfortable seat for your arse. Put yourself at ease for the northern watch is yours for now. You can alert me when the pursuit comes.'

With that, she turned on her heel and stalked away from the warrior, deep into the trees.

***

But the pursuit did not come.

Four days passed without activity of any kind on the three routes, apart from the occasional sighting of a trader or solitary traveller. With each passing day, the *bandraoi* felt her morale plummet further.

By the morning of the fifth day, Bodhmhall had no choice but to accept that something was amiss, that she'd made some error of judgement. The lack of pursuit no longer made sense. The Adversary wouldn't have risked the trail growing cold.

The *bandraoi's* confidence wasn't improved by her dreams, increasingly unsettling nightmares that had worsened progressively after that first odd reverie on the day of their arrival. Over the first two nights, they'd been relatively benign, simple sleep memories that reflected their location on the mountain and the boring routine to which they'd restricted themselves. Even within those dreams however, the *bandraoi* could not shake off the continuing impression of being watched.

At first, she'd put this down to an echo of her fears at Cathal Bog's surveillance back at Dún Baoiscne and thought little more about it. On the third night however, a strange, unsettling figure had appeared in her dreams. Never quite close enough for her to make out in any detail, that figure had always kept its distance and when she'd attempted to approach, it had quickly glided out of reach. Despite this apparent shyness, it continued its silent observation with a skin-crawling intensity that made her shiver.

The previous evening, this passive figure had become dramatically more forward in his behaviour, wandering through her dreamscape in a distracted but almost brazen manner, giving her the strangest impression that he was searching for something. This time, determined to confront it, Bodhmhall had moved forward at great speed, surprised to discover it making no attempt to move away. Up close, she'd been disturbed to discover that the figure had no face, nothing but a smooth, black surface where hair and facial figures were normally to be found. Affronted, the figure had turned its head to regard her with such a focus of unbridled hostility it had actually woken her up.

The scuff of bare feet on rock alerted her to Fiacail's return from the far side of the plateau. Some tension remained from their earlier argument but she found herself grateful for the distraction.

The warrior took up position alongside her, chewing on a tuber as he stared out at the forested panorama below. 'Have you seen the enemy set foot in *Clann Baoiscne* territory?'

'Not so much as a toe of them.' The *bandraoi*'s response was curt, reflecting her frustration.

Fiacail frowned and scratched his head. 'I don't understand. It's been five days since we left Dún Baoiscne.' He sniffed and wiped his eyes then looked at her sideways. 'Maybe the Adversary struggles to get men in place.'

The *bandraoi* found that she couldn't look at him. The Seiscenn Uarbhaoil man was trying to be tactful of course, to come up with some logical explanation to explain their absence. But it was way too late for that now. Although she felt grateful for the attempt, it actually made her feel worse.

'That would go against every pattern of behaviour we've seen of the Adversary so far. He's never shown any shortage of resources or men and he's always had a reserve plan to his foremost action. Three years ago, he had two *fian* and a Tainted One to find Muirne. In his efforts to trap us at An Glean Teann, he had a false *techtaire* and an additional two *fian* in place.' She shook her head. 'No. This is a man who'll have placed resources to hand for fear of losing the boy once more.'

As she sat on the ledge, her fingers drummed a nervous cadence along her thigh as she picked furiously at her worries.

'I think that we should leave this place Fiacail. I have the sense I've made some mistake although it baffles me as to where I did so. I had thought to come at this from every angle; from behind, from the front and even from the side.' She paused. 'I also have a sense of hostile parties drawing ever closer. I fear we may have to move.'

The warrior looked doubtful but he refrained from comment. Instead, he reached over to pat her silently on the knee.

They were still sitting in silence when Demne came barging from the trees, his face pale and a gleam of fear in his eyes.

'Warriors, *a Aintín*! Many warriors. Coming directly towards us.'

Chapter Fifteen

Thanks to Demne's impressive eyesight, the enemy was still some distance from the base of the mountain. Peering down over the dense forest canopy from the western lip of the plateau however, Bodhmhall struggled to make out any sign of human activity. For a moment, she'd almost convinced herself the boy had been mistaken then a flicker of movement in the trees far below dashed that possibility.

They're here.

'Fiacail.' She looked to the Seiscenn Uarbhaoil man with growing alarm. 'What can we do?'

'Little enough.' There was a hesitant, almost fatalistic, resonance to the big man's voice, a quality she'd never heard over all the many years she'd known him. Combined with the uncharacteristic droop to those broad shoulders, it brought the brutal reality of their situation to the fore.

'There's but a single trail to this summit.' His fingers stroked the end of his moustache. 'We're snared here at their leisure but with Dún Baoiscne so close, they'll be loath to delay.'

'But the track is narrow.' The *bandraoi* gestured urgently to the natural path that meandered up towards them through the dense forest and lush, green undergrowth. 'Less than two paces wide. Can we not hold it?'

The Seiscenn Uarbhaoil man sighed. 'The path is narrow,' he acknowledged. 'But the growth to either side poses no barrier to a determined man. They'll outflank us without difficulty. If I had two other fighters or a supply of javelins, I might hold the path for a time but even then ...' His words trailed away and he considered the *bandraoi* gravely. Bodhmhall felt all hope, all prospect of survival, slipping away.

'I'll fight them to my last breath, Bodhmhall. But I'll not be able to stop them from reaching you and the boy.' He hesitated. 'And, therein lies a hard choice.'

She stared at him then, doing her best to ignore the nausea rising in the pit of her stomach. She knew exactly what he was going to say.

'When they come, we can fight but we'll most certainly be overcome. We can surrender and hope for clemency but these are brutal, ruthless men and ...' He left the rest unsaid. 'There is one last option that remains.' His eyes drifted to the northern side of the plateau, just visible through the trees, where the ledge projected outwards from the cliff.

Bodhmhall fought the sudden urge to vomit. Having already launched herself from a great height once to escape the Adversary's men, the mere prospect of doing so again was enough to make her quake with terror. This was also a leap from which there'd be no return.

She shook her head. 'We don't surrender, we don't leap to the ancestors.' She inhaled deeply. 'We fight, Fiacail. We fight and we cut them deep. We make them bleed for all they've done against us and those we love.'

With tears in her eyes, she turned to her nephew, dropping to one knee so that she could look directly into his eyes. 'Forgive me, *a bhuachaill*. I'd hoped for such great things for you, I'd hoped that one day you might ...' Overcome by emotion, she paused and inhaled deeply.

'Nephew, I would have you withdraw to the ledge and leave the fight to me and Fiacail. These men have been seeking you for a very long time. It's just possible they'll let you live.'

'*A Aintín*, no! I ...'

'Demne!' She cut him off sharply. 'There is a slim hope you'll survive and you must grasp that prospect with both hands. When you're full grown and the opportunity arises, you can seek vengeance in my name, in Fiacail's ... and in Liath Luachra's.'

To her surprise, the boy shook his head, the tears in his eyes doing nothing to reduce their fiery determination. 'No, *a Aintín*. Not without you. If you fight, so will I and ... ' His voice was shaking. 'I won't let them harm you.'

Unprepared for the ferocity of her nephew's resolve, the *bandraoi* stared, speechless.

Fiacail, who'd been watching in silence, took that opportunity to reach out and place one mighty hand on each of their shoulders. 'There's much I regret in this life but these last few days spent in your company ...' He hesitated. 'Well, that's enough for me to face death satisfied.'

With that, he straightened up and shifted the harness holding his two battle axes.

'Very well. We fight.'

***

By the time the enemy warriors had made it halfway up the mountain, Fiacail had outlined the defensive positions on his chosen battleground, a relatively flat section of trail just below the western lip of the summit. Locked in on all sides by dense forest, it was a restricted space that would confine most of the fighting to the trail, allowing him optimal reach with his axes. If the enemy used javelins, the plateau was close enough to retreat into the cover of the trees.

'I have a plan,' the big man informed them. 'But, at its heart, this is how the fight will be.' He paused then, considering them both carefully before he continued. 'I'll hold the main approach with the aid of the Two Sisters. The Adversary's men have the numbers so they'll make to rush me.' He paused and turned to Demne. 'And that is where you'll step up, *a gharsúr*.'

The boy swallowed but managed to keep chin high and his lips from quivering. Bolstered by this new responsibility, he abruptly pulled a metal sword from the satchel he'd carried all the way from Dún Baoiscne.

Fiacail eyed the metal weapon which the boy was struggling to brandish, the weight of it requiring him to grasp the hilt with both hands. 'No.' He shook his head. 'It takes a ripe man to use such a weapon and you're still fresh green. Use the sling for the Grey One taught you well with that. If you wish to honour her, you will not miss, eh?'

Recognising the sense of the warrior's argument, Demne nodded and laid the sword aside. 'I will honour her,' he croaked.

With that, Fiacail turned to the *bandraoi* who stood slightly to his left, a rock in her right hand and several other of similar size in a small pile at her feet. 'And you, Bodhmhall. You must cast your stones equally well. Once I engage the first opponent, it's your accuracy alone that'll prevent the others from taking me from the rear. That should allow me space for a second opponent, possibly a third. But then …'

He paused but then he shrugged at the reality of what he had to say.

'But then I will fall,' he continued at last. 'I will fall for no one man can defeat such odds. When I do, my counsel is to fight on. Cause them great grief and do not to give into despair.' His eyes turned directly to the *bandraoi*. 'And remember, it is you who holds the power of choice over your depart. The ledge is a short run.'

With that, he lapsed into silence, suddenly out of things to say.

'You mentioned a plan,' Bodhmhall said, her voice hollow.

'Yes.'

'What is the plan?'

Fiacail paused. 'If good fortune is with us, I'll have a moment to choose my first opponent. If I do, I'll choose their leader. Once I've killed him I'll start working my way down to the lowliest *óglach*.'

Bodhmhall looked at him incredulously. 'That's a shit plan.'

His answer was a quiet smile and the *bandraoi* realised he'd been making a joke in an attempt to raise their morale. 'Not if the remainder are so demoralised by my battle skills they flee back down the mountain.'

Noting the *bandraoi*'s obvious terror, he placed one hand on her shoulder and squeezed. 'I wish we'd had more time, dear one. I think every

man facing death must have uttered those same words at the end but …'
He shook his head, his shoulders heavy with sadness. 'The truth does not belittle them.'

Too scared and too upset to reply, the *bandraoi* just quivered.

The big man straightened up abruptly and slapped Demne on the arm. 'Hold fast to your arms,' he told him. 'Until the hard fight is ended.'

Without another word, the warrior stepped down from the lip of the plateau and walked several paces downhill. Moving around on the narrow path until he found a position that seemed to satisfy him, he unsheathed his axes then turned to glance back over his shoulder. 'Do you have a clear line of sight?'

Bodhmhall and Demne nodded, unable to speak.

Satisfied Fiacail turned to face the direction from which the enemy would come, allowing the weight of his axes to drag his arms downward and letting his head droop so that his eyes were fixed on the ground at his feet. Watching from uphill, Bodhmhall saw how his entire body seemed to relax into itself.

He prepares for death.

The realisation prompted a stifled gasp. The *bandraoi* felt hot tears well up in her eyes and, raising her right sleeve, roughly wiped them away, unable to tell if they were tears of grief for the big man's sacrifice or simply tears of fear for her own life.

Is this truly the end?

She wondered at that, her distress lodged like a lump at the back of her throat, making each breath she took sound short and gasping.

A chest-full of regrets, of sorrow for lost opportunities, for loved ones I'll never see again.

The sound of hard movement from down trail drew her attention: mud-muffled shuffling, a stifled curse, the clang of metal against wood and the beating of foliage. The noise grew louder as the enemy force drew closer, making no attempt to conceal their presence. These men were confident in their success, eager to attain their prize and depart *Clann Baoiscne* territory as quickly as possible.

Bodhmhall realised her hands were shaking, the rock gripped so tightly in her right fist her fingers had gone white. Less than thirty or forty paces down the trail she caught a brief glimpse of shadowed movement. Then, suddenly, everything went eerily quiet.

The branches in the upper forest canopy shifted back and forth in the breeze, the brushing of leaves creating a long, undulating whisper. A sharp scent of pine rolled up from the forest, embroidering the air with a tangible

267

tang. Despite the hush, the *bandraoi* felt the weight of many eyes and looking out from the shelter of an ash tree, she had the oddest sense that the world was holding its breath. As the silence extended, her nerves began to fray, her injured arm ached with an intensity she'd not felt at any time over the previous days and a great wave of weakness washed over her. She felt an urgent, desperate need to piss.

Several paces below, Fiacail stood calmly, head down as though oblivious to the cares of the world. The leather loops in the hilts of the Two Sisters were wrapped about his wrists and both weapons dangled lazily, the metal sheen of the blades twisting and gleaming bright in the sunlight.

'Well, now!' came a husky voice. 'Here's a fine pig for scalding.'

Gob an Teanga Gorm.

The hatchet-face man stepped out of the trees much closer than Bodhmhall had anticipated, less than twenty paces away. A number of warriors followed him out and although the greater part of them remained clustered to his rear, two or three were already pushing their way forward into the surrounding undergrowth.

Just as Fiacail predicted.

Bodhmhall quickly counted those shadowed shapes she could make out clearly: two, three, eight … Her heart sank. They didn't stand a chance.

Rough laughter accompanied the tall *rígfénnid* as he strolled confidently forwards, the gloomy shapes of the warriors behind him becoming more distinct as they emerged into the open. She twisted the rock in her hand, forcing herself to grasp it in readiness to fling. Glancing down at Fiacail, she recalled his earlier words.

I will kill their leader.

Had he meant that or had that just been another one of his jokes?

Meanwhile, Gob An Teanga Gorm had halted, retaining a defensible distance between himself and the Seiscenn Uarbhaoil man. Slowly raising his head, Fiacail considered the *rígfénnid* with detached, almost aloof disinterest. Gob, for his part, seemed to study the big man with even greater intensity for creases of concentration had formed along the length of his forehead.

'I remember you! At Ráth Bládhma. *An Clab Mór* - The loudmouth on the ramparts.'

Fiacail sighed and laboriously blew air from his cheeks, as though dismayed by such crass interruption. Even under such desperate circumstances, the *bandraoi* had to appreciate his display of aplomb.

'You were at Ráth Bládhma?' The Seiscenn Uarbhaoil man spoke ponderously and seemed to give the possibility some genuine consideration but then he slowly shook his head. 'No. You could not have been at Ráth Bládhma. I killed everyone. Except those who ran at the first sight of blood.'

The *rígfénnid* stiffened, his smile fading as his face closed over. 'Those are rash words, dead man.'

'Aaah, hardly dead. And Fiacail mac Codhna is the name on me.'

Gob smiled a malignant smile, a bitter crack of the lips that held all the appeal of a blood-stained nettle. 'No one cares, big man. You'll die a hard death on the mountain. No-one will remember your name.'

Once again, Fiacail displayed a somnolent lack of interest. 'Others have made that boast,' he drawled. 'And I'm still here, standing alone in the chirp of crickets.'

The Seiscenn Uarbhaoil man's interminable calm seemed to ruffle the *rígfénnid's* composure. 'You rash-arsed dog!' he shouted. 'You itchy-arsed shit sucker! You think you can stand there like a lone gull on the strand and expect to repel the incoming tide.'

His men liked that one. A chorus of snorts and guffaws echoed from behind.

Suddenly Gob shifted his weight and turned to stare up at the *bandraoi*. His features rearranged to form a malevolent leer. 'I see you up there too, Bodhmhall Ua Baoiscne. You've led me a merry chase but your dash is done. Tonight you'll recompense for the trouble you've caused.'

Bodhmhall shuddered as a similar smile twisted each of the *fian* warrior's lips. Her knees turned to mush and she'd have collapsed if an unpleasant but distinctly familiar prickle hadn't suddenly flared inside her head, triggering a surge of fury that eclipsed every other emotion.

'Know that when our task here is done,' Gob was saying. 'I'll return to that flea-pit at An Gleann Ceoch. Wild dogs will rut in your empty settlement once I'm finished. Crows and magpies will nest in the thatch of your broken homes. The bleached bones of your people will shine in th-'

'Where's the one who directs your footing?' the *bandraoi* interrupted curtly. 'Where's the owl who sends the fieldmouse on his errands.'

Startled by this unexpected defiance,' Gob regarded her angrily. 'By the ancestors, I'll ha-'

'You're down there,' she called out, ignoring the incensed warrior as she levelled her gaze on a cluster of trees below the plateau. 'I can feel your foul touch. Come out now. *Draoi* knows *draoi.*'

Even as the last words left her lips, a lean, bearded figure clothed entirely in black, stepped out of the shadows and onto the track. Looking up towards the startled *bandraoi*, his lips cracked into a cruel smile. In the odd half-light, those lips looked strange, a striking red colour like winter berries against the snow. Bodhmhall realised she'd seen this man before, many years ago at a gathering of the Druidic Council.

Tadg mac Nuadat.

Bodhmhall stared in shock.

Tadg mac Nuadat. Draoi of Almhu. Father to Muirne Muncháem.

Even as the realisation settled in, the *bandraoi* had the sense of certain elements slotting into place in her head. And yet, other parts remained stubbornly out-of-place. The presence of Tadg mac Nuadat, the renowned and much-feared *draoi*, explained much but many questions remained.

'Bodhmhall ua Baoiscne,' the black-clothed figure said at last, his voice carrying clearly across the distance. '*Draoi* knows *draoi*, a *Cailleach Dubh*.'

As he and the *bandraoi* considered one another, everyone else looked on, intrigued but instinctively sensing some significant occurrence beyond their ken was taking place.

Fuelled by her anger, the *bandraoi* dared to cast the question that had been burning inside her for so long.

'Who was it betrayed us? Lonán, Becal or Cathal Bog?'

Tadg mac Nuadat slapped the question away in the same way he might have slapped a bothersome fly. By then, he'd already shifted his gaze and as Bodhmhall followed that concentrated stare to her trembling nephew, she realised she was no longer relevant to the *Draoi* of Almhu. It was Demne alone who commanded his attention.

'That's the Adversary?' Several paces downhill, Fiacail mac Codhna's voice sounded distinctly unimpressed. He leaned forward casually, as though peering at the *draoi*. 'I wouldn't follow him. See his nose. He looks like he walked into a tree.'

And without warning, he attacked.

The enemy warriors were taken by surprise. Secure in their superior numbers, lulled by the slow, almost lethargic behaviour of the Seiscenn Uarbhaoil man and diverted by the *draoi*'s dramatic entrance, in their minds the outcome of this encounter had already been decided. There was no escape from the plateau. Opposition of any kind was clearly futile. It made no sense for their quarry to take the offence.

And yet, that didn't prevent Fiacail mac Codhna from crossing the distance between himself and Gob An Teanga Gorm in a blur of speed, his right axe swinging into motion.

Although taken by surprise, the *rígfénnid* reacted with impressive alacrity, raising his sword quickly to deflect the incoming blow. Despite his rapid response, the defence proved inadequate against the power of the first Sister's momentum. Smashing against the sword blade with incredible force, it blasted the weapon right out of Gob An Teanga Gorm's hand. Before the *rígfénnid* had time to realise what had happened, the second Sister came sweeping in, this time in a upwards direction to catch him under the jaw with such force it lifted him clean off his feet. The *rígfénnid* went flying backwards onto the ground, his lower jaw smashed and a bloody gash across his throat.

The other enemy warriors immediately leapt into action, flocking forward to assist their leader. For Gob An Teanga Gorm however, it was all too late. His body twitched on the ground, his life's blood spilling out around him.

Although the *bandraoi* had noted the big man inching forward during the restricted interaction, she too had been taken aback by the blistering speed of his attack. A whoosh of air to the left alerted her to the fact that Deme had released his shot and she caught a glimpse of the warrior attacking Fiacial's left side go down, clutching at his leg. Flinging her own rock at a warrior coming in on the right, she saw it clip his shoulder and although the blow wasn't strong enough to injure him, it made him stagger to a halt. Startled, he glanced in her direction and snarled.

But it was all too little, of course. Fiacail's attack was over even before it had truly gained momentum, faltering as the enemy warriors swarmed in tight around him. Driven back by the superior numbers, he managed one last strike with his right axe before he was overwhelmed. With a cry of despair, Bodhmhall saw the Seiscenn Uarbhaoil man take a spear high in the chest, the blow causing him to drop the axe in his left hand. Then he was down, overtaken by the rush of enemy warriors, moving in on him like a pack of hungry wolves.

Two enemy warriors who'd circumvented the central skirmish, made directly for Bodhmhall and Demne, approaching too fast for either to cast again. As they closed in on her, the terrified, *bandraoi* frantically brandished her second rock, knowing that if she cast it at one of them, the other would attack. Her visible desperation tickled the two warriors. One of them smiled a gap-toothed smile and released a coarse guffaw.

'Hold!'

Tadg mac Nuadat's command rang out with startling authority, even above the echoing remnants of the violent scuffle.

'Let them be'.

Thwarted at the moment of victory, the two warriors twisted around to look back at the *draoi* in disbelief. Confused, Bodhmhall too redirected her gaze to Tadg mac Nuadat's lean form and saw that now there was a second figure standing alongside him, holding a knife blade to his throat.

Liath Luachra!

The *bandraoi* experienced a surge of emotions, so chaotic, so intense she was unable to form a coherent thought. Thunderstruck, she stared at the unlikely pairing, her mouth hanging open.

Liath Luachra!

Absorbed in her own perilous circumstances, the Grey One wasn't looking in her direction but moving forward carefully, attempting to use the *draoi* as a shield against his own men. Bodhmhall saw her jab her unyielding hostage, prompting him to issue a fresh set of commands.

'Lay your javelins on the earth. Move down trail from where I stand.'

Despite her shock, Bodhmhall couldn't help but notice that the dark *draoi* didn't look frightened by the situation. If anything, his commands rang out with complete confidence, absent of any trace of uncertainty. The enemy warriors remained where they were, unsure how to respond without their *rígfénnid* to guide them.

'Do as I command. Now!'

There was an intensity, a power to his voice that shocked them all and even the *bandraoi* felt its compelling tug. Slowly, grudgingly, the warriors did as instructed, those with javelins tossing them on the ground and following their comrades down the trail. As each passed their captive leader, they glared savagely at the warrior woman. Unmoved, her grip on the blade at the *draoi*'s throat remained steady.

When the enemy warriors had assembled in a loose, glowering band thirty paces or so down the trail, the woman warrior whistled. Bodhmhall spotted a brief shuffling in the bushes behind her just before a youth emerged onto the trail.

Fintán mac Gleor.

Wasting no time, the *Lamraighe* youth ran uphill, gathering the abandoned javelins as he did so. Hurrying up to the edge of the plateau where Bodhmhall and Demne were standing, he dropped the greater proportion of the missiles onto the ground with a woody clatter. Five of the javelins, he retained: four stabbed headfirst into the earth in front of him, the last held aloft in preparation to cast. When he was done, he nodded down at the warrior woman and the Grey One immediately started backing uphill towards them, pulling the hostage *draoi* with her.

If I had two other fighters or a supply of javelins, I might hold the path for a time.

Recalling Fiacail mac Codhna's words, the *bandraoi* finally understood what the woman warrior had in mind. Fintán had gathered almost twenty javelins. Given the narrowness of the trail and the open ground the enemy would have to traverse, that was more than enough for him and Liath Luachra to hold them off or, at a minimum, inflict very serious casualties.

Manhandling her captive backwards, the woman warrior paused to glance down at the body of Gob An Teanga Gorm. Spread-eagled on the earth, a puddle of blood was soaking into the ground around the corpse's shattered head.

Heart pounding, Bodhmhall shifted her attention to the nearby body of Fiacail ma Codhna, only to stiffen in shock when she realised the fingers of his right hand were moving.

Fiacail lives!

Without pausing to think, the *bandraoi* started down the gentle incline and rushed towards the warrior. Dropping to her knees, she examined him closely. Blood was streaming from several wounds in his chest and hands. Seeing her, he tried to speak but bloody foam bubbled from his lips.

Furious beyond belief, she turned to glare up at the *draoi* held in place mere paces from where she was kneeling. 'Why?" she demanded. 'Why do you seek to cause us such injury? What have we done to deserve your wrath?'

The *draoi* simply ignored her, coolly shifting his stance with care so that he could face Liath Luachra instead.

'Release me. I've done as you asked.'

Bodhmhall could see the conflict in the Grey One's eyes, the slight tremor of the blade as she fought the itch to cut his throat. Tadg too must have seen that fuming indecision but it didn't seem to unsettle him.

'You and yours remain unharmed. I have lost my most valuable servant.' His eyes flickered to Gob An Teanga Gorm's now motionless corpse before returning to the Grey One. 'And lest you forget, my warriors will retire only so long as I remain unharmed.'

Liath Luachra held his gaze for several heartbeats but then, grudgingly, released him. Taking a step away from the woman warrior, Tadg mac Nuadat raised his hand to touch the graze on his throat where the blade had sliced the skin then raised it further to touch his swollen nose. The silent, deep-rooted hatred in those dark eyes was impossible to misinterpret.

'You've won this day,' he hissed quietly. 'Your luck has held but the next time we meet this matter will be settled. Once and for all.' He stared at her meaningfully then finally deigned to turn his eyes to Bodhmhall. 'And you, *Cailleach Dubh*. Farewell. You'll see me in your dreams.'

With this, the *Draoi* of Almhu, turned and started downhill.

The two women did not hesitate. Grasping the Seiscenn Uarbhaoil man, between them they hurriedly hauled him back up to the lip of the plateau. There, the Grey One immediately left him in Bodhmhall's care, rushing to retrieve a javelin and stand alongside the *Lamraighe* youth, overlooking the trail.

Below them however, Tadg appeared to have finished conversing with his men. With a sick feeling in her stomach, Bodhmhall saw the *Draoi* of Almhu cast one last lingering look at Demne. Finally, turning, he led his men away.

***

Bodhmhall remained the edge of the plateau for a long time after the *fian* had gone, drawing on the *Gift* to search through the trees below for the merest flicker of lifelight. Initially, when she'd watched the *fian* descend the mountain track, the warriors had seemed to move erratically, like a wavering swarm of fireflies. Once they'd reached its base however, those lifelights had converged and veered off to the west, quickly fading even from her enhanced sight. That had surprised her at first. She hadn't expected Tadg mac Nuadat to hold true to his word and assumed his actions had more to do with escaping *Clann Baoiscne* territory than with any genuinely honourable intent.

Ironically, it was only then that the trembling started, commencing in her chest but rapidly spreading to her limbs and ultimately, throughout her entire body. Shaking uncontrollably, the *bandraoi* was forced to a crouch, clutching herself in an attempt to suppress the tremors and throwing up violently until she'd physically expunged the terrors. When the shakes finally ceased, she stumbled to her feet, mortified to find that Fintán had been nearby the whole time. Assigned to watch over the trail with his collection of javelins, he'd done his best to turn away and offer what little privacy he could but even with that she could sense his discomfort.

Leaving the *Lamraighe* youth, she returned to the campsite they'd established in the trees at the centre of the plateau. Demne, sitting on a rock by Fiacail mac Codhna, looked up as she arrived.

To the *bandraoi*'s surprise the Seiscenn Uarbhaoil man was conscious, lying without complaint on his makeshift bed of fern and moss. She crouched to re-examine the wounds on his bare chest. The green *léine* was gone, removed for it'd been drenched in blood from the various gashes to his upper body. She'd managed to staunch the blood loss with moss compresses but she knew Fiacail had been remarkably fortunate for none of the cuts and blade thrusts seemed to have penetrated a vital organ. She was however concerned by the deep wound from the spear thrust to his chest and an alarming gash down his right arm where wet muscle gleamed almost to the bone.

With Demne's assistance she cleaned the wounds with boiled water, then packed them with a hastily prepared paste of herbs to prevent blood poisoning. Afterwards, she'd sewn the wounds shut, Demne holding the skin in place as she pushed a sharp bone needle through the flesh and completed the stitches.

When she was finished, she covered the wounds with a fresh compress, held in place by a loose bandage. Sitting back exhausted, she regarded her work with a critical eye. She'd done everything she could think of, had used all her healing skills and experience, but now the fight was Fiacail's alone. If the warrior slept through the night without fever he had a fair chance of survival. If he didn't …

Having thought to see him die once already, she was loathe to consider that possibility further.

Typically, the Seiscenn Uarbhaoil warrior attempted to put on a brave face, despite the fact that it was white and twisted from pain.

Just like old times!

'Your needle bites like an irksome midge, *Cailleach*.' Although he was bleeding from the mouth and his lips were swollen from the beating he'd taken, he attempted a grin. Sweat glistened on his forehead in the afternoon sunlight.

The *bandraoi*'s glare gouged some of the foolishness out of him. 'Better a bite than the fevers. I'd not have the wolves bother me when they come gnawing on your corpse.'

Reaching around, she retrieved the skin of *uisce beatha* that she'd had the foresight to bring from Dún Baoiscne. 'Will I dampen your lips?' she asked.

The warrior looked at the skin in surprise. 'Isn't the drink tainted?'

She shook her head. 'The effect of the herb lasts a short time in liquid, particularly in a drink of such strength.'

'Oh, well then ….' Fiacail needed no further convincing. 'It's true that killing puts a fierce thirst on a man.'

Unable to lift the container by himself, she had to raise it to his lips and hold it for him as he swallowed, gulping down one mouthful, then a second and a third.

'Aaaaaaah!'

The *bandraoi* considered him with concern. Between the wheezing and bloody lips, it was hard to tell if the exclamation was prompted from discomfort or from pleasure. 'Pain?' She asked

'No. You're kind but I have enough.' He gave her another blood-smeared grin.

Bodhmhall sighed but then reached down to put a gentle hand on his shoulder. 'You are a fool, Fiacail mac Codhna. A wholly marvellous and courageous fool.'

Fiacail smiled but this time there was an unfocussed glaze to his eyes. As she watched, that gaze grew duller. When he attempted to speak again, nothing but dribble and mumbles escaped his lips. He managed a brief look of bewildered outrage before his eyes rolled back and his head fell to one side.

Dispatching her nephew to join Fintán, the *bandraoi* yawned and sat back to regard the unconscious warrior. In an odd way, she found herself envying his unconscious state. At that moment, the prospect of a few moments' oblivion, of a temporary respite from the reality of existence, seemed immensely appealing.

'The Great Wild breathes a sigh now Fiacail mac Codhna sleeps.' Liath Luachra's voice carved through the silence of the little campsite. 'He'll still be yabbering the day they lay him in his grave.'

The *bandraoi* felt her heart lighten as she turned to face the woman warrior. With the Grey One's insistence on ensuring the safety of the plateau and her own treatment of Fiacail's wounds, the two women hadn't had a moment to speak since the confrontation with Tadg mac Nuadat's *fian*. Up close however, Bodhmhall now found herself genuinely appalled at the woman warrior's haggard appearance. Gaunt and drawn, her skin was stretched taut over her high cheekbones and she'd lost far too much weight. The flowing locks had been reduced to a ragged stubble, her eyes were blackened, and her cheeks were badly bruised. It seemed a wonder the woman warrior was capable of standing.

The *bandraoi* did her best to hide her concern as they embraced, drawing the woman warrior close, yet pressing against her carefully, fearful both for her own hand as well as the other's injuries.

'*A rún! Liath Luachra, a rún.*'

Returning the *bandraoi's* embrace, the woman warrior attempted a laugh but it was a weary, tearful thing, as though the effort had caused something to tear deep inside. Bodhmhall drew back, raised one hand to stroke the Grey One's cheek and then tenderly ran her fingers through the close-cropped stubble. 'I thought I'd lost you, Grey One. I truly thought I'd never see you again.'

Liath Luachra laughed sadly and kissed her full on the lips.

'You'll never lose me. You ...' Her voice caught and, for a moment, the *bandraoi* thought she was going to cry. '*Leatsa go deo, a Bhodhmhall. Leatsa amháin.*' Always yours, Bodhmhall. Only yours.

Taken aback by such a rare display of emotion from the Grey One, the *bandraoi* stumbled momentarily, falling back to the topic of practicalities while she regathered her thoughts. 'You've satisfied yourself of our safety?'

Unable to speak, the woman warrior nodded stiffly.

Taking her by the hand, Bodhmhall led her to a log some distance from where Fiacail was sleeping so that they could sit themselves down. 'I've not felt death's touch so intimately before, Grey One. I was terrified, *a chroí.* Truly terrified. Even more so than during the attack at Ráth Bládhma and An Gleann Teann.' Her voice had an audible quaver as she squeezed Liath Luachra's hand. 'Your timing could not have been better. Or more welcome.'

The woman warrior sniffed and wiped her eyes. 'Do not torment yourself, Bodhmhall. The thrust of violence cuts different every time. It's never truly the same. But ...' she paused to look away as though embarrassed by the display of emotion. 'In truth, there was little fortuitous about our timing. We chanced upon the *fian*'s trail two days ago and followed, knowing they'd close in on you eventually.'

Regarding the *bandraoi* uncertainly, she chewed on her lower lip. 'In truth, I too felt the draw of the ancestors. There were ten fighting men in that *fian* and I didn't think to survive this encounter.' She coughed briefly and cleared her throat. 'Then I saw Tadg step out alone from the trees and knew what could be done, what opportunity I could grasp. Why take on ten and lose when I could take one and win.'

Bodhmhall clasped the woman warrior's hand and closed her eyes, struggling to cope with the combined rush of relief and gratitude and the dreadful potential of what might have been. Taking a deep breath, she addressed the Grey One again. 'Did you know Tadg was leading the *fian*?'

'Through Gob An Teanga Gorm? Yes. Cargal Uí Faigil crossed my path and spilled that secret.'

'Then you achieved far more than I. My great scheme to identify the traitor proved worthless.' She shook her head dismally. '*An Cailleach Dubh.* The Black Hag and her wisdom. Ah, yes. I thought myself so very clever.' Bodhmhall could not disguise the bitterness in her voice.

Liath Luachra nodded in sympathy. Demne had already explained the *bandraoi*'s plan to her. 'Do not dismay, Bodhmhall. The trap you set for the traitor was a clever one, even if it was the Adversary who set his foot in it.

277

Besides, you couldn't have known Tadg would find you through your dreams.'

The *bandraoi* considered her in surprise. 'You know of that?'

The woman warrior paused as she recalled her own dream. 'I too have attracted *An Fear Dubh's* attention.'

Both women lapsed into silence for a time, recalling their individual experiences with the faceless entity.

'In my dreams ...' the *bandraoi* said suddenly. 'When I finally recognised *An Fear Dubh's* presence for the infiltration it was, I detected an ... aftertaste, a sense I'd only ever felt once before.' She held the Grey One's eyes. 'With the Tainted One.'

Liath Luachra shuddered. Of all those at Ráth Bládhma three years earlier, she'd been the one most exposed to the Tainted One's blemish and it wasn't a memory she cared to dwell on.

'Which suggests ...' The *bandraoi* frowned as she worked through the ramifications. 'Which suggests it was Tadg who set the Tainted One after Muirne. It's even possible he had a hand in creating the Tainted One.'

Again, Liath Luachra felt a chill run down her spine. 'Is that possible? And why would he set such a creature after his own daughter?'

Unable to answer the question, the *bandraoi* could only shake her head helplessly. 'Probably for the very same reason he seeks to get his hands on Demne. Sadly, there are but two people who could answer that question.'

'Perhaps but one. When I questioned her, Muirne did not seem to know.'

Once again, they grew quiet and it was some time before Bodhmhall broke the silence. 'You know, my scheme to identify the traitor was successful in a single aspect but it's one that now troubles me greatly.'

The woman warrior winced. 'I dread to think there's anything worse than what we've already endured. What is it that troubles you?'

'The pursuit. It did not come from any of the routes I outlined to my father's three advisors.'

'So ...' The woman warrior hesitated, unsure what the *bandraoi* was trying to say. 'You mean ...'

'I mean that none of my father's three advisors is the traitor. In a way, Tadg himself confirmed that when I asked him outright and studied his reaction. It was evident that none of their names were familiar or held any interest for him. The traitor must be someone much closer than we'd originally believed.'

There was yet another silence as the two woman thought through the ramifications of that statement, what it meant with respect to their people back at Ráth Bládhma. The possibility that there could be a traitor amongst them wounded the *bandraoi* deeply but she could think of no other likelihood.

'Perhaps there was another reason,' Liath Luachra suggested at last. 'Some reason of which we're unaware.'

Bodhmhall shrugged. 'It's possible', she admitted. 'But I don't think so. If what Cargal Uí Faigil told you is true, somebody provided Tadg mac Nuadat with a strand of our hair. That could only be someone we allowed close.'

The *bandraoi* sighed, suddenly overwhelmed by the sheer scale of the future challenges, the potential battles they still faced. 'Our lives hang by a single thread,' she told the woman warrior. 'Here we are, in unfriendly territory without friends or provisions and barely a fit fighter amongst us. Our allies our scattered, our people are at risk and there's no safe refuge to be had for my nephew. And now, to make matters worse, we must also discover a means to counter the Adversary's charm.'

Liath Luachra reached up to brush a strand of hair away from her eyes. 'We will, *a chroí*. We've bloodied Tadg mac Nuadat's nose on three separate occasions. We will do so again.'

The woman warrior was leaning over to place a comforting arm about the *bandraoi*'s shoulder when a rustle of branches in the nearby bushes drew her eyes. As both women turned to watch, Demne emerged and pushed his way forward into the little camp. Despite her brooding heart, Bodhmhall forced a smile but her nephew's gaze had already bypassed her to fix on the woman warrior.

'Grey One! Fintán continues to guard the trail but grows weary and asks that you relieve him.'

Bodhmhall watched the woman warrior suppress her great frustration and nod assent with a jaded sigh.

'Very well. I'll take the next watch. Bodhmhall, with your *Gift* you're better suited for the night watch with Demne.' She glanced at the *bandraoi* for her consent and Bodhmhall nodded acquiescently.

Grimacing in pain, the woman warrior rose to her feet with a haggard clumsiness the *bandraoi* had never associated with her before. Seeing how thin, how haunted, the Grey One truly was, she felt a shudder in her chest, as though some essential support had crumbled. The latest battle might have been won but the cost to the warrior woman had truly been monumental.

With growing melancholy, she watched the Grey One limp towards the trees but then Demne suddenly lunged forward, throwing himself around the woman warrior to hug her tightly.

'Liath Luachra! I'm so glad you're back!'

The Grey One's face went pale from the obvious agony of the boy's grip but she uttered no word of protest. To the *bandraoi*'s great surprise, the warrior woman smiled and returned the boy's embrace.

And this time, she did, indeed, cry.

Epilogue

The sky had turned silver when Bodhmhall returned to find her at the western vantage point. Haunted, ragged and swaying on her feet from tiredness, the Grey One was still so beautiful to her, the *bandraoi* winced.

Using the *Gift* to confirm their seclusion, Bodhmhall took her by the hand, leading her to the long grass overlooking the moonlit landscape. There, drawing close, she helped the Grey One shed the battle harness and treated her wounds as best she could, relieved to find no sign of blood rot. Afterwards, oiling her hands, she kneaded the woman warrior's back, massaging the knots of tension from her neck and shoulders.

Although she hadn't planned it, stirred by the Grey One's hard belly, her muscled arms and the sensual curve of her jaw, the *bandraoi's* fingers spread much further than intended, working their way between the woman warrior's thighs and warming the tinder of her exhausted body. Despite her physical fatigue, the Grey One responded to the kindling sensations, gradually tensing and then stiffening to finish with a shudder.

Later, lying in the hollow of each other's arm, they stared skywards, watching as a fiery star burned its silent path across the heavens. A moment later that star was followed by another and then another until the night sky was full of fire. Enthralled, the two women watched in mounting fascination until the Grey One finally turned to face the *bandraoi*.'

'My head is full of bees,' she confessed. 'But did you also provoke Father Sun?'

'Yes,' Bodhmhall said shamelessly, causing both women to chuckle.

'I've heard the Elders say,' the Grey One continued, 'such signs are portents of great change. They also say these are the moments best suited to seek entreaties from the ancestors, entreaties for your true heart's desire.'

'Then I would ask them that we grow old together, Grey One. Even on the coldest days, the thought of you ...' She took a deep breath and exhaled slowly. 'It keeps me warm.'

At first, the warrior woman appeared to make no response but then the *bandraoi* noticed her shoulders shaking. With that, her mirth became more apparent. Starting with a soft chuckle, it quickly escalated to booming laughter, spilling off the mountain top and spiralling out across the landscape. Bemused by the display of such uncharacteristic good humour, Bodhmhall felt an immense unfolding of tenderness towards her.

Wiping the tears of laughter from her eyes, the Grey One sat up to clasp the *bandraoi's* hand. 'You too are a bright star within the darkness, *Cailleach*

Dubh. A star that outshines all others. In all these years, I've often wondered why you stayed with me. Had you desired, you could have held a role of immense authority: *bandraoi* with the Druidic Council, leader of *Clann Baoiscne* in your own right.' She shrugged as though this was all some mystery beyond her comprehension. 'And yet, here you are with a lonely blackbird on a bleak mountain top.'

Touched by the woman warrior's words, Bodhmhall mulled over what she'd said for a very long time.

'When I was a child,' she said at last. 'My father accused me of lacking ambition. He said I wanted far too little from the world. To be honest, that accusation chafed for I suspected an element of truth to his words and I didn't know whether that was good or bad.'

The *bandraoi* sniffed and shifted her weight to make herself more comfortable.

'Ten years ago, when I met you, I finally understood the truth. My father had been correct in one critical regard, for when I'm with you I want nothing else from the world. When I'm with you I have everything I could possibly need.'

The Grey One considered her in silence for a time and although she said nothing more, she leaned forward to press her lips against the *bandraoi's* forehead.

Retrieving her cloak, she wrapped it around them both and they remained on the mountain top to await the sunrise.

*The story will continue in Book Four, **FIONN: Stranger at Mullán Bán**.*

*Thanks for taking the time to read Fionn: The Adversary. If you enjoyed the story I'd really appreciate if you could leave an honest review at **Goodreads** or **LibraryThing** or on your preferred ebookstore.*

We're a tiny publishing company and independent reviews are very important to us, not only in terms of visibility but feedback as well.

Thank you

Glossary

Some of the Irish terms/concepts often used in this novel:

Aintín – Aunt
Amadán – Idiot/fool. (Plural: *Amadáin)*
Ar aghaigh linn – Let's go
Bandraoi – Female druid
Beacáin scammalach – Literally, 'cloudy mushroom'. A fungus with hallucinogenic properties.
Bod – A penis
Brocach – A den
Brón – Sadness
Buachaill – Boy. When speaking to a boy it's expressed as '*a bhuachaill'*
Buaile – A feeding or milking place for cows. Usually refers to the transfer of cattle to summer or winter feeding areas.
Cabóg – A clumsy/awkward person
Caiseal – A circular defensive fort, usually made out of stone
Cara – A friend. When speaking to a friend it's expressed as '*a chara'*
Conradh – A champion/ battle leader
Derbfine – Member of a patrilineal group
Díberg – A band of warriors, usually a raiding party or reavers
Dornfhásc – Tickling (of fish)
Draoi – A druid
Dún do chlab – Shut your mouth (beak)!
Éblána – A tribe
Éclann – Clanless state. A person not affiliated to any particular clan
Fian – A band of warriors or war party
Fidchell – an ancient board game used in Ireland believed to be similar to chess
Gaiscíoch – a hero warrior, a fighter of great prowess
Garsúr – Boy. When speaking to a boy it's expressed as '*a gharsúr'*. It's actually a more modern term but used in this novel for variation.
Gléas Gan Ainm – Literally 'Tool Without a Name'
Imbas forosnai – A divination/prophetic ritual
Lamraighe – Name of a tribe
Léine – Ancient shirt-like garment
Lis – Circular courtyard of a *caiseal* or *ráth*
Na Cinéaltaí – The Friendly Ones
Óglach – A young, unblooded warrior (plural: *Óglaigh)*

Ollamh – Chief/Head Druid

Plámás – Soft talk or sweet talk

Ráméis – Nonsense talk

Rechtaire – A title for someone acing as an administrator/ steward

Rí – Literally translated as 'king' but generally refers to a tribal leader

Rígfénnid – Leader of a *fian*

Síd – Ancient burial mound

Slat – Slang word for penis (cock/dick)

Stiúsaí – Hussy/trollop

Tánaiste – Successor to the rí or leader

Techtaire – Messenger/envoy

Tíolacadh – A paranormal gift or skill

Uí Cuaich – A tribe

Uí Barraiche – A tribe

Uisce beatha – Water of life. Modern-day translation is whiskey

Basic Pronunciation Guide:

Characters:

Muirne Muncháem:
This is pronounced roughly as 'Mir-neh' and 'Mun – cawm' in English. I'd recommend checking the audio guide at **irishimbasbooks.com.**

Bodhmhall ua Baoiscne:
This is pronounced 'Bough-val' (the 'mh' in Irish produces a 'v' sound). There's really no easy way of pronouncing 'Baoiscne' for non–Gaelic speakers. Please just check out the audio guide at **irishimbasbooks.com**

Liath Luachra:
This is pronounced 'Lee-ah' (the 'th' is silent) and 'Luke-rah' in English

Fiacail mac Codhna:
This is pronounced as 'Feek-ull mack Cow-nah' in English.

Place names

Ráth Bládhma:
This is pronounced 'Raw Blaw-mah' in English (the 'th' and the 'dh' are silent. Irish speakers love long silences – not!)

Dún Baoiscne:
'Dún' sounds like 'Dune' in English. Again, for 'Baoiscne' I'd recommend you go to the audio guide at **irishimbasbooks.com**.

Seiscenn Uarbhaoil:
Again, quite difficult for non-Gaelic speakers. Seiscenn sounds like 'shesh-ken' but best to check this out at the website pronunciation guide.

Historical and Creative Note:

Like the preceding books in the series, FIONN: The Adversary introduces one or two new cultural concepts from Ireland's prehistoric period (i.e. pre-fifth century A.D.). One of these is the *imbas forsonai* ritual (previously referred to with respect to Bodhmhall's past and which will probably be elucidated further in later books).

In essence, *imbas forosnai* was an ancient ritual used for prophetic purposes or when seeking advice from the Otherworld (probably through the intercession of ancestors). In some respects, it might be best to think of it as a Celtic/Gaelic equivalent of those ritualistic processes used by other contemporary ancient cultures (in terms of its objective, at least) such as the Greek oracle at Delphi, the Nechung oracle in Tibet and so on.

There's plenty of evidence to indicate *imbas forosnai* was a relatively well-known rite in pre-historic Ireland however over the course of many centuries of colonization and competing cultural belief systems (Christianity), that ritual was proactively eroded from cultural memory by those who felt threatened by what it represented. Fortunately several references still remain in the ancient Irish literature. The most well-known of these is the *Sanas Cormaic* – a ninth century Irish glossary/dictionary that attempts to explain many ancient words or expressions – which describes the ritual in some detail. Unfortunately, when you read *Sanas Cormaic* it's pretty obvious the author isn't personally familiar with the subject he's writing about. Even by the ninth century, the ritual he's describing has already faded into antiquity.

Fionn mac Cumhaill has a very strong association with the ritual and there are also several references to it throughout the Fenian Cycle (in the earliest stories, Fionn is actually portrayed more as a 'seer' than a warrior or a leader of men, a narrative development that happened much later during the early medieval period). The *imbas forsnai* ritual is also believed to form the basis of Fionn's prophetic ability, achieved in the stories through the sucking or biting of his 'magic' thumb.

If you go online, you'll find numerous references to *imbas forosnai* but you'd probably be better off ignoring anything that doesn't have a significant body of contemporary academic analysis to support it. Like the author of *Sanas Cormaic*, some people attribute all kinds of mystical interpretations to something they don't fully understand and they forget how difficult it is for someone from contemporary times to fully comprehend the context behind such ancient references. People from different cultures and different societies do not always think in the same manner or have the same value systems. Applying our own modern cultural and values systems to ancient cultures, invariably leads to misinterpretation.

[This isn't intended as an advertisement or hard sell but anyone interested in the character of Fionn mac Cumhaill can find a lot more of this kind of information in my book **Beara Dark Legends.** This provides far more detail on the character of Fionn and his mystic abilities than I can provide in this series.]

One new character introduced in this novel (again, briefly referred to in the previous books) is Tréanmór. Within the Fenian Cycle, the character of Cumhal (Fionn mac Cumhaill's father and Bodhmhall's brother) is sometimes referred to with the patronymic "*mac Trénmóir*" ("*mac Tréanmór*" in modern Irish) which, literally, means 'Strong-Big'. This unlikely name is believed to have been introduced by genealogists of seventh century Leinster families who were keen to link the famous hero to their own ruling dynasties – even if they had to bend the truth to do so. Essentially, they were the 'spin doctors' of their day. Apart from those references, there's no other mention of Tréanmór within the other historical narratives (hardly a surprise).

The lack of definition around this character in the Fenian Cycle means that the scenes in which he appears are pure invention. The type of tribal politics he's associated with however, would probably have taken place. In addition, the presence of *Na Cúig Cairde* – The Five Friends – would not have been *too* unusual. The taking of enemy heads would appear to have been a relatively common practice in prehistoric Ireland. In ancient societies, the head was seen as containing the essence of an individual (which is still true) so desecrating the head of a defeated enemy was an expression of complete dominance (and an insult) over one's enemy. As to whether any tribe would have put up with their leader degrading heads to the extent that Tréanmór does in this book, is of course a lot more unlikely.

But, hey! This is fiction, after all.

If you're interested in progress on the next book in the series (and others), aspects of the creative process, bits and bobs on Irish culture/mythology and other articles, please feel free to sign up to 'Vóg' (my monthly newsletter) at irishimbasbooks.com.

Thanks for following the FIONN series.

Brian O'Sullivan
February 2017

Other Books by Brian O'Sullivan

See Brian's blog and website at *irishimbasbooks.com* for contact details and updates on new and upcoming titles.

Beara: Dark Legends
[The Beara Trilogy – Book 1]

Nobody knows much about reclusive historian Muiris O'Súilleabháin (Mos) except that he doesn't share his secrets freely.

Mos, however, has a *"sixth sense for history, a unique talent for finding lost things"*.

Lured from seclusion by the prospect of a challenging historical puzzle, Mos is hired to locate the final resting place of legendary Irish hero, Fionn mac Cumhaill. Confronted by a thousand year old mystery, the distractions of a beguiling circus performer and a lethal competitor, Mos must draw on his knowledge of Gaelic lore and mythology to defy his enemies and survive his own family history in Beara.

Beara: Dark Legends is the first in a trilogy of unforgettable Irish thrillers. Propulsive, atmospheric and darkly humorous, *Beara: Dark Legends* introduces an Irish hero like you've never seen before. Nothing you thought you knew about Ireland will ever be the same again.

A sample of what the reviewers say:

"This is a tale that starts in two different times and later merges into one. It develops characters and backgrounds with depth and substance, transporting the reader on a dramatic, sensitive and often humorous journey. While other authors often seem to trot out trite story-lines with readily guessable conclusions, Brian O'Sullivan weaves unusual plots, using realistic dialogue and producing often surprising events and outcomes."

"O'Sullivan has done an amazing job of introducing a culture that many would say is dying and using it as the basis for a unique and exciting thriller. I think I've learned more about Irish history and the Irish language in this one book than I have in many years of school and television, without it once feeling forced or jaded."

"A great mixture of a strong story and strong characters, dark (some very dark) themes and wonderfully evocative descriptions of the wild Irish landscape, interspersed with ancient Irish lore running throughout the book."

"Excellent story, very well throughout, many twists and turns that weren't expected. Thoroughly enjoyed the main character Mos and his no nonsense-take, no crap attitude to life. He says what most of us often probably think but are too polite to say. Highly entertaining!"

"O'Sullivan's cast of international characters enliven this tale of archaeological intrigue, magic, murder and sex, set mainly in West Cork, Ireland. Dual story lines, across different time zones, reveal secrets of Irish spirituality, ancient lore and language."

"Irreverent, informative and astoundingly original."

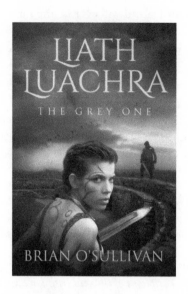

Liath Luachra: The Grey One
[*Recently adapted for the Screen*]

Ireland 188 A.D. A land of tribal affiliations, secret alliances and treacherous rivalries.

Liath Luachra, the young – and deadly – woman warrior has survived two brutal years with mercenary war party "The Friendly Ones" but now the winds are shifting.

Dispatched on a murderous errand where nothing is as it seems, she must survive a group of treacherous comrades, the unwanted advances of her battle leader and a personal history that might be her own undoing.

Clanless and friendless, she can count on nothing but her wits, her fighting skills and her natural ferocity to see her through.

Woman warrior, survivor, killer and future guardian to Irish hero Fionn mac Cumhaill – this is her story.

"Dark, dangerous and strikingly original."

A sample of what the reviewers say:

"Raises Irish mythology and historical fiction to an absolutely new level! Liath Luachra has got to be the most authentic and most exciting Irish fantasy on the market."

"A fast paced traverse through bush trails and battles with a female heroine who is commanding and fascinating."

"A darker tale than the other books in the Fionn mac Cumhaill series, this stand-alone prequel is more satisfying in many ways. Liath Luachra, the troubled and withdrawn woman warrior, has always been one of the best things about the series and O'Sullivan does a tremendous job relating the events of her early life, presenting her as a much more vulnerable character - although just as resilient."

"In the legends of Fionn mac Cumhaill, Liath Luachra is an intriguing name with minimal context, but in Brian O'Sullivan's adaptions she becomes a most fascinating and formidable character in her own right. Her backstory is a great read; brigands and bloodshed, second-guessings and double-crossings. This is an Ancient Ireland that is entrancing and savage, much like Liath Luachra herself."

"The plotting is riveting – full of twists and turns – and the action is full on, hell for leather. If you like Games of Thrones style dramas with a strong splash of Celtic culture, this is a book you'll enjoy."

The 'Liath Luachra' prequel provides us with the background story to 'The Grey One', which O'Sullivan develops further in the Fionn series. Liath Luachra is an engaging protagonist – deliciously sensual, yet calculatingly violent when the cause demands it. Never a dull moment, difficult to put down.

CPSIA information can be obtained
at www.ICGtesting.com
Printed in the USA
BVHW032154130123
656318BV00016B/61

9 780994 146816